# SUN STRIKE

## J L PAWLEY

Nineteenth House Publishing

Getting the ability to fly would be so uplifting.

Cover design by Damonza.com.

An earlier edition of *Sun Strike* was published on Amazon by Steam Press, an imprint of Eunoia Publishing, Ltd.

This edition published by Nineteenth House Publishing

Auckland, New Zealand

Print ISBN-13: 978-1-0670439-0-2

eBook ISBN-13: 978-1-0670439-1-9

# 1

# CONDOR

I sprinted through the dusk.

My breath surged. Dark feathers sliced freezing air. The sky was still light. Too light.

Ahead, white-blonde wings flapped. A soft voice murmured between the hissing thuds. Dove was praying, just as I was.

*Oh God, please … don't let them find us. Please.*

There was the little church. An idle factory. Beyond, crop fields. Below, a leafy suburb and quiet roads.

Beside the church, a nature reserve. Barely an acre of trees.

We'd made it.

*Oh, thank you.*

Dodging the steeple, I slowed and angled my wings to land. Dropping onto the frosty grass with a crunch, Dove and I barely paused to compress our spring-loaded tails, and ran for cover.

As I slipped into the trees, I reached out and took Dove's trembling hand.

"Are you okay?" I whispered.

Breathing hard, she nodded. "*Oui.* But it was too close."

"I know." Shuddering, I tried to flick away the tension, and bruised my wing-arm on a branch. "Let's find the Flight."

In the trees ahead, someone counted quietly. Silhouettes moved through the shadows.

"One, two, three, four, five." It was Tui. "Where the bloody hell are Condor and Dove?"

Hawk's muffled voice answered. "They'll turn up."

"We're here," I said, pushing past a spiky shrub.

Falcon was having an argument with an 'evil bush', and losing. "Took you long enough. Thought the Evos got you this time." He yanked his wingtip out of the twigs and tried to smooth the feathers back into shape.

"Thankfully, no," I said, while Dove shivered. I didn't take Falcon's anger personally. After several weeks on the run, in rapidly-dropping temperatures, with barely enough to eat, we were all exhausted, starving, and stressed. This latest empty-handed narrow escape wasn't helping.

Falcon threw himself on the ground next to his girlfriend. "I'm hungry."

"We're all going hungry, Fal." Tui patted his shoulder, and he buried his head into her side.

Kestrel extracted some chocolate bars from a pouch on her flight harness. "You'll have to share, but it'll keep you alive for a few more minutes." She tossed one over.

Falcon caught it left-handed and pointed at Hawk. "I'm not sharing with him."

"No one said you had to." Kestrel offered the second bar to her boyfriend, but he shook his head, while massaging his temples.

"I'm all right."

"Headache?" I asked, sympathetically, gratefully accepting the third bar from Kestrel.

Hawk grimaced. "Not too bad. I think I've held onto everything this time."

Nodding, I sat next to Dove. She was shivering from both the adrenaline and the cold of falling night. I wrapped my wing around her and divided the chocolate between us.

Raven was standing near a gap in the trees, staring at the pale sky. "See anything, sis?" Tui asked.

Raven signed *no*. She'd once again been mute since our escape from the Evolutionaries. Since Owl had … died.

Kestrel had her phone out. "Better see how famous we are today, then," she said, resigned. Tui and the others also had phones in hand, but I concentrated on the chocolate, and Dove.

The cheap phones from Jenny, our vet friend, were all registered under fake names and email addresses. We used the occasional stolen credit card to keep them connected. Without them, we'd have gotten lost and starved weeks ago – and nearly had, anyway, when we tried to take a shortcut across a national park and lost cell service. Now, we stuck to road directions.

Hawk groaned. "Oh, for Flight's sake."

"Well … shit," Tui said. Dove flinched. Falcon muttered something obscene, threw his phone into the 'evil bush', and began taking out his frustration on the branches.

"What?" I leaned over Kestrel's shoulder.

The screen showed an eyewitness video of us bailing from the latest house we'd burgled. In handheld HD, seven winged figures scattered into the twilit sky and disappeared over the roofs of the factory town suburb. It was being replayed in slow motion. Of course.

"The Evolutionaries are on their way." Hawk shuddered, his brown wings looking black.

"Yeah, we know," I said, quietly. The Evos had been only a step or two behind since we'd escaped a few weeks ago. We'd tried to throw them off by turning northward into the advancing winter, but now they had an exact location.

My chest ached, and it wasn't only from the frantic sprint to the rendezvous.

"The cops are looking for us too," Kestrel said, watching a reporter gesture energetically outside a house surrounded by police tape. "They're accusing us of all the local burglaries from the last couple of weeks."

"To be fair, we are guilty for most of them," I said. Dove sighed, and murmured in French.

"What do we do now?" Falcon demanded, emerging from the bush with a phone in his hand and twigs in his afro. I opened my mouth, but he glared at me. "*Except* call the Angelists!"

"Actually, I was going to say we could look up local campgrounds," I said, calmly. "You know, summer camps that will now be shut for winter with no one around, but a whole lot of cabins we could shelter in?" I'd had the idea earlier, but hadn't had the chance to suggest it before we were busted.

Falcon's broad smile flashed in the gloom. "That's not a bad idea!"

"Will there be anything like that conveniently nearby?" Hawk asked, sceptically.

"Guys, we have to make a decision, and fast. We're viral." Kestrel showed us her social media tracker. We occupied the top three spots on the trending list, and more further down.

Tui rubbed her eyes. "We're screwed."

"Forget about the hashtag storm." Hawk abruptly stood up. "Evolutionaries are mobilizing in this direction, right now."

"Don't forget the viral-fame-hunters and news crews," Falcon said.

Hawk nodded. "Why are we still here, again?"

Raven appeared next to me and signed, *Someone's coming. Let's go.*

"Maybe we should stick to the ground, this time," Kestrel whispered. "They'll expect us to be flying."

"See, I said you were the smart one." Hawk grabbed her hand.

Falcon pretended to pout. "What about me?"

"You're the pretty one," Tui said. I snorted, using my wing elbows to lever myself to my feet.

"You're just jealous," Falcon muttered to me as he passed, his arm around Raven's tiny form.

"Yes, I'm green with envy."

Falcon chuckled, and disappeared into the dense trees after Tui, Hawk, and Kestrel. Clasping Dove's hand in mine, I followed.

We didn't get far. The patch of trees ended at the edge of a wheat field. Thigh-high golden grass stretched to the cloudy horizon.

"Why couldn't it be corn?" Falcon moaned. "Beautiful, green, and most importantly tall and easy-to-hide-in corn plants."

"Also could have made some crop circles, and called your mothership for help, eh," Tui said. Falcon let out an amused *heh*.

"Plan A, we take cover in the trees till it's dark, hope no one flushes us out, and then fly for it," Hawk said. "Or, plan B, we make for the tractor tracks." He pointed at a dark line in the wheat, a few hundred yards away. "And we crawl."

The Flight glanced at each other. Even Raven wrinkled her nose. But distant voices left us with no choice.

Following Hawk, we slipped along the boundary between field and trees, instinctively hunching our backs and wings. Twice Hawk hit the ground, the rest of us copying a second later, trying not to breathe.

*Oh, Lord, please. We can't take this much longer.*

Living day-to-day was straining us to the breaking point. We hadn't had a chance to stop and think about anything beyond tomorrow, let alone a long-term solution to our situation. Dove and I had stopped suggesting we ask the Angelists for help more than a week ago, though we hadn't stopped wanting to. I had to keep the Flight together. Since Owl's death … I couldn't bear losing a single person more.

The sky was still pale when we finally reached the tire tracks.

"I'll go first." Hawk reluctantly turned to his girlfriend. "Kess, babe, I need you to bring up the rear. Your wings will camouflage into the wheat, and shield everyone else from view."

Jaw and eyebrows tightening, Kestrel nodded, and stood aside as Dove, Tui, Raven, Falcon, and I lined up behind Hawk.

"This is gonna suck," he said, "but just remember, it's better than those damn Evo cells."

"It'll be properly dark soon, anyway," Falcon said, helpfully.

"We're right behind you, Hawk," I said. Tui agreed, and Kestrel gave two thumbs up.

As the voices in the trees grew louder, Hawk dropped to his knees and commando-crawled into the narrow gap in the wheat. I was hard on his tail, copying his movements. Dove, Tui, Raven, Falcon, and then Kestrel followed.

My legs were soon aching. My jacket didn't cushion my elbows from the muddy ground, but at least months of flying meant my neck and back were strong enough to cope. All I had to do was picture the demonic grin of Frederik Larrsson, Junior, and I could push through the pain.

"Get down!" Tui hissed.

I hit the ground with my chest and face.

Awkwardly, I glanced over my shoulders, past Dove and the others. At the end of our ragged line, just visible around the curved track, Kestrel crouched with her blonde wings partly spread into the wheat stalks on either side.

In the distance, people spoke. With our sharp hearing, plus adrenaline, it was easy to recognize the voices of the news crew. I begged the Lord to draw their attention away.

As the voices drifted further to the left, Hawk whispered, "Keep moving."

Taking a deep breath of damp dirt and musty grass, I passed on the message and lifted myself back to my bruised elbows.

The Flight crawled through the crops as night slowly darkened the cloudy sky. Eventually, not even prayer could distract me from the agony in my muscles and joints.

By the time Hawk called a halt, it was obvious everyone was suffering.

"How is everyone holding up?" Hawk asked, rubbing his arms.

"Apart from feeling like my knees and elbows have just built a house, and that my stomach lining was used for the carpet, I'm fine," Falcon growled.

"How poetic," Kestrel said, wiping hopelessly at the layers of mud. Still, somehow, she grinned.

Hawk rolled his eyes. "Okay, let me be more specific for the cynic in the front row: we're all hungry, we're all in pain, we're all stuck in this muddy wheat field until it gets dark, people are actively hunting us in this area, and it's about to rain, so how far do each of you think you can fly in search of shelter and food right now?"

"As far as I have to, bro," Tui said.

Raven signed *Me too*, and Falcon nodded. I glanced at Dove, her head hanging and arms clutching her chest. The Flight had been living rough for months before being snatched by the Evos, but Dove had never adapted to such physical demands, let alone the mental and spiritual challenge. Since we'd given up suggesting the Angelists as a sanctuary, she'd been quieter and quieter, until she was almost as silent as Raven.

"How far is the next town?" Kestrel asked.

Hawk checked his phone, shielding the glow with his wing. "Continuing in this direction, the next town – let's call it Town A – is about forty miles away. Probably about an hour, in our condition and this wind. Town B is only half as far, but we'd have to go back around the factory and houses to get there, and it'll be the first place the Evos and cops look for us. Or, option C, we look for a barn to hide in and conserve energy."

"Will this hypothetical barn have food?" Falcon demanded.

"And a lavatory?" Kestrel added.

Hawk just gave them a Look.

"I vote for Town A." I shivered. We had to keep moving, both for safety and for warmth. Rain was advancing across the field.

Raven grabbed my sleeve, and I looked where she was pointing. Flashlight beams flickered in the distance, and something was making a weird buzzing noise, whining as it grew louder.

Falcon squinted. "Crap. They've got a drone."

Ice flooded my chest. Dove whimpered.

"Bloody hell. Time to go." Tui pulled her flight glasses over her eyes, urging the Flight to our feet. "Hawk, take point, bro?"

"Roger." Hawk broke into a run. With a couple of hard flaps, he launched. The sound seemed to echo.

Tui shoved me after him. "Go, quick!"

The flashlights swung our way as the Flight leaped into the air. Hawk was already flying in a different direction to our actual goal; in our sore, hungry states we fought to make altitude.

Below came excited exclamations, but no gunshots. Instead, the drone's motor whined as it accelerated after us.

"I'm getting too old for this," Falcon muttered beyond my right wingtip.

Tui scoffed, a bit breathlessly. "Yeah, nah, you old fart. Seventeen going on eighty."

"Flying, not flirting!" Hawk called.

Falcon snorted. "Obviously you've got no idea what flirting actually looks like."

"Come on, guys," I said, pulling ahead of them. My chest burned trying to keep up with Hawk and Dove. The first wave of rain splashed my face.

Falcon and Tui kept hard on my tail, with Kestrel and Raven just behind them. I heard Kestrel's whimper as the frantic sprint strained the not-quite-healed scars in her belly. I could only imagine the pain. Her wings were jerky. But I couldn't help.

I glanced back. Three dark figures were crashing through the wheat, and the drone was a dot. It was too small to keep up with seven panicked Icari, especially in the rain.

Ahead, Hawk touched the lowest cloud level and vanished. One-by-one, the Flight followed him into the disorienting fog. Everything ached, and I didn't know if I was still climbing. But, after long, anxious moments, I burst into rainy air, my wing sending ripples of cloud rolling away in all directions.

The Flight regrouped into our usual V, with Hawk on point. Dove was the last to fall in, so of course I was at the back of the V with her.

It wasn't a very tidy V. As Dove struggled to keep up with the others, the distance between us and the Flight increased until we'd nearly fallen out of the formation's slipstream.

When Dove finally spoke, I realized it was deliberate.

"Condor," she said, quiet and breathy.

"Yeah?" Instinctively, I kept my voice low, too. The wind direction and sound of wings would mask our conversation from the Flight.

"I want my home."

"I know, Dove. We all want a home."

She grunted in frustration. "No, Condor. I want to go to my home. To France."

Startled, I dropped a few feet before regaining my rhythm. "Not the Angelists?"

"I want Maman and Papa." Her voice broke. "I want my home."

My mind whirled. After the Change, Dove's parents' search for answers eventually brought them to America to join the

Angelist megachurch. Her mom and dad were probably still there, worrying about their daughter.

There was no way to reunite Dove with her parents, let alone return to France, without involving the Angelists. They were her family's sponsors and protectors. But the Flight didn't trust them. After Kestrel, Dove and I had been so easily and rapidly kidnapped while on their watch, I wasn't sure how far we could trust them, either. I still wanted to talk to the church, but I didn't think I was ready to be a full-time angel.

"Condor," Dove said, breaking into my thoughts. "You should come too."

"To the Angelists?"

"To France."

I nearly fell out of the sky again. Anxiety and hope grappled in my chest. I didn't want to leave the Flight, my friends, but did this mean Dove might have ... feelings for me?

Just like I was developing for her?

"Just think about it, *mon amie*," Dove said, and smiled through her exhaustion.

"Yeah," I said, vaguely. "I definitely will."

# 2

# FALCON

"Man, I need to shave. A hunting knife really isn't cutting it."
I paused. "Get it?"

A few groans came from the darkness.

"Please don't try that while we're flying," Tui said. "Next
stop, I'll find some razors. All right?"

"Thanks, babe. I'm also thinking of nail clippers,
tweezers…"

Hawk, currently checking the map, grunted. "I'll get you a
whole beauty kit if you shut up."

"Yessir." I flicked a salute. "Are you taking us somewhere
that will have some toiletries available? Ooh, maybe some of
those little hotel soaps. Easy to carry."

"Shut up, Falcon."

"How wude."

Hunger and cold had numbed my wings, but I kept sliding
them through the sky and resumed daydreaming about being
rescued and recruited by a secret organization of mutant
superheroes.

I was so zoned out, I nearly overshot Hawk when he finally
decelerated.

There were lights ahead in the flat, boring landscape. Hawk,
however, was not aiming for the town. He'd spotted a dark

farmhouse with several barn-type buildings and a silo; all mere
lumps in the landscape, even with our sharp nightsight.

Only minutes later, we'd landed behind the biggest shadow
and had slipped in through the unlocked back door.

"Nice work, Cadet Captain Bro," I said, as Hawk opened the
first cupboard in the farmhouse kitchen and was hit in the face
by a falling packet of cookies.

"The farmer's probably just at the pub," Kestrel said, anxiously,
"so let's stock up and retreat."

"Here you go." I handed her a packet of soup stock. Kestrel
groaned, and threw it at my head.

As I ducked, I saw a brilliant opportunity to crack a joke about
nuts and Hawk's intelligence.

The Flight soon banished me from the kitchen for too many
food puns. Still laughing at my own comic genius, I relieved
Raven of watch duty, and lurked at a window while munching
on corn chips.

I was into my third bag when headlights turned into the long
driveway.

"Time to go, guys!"

As a pickup pulled up to the front of the farmhouse, the Flight
bailed out the back and ran for the barn.

Two men laughed and joked, one obviously very drunk as his
friend cajoled him inside.

Anxiously, we waited to see if they'd notice the home invasion
and missing food, but the house soon fell quiet.

"I can't decide whether to say, 'That was close,' or not," Kestrel
said jerkily, tucked tightly under Hawk's wing.

Tui sighed. "I never want to have to say it again, eh."

"How long can we live like this? How many times can we just barely escape?"

"It is getting a little repetitive. But look." I pointed into the hayloft. "We could sleep there tonight."

For once, the Flight actually listened to my suggestion, and wearily climbed the ladder.

"This always seems so much more comfortable in movies," I grumbled, trying to arrange the dry, scratchy grass.

"It's better than mud and rocks," Tui said, as she examined Kestrel's abdominal wound. Kestrel murmured in agreement, wincing as Tui poked her.

"I guess."

Hawk had collapsed onto a hay pile, brown wings draped across half the floor. "Rather be here than in a cell."

Dove shuddered as she put away her insulin kit, her feathers rustling. Condor put his wing around her, and he nodded at me when I caught his gaze and raised an eyebrow. However, he looked away too quickly, and I wondered what the heck was going on *now*.

I was too tired to care much and was just happy they'd stopped banging on about the Angelists.

Snuggling up to Tui, I announced, "Shotgun first sleep shift."

Hawk sighed and pushed himself to sitting. "I'll take the first watch, then. But we need a plan before morning."

"What's the point?" Kestrel said, exhaustedly. "The Evos will be swarming the area. They'll catch up with us eventually. Even if they don't, even if we find somewhere to stay, then some douchebag with a camera and no shits to give about people's privacy will throw us all over the internet and ruin everything again. What's the POINT?"

Kestrel burst into tears. Raven threw her arms around her and buried her head into Kestrel's side.

Hawkwardly, like always, Hawk hugged both of them and looked at me and Tui for help. But Tui was now staring at the ground and I couldn't think of a single joke to lighten the mood, which was pissing me off even more.

Mad at the whole frickin' world, I started shredding bits of hay and tossing them over the side of the loft. It had been nearly a year since the Change and we were still forced to live like fugitive raccoons. And the only alternative anyone seemed to be able to come up with was to flock off to the Angelists, where there'd be freaky religious morons fawning all over us, beginning by bringing us peeled grapes and blessed wine and sacred sausages and golden computer tablets to write the new Commandments on, or something equally messed up. And if we didn't come up with something convincingly holy, we'd probably be burned at the stake. Possibly literally.

It didn't help that I understood Condor's desire to do some good in the world. It was awesome that he wanted to help people, but then he had to go and ruin it by making it all about divine will, that we had to do what God wanted or we'd be punished by going to Hell, which was no fun at all. Why couldn't we just try and do good in the world because it was the right thing to do?

Couldn't we be superheroes and help people without the pressure of being perfect angels?

*If we were going to be superheroes, then first we'd need a safe base.*

"We need a base," I said, out loud.

Tui snorted. "We're not going to be superheroes, bro."

"Are you sure? Because you just read my mind." I ducked as her wing swiped at me.

However, I was still at the edge of the loft, and I slipped. Swearing, I was about to fall ass-over-tail when her hand grabbed mine and yanked me back.

"My hero!" I pretended to swoon. "Sorry, heroine."

"Egg," Tui said, but at least she was smiling.

Kestrel had stopped crying; she leaned on Hawk's chest, her exhaustion clear even in the shadowy loft. Raven peeped out from under their arms. She blushed and hid her face when I waved at her.

"Sorry, guys," Kestrel said, quietly. "I'm just tired."

"It's okay, sis." Tui yawned and stretched. "We'll figure something out, eh. Maybe we can nick a car and take a break from flying."

Condor sighed. "Can we find a solution that doesn't involve stealing? Please?" Dove nodded in agreement.

"Also, Evolutionaries will be all over the place with their drones and infrared and sonic x-ray vision tech," I added.

"That's not a thing," Condor said.

"Is too! The military's had wall-penetrating radar for years–"

"Guys!" Hawk shook his wings, letting go of Kestrel and Raven. "Don't worry about all that. I've had an idea. Just find us the closest major road, Tu."

"What are we going to do, hitchhike?" I demanded.

"Sort of." Hawk smirked. "But we're going to do it the smart way."

Tui arched an eyebrow. "And which way is that, Sergeant bro?"

"That's Cadet Captain Bro, thank you very much." Hawk tried to look dignified, but it was difficult with hay in his hair. "And it's my way."

Then, for some reason, he turned to me. "Falcon, what do you know about the science behind tinfoil hats?"

Late next morning, a big rig trucker slammed on the brakes just before hitting a large broken branch. While he was cussing, dragging it off the interstate and tossing it into the nearest field, seven Icari dropped out of a tree and onto his cargo unit. We'd hoped for an enclosed boxy thing, but this guy had a load of steel frames under a tarp. As we'd already let a couple of oil tankers and a huge flatbed hauler leave without us before replacing the branch in the road, this would have to do.

It was hard, squeezing into the narrow spaces under the tarp, especially as the truck took off with a lurch, but in the middle we found some hollows to nestle into. Tui curled up against me in one space, and Raven, who hadn't strayed more than a few feet from Kestrel since her breakdown, crawled into another with her and Hawk. Condor and Dove found a third.

It was cramped and claustrophobic, but I had Tui all to myself. As a bonus, the stacked steel all around us should deflect any Evolutionary tech. Which had been the reason Hawk wanted to pick my brains about tinfoil.

At first, Tui seemed like she just wanted to nap, but as I took advantage of the rare moment of privacy and snuggled my nose into the crook of her neck and my hands into her curves, she soon rolled over in my arms and pulled my face to hers.

It was hardly a romantic bridge in Paris, as Hawk had once teased. But the steel frames were going to make *some* sort of strong structure somewhere, so it was doing quite well as a substitute, especially considering it was being quite a lot more useful in saving us from certain doom and disaster than the aforementioned Parisian bridge.

As the day wore on, and under the masking rumble of the road, Tui said some things in my ear that I'll never share with anyone else because she would never admit to saying such lovey-dovey things, and I said quite a few back, and somehow I was even more in love with her by the time the big rig finally drove into a truck stop, and I told her so.

However, I was also cramped and hungry, and prepared to get pretty pissed off with Hawk if his grand plan didn't have a decent Part Two.

As the driver wandered off for a well-deserved break after traveling nonstop all afternoon and into the first part of the night, the Flight eased out of the trailer and into the shadows between the quiet giant vehicles.

"It's been twenty-four hours since we ate," I said, helpfully.

Hawk grunted. "You think my own stomach hasn't already told me that fifteen times?"

"In just the last hour?" Kestrel added.

Grimacing, Hawk checked our location on his phone. "We don't have to go far. Just need to wait for the place to close for the night."

'The place' was a department store and its associated mall. From the dark sky overhead, it wasn't hard to find the part shoppers didn't usually see, and drop down behind stacks of new stock waiting to be forklifted into the building. The tired, underpaid workers weren't exactly on high alert.

Eventually, the staff clocked out, and the Flight sneaked in through the loading dock just before the door was lowered and locked. We were alone inside the giant gloomy complex.

It was easy to see with the ambient light from various displays that hadn't been turned off, and the city glow coming through the large skylights. Also, even though there were still weeks to go till December 25, there was a giant Christmas tree and glowing icicles and fairy lights everywhere, which also helped. The hardest part was moving quietly, because every sound echoed through the tiled halls.

The first store we raided was the supermarket. Obviously.

I was halfway through my first course when Tui took the chocolate out of my hand and replaced it with an apple. I didn't argue when I saw the bar go into her back pocket and I knew I could try out a few smooth moves to retrieve it later.

When we were finally full, with bags of rations over our shoulders and favorite beverages in our hands, we moved into the fake-snow-covered department store to help ourselves to a few more urgent items, like clean clothes and thicker socks, razors, toothbrushes, hair ties for the girls, and insulin for Dove.

Me and Hawk were hassling each other in the male restroom, about who had the most head hair and manliest facial hair to groom off (neither of us, really – we were both scraggly messes looking even worse under the fluorescent lights we'd found the switch for), and debating whether we should look for sleeping bags. Condor was ignoring us and trying to wash some of the dirt out of his newly-chopped hair with liquid soap, having refused to steal any shampoo.

"Wonder if Dad got my letter yet," Hawk said, as he wiped bits of hair off his neck.

I snorted. "It's called snail mail for a reason." The other two chuckled.

About a week ago, Hawk had posted an actual handwritten letter to his parents, via his grandma's house. In it were the details of his fake email account, suggesting they get a burner-type phone and do the same, so we could communicate secretly even if someone had hacked or tapped their existing devices. That was the reason none of us had risked messaging our families, encrypted apps or not.

"Have you decided if you're going to write your folks, yet?" Hawk asked.

"Nah. I'll wait and see if it works with yours, first. Then if it all blows up in your face, my mom and dad will still be safe."

"Gee, thanks," Hawk drawled.

Then he stiffened, tilting his head and listening.

"What?" I asked, voice low. Condor froze in the middle of drying his hair with paper towels.

Frowning, Hawk sidled to the door and peered around the corner. "Was there a cleaner's cart outside before?" he whispered.

Condor paled. I gulped. "Don't think so."

Hawk clenched his hands. "Damn it."

Tui's and Kestrel's voices were echoing along the passage, like ours would have been moments before. Now someone knew we were here. Most likely some poor minimum-wage cleaner, who'd understandably bolted.

"There goes my nap in the mattress section," I muttered, sweeping my 'shopping' into my new backpack and grabbing the extra bag of food, feeling doubly-bad for the cleaner when I saw the explosion of snipped hair all over the sinks. I had intended to tidy it all up. I swear.

Hawk's wings were already disappearing out of the men's as he ran to alert the girls. Condor and I followed.

Kestrel and Tui shrieked as we dashed in. I got a great eyeful of Tui's bra and tattoo before she hurled her jacket at me. "What the frickin' hell, bro!"

Hawk and Condor had thrown their hands over their faces. "Sorry, but we gotta go!" Hawk said.

"We're all kinds of busted," I said, dropping my stuff, untangling Tui's jacket from my neck and holding it out for her. "Sorry, babe."

She left me hanging as she threw on other layers before finally accepting my help. Dove appeared from one of the stalls, and Raven peeked out from another, her hair tied up in sprigs like a little kid. She came out when I waved her over. Thankfully, fully dressed.

Kestrel and Hawk had their heads bent over a phone, frantically searching for somewhere to flee to.

"That'll have to do," Hawk said, shoving the device into his harness. "Let's go."

Loot in hand, we ran for an emergency exit, the smiling models in towering ad banners mocking us as we went.

Dashing down a narrow corridor, Kestrel slammed the bar and threw open the exit. An alarm instantly began to wail, of course.

"Freeze, or I'll shoot!" a man shouted. One set of shoes pounded towards us.

I shoved Hawk after the others then, slowly, lifted my hands, and turned.

A gun glinted in the flashlight; both were aimed straight into my face. I couldn't see any other details beyond the painfully bright bulb, which was obviously the point.

"Drop your weapons!" He sounded young, which did not make me feel any better as the gun and flashlight shook along with his voice.

"I don't have any," I said, every video of black men gunned down by white cops flashing through my head. "I promise. We're homeless and starving, and people are trying to kill us." *Please don't be one of them.* "Come on, man, it's nearly Christmas, and we've got nothing."

He hesitated. "Why is someone trying to kill you?"

"Don't freak out," I said, and partly opened my wings.

"Oh ... shit," he said.

"I know, right?" I said. "There are these douchebag humans who think they're *so superior* to us and they want to cut us up but the only reason they'd want to do that is because they're actually subconsciously scared that *we're* better than *them* and they want to know how and why. You'd think they'd never seen a superhero mutant movie–"

"Shut up!"

Under the alarm, I heard the safety click off.

I shut up.

"Put your hands on your head and your ... uh..."

"Wings," I reminded, helpfully.

"Jesus," he muttered. "Put your … wings away and get down on your knees."

"I can't kneel properly if they're folded, they're too long," I lied, stalling. "Look, man, I swear I'm no threat, I never hurt anyone, and I don't want to hurt anyone except the bastard who murdered my friend and–"

*CRASH*

The cop flinched, his gun and flashlight jerking toward the thunderous banging overhead. A hand grabbed my wing, yanking me through the exit.

"Move your ass, Fal!" Hawk shoved a dumpster in front of the door. There was a clang as the cop tried to follow us out and the door hit the metal bin.

Already bolting, I flapped frantically to get airborne, Hawk right behind me. The girls and Condor launched off the mall roof, leaving behind a pile of broken wood and other trash.

"Thanks for the rescue," I said, as cop cars screamed into the vast parking lot.

"Thanks for covering our exit. Let's get the flock out of here."

"Aye aye."

As the Flight met up and began racing out of the city's light pollution, I couldn't help chuckling. "So, how did your plan go, again, Hawkie?"

Hawk flipped me the bird. "At least we're refuelled and resupplied."

"And there were no cameras this time," I added.

Kestrel cleared her throat. "Uh, security CCTV?"

"It was dark," I said, confidently. "Ish. That stuff is always grainy and crap anyway."

"Couldn't be anything worse than what people have already filmed, eh," Tui said.

"Exactly," I said, cheerfully. "Nothing to worry about."

But, when the sun woke us from our huddle under the trees on the hills east of the city, we found that we were very, very wrong.

Because the cop had been wearing a body cam.

And the footage was going viral.

Crap.

# 3

# FALCON

To say that I was 'in trouble' would be like saying the Evolutionaries were 'a bit of a pain'.

Tui was apparently so mad at me, she'd actually said nothing. I knew I was in the shit then, if she was so incandescently enraged that she couldn't even find the words for it. She seemed to have passed through anger and was now hovering above it, buoyed up by the incredible heat rising from the rage-flames below. Kind of like the hot air balloons floating in the blue morning sky over the city a few miles away.

"The only good thing is you didn't actually name the Evolutionary Corporation," Kestrel said, tightly. "Everyone loves them. No one would have believed you."

"Actually, it's the perfect conspiracy claim. It fits perfectly with the facts because it's the truth," I pointed out, but Hawk and Kestrel still glared at me.

Condor and Dove sat a little distance away, talking quietly, glancing over at us occasionally. Tui had her wings to everyone, hugging her knees on a boulder and staring across the plain to the city.

In an annoying paradox, on that morning the sky was too clear yet too busy for us to fly. No clouds to hide in, and too many hot air balloons, planes, drones, and other airborne stuff. And, after the Mall Cop Incident, too many people were looking up. With nothing else to do and nowhere else to go and no way to get there safely, the Flight stayed put.

It was so calm and beautiful, it was hard to comprehend the insanity unfolding online.

"Did you have to claim that we're superior to humans?" Hawk asked, exasperated.

"I didn't!" I crossed my arms. "That is not what I said!"

"That's what people heard."

"You try debating perfectly when an alarm is blasting your brain and you've got a loaded gun and an itchy trigger finger in your face, and tell me how that goes for you."

Unexpectedly, small arms slid around my waist. Raven hugged me tight, and I hugged her back.

"See, someone appreciates how well I held up under terrifying pressure," I said to Hawk and Kess.

Hawk rubbed his face. "Damn it, Falcon."

"Don't damn me, damn the Evos!"

"I said damn *it*." Hawk flapped his hands. "Just everything. All of it. This, that, *them*."

"Yeah, that I agree with."

Kestrel rolled her neck, her angry energy fading into gloom. "We are so screwed."

"Technically, we've been screwed for months," I said, but Hawk flicked his wing between me and his girlfriend, using it to push me away.

"Go and think about what you've done," he said, with a half-grin.

"Yeah, yeah." With Raven clinging to my waist, I wandered over to Tui. Probably not my wisest move, but it was one way of ripping off the band aid, or whatever.

She wasn't gazing out across the view; she was scrolling on her phone.

"Don't you know social media is bad for your health?" I said.

Unexpectedly, she budged over so me and Raven could squish next to her on the rock, and actually smiled. "You're such an idiot, bro."

*Maybe she's not mad at me after all? Somehow?* "A sexy idiot?"

"No comment." She harrumphed. "But, apparently, every single other person on the planet has been making heaps of comments. Like it's actually any of their bloody business."

"They say there's no such thing as bad publicity."

"Falcon, there is so much bad publicity out there right now, we're not just in danger from the Evolutionaries, but every agency on the continent, and a bunch of citizen vigilante slash bounty hunter wannabes too."

I shrugged. "So, what's new?"

"The online shit-slinging about how we're escaped lab experiments and a danger to society, and crap like that, you spoon."

Before I could assemble a witty retort, Raven tapped my knee, and put her phone in my hand.

"Hey, it's not all bad." I showed Tui. "There's a bunch of people offering us a place to stay. You know, because I said we're homeless. They want to help!"

Tui looked at me like I was actually a talking spoon. "And we can trust exactly zero of them, you know that, eh? They've announced a reward for dobbing us in."

"But not everyone thinks we're evil and abominations and stuff. Even if, say, ninety-nine percent of these people are in it for the fame and fortune of capturing us, that leaves one percent of people who are genuinely on our side. Out of millions of people, that's ... uh, quite a lot."

"And how do we tell who is who, exactly?"

"I'm still figuring that out. But it's an information war now. We're out of the shadow and into the light. No more hiding," I said, dramatically.

Kestrel and Hawk came over. "What the hell are you on about this time?" Hawk asked.

Giving back Raven's phone, I sighed. "It's all about our image, now. People have seen us, heard us, but have about a tenth of the story. Of course one mistake will cause a storm of bad publicity."

Tui stood. "All we need is a good publicity stunt then, eh?"

I jumped up too, wings flaring. "Exactly! Oops, sorry, Raven."

"Oh, gods." Tui groaned, throwing her hands in the air. "I was kidding!"

"Accidental genius is still genius. What if, instead of hiding, we open up and ask for help?"

"Falcon, you'll get us all killed, or worse," Kestrel said, sourly.

"No, seriously, think about it! It's like safety in numbers, right? If everyone knows about us, that makes it harder for the Evos to make us disappear, not easier." Encouragingly, Tui looked thoughtful instead of mad. "We can't hide forever, babe. There are people and cameras everywhere."

"Yeah, I think we've all figured that out by now."

"Raven, what do you think?"

Our little Flight sister hid her face behind her hands. Her hair was still sticking up in tufts.

"Okay, that's fine." I rallied myself. "I'll put you on the To Be Convinced list. Condor? Dove? Thoughts?"

"That was kind of the theory we had about the Angelists," Condor said, carefully. When I rolled my eyes, he held up a hand. "I'm not asking the Flight to go to the Angelists. But Dove…"

He looked at her, and she nodded.

"Guys," Condor said, "Dove wants to go home to France."

The five of us looked at the two of them in silence. I wasn't sure what the others were thinking, but I was fighting a wave of hurt that the 'new girl' didn't want to be part of our little family anymore. At the same time, I understood why she'd want to go home. Not everyone could hack the rough life of a vigilante superhero living on the outskirts of civilization.

"Okay," Kestrel said, eventually. "We'll figure something out. We'll get you home, Dove."

The Flight nodded. Dove burst into tears. "*Merci, merci,*" she sobbed, rushing around to distribute soggy hugs.

"I think everyone needs to rest, now," Hawk said, 'hawkwardly' unpeeling the French girl from his shoulders. "It's been a hell of a few days, and we can't go anywhere today. We'll have a Flight meeting later. Okay?"

Condor and Dove nodded.

"Aye aye," I said.

"Yep," Tui said. Returning to her rock, stretching back on her open wings, she put her hands behind her head and shut her eyes.

Kestrel and Hawk wandered off into the woods, while Condor and Dove found a patch of ground. Raven sat in the shade of a tree, and started scratching in the dirt. I had such a strong sense of déjà vu, I nearly looked around for Owl.

It only made me more determined to DO SOMETHING.

The morning dragged on as I tried to think of the perfect plan, but I kept getting distracted by the growing hunger. Hawk and Kestrel returned just in time for Cadet Sergeant Captain Bro Sir to stop me raiding my own rations.

"We have to make it last, Falcon," he said.

"Yeah, yeah, I know, Hawkie. I'm just so sick of being hungry!"

"Fine. Eat whatever you want. But once you've run out and you're starving, you're not getting any of mine!"

Grumbling, I surrendered to Mr American Hero and followed his advice. He did actually know what the hell he was on about. And I wouldn't play the bumbling, sacrificial redshirt in this drama. No way.

Later, when night was once again rolling over us, Condor was napping, while Raven was thrashing my ass in a game of tic-tac-toe in the dirt, as Tui and Dove spectated. Kestrel was reading an ebook, apparently. Hawk was messing around on his phone when there was a weird alert tone. He yelped.

"Did it bite you?" I teased, as Condor jerked awake.

"No," Hawk said, through a massive smile. "It's an email from my dad."

Kestrel clapped her hands. "See! I told you he'd get the letter eventually."

"Yeah, he set up a dummy account through a brand-new burner device, like we suggested."

"What did he say?"

"Mom is fine, he's back at work part time but still doing rehab for his shoulder. And Cherie – he's referred to her as Sherry, she couldn't say Cherie when she was real small, I guess that's to throw off Evo spy programs – she's dropped ballet and is taking karate instead. She's already an orange belt!"

I could almost see the ends of Hawk's smile from the back of his head as he kept babbling and showing Kess the photos his dad had sent, while she did the expected gushy supportive things. Tui had frozen. I was reaching out when she jumped up, ran, and leaped into the air.

I knew what was up. "We'll be back soon, Rave," I promised. "Look after the others for me?"

Raven nodded as I turned. My wings scooped, my ankles joined and my tail opened. Catching the air, I raced after Tui.

She hadn't gone far, just further back over the hills, away from the city and its distant lights.

When I caught up, she was staring down, wings not moving much as she coasted in the weak thermals.

"You okay, babe?" I called, falling in beside her.

She didn't answer.

I tried again. "Thinking about Ria?"

Obviously, I'd never met Tui's family. Though she avoided talking about them, I knew how much she missed her mom and little half-sister. My brain-injured dad had been distant mentally for years, and Mom was distant physically as she travelled for work, so I didn't miss my own folks too badly. At least, when I did, I focused on Tui instead.

"Ria will be three, now," Tui said, almost inaudible in the breeze. "She'll be forgetting me."

"I'm sorry, babe." I wanted so badly to put my arm and wing around her, but pretty much any gentle contact was impossible in the air. It was like the one disappointing part of flying.

Knowing Tui wasn't the talk-about-it type, I stretched my brains for another way to show her I cared. I knew she knew already, but that wasn't the point.

Her altitude was slowly dropping as her thoughts flew back to New Zealand, on the other side of the world. The tip of her feathers slid below mine.

I had my idea. Carefully, I drifted sideways till my body was over her wing. Then I reached down, and softly ran my hand along her wing-arm.

She gasped and glanced over her shoulder. Her eyes touched mine, and a smile curled the side of her mouth. I wanted to kiss her, but settled for caressing her wing-arm again. Her dark brown feathers shivered in pleasure. We hadn't helped each other preen in a while. Running my fingers through them again, I decided to make up for lost time once we landed.

"Keep doing that, and I might have to tackle you, eh," she said.

I couldn't stop the grin. "Catch me if you can."

She lunged. I dodged, laughing. Twisting through the air, I entered a deep, tight spiral. Tui was right on my tail, and I let her nearly grab it a few times.

We were out of altitude when I swung hard around a tall tree and aimed for a ragged gap on the hill. Tui deliberately landed on top of me, knocking us both over. She pinned me down. I was not complaining.

"Got you," she said, her chest heaving as she panted. I was so happy to see her smiling again, I forgot my witty comeback and grabbed her face so I could kiss her. Hard.

She liked that.

As we were making out, I remembered the other thing I was after. Slowly, I slid my hands down her sides, expertly splitting my attention between my girlfriend and my sneaky search.

Okay, maybe not that expertly.

As my hand slipped into her back pocket, Tui broke the kiss. "Looking for something?"

"My chocolate bar," I confessed. "I'm sure this is where I last saw it." Grinning, I pushed my hand deeper into the pocket, feeling around.

Tui giggled, her chest pressing into mine. "You're not going to find it there."

"Are you sure?"

"Yep."

"Can I keep looking, just in case?"

"You could, or you could help me eat this." She pulled the missing chocolate from a pouch on her belt.

"Oh, I love you," I said.

She smirked. "Are you talking to me or the chocolate?"

"Both," I said, and dodged as she pretended to swipe at me.

"You know I will eat this all by myself, eh."

"That would be a cruel and unusual punishment which I'm sure is prohibited under the Geneva Conventions."

Calmly, she broke off a piece, and put it in her mouth, watching me watch her.

"Flock it," I said. Pitching her off my chest and onto the ground. Now I was pinning *her* down. I kissed her hard while her mouth was full of the chocolate. The rest of the bar was ignored for a while after that.

Eventually, we lay side by side, looking up at the patchy stars and finishing off the chocolate in a more democratic fashion.

"I love you, Tui," I said.

I could hear her smile. "I know."

"Don't you love me too?"

"Babe," she said, snuggling closer, "you're the only thing that's right in my whole messed-up world."

"Does that mean we can go all the way, one day?" I asked, brightly. I'd been thinking about it occasionally. Okay, a lot. But it wasn't like we'd had many (i.e. any) opportunities to even talk about it, let alone actually follow through.

She rolled her head onto my shoulder and met my gaze. "I haven't had sex before. Not properly."

"Don't you want to? With me, preferably."

Tui giggled. "Well, yeah. Have you done it before?"

"Not properly," I echoed. "I mean, I've messed around with old girlfriends–"

"I could tell," Tui said, giggling again.

"–but I've been saving myself for you, babe."

"Uhuh. Sure."

"I could've had a load of sex before if I wanted to," I said, defensively.

"Falcon," Tui said, putting her finger on my lips, "stop talking."

"Okay."

My pocket buzzed. It was a text from Hawk.

*You lovebirds done yet?*

I looked at Tui. "Are we?"

She sighed. "Yeah. Guess we are."

Another message, this time from Kestrel. *Dinner's waiting.*

"Yeah, we're done," Tui said, more energetically, and I laughed. Hauling ourselves up, we wandered hand-in-hand down the hillside to find the others and, more importantly, food.

# 4

# KESTREL

I was so sick of sleeping on the ground.

Curled up with Hawk, and with the others huddled close by, I watched my breath condense above me in the dull light. It had been freezing, literally, all night. Thick frost crusted everything. Without the tarps Hawk had rigged as shelter for the seven of us...

Shivering, I snuggled closer to my boyfriend, and counted myself at least a little bit lucky, even as the wounds in my belly ached.

The others soon stirred. Bunched together, we shared the remains of our mall raid for breakfast, and delayed the inevitable argument about what the flock we were supposed to do now by checking phones, finger-combing our hair, and pretending we were halfway normal.

Then Hawk sat straight up. "Holy shit! Look at this!"

Heads and wings bumped.

"Why is it always YouTube?" I muttered as Hawk started the video again. But my heart nearly stopped when I read the title.

*WE GREW WINGS! PLEASE HELP!!*

The video started like an 'anonymous witness' clip from a documentary, with a shoulders-up view of the person silhouetted against a window, the face blurred, and the voice digitally altered.

*"A few weeks ago, my sister and I got really, really sick. We thought we were dying – but then we remembered those viral videos, you know, the skydiving bird boy, from a few months back, and then the crazy incident in LA. And we realised. We were growing wings."*

The video cut to a new shot. Even Raven squeaked as the Flight swore, and yelped.

The camera was now close up on a bare back, which was bulging unnaturally. As the person turned, folded wings were clearly packed tightly inside the skin, shoulders to butt, the tips disappearing beneath a pair of jeans. The darkness of the feathers filtered through the thinned-to-breaking-point skin, a few freckles stretched into tiny lines. The feathers were birth-size, packed together like giant cells. Because we knew what it was – because we had *felt* that exact same thing – we could see every detail. The final stage of the Change had begun.

Hawk swore again, and I released a strangled whimper.

"This must be right before they burst," Falcon said, dazedly.

The anonymous Icarus slowly turned from side to side, letting the camera person record, in excruciating detail, the fledged wings inside their body.

Tui practically had her nose on the screen.

"It's a video, Tui, you can watch it again in a minute," Hawk said, gently pushing her shoulder back so everyone else could see.

Tui moved about foot, and no more, not taking her eyes from the phone.

The distorted voice listed all the symptoms they'd suffered. We knew every single one. Fever, back pain, extreme hunger, the weird swelling, the itchiness, the urge to hide from everyone and everything. Hawk impatiently dismissed a popup ad.

*"While we were recording, it ... happened."*

The close-up of the cocooned wings jerked. The voiceover was drowned out by a scream of pain. The Flight flinched as the Icarus fell to the floor. A censoring blur covered the head as they curled up on their knees, rocking and wailing. Another, distorted voice cried out. The camera fell to the floor. Feet and legs appeared in frame, and in the background, there was some equipment that suggested they were in a hospital ward.

The Flight gasped.

A dark jagged line tore through the wing-sheath from the shoulders. Like a lightning bolt, it ripped further and further down the spine, an earthquake wrenching open the skin. With a final yell, the Icarus visibly pushed.

Two arm-length black wings burst out, spraying body fluid and blood everywhere.

The Flight gasped, groaned, cried out.

Helplessly, we watched the Icarus stop moaning and rocking, and just lie there. Shredded fringes of skin dangled from their sides. The new skin was blemish-free and lighter brown, mottled only by the shadows cast by the new black wings. Slowly, joint by joint, they folded down, glistening wet.

Hawk hit pause. "Is it just me, or does that person have a wing bulge, too?" he demanded, poking at the screen where another blurred figure leaned over the new Icarus.

"Must be their sibling," I said, dazed. "Twins?"

"Maybe we'll find out if we keep playing?" Falcon said, impatiently.

Tui tapped the video before Hawk had a chance.

It cut back to the silhouette. *"We're really scared. But when we saw the mall cop video, we had to try and communicate. We're like you. Please, help us."*

Abruptly, the video ended.

The Flight was silent.

"So, that's what a wing-birth looks like from the outside," Falcon said eventually.

"And now the whole world knows, or will soon," Hawk said. "Uploaded three hours ago, already at fifty million views, and counting."

Raven was perfectly still, her eyes staring at nothing. I realised she must have seen another's wing-birth in person before. Her pain echoed through the Flight as we tried to comprehend what we'd just seen, the Owl-shaped hole in the Flight tearing wider.

With stiff fingers, I took the phone. "Upload data says they're in Hawaii."

"Evolutionaries will be tracking them down." Hawk shook his head. "How do they think we could possibly help them?"

Tui was waiting for the video to load on her own phone. "I don't know, but we've got to try."

"They've asked for our help," Condor said, quietly. "We have to do something."

Dove nodded emphatically. "It is so scary being alone. But, they are two."

As I blinked and shivered, Hawk pulled me close. "What do you reckon we should do?"

"How are we supposed to contact them, though?" Falcon said, crossing his arms and wings. "Their inbox will be exploding!"

"Hey, Rave, don't cry, honey," Tui said, suddenly, dropping her phone and crawling to the Flight's little sister.

Raven's shoulders shook, her face scrunched up and wet as she sobbed silently. Tui wrapped her up in her arms and wings, and Falcon's added another layer.

Gently murmuring and rocking our friend, who had the mental age as well as the size of a nine-year-old, Tui began humming a Māori lullaby she'd sung for us before.

After a while, when everyone had withdrawn into their own thoughts and space, Falcon said, slowly, "You know, there is one way we can pretty much guarantee that they see our warning…"

The remains of the Flight turned to him. I dreaded what he was about to say.

He grinned. "We make it go viral."

"Go on," Hawk said, frowning.

Falcon sat up straighter, his wings dragging through the dirt. "If we make a video message for them, and post it online with all those hashtags, it'll erupt! There's no way they, or anyone else with wings, will miss it."

"Which will also be a neon billboard of an invitation for the Evolutionaries to come and pick us up, you know that, right?" I said, feeling sick, the scars in my ab muscles pinching with the thought. "The second we post it, they'll track us down."

Falcon the lunatic grinned at me. "Then we'll schedule the publishing for some hours later, delay it till after we've hidden our phone signals and bailed from the area."

Hugging her knees with one arm and Raven with the other, Tui sighed. "It won't make much of a difference after that cop cam thing, eh. I know it's frickin' freaky, sis, but my mad-ass boyfriend has a point."

Hawk slid his hand around mine. "It's better to do it here, where they already knew we were, and sneak out while we still can."

"You're agreeing with him on this?" I gaped at Hawk.

He slid his hands to my shoulders and met my gaze dead-on. "The only reason I am is because we've got you. You can cover our digital tracks with encryption, fake accounts, and whatever else we can do to make the Evos' lives difficult."

"It won't just be the Evos," I said, miserably, my wings sinking to the dirt, and my voice rising along with the panic. "The government, the Angelists, conspiracy theorists, frickin' big game hunters–"

"*Kāti*, Kestrel," Tui said, sharply. "Don't flip out on me, sis. You wanna help them, right?"

Breathing deeply and slowly, I nodded. "Of course!"

"We won't be in any more danger than we already are," Falcon said, helpfully, and Tui shoved him away with her wing.

"Not helping, bro." She stood up, pulling Raven with her, and started brushing off the dirt. "We gotta do something, and we don't have heaps of time to do it. We're moving on today anyway, eh, Hawk?"

He nodded, and squeezed my hands. "You trust us, don't you, babe?"

The panic was subsiding into a weird past-the-point-of-fear calm. "Okay. But I don't have to be in it, right? And I don't think Raven should, either." Raven shook her head violently.

"I thought every girl wanted to be Instagram-famous," Falcon said. "Ouch! Okay, okay!"

As Tui removed her fingers from Fal's earlobe, Condor and Dove exchanged looks. "We don't mind going public," Condor said, quietly. "It's what will … would happen if we went to the Angelists, anyway. We can actually do something to help."

"Yeah, but we're not going to call ourselves angels, all right?" Falcon said, so aggressively that the rest of the Flight stared at him. He looked surprised.

"Come on, guys! If one garbled clip of me has set everyone off, how do you think they're going to cope if Condor and Dove pop up, claiming they're real live holy angels? That's a whole level up from pretending to be a prophet, and only one little step down from saying you're actually a god yourself."

"Oh," Hawk said. "Yeah. That would annoy a few people … and not just me."

"Understatement," Tui said, flatly.

"I didn't say we should call ourselves angels!" Condor protested, his black wings flaring. "I said it would have happened that way if–"

"Yeah, we get it," Falcon said. "But I still don't think we should put the so-called White Angel in the video. No offence to you, personally, Dove, but we can't let the Angelists hijack this and start putting words in our mouths. Okay?"

Dove blinked, looking bewildered. Her wings, half-white and half-blonde underneath the accumulated dust and dirt from the last two weeks on the run, flexed anxiously. "I just want to help."

I shook my head. "Falcon's actually right, guys. If we want to avoid links to the Angelists, that means we can't have Dove, or Condor, or me in it, not after the live broadcast of our visit. Anyway Dove, if you want to go home to France, it would be safer not to become super famous, right?"

"Ah, *oui*. You are right." Dove nodded, and even seemed slightly relieved. Condor wisely kept his mouth shut.

"But I'm safe to go on TV," Falcon joked.

"And I've already gone viral once myself," Hawk added. "So I don't mind doing it again."

Tui looked thoughtful. "If we do go viral, then my mum might see me. All our families might see us. We could send them a message, too."

"Yeah, I'm definitely not appearing in this," I said, trying to sound light-hearted, but flinching at the thought of my stepdad and stepsister. "But I'll do my best to make it hack-proof."

"It's our chance to share our side of the story," Falcon said, enthusiastically.

The others nodded, and Tui crossed her arms. "Cool. Let's get on with it."

After setting up the most difficult-to-hack fake social media profile I could, with self-destructing email accounts and several fifty-character passwords and a few other tricks I remembered from my misspent youth, we argued about what to say and what to show. Soon, it was time to do the video.

As Condor and Dove provided encouragement, and Raven watched, I recorded the Flight's message. Hawk kept forgetting what he was supposed to say, and Falcon kept going deliberately off-script, so Tui ended up doing most of it. At least we'd agreed to keep it less than a minute long.

Then it was all done, and uploaded, and it was time to schedule the post. Taking a deep breath, I tapped the final confirmation button.

"The countdown is on," Falcon said, triumphantly. "Let's get the flock out of dodge."

As we launched towards the south, we levelled out just above the trees. With Hawk leading us along the winding route we'd mapped on his phone, we hoped we were minimising our chances of being spotted.

In just a few hours, people would be too busy gawking at us online, anyway. The video would instantly go viral, and everyone would see–

–*Tui standing in front of Falcon and Hawk, arms crossed, face grim. Long dark stripes reach the ground behind their legs and boots.*

*"My name is Tui."*

*"I'm Falcon."*

*"And I'm Hawk."*

*My friends partly-open their wings. Tui continues. "A few months ago, we were changed. No one asked us, no one told us it was going to happen. We found each other, tried to figure everything out, but then they came for us."*

*"The evil guys," Falcon interjects. "So far beyond bad, you can't even begin to imagine."*

*"They kidnapped us, tortured us, in the name of science," Tui says. "They killed our friend when we tried to escape, and now we're running for our lives. We're sorry if you've been one of the people we've had to steal from along the way, but if we hadn't, we'd be dead."*

*"Or worse," Falcon adds.*

"We've realised we can't hide forever. And now we know there are definitely more of us. Homo sapiens icarus, they call us."

Hawk smiles, lopsidedly, probably making a million hearts backflip. "We call ourselves the Flight."

"One Icarus, seven Icari," Falcon says. "Or more. Let us know if you're out there!"

"And if you are one of us," Tui says, stepping forward and opening her wings, "and ESPECIALLY if people have seen you, then run. Hide. They are coming for you."

"And they'll kill you," Falcon says. "Eventually."

"Tell your family you love them," Hawk says.

Tui smiles, briefly. "And good luck." She adds something in her own language, telling her mum that she's sorry, and that she loves and misses her.

Then they jump into the air and fly out of view.

Cut to black—

—and the online crowd would go insane.

I shuddered. Only a few more minutes, and the video would be live. No going back.

I'd had to set up an online account, obviously, to post the video. And we'd had to come up with some sort of handle. After Falcon's enthusiastic suggestion of 'The Awesome New Icarus Generation', we'd settled on something much simpler.

Generation Icarus.

# 5

# HAWK

"I've never been this popular in my life," I said, laughing awkwardly.

Falcon scoffed. "It's not you, it's totally me."

Tui and Kestrel ignored us as they struggled to turn off the avalanche of notifications, currently rendering Kestrel's phone almost unusable. Every time she tried to tap something, another pop-up would get in the way. Out of our two million new followers, about seventy-five percent had decided to message the account directly. Multiple times. Or so it seemed.

"So that's all it takes to be internet famous," Tui muttered. "Get tortured for months."

Kestrel huffed. "And have a huge genetic mutation."

"I think the flying part might help, too," I said.

Wings outspread, Falcon did a terrible dancer's spin and struck a pose. "Not my good looks?"

"No!" the Flight said together, and Raven shook her head. Falcon laughed.

Finally, Kestrel sat back on her wing elbows with a sigh. "Okay, I can think straight again." She looked out across the agricultural landscape from the steep hillside ledge.

"What's the stats?" Falcon asked, dropping down next to Kestrel.

"Millions of views, hundreds of thousands of comments and shares, and the inbox keeps updating so fast, I can't read anything."

"Oh."

Everyone looked at Fal.

"You okay, Falcon?" Condor asked, grinning wryly.

Tui nudged her boyfriend when he didn't answer. "What's up?"

Falcon picked at his tail straps. "I was hoping the new Icari would reach out. But with so many messages…"

"They'll have the same problem, which is why we did the video in the first place," Kestrel said. "Your plan succeeded too well, huh?"

"We could read through a few," I suggested.

Kess held out the phone. "I've blocked direct messages now, so at least no more can shove their way in. Good luck."

"You're brave, bro," Tui said.

Falcon snorted. "Or stupid."

"And whose idea was this, again?" I started scrolling. Within seconds, I was agreeing with Falcon, as I realized just how monumental the task was. And how many people had sent messages in ALL CAPS.

"People either love us or hate us," I said, deleting a message which told us to cut off our wings and jump into a lava lake because it was a shortcut back to Hell, which was where demon-spawn freaks like us belonged, and then another message which offered to have my babies. "Or want to use us to make money."

"A makeup sponsor? Really?" Tui peered over my shoulder. "Should I be offended by that?"

"You have glorious natural skin, babe," Falcon said. "Second only to mine."

Tui threw a wad of food packaging at him, which he caught and began kicking around like a hacky sack.

"Come on, Hawk. Bet I can still beat you at trashball." The ex-basketball star bounced it off his head.

I waved a hand. "I've still got seventeen hundred trolls, fifteen hundred proposals of marriage, twenty thousand requests for nudes, and about a million religious rants to delete. Give or take."

Condor twitched, while Dove looked confused. Most likely, she didn't fully understand what I'd said.

"Hasn't anyone got something relevant to say?" Falcon demanded. "Like, hey, I've got wings too, wanna catch up sometime?"

"A few people have tried it on," I snorted as I deleted another one, "but nobody's offered proof."

I'd thought I'd known what the cyberbullying onslaught would be like, but some of the insults were beginning to sandblast away even some of my thick biracial skin.

During elementary, I hadn't been black *or* white enough for some people. Once I'd started combat training and accelerating up the CAP cadet ranks, though, it had faded away. People had moved on to easier, less-likely-to-kick-their-ass targets.

But now, safe behind their screens, the internet trolls had no fear, and no morals. Just a lot of words like 'abomination' and 'freaks' and 'do the world a favour and kill each other'. Someone had spent a considerable amount of time describing exactly how our mothers had mated with vultures to create us, but not even two seconds to fix the autocorrect.

For some reason, someone else had photoshopped Tui's head and wings onto a naked woman's body. Badly. And then sent it to us. I didn't bother reading the message that came with it, or even mentioning it to Tui herself. Just deleted it and moved on.

At least the next one was a text-only love poem. Going by the first two lines, it was agonizingly cringeworthy, but at least it wasn't smutty. By now, I was hoping my dodgy memory would actually come in handy by erasing most of these messages from my brain as well as from the phone.

Kestrel was curled up against her new backpack in the lee of a rock, with Raven snuggled next to her, sheltering from the cold breeze. Now Kess propped up her head on one hand.

"What if someone tries to make contact with us the same way? Publicly, I mean."

"Anyone want to check the hashtags? I'm a bit busy," I said, staring at a sketch of a giant bird house which, apparently, someone thought was a really good idea for us to live in, with a pole for a front door mat and all. *Yeah, right,* as Tui would say. Delete.

The next person had simply sent us a link. It took me a moment to decipher the URL.

"Hey, Falcon?" I said, chuckling. "Someone's written a fanfiction about you."

Falcon missed the trashball. His frantic recovery attempt sent it sailing over the side of the cliff.

Tui pointed. "Fetch."

"But, babe–"

"Rubbish first, then reading."

Groaning, Falcon dived off the edge.

"While he's gone," Tui said, crossing her arms, "are you serious, bro?"

"Yep," I said, grinning, as it loaded. Soon I was laughing so hard I couldn't see straight.

Tui snatched the phone. "Well, okay then. That's … a thing," she said, blankly. I could hardly hear her over my howls of hilarity.

"Okay, Hawk, don't hurt yourself," Condor said. I couldn't answer.

Falcon returned with a flump. "Remind me to tell you about the new game I just invented," he said, chucking the trashball at my head. "After I've read this masterpiece about me."

I was literally crying with laughter and struggling for breath. Tui handed him the phone and stuffed the trashball in her pack, then sat back to wait.

"I don't know what you're on about, this is great," Falcon said, within seconds.

"Wait for it," Tui murmured.

Falcon kept reading.

"Wait for it," I repeated with a gasp.

Then:

"What the FLOCK?"

"There it is," Tui said, smirking.

Falcon stared from the phone to me and back again. I staggered upright for a second look.

"This is…" Falcon struggled for words. "This is … AMAZING!"

"I know, right?" I was giggling, full-on giggling, as I glanced again at the fanfiction.

Falcon grabbed my shoulder. "Hey, baby, it's all so clear now! We are meant to be! Sorry, Tui! Sorry, Kess!"

"I don't know how I didn't see it before," I said, throwing a hand to my forehead. "How blind I've been!"

"Falcon and Hawk forever!" Fal pointed to the sky for the briefest moment before dissolving into the loudest giggles I'd ever heard.

"And our ship name is apparently *Fawk* which sounds just like–"

"I KNOW!"

Falcon and I collapsed, laughing so hard no noise actually came out.

"What just happened?" Condor stared at us. Snorting, Kestrel explained it to him, Dove, and Raven, while Tui chuckled.

Eventually, Kestrel tried to get our attention. "If you're both quite done?"

Fal and I paused, looked at each other, then burst all over again, racing each other with the terrible jokes.

Finally, after my stomach was cramping and my throat hurt, I sprawled on the rock and stared up at the sky. "I needed that," I said, still trying to breathe. "I haven't laughed that hard since ... I can't remember when."

"Me either," Falcon wheezed, "bae."

Too weak to chuckle, I whacked him weakly with the end of my wing. "If Tui ever gets sick of you, I'll be waiting."

"You're not the only one waiting," Kestrel said.

Struggling up onto my elbows, I grinned at my girlfriend. "Sorry, Kestrel. But seriously, you have to read it."

She smiled. "I get enough of your bromance in real life without reading a slash version. Please come look at this?"

Crawling over, I wiped my eyes and tried to focus on the screen.

She'd been scanning the hashtags, turning up messages both better and worse than those I'd been trying to screen. Biological debates about how a human body could fly; deniers and believers going head-to-head about whether we were a hoax; religious nutters *and* atheists having nuclear meltdowns about angels; all-caps screaming fits about fake news designed to distract the world from the real menace of the government/aliens/terrorists/the political right/the political left. The word 'abomination' was trending, which everyone avoided mentioning.

We were being claimed by every minority group I'd ever heard of and many I hadn't; people were writing poetry about flying, wishing they were one of us; some were even posting fan art of me, Falcon, and Tui, for Flight's sake.

Condor and Dove were noticeably quiet. But all of us were overwhelmed, it seemed.

"How do people come up with this stuff so quickly?" I asked, dazed.

"People live online," Kestrel said, shrugging. "And when inspiration strikes, they just throw it out there. There's already a bunch of accounts on all other social media using the same 'Generation Icarus' username. Even weirder, there are at least two whole websites dedicated to us, either dreaming up conspiracy theories like the Icarus Truthers, who seem a bit unhinged, so I'll leave that one for Falcon to enjoy–"

"Hey," Falcon complained, amiably.

"–or for hardcore fans, like one lot calling themselves the Flight Fam. They're designing Flight clothes and gear, wing-appropriate furniture, making art and fanfiction and stuff … some have even suggested setting up an Icarus charity fund."

"Both will be infiltrated by the Evos," I said. Tui nodded, and Falcon huffed in resignation. Raven and Dove frowned as they tried to keep up. I put an arm around Raven's shoulders, and was extra-glad that Kestrel had insisted on keeping Raven a secret. I hated to imagine what internet creeps would have made of her.

Kestrel also nodded. "But that's not what I wanted to show you. Have a look at this."

It was the inbox of our @GenerationIcarus profile. She'd logged in on another phone, and there was a new unread message at the top. From the account that had posted the wingbirth video.

"I realized you could restrict DMs to people you follow and who follow you," she said. "As soon as I linked with that account, this appeared."

*Thanks for the warning. We're currently safe. Can we talk?*

"What should I say?" Kestrel asked.

I floundered. "Uh…"

The phone blooped. Another message; a screenshot of an app's info and download page.

"Oh, cool!" Kestrel said, appreciatively. "It's an encrypted comms platform. Much better than this social media crap…"

Soon, she had it downloaded, had logged in, and had used a one-off code to connect with the other Icarus.

Kestrel's thumbs hovered over the digital keyboard. "Okay … now, what do I say?"

Unexpectedly, Dove spoke first. "We call him?"

"Yeah!" Falcon nodded enthusiastically. "Just video call them!"

"Is that really a good idea?" Condor asked. "Would it be safe?"

As the others descended into a heated discussion, I sat back on my heels and wing elbows, trying to think through the pros and cons of the idea. Next thing I knew, the phone was already ringing, and I was losing my place next to Kestrel as the Flight jostled to see.

"Don't think they're–" Kestrel was saying, when the thirtieth-odd ring cut off.

There was the usual awkward delay and muffled shuffling as the screen claimed it was *Connecting…* and then, there they were.

The guy had surfer-length, wavy black hair, and the girl had long curly red hair falling down around her glasses. While he was tanned, and she was pale and freckly, their pale green, Icarus-stretched, almond-shaped eyes and slim noses immediately showed they were related and, I guessed, part-Japanese. After a moment of staring, their identical broad grins further emphasized their shared genes.

"Oh, wow!" the girl said, her voice American and so loud it rattled the phone speaker. "There's so many of you!"

"Classy opening line, Rory." The boy snorted. Dark wings flicked and resettled behind him.

"Didn't hear you coming out with anything more epic or memorable." The redhead nudged him with her wing elbow, and grinned. "Aloha, guys. I'm Aurora, you can call me Rory, and this is my brother, Benji."

"Are you twins?" Falcon demanded, pushing closer and dominating the camera.

"Falcon!" Tui hissed. "Rude, bro!"

Rory and Benji laughed. "Don't worry, we get that a lot," Rory said. "Yes, we are twins, but I take after Mom and Ben looks like Dad."

"You're Falcon, right?" Ben asked.

"That's me!" Falcon smirked at me. Later, he'd definitely brag about being recognized first.

Shoving him out of the way, I took up a more secure position at Kestrel's side, as my girlfriend tried to angle the phone camera to catch all of the Flight. "You probably also recognize Tui, and Hawk. I'm Kestrel. This is Raven, and Condor, and Dove."

"I love your bird names!" Rory gushed. "I want a bird name!"

Benji peered at us. "Were some of you at the Angelists about two, three months ago?"

Condor shyly put up a hand. "That was me and Kess. When we met Dove." The blonde French girl waved and smiled but kept back from the main huddle.

"There are seven of us," I said.

Benji nodded. "You're the skydiver, right? And all of you were in LA during that crazy street chase?"

"Guess you saw us on the news," I said, wincing as I remembered hitting a truck at freeway speed. My healed ribs twinged.

Rory grabbed the phone from her brother. "We saw you, and we saw the winglets on your legs – so brilliant! We were so excited! Thanks to you guys, we were finally able to fly. Took a bit of experimenting but–"

"Whoa, what?" I tried to wedge a word into Rory's insanely fast chatter. "You guys aren't newborns?"

"Huh?" Derailed, Rory blinked through her glasses.

Kestrel put her free hand on my arm. "We thought your wingbirth video was recent."

"That was a deliberate misdirect. In fact, we started transforming shortly after Tyler – uh, Hawk – crashed," Benji explained. "We guessed it might be the same thing, you know, wings, so we kept a video diary of the process."

"It was so boring being locked in a hospital ward." Rory groaned theatrically.

Benji continued, obviously used to his sister's interruptions. "Mom's a doctor." Tui perked up and pushed closer. "As soon as it started, she arranged immediate transfer to UCSF–"

"We had a medical evacuation from Honolulu and everything. It was insane!"

"–we were supposed to be kept in isolation, but of course it leaked. People were poking around too much. Then when the transformation had finished and we were stable, Mom and Dad sneaked us out of the hospital, and we've been in California ever since."

"It seemed to be the hotspot for others, i.e. you guys." Rory grinned. "But then it went quiet, and even the Angelists hadn't put up any new angel stuff, so we decided to be more proactive."

"We used the video diary clip, posted it online, and now, here we are," Benji finished.

"Rory, how come you wear glasses?" Falcon butted in, apropos of nothing.

Rory struck a librarian-esque pose with her glasses halfway down her nose. "Just for reading. I used to need them all the time, but then the wings thing happened, and suddenly I could see really far! It's amazing! But my short sight is still a little out of focus. Do any of you need glasses, or did you need them before transforming?"

"No." Kestrel glanced around for confirmation, seeing only shaking heads. "And, by the way, we call it the Change."

"Oh, that's much better! I love it! And your winglets? What do you call those? And what are you wearing? Those belt things?"

Kestrel started to answer, but Benji dragged the phone away from his sister's nose. "This is exciting, talking to you and all, but it might be easier in person? What do you think?"

"Uh, yeah!" Falcon said, eagerly.

Tui elbowed him again, hard. "What are you suggesting, bro? You're still in California?"

"Yeah, it wasn't safe to go home to Hawaii. That's what Mom and Dad said, anyway," Rory said, sighing. "They're a little paranoid."

Benji smiled. "But Mom and Dad also said that if you guys are for real–"

"And obviously you are!" Rory waggled her red wings.

"–we can invite you to visit us here."

"Where's 'here'?" Kestrel asked, before I could.

Rory and Benji exchanged glances. "We've got a place away from everything," Benji said, clearly being deliberately vague, "but Dad said we'd meet you somewhere neutral and then bring you in."

"Not that we don't trust you guys. Birds of a feather, right?" Rory winked as her brother groaned. "But it would be safer than sending information about our exact location over the tubes of the interweb. Even if it is encrypted." Benji now covered his eyes and his sister giggled. "We've got plenty of room. And food. Lots of food."

Rory grinned, knowingly, as Falcon jiggled excitedly. I wasn't far off it, myself, but Kestrel's hand was still on my arm.

"We have a few things to take care of, first," Condor answered quickly, surprising me. But then I caught his glance at Dove.

"We'll have a chat and get back to you, okay, bro?" Tui said. "Even if we don't come visit straight away, we'll keep in contact."

"Fair enough," Benji said, his sister nodding rapidly.

"Okay, uh, I guess we'll text you, then," Kestrel said.

The Hawaiian twins nodded, and waved. The call ended.

The Flight was quiet for a few moments.

Falcon said, "And then there were nine."

# 6

# RAVEN

The Flight were talking fast again. Talking, talking, always talking.

I missed Owl.

I could not remember a time that he had not been there. Just knowing. Knowing what I was thinking, what I wanted. What we could do next.

Now he was gone. My heart hurt and didn't stop.

I rubbed my arm so it hurt more. The place where She had Tested me. If I pressed hard enough, the pain would be louder than the Owl-Gone.

But I couldn't forget.

The Flight suddenly stopped talking. Hawk and Kestrel and Tui and Falcon were looking at Condor and Dove, so I looked too.

"Are you sure?" Hawk said.

Falcon made a loud noise. "Jeez, dude, of course she's sure. If your home was safe, you'd be going straight back there too. Don't deny it."

"I'm not denying anything," Hawk said, his wings moving up and down. Shrugging. "But that would mean returning to the Angelists first, Dove, and you've seen what happens when we get exposed online."

Condor's feathers went fluffy in the worried-angry way. "Dove was with the Angelists for a long time before me and Kestrel showed up. She knows better than you what it'll be like to go back."

"I do not want to go to the Angelists," Dove said, making the word Angelists very loud and putting her arms across her chest. Her not-white wings opened wide. "I want to go home to France! With Maman and Papa!"

"If nothing else, we need to tell her parents she's okay," Condor said. "It's been two or three months since we were kidnapped. They must be going out of their minds with worry."

The others talked all at the same time, but Condor held up his hands. "I know, I know, it's been a safety thing, Evos bugging their phones, yadda yadda. But now we've gone viral, it's all a bit moot, don't you think?"

I didn't know what a moot was. But I thought I knew what going out of a mind was. In the Facility, She had told me that I was a new person in another body.

I think She wanted the other person back.

And if She put the other person back in me, where would I go? Would I go to where Owl was now?

Maybe that would be a good thing. Maybe the hurt would end. Maybe the other person would be better in this body.

Maybe I should go back to Her.

"I just want to be sure that this is what you really want, because there would be no coming back," Hawk said, and I blinked. It was almost like he had understood my thinking, just like Owl did ... used to.

But Hawk was not looking at me.

Dove nodded. "I want to go home. I like you. I like the Flight. But I do not like living like this."

"None of us do," Falcon said, putting his hands on his hips. "And now we've met Rory and Benji – or, we're going to meet them – we might have another option."

Tui put her hand on Falcon's shoulder, and his wings folded. The girl with the brown skin looked at Condor and Dove. "Sis, if this is what you want to do, we will help you do it," she said, her voice quiet, and she made a little smile. "If I could go home, I definitely would, eh. I just don't feel it's safe for me. But if you think it's the best thing for you to do, then we will make it happen. All right?"

The last two words she said much louder and with a scary face as she moved her looking to Hawk and Falcon.

The boys put up their hands. "All right, all right," they said.

"Just had to be sure," Hawk said.

Kestrel let out a long breath. "Because surviving day-to-day by burgling houses, and sleeping on freezing ground, is *so* much fun."

I thought the boys would be upset, but they laughed.

"And if we went back to Los Angeles, maybe I could drop in and visit my parents, too," Hawk said, rubbing his face.

"That's a long detour," Falcon said.

"Still going in the right general direction, though." Tui stood and stretched. "And, judging by what you guys have said, the Angelists would race out to meet us anywhere we wanted, if we asked them. With a whole welcoming committee."

"That's what I'm afraid of," Hawk said, his voice quiet.

"Oh!"

Everyone jumped when Kestrel made the loud noise.

"What?" The Flight said, and I wanted to hide. It didn't sound like a good noise.

As the others leaned in to look at Kestrel's phone, I pushed close to Falcon. His arm and his wing folded around me and he hugged me tight. I closed my eyes and tried to pretend it was Owl. But Falcon smelled wrong, and his voice was not deep in his chest under my ear.

"What's happened, Kess?" he said.

Kestrel sounded happy-worried. "The ex-Reverend is now the ex-Bishop. Look. He's left the Angelist megachurch."

"Why?" Condor and Dove said, loudly.

I opened my eyes and tried to see around Falcon without letting go.

Kestrel showed the phone. "Someone leaked it to the media, so they've released a proper press announcement to counter the rumours. The official Angelist statement says they've had a mutually-agreed parting of the ways … that he fulfilled his role in bringing the Angels' message to the megachurch to allow them to spread it further … and now he's going to seek further personal spiritual growth like the hermits of old … or some such rubbish."

"You think they kicked him out?" Falcon asked.

Tui walked around the Flight, her hands behind her back and under her wings. "Sounds like he lost the power struggle. His little congregation would have been swallowed by the huge church."

"He was always very kind to me," Dove said, worried-sad.

"His wife and son were also really nice," Condor said. "Wait … if he's left, then his family must have too, right?"

"Depends how the cult's structured at the top," Falcon said.

Condor made an angry face at Falcon. "We've been over this, Fal. They're not a cult."

"Yet," Falcon said, quietly.

Kestrel stood up. "Actually, this is perfect."

"Huh?" Even Tui stopped to look at Kestrel.

"Think about it. We need to contact Dove's parents, but the only way we thought we could was through the Angelists. Now the Bishop – uh, Mr Carter, has left, we can try contact *him* and see if he has any idea if Céline's mum and dad want to leave as well."

"He might try to manipulate the situation to his advantage," Hawk said. "Use us to get power back in the church."

Condor, Dove, and Kestrel looked at each other. "I don't think so," Condor said, slowly. "I mean, we only knew them for about a day, but they didn't strike me as that kind of people. They were totally out of their depth in the megachurch. Carter was trying and trying to get the Archbishop to visit us, because we were desperate for their help to save you guys from the Evos–"

"Aww!" Falcon said. "You do care!"

"Shut up, Falcon," Tui said, squeezing his shoulder, but her voice was not angry.

"–but I think, even then, there was some power play going on."

"Marlene, his wife, was very sweet," Kestrel said. "And Luke was nice."

"Who the flock is Luke?" Hawk asked, loudly.

Kestrel smiled. She had told us before, but Hawk was still forgetting some things. "Carter's adopted son. Our age. He was trying really hard to be friendly without being rude. Kept checking on us. He obviously felt bad for the way the adults were treating us."

"Or he didn't have anything else to do," Falcon said, doing the nose thing again. It was even louder with my ear on his side.

Kestrel laughed. "I guess being the black adopted son of a white pastor whose crazy angel predictions were suddenly coming true, and shifting from a tiny town into a huge LA megachurch would mean you ... were..."

Her voice slowed and stopped, and she stared at the trees.

"Uh, Kess? Hello?" Hawk waved to her face.

Kestrel shook her body and wings. "Sorry. Just realized. He must have been so lonely. Now his dad's left the church–"

"Or been kicked out," Falcon said.

Condor folded his arms. "Or chose to leave."

"Point is," Kestrel said, loud, "I can probably find Luke through social media, and talk to his dad that way."

"Kestrel is right," Dove said. "The Carter family is very nice. If they have left, they will help Maman and Papa leave, too."

"Makes sense," Tui said. "We'll miss you, sis, but we'll get you home somehow."

Falcon squeezed me tighter and then let go. "Can we eat first?"

"It doesn't take all seven of us to use Google," Kestrel said. Then she looked at me. "Hey, Raven, are you okay?"

All the Flight looked at me, and I blinked. Then I let go of my arm.

There were dents in my jacket.

"Raven?"

*I'm okay*, I said with my hands. My arm hurt.

Kestrel looked at the others with worry, but then smiled at me. "It's getting colder. Can you come sit with me, and we'll keep each other warm while I trawl the internet?"

"And we'll get dinner and a fire going," Tui said. She started telling the others what to do.

Kestrel put her yellow wing around me, and we sat on a rock. She held her phone so I could see while she looked at the messages.

"Rory and Benji have sent us coordinates," she called. "Should I tell them about our change in plans?"

"Why don't we wait till we actually have another plan in motion?" Hawk called back.

"Good point." Kestrel opened the app of the internet and typed some words. LUKE CARTER.

*About 74,600,000 results (0.33 seconds).*

"Of course, it wouldn't be that easy," she said to me. I wasn't sure if it was right to smile, so I just did a little one. She squeezed my hand and typed in more words.

The Flight had been doing that a lot since we had escaped. Without Owl. They had been hugging me, and touching me, and squeezing me. Kissing the top of my head. It made me feel safe.

It did not make me happy.

Without Owl, I would not feel happy again.

"'*Luke Carter Angelist Reverend Bishop son*' is not helping either," Kestrel said, tired-annoyed. "Any ideas, Rave?"

I knew now that the Flight changed my name, made it shorter, not because it was easier to say but because they were showing I belonged to them. Like when the Team called me One. Like how I had chosen the name Raven, and the Flight had chosen their bird names too, to show we belonged to ourselves now.

On my own phone I typed, *Maybe Luke is his Angelist name.*

Kestrel stared at my screen. "Raven, you are a genius."

I watched as she tried some different words and listened as she talked quietly to herself.

"Luke might be short for Lucas. No, that's not enough. Carter adopted him … he might still have his biological dad's name … that won't help either. Um … oh, what did he say?" Kestrel's thumb tapped her phone. "Oh! Yes!" She looked at me. "Remember when we first met? When you guys were trapped in the bookshop by the fight between the original Angelists and the Evos, and me and Condor rescued you out the back window while Hawk made a diversion?"

I nodded.

Kestrel smiled. "Luke was there, that day. He told me. That town was where Mr Carter was pastor, so that must be where they lived. So if I put in the town's name…"

Soon, Kestrel had found a website of a school. She looked at some photos.

After some time, she found Luke.

"Yep, he's a Lucas," she said, happy. "Now, let's see if we can find his social media, because I suspect he's not at this school anymore…"

Hawk and the others came to sit with us and gave us the food they had made hot. We ate, and Kestrel kept looking.

"Oh, the school has an account! Let's see if it ever starred our ex-Angelist friend."

"Here, let me have a turn," Condor said. "I've finished eating, and yours is getting cold."

"And after I worked so hard on making fire," Hawk said, with a silly-happy voice.

Kestrel tapped the phone. "This is him."

"Yes, I remember," Condor said. "I'll recognize him."

Dove leaned on his shoulder and nodded. "I will help."

They looked at the photos and the videos for a long time, and the Owl-Gone got bigger again. They could find pictures of someone they only met one time.

And I had nothing of Owl. No face. No voice.

Nothing left but the hurt.

"Raven, leave your arm, sis," Tui said, soft, and pulled at my hand.

I let my arm go.

"Here," Condor said, as Tui hugged me. "I think that's him in the back one, there. I'm about seven months deep, now."

Kestrel looked close at the phone. "Yeah, that's him. Don't suppose anyone has helpfully tagged him in it? Or in the comments?"

"Not that I can see, but it looks like some sort of big event so maybe there are other posts ... here!"

"Got him," Kestrel said, very happy.

"Nice detective work, babe," Hawk said, holding up his hand. Kestrel clapped it with hers.

Condor laughed. "What am I, molted feathers?"

"I can't call you babe as well." Hawk used his silly-happy voice again.

Falcon did the nose noise. "And *I'm* the one who gets Hawkie-bae."

Hawk pushed Falcon off his rock. "Next time you call me Hawkie, I'll push you off the edge instead."

"Aye aye, Cadet Bro Captain Sarge Sir."

Kestrel took the phone back from Condor. "Okay, I'm running low on battery, and we're all out of daylight. Did the last person to use the extra battery remember to recharge with the solar panel?"

"Here, sis." Tui took a hand-sized block from her flight harness and gave it to Kestrel. "Should have at least half a charge."

"Thanks."

Dove whispered to Condor, and he nodded. Then she talked to the Flight. "Snow is coming."

Hawk and Falcon looked around and sniffed. It was very dark, but we could see. The sky was very cloudy. Weather was still strange to me, sometimes. I tried sniffing, too, but I could not smell anything but the dirt.

There was a lot of dirt Outside.

"Okay, we'll erect the shelter," Hawk said, standing up. Falcon fell off his rock again, this time, because he was laughing.

Dove also looked confused as the rest of the Flight groaned and told Falcon to grow up.

"What is funny?" Dove asked.

*Me too*, I said with my hands, to show I didn't understand.

"Uh ... I could explain later," Condor said, and his face changed color. Going red. "Someone else want to enlighten Raven?"

"I'll give her the talk when it's time," Tui said, happy but quick. "Once I've figured out a bit more of Icarus biology, so I know what's necessary and what's not."

Falcon rolled onto his knees in front of Tui. "Ooh, I can help with your research!" He quickly closed one of his eyes. Winked.

The rest of the Flight made more groaning noises, and this time Dove was red.

I was the only one who didn't understand. Again.

"Can we make a tent now?" Hawk said, happy-annoyed.

I helped, and so did Kestrel, when she had sent the message to the person she thought was Angelist Luke.

"What did you say?" Hawk asked Kestrel, as he made knots and she held one of the ropes tight.

"I said: Is this Luke? This is Victoria. We met on the way to Eden."

"You did what where?"

"That's what they call their apartment block. So, Condor, Dove and I were kidnapped from Eden. Ironically."

"Huh." Hawk pulled on a rope. "Okay, I think that's as good as it's going to get. It's not the Paradise Apartments, but…"

"It has fabulous indoor-outdoor flow," Falcon said, in a silly voice and waving his arm. "The air-conditioning is to die for."

Tui laughed. Hawk looked at the sky. Small bits of white were falling. Snow.

"I'll take first watch," he said. He kissed Kestrel, and then began picking firewood from the ground and the trees. Kestrel took my hand, and we girls went into the woods to urinate. It was already very cold, and I was happy to get back to the fire and the tarp tents, where Tui made us wash our hands and faces and brush our teeth with water from the drinking bottles. Dove quietly injected herself with the medicine she needed, and Tui checked the five doses she had left. Then Kestrel, me, and Dove went into one of the shelters, and Falcon, Tui, and Condor into the other.

We lay down together, very close, to keep warm. Just like me and Owl did in the Facility, when we were only One and Two. And the Owl-Gone got so big I thought I would break.

But my eyes stayed dry.

Owl was gone. He was gone because of Not-Owl. The one who looked like Owl, but wasn't. The one who got so angry whenever he saw my Owl. The one who had hated us. Hated us enough to kill Owl.

Why?

# DIRECT MESSAGES

Is this Luke? This is Victoria. We met on the way to Eden. :-)

Hi Victoria

Sorry I think that came across really unfriendly, it took me so long to figure out how to reply without sounding like a weirdo and then I sent it and instantly regretted it

And now I'm just making it worse, aren't I

But yes, this is Luke :)

03:16 @GENERATIONICARUS

lol please don't panic. We're actually normal teenagers too

03:17 @LUCAS.DARKMATTER:

Wow you're up late

03:19 @GENERATIONICARUS:

Could say the same to you ;-p it's my turn on watch.

03:22 @LUCAS.DARKMATTER:

What, like in action movies? I was going to say that staying up late is actually very normal for teenagers...

Sorry that was rude

Your message woke me up because I'd put the volume up loud because I didn't want to miss it. And now I'm not really thinking straight and regretting my life choices (again)

03:25 @GENERATIONICARUS:

haha I can relate

Please go back to sleep, I didn't mean to wake you up

03:27 @LUCAS.DARKMATTER:

Nah it's okay, I'm awake now.

So what can I do for the Gold Angel?

03:30 @GENERATIONICARUS:

For starters, you can call me Kestrel. I'm not an angel. And I only get called Victoria when I'm in trouble with my mum ;-)

03:34 @LUCAS.DARKMATTER:

Oh, ok. Sorry

So... this is probably going to be rude again, but why are you messaging me?

I don't mind btw!! I'm just confused

03:40 @GENERATIONICARUS:

Don't worry. Now it's my turn to be possibly rude. I messaged because we saw the news about your dad, and the church...

03:42 @LUCAS.DARKMATTER:

You're messaging me because we're NOT Angelists anymore?

03:44 @GENERATIONICARUS: Yeah, pretty much

And we need your help.

03:47 @LUCAS.DARKMATTER:

Is it an emergency? Should I wake mom and dad??

03:48 @GENERATIONICARUS:

No no it's ok

I promise we're all right at the moment. Just cold. Snow sucks when you only have a plastic sheet for a roof

03:51 @LUCAS.DARKMATTER:

Yikes that sounds rough

Do you need somewhere to stay?

I know mom and dad would let you stay with us, no strings attached

I mean, we don't have a house at the moment either. We're actually in a motel. But at least it's a building.

03:56 @GENERATIONICARUS:

That's really nice of you to say. But we've survived this long. We'll figure something out. You guys have enough to worry about as it is without seven random teenagers crashing on your motel sofa, let alone the wings thing.

However, Dove isn't really having a great time, and she's decided she wants to go home. That's actually why I messaged.

04:00 @LUCAS.DARKMATTER:

Dove?

04:02 @GENERATIONICARUS:

Oh, sorry. I mean Céline. We call her Dove. We all took bird names (NOT angel names. Again, NOT angels)

Céline wants to go home to France. And we've been assuming that her parents are still at the Angelists?

04:05 @LUCAS.DARKMATTER:

Yeah, as far as I know they're still there.

Put it this way, they were when we left last week.

04:09 @GENERATIONICARUS:

Do you think maybe your dad can help Céline and her parents get home?

04:11 @LUCAS.DARKMATTER:

I'm sure he will want to help. I'll ask him first thing in the morning.

04:12 @GENERATIONICARUS:

Thank you so much

You should probably get back to sleep now. I feel bad keeping you up

04:15 @LUCAS.DARKMATTER:

It's really not a big deal. It's not like I have school in the morning

04:16 @GENERATIONICARUS:

haha yeah me neither. But I really should be actually keeping watch instead of looking at my phone

04:17 @LUCAS.DARKMATTER:

Oh, got it. Sorry

04:18 @GENERATIONICARUS:

Don't be sorry! :-) I'm the one who woke you up

04:20 @LUCAS.DARKMATTER:

Can I ask one last question?

04:21 @GENERATIONICARUS:

Sure

04:25 @LUCAS.DARKMATTER:

How did you know this was my account?

04:29 @GENERATIONICARUS:

I remembered what you said in the Angelmobile. About how you and your parents and your church were at the bookstore that day. I figured you probably lived in or near that town. Found the only nearby high school, and you were tagged in some photos the school had posted about seven or eight months ago.

04:30 @LUCAS.DARKMATTER:

That's kinda creepy lol

04:31 @GENERATIONICARUS:

IKR. Angel stalker. Sorry!!

04:33 @LUCAS.DARKMATTER:

I think I'll get over it haha :p

04:35 @GENERATIONICARUS:

Thanks, Luke. Appreciate it. Talk in the morning?

04:37 @LUCAS.DARKMATTER:

I'll be here :)

# 7

# CONDOR

"Condor, hey, Con, psst."

Resisting a groan, I glanced over through the freezing gloom. "What, Falcon?"

"What do you call a nocturnal Icarus?"

"I don't–"

"Batty!"

This time I did groan, as did several other shadows in the Flight. The night burned my lungs. "Please stop," I said. "Please?"

Falcon was too busy laughing at his latest terrible joke to respond.

"How much further?" The strain in Kestrel's voice was clear.

A flash of light ahead. Tui was checking the digital map. "About six kilometers. You going to make it in the air, sis?"

"Yeah. Don't land. I'll push through. We're so close now…"

Hawk called from the rear. "Where are we going? I forgot. Sorry."

With patience, Tui answered. "We've been offered a safe house. We're in Colorado."

"So that's why I'm so cold," Hawk complained.

"The glowing white snow covering everything beneath us didn't give it away?"

"Shut up, Falcon." Hawk paused. "Wait, a safe house? From who? Don't tell me Carter actually came through?"

"Yes," Dove said, firmly, to my left. "The Bishop, he has promised to help us."

"He's not the Bishop anymore," I gently reminded her.

"*Oui, oui*, I know. But to me, he is."

I let it go. As the White Angel, Dove had spent a lot of time with Carter. Now, it seemed, he really had walked away from his Angelist movement. His message had been broadcast to the world, supported by the Archbishop and his experienced, well-established team. After less than a year – and the loss of the Angels – Carter had left it all behind.

Left ... or been thrown out?

The media were sharply divided on the matter, speculating about the imminent collapse of the religious and financial behemoth. The public explanation only mentioned 'differences in direction going forward', and other chunks of corporate speak that sounded official but meant nothing.

How I missed the Catholic Church.

Now, we needed Carter's help to get Dove back home to France.

And she wanted me to go too.

The conversation had faded again. As always, Raven had been silent.

Raven was a slight shadow near the back of our loose group. After slogging through the night for so long, no one could be bothered remembering who was next on point for a proper V. Our wingarms and chests burned while our faces and lungs froze. Every flap felt heavier, and heavier. But still we pushed on. Tui, with the map, guided us from the front as Falcon lazily swept his wings through the air beside her. Kestrel and Raven stayed close to Hawk, at the back, leaving me and Dove in the middle.

A few hundred feet below, the wintry Colorado landscape slipped past. After weeks flying at night and hiding during the day, I could guess the time by how busy the roads were and how many houses had lights on.

Going by that measure, it was now so late, it was early.

"Taking the next highway off-ramp," Tui called.

"Wait, let me just get in lane!" Falcon chortled, sliding sideways, his silhouetted 'indicating' hand waving against the city lights ahead.

"Wasn't funny two weeks ago, and it's still not funny now," Hawk grumbled.

Falcon snorted. "How would you know?"

"Everyone shut it," Tui ordered.

"Yes, ma'am, GPS lady ma'am!"

Tui ignored her boyfriend as she followed the last few directions over a sleeping suburb.

"That cul-de-sac." She pointed, and tilted her wings. "Number ten."

After one circle to double-check the street number, the Flight landed between the ice-laden trees of the back yard. These days, or nights, we had to end each long, exhausting flight by hovering. Flapping hard, we unhooked and folded our tails with careful nudges, before dropping into knee-deep snow. Hopefully the neighbours were sound sleepers, or would assume the brief moment of heavy, overlapping flapping was distant thunder.

Falcon, while muttering something about wishing he was an elf (I wasn't going to ask), forged a path through the drifts towards the porch, Tui hard on his tail. The Flight trudged after him in a ragged line. In the weak moonlight, everyone's feathers were silver-tinged gray or black, the tips dragging wearily. Hawk had his arm and wing hooked firmly around Kestrel's slumped shoulders, while Dove and I helped Raven step over the bigger drifts.

"I can't remember the last time I knocked on a door and actually wanted someone to answer," Falcon joked, as he raised his hand.

Yet again, I silently asked forgiveness for us for all the burglaries we'd been forced to commit recently. Then, shivering, I pulled out the stolen, rolled-up parka from my cobbled-together flight harness, and draped it over my wings. Without the strenuous exercise of flight keeping us warm, the cold bit deeply. Our rapid breaths were condensing and hanging in the still air, gathering around the Flight.

"Wait, why am I the one at the door?" Falcon suddenly said, looking at me and Dove. "Come on, Angels, do your thing."

Till that moment, I'd been too tired to be nervous. But, as the other five moved aside, my heart beat quicker and my fist shook as it rose.

Before I could panic, I knocked, hard.

After a moment, there were muffled voices. A light switched on.

The door cracked, and a dark face peered around the jamb. Luke.

"Dad! Mom!" he called, yanking the door open. "They're here!"

"Shh!" Instinctively, I glanced over my shoulder. The Flight squinted into the light and shifted nervously, the porch creaking underfoot and wings rustling.

Luke ducked his head, though his wide eyes moved across the Flight without pause. "Sorry," he whispered. He shivered in his T-shirt, track pants and bare feet.

An African American woman in a pink headscarf and matching pink fluffy robe hurried into view. Luke's mom, Marlene.

"What are y'all doing out there?" she exclaimed. "Luke, didn't I teach you anything? Get them in the warm!"

"Sorry, Mom."

Marlene beckoned us all inside. "Michael, honey, and Céline! Sweetheart, we've been so worried. And Victoria! Are you okay? These your friends? No, don't introduce us now, y'all get inside…"

Marlene closed and deadbolted the back door, then ushered the Flight through the house towards a smouldering fireplace surrounded by large sofas.

"…we were hoping the house would be big enough. It was hard to tell by the photos. Who builds a house with five bedrooms and one teeny living room? But it was the only one available on the vacation rental site for long enough. So we'll make do. Come on, sit yourselves, get comfy, and I'll get y'all something to warm you up from the inside…"

Marlene continued bustling and chattering as she went into the kitchen. The shell-shocked Flight stared at each other as we sank onto the sofas. Luke hovered awkwardly at the door, glancing between us and his mom.

"…Luke, honey, why don't you stoke that fire?"

"Oh. Right. Sure, Mom."

My face was already thawing. As Luke inexpertly poked a log into the embers, the tingles became the full burn of extreme temperature change. I wasn't the only one, as the rest of the Flight were flushing and stripping off their outer layers. Soon, even the innermost sweater was coming off, exposing our shirt wraps to the air for the first time in a week or two.

And, unfortunately, it also released the smell.

Luke wrinkled his nose as he turned. "What's that – oh, um…"

"Oh, my," Marlene said as she entered with a tray of steaming mugs. But her smile didn't waver as she placed the tray on the coffee table. "Drink, then there are hot showers and clean beds waiting for you. At least there are two bathrooms!"

"Thank you," Tui said, finally getting a word into Marlene's welcoming chatter. "We're really sorry about the smell, eh. Haven't been able to shower for … ages."

Marlene waved one hand as she passed out hot chocolates with the other. "Don't worry about it, honey. Thomas should be joining us – ah, here he is."

The ex-Reverend, ex-Bishop Carter quietly entered the room, apparently not noticing the smell of seven unwashed teenage bodies and musty wings. "Welcome," he said, gently. It appeared he'd taken the time to get dressed while his wife got us settled, which I was oddly grateful for – I wasn't sure I was ready to cope with meeting a preacher in his pyjamas. Still, it was a little jarring to see him clean-shaven, and in an ordinary button-down shirt and pants instead of robes. At least his cross was still around his neck. "I'm very glad to have you all here, safely."

"Thank you for helping us," I said, awkwardly. "This is Tui, Falcon, Hawk, uh, Tyler, and Raven. You know Kestrel. I mean, Victoria."

"You can keep calling me Victoria, if you like," Kestrel said, tiredly.

Marlene and Carter glanced at each other, then at their son. Luke didn't notice, as he was busy trying to make himself small in the corner while still getting a good look at all the new faces, and the spectrum of feathers that were hooked awkwardly over sofa backs and arms.

"We'll use the names you prefer," Marlene said, gently.

"And that includes not using the name Angel." Carter chuckled ruefully. "I fear the term has been somewhat tarnished, recently."

Dove, who'd been fidgeting with her mug, burst out, "My parents? Are they okay?"

"Yes, sweetheart." Marlene reached over and placed a reassuring hand on Dove's. "They're still in LA, but the Angelists are looking after them." She patted Dove's pale arm. "You must miss them. I know they are missing you."

Tears glistening in the firelight, Dove nodded.

There was a long, awkward pause. I desperately wanted to ask why the Carters had left the Angelists, and why they were helping us, but I couldn't think of a polite way to bring it up. It seemed the rest of the Flight were too tired to talk, but too tense to relax.

After a long pause, Luke jumped to his feet. "I have something for you guys!"

His parents seemed just as bemused as the Flight as Luke dashed out of the room, but he was back in moments. Gripping a small bag, he trembled with nerves.

"When you visited us in LA, and you were … then you … you left…" He cleared his throat. "I kept these safe for you."

Anxiously, he thrust the bag at me. Automatically, I took it in one hand as I set down my mug with the other. Luke kept babbling.

"I found chargers for all of them and when you said you were coming, I made sure they were all plugged in, so hopefully they all still work…"

Finally, it clicked. The bag was full of cell phones. Our cell phones. The phones that the rest of the Flight had lost when they were taken by the Evolutionaries in the mountains; which Kestrel had carried when she and I had fled to the Angelists, where they had been left after the Evos came for us, too.

Shocked, I pulled out the phone I'd been given by my ex-boss Juan in Mexico City, and passed the bag to Tui. The phone turned on immediately. As promised, it was fully charged.

"I didn't know you had those, son," Carter said to Luke, but he didn't sound angry. More like proud.

Luke blushed and dropped his head again. "I didn't want … *them* getting into the Ang – their private stuff," he muttered.

Carter nodded, and Marlene squeezed her son's shoulder, smiling.

"Oh!"

Kestrel's pained gasp turned all eyes her way. Tears spilled from her big gray eyes. Shakily, she showed the Flight her satellite phone.

The screen background was a group selfie of the Flight from some months before. Before the Evolutionaries, before we'd met Dove.

Before Owl had been killed.

The sight of his healthy face, with its somewhat-puzzled, faint smile, squeezed in among the rest of the laughing Flight, was a shotgun to my chest.

Falcon buried his head in his arms. Tui was already rubbing his shoulders as he leaned into her. Tears trickled over her deep frown and tense jaw. Kestrel's hand clamped to her mouth. Face reddening with anger, Hawk's fists and neck clenched until Raven, who'd frozen, let out a high-pitched keen and collapsed. Hawk scooped her up. He held her tight as the Flight's little sister cried properly for the first time since her soulmate had been killed.

The poor Carters backed off, horrified. Luke bit his lip and his eyes brimmed. Clearly, this was not the reaction he'd been hoping for.

Taking a deep breath, I forced myself off the sofa, and approached our stunned hosts.

"I'm sorry," I said, softly. "We just…"

Marlene ushered her husband, her son, and me into the kitchen. "What happened, honey?" she asked, ever so softly.

With a tight throat, I explained. "The people who took us, they, uh, tortured us. And I mean … literally."

Weakly, I pulled aside my shirt-wrap to expose the charred scar of my crucifix, where it had been cremated and seared into my flesh by Frederik Larrsson, Junior. Heir to the Evolutionary Corporation; a genetically modified human, and a murderer.

Luke swallowed hard, and Marlene steadied herself on the table. "Oh, honey…" she whispered. "You poor things."

Carter's face was thunderous. A flash of the fevered, determined Reverend we had first met, so long ago, was briefly visible in his eyes. "How did you get away?"

My hand fell from my chest. "We had a little help, but we nearly didn't make it. And ... not all of us did. This..." I held out my phone. "This is Owl. He was ... killed."

"By who?" Carter asked, tightly.

Gazing down at Owl, my vision blurred. "His own brother."

The Carters gasped. "His brother?" Luke's voice shot higher. "Does ... did his brother have wings, too?"

This shocked me out of the daze. "No. And ... I think that's why he was killed. Because when his brother found out his twin was one of us, he was ... disgusted. Or something." Shrugging, I slipped the phone away into my harness. "We still don't fully understand anything the Evos did to us."

"Wow," Luke said, weakly. "Now my experiences don't seem so bad."

Marlene began to correct her son, but Tui beat her to it.

"Our pain doesn't invalidate yours, bro," she said, sharply, as she entered the kitchen, Hawk on her heels. "What did the Angelists do to you guys?"

Confused, I blinked at her, then at Luke and his parents. "What do you mean, Tu?"

"The Angelists must have been doing something you didn't like." She crossed her arms and stared at the family, wing twitching. "Otherwise, why would you leave?"

Carter smiled thinly. "You are correct, young lady," he said, with a trace of his preacher voice, and then Marlene's touch caused his jaw and shoulders to soften. "I was never sure about turning the Angels into a spectacle of quite that scale, but the Archbishop had convinced me it was the best way to share their message in the Internet era. Their reaction when you were kidnapped…" He shook his head. "They seemed to think it was my fault."

"Huh?" Hawk and I blinked at him. Tui lifted an eyebrow.

Carter ran a hand through his graying hair, and placed his other arm around his wife. "It took me longer than it should have, but I came to realize they disapproved of my family."

"Disapproved?" Unexpectedly, Luke threw his hands in the air. "They hate me and Mom!"

"Hate is a strong word, honey," Marlene said, but Luke cut her off.

"They hate us, and you know it. They hated that the Angels had come to a white man who'd married a black woman, who'd already had a gay son out of wedlock. They hated me. They still hate me. And they will always hate me." Shaking, Luke turned to storm out of the room, but his parents caught him.

"And that's why we left, son," Carter said, gently, then turned his eyes to Tui. "That's why we left."

I was reeling from Luke's outburst, and Hawk openly gawped, but Tui didn't seem surprised. "I'm sorry," she said, softly. "Seems we've all been treated like shit, eh?"

I had no air left to gasp at Tui swearing in front of a priest, but Carter just chuckled. "Indeed, young lady. Indeed."

With a nod, Tui seemed to make a decision. Dropping her arms, she told me and Hawk to go get clean and stop stinking up the place. But before Hawk obeyed, he looked Carter straight in the eye.

"Thank you, sir," Hawk said, offering his hand.

Carter smiled. "Please, call me Thomas."

# 8

# CONDOR

Yawning, and squinting into the afternoon sun bouncing off the ice-crusted view, I wandered into the living room. It sounded like Falcon and Hawk would be continuing their snoring contest for a while yet, and the gap under Céline and Raven's door had been dark. Only Tui and Kestrel were at the table with Luke, their hands wrapped around still-steaming mugs next to empty bowls and crumb-scattered plates.

Luke knocked over his chair as he leapt to his feet. "Oh, hi, Ang– uh–"

"Chill out, bro, we told you," Tui said, smiling. "Just call us by our names. That's Condor, remember?"

"Or Miguel," Kestrel added, at the same time as I said, "Or Michael."

Luke froze, panic plain on his face. Kestrel and Tui made a show of swiveling in their seats to stare at me, Tui with eyebrows raised, while Kestrel's lowered in a frown.

"Michael?" Tui said.

Kestrel's wing flicked. "That's right ... I never got a chance to ask you, Con. Why?"

"Why what, sis?" Tui turned her dark, bewildered gaze to our blonde friend. Kestrel continued frowning at me.

"When Condor and I dropped in on the Angelists, Condor introduced himself as Michael. I didn't get a chance to ask before the Evos turned up."

Luke inched towards the door. "I'll give you guys some space."

"No, it's okay." I waved a hand, and sighed. "The name on my birth certificate is Michael. I prefer Miguel, now, after … living in Mexico. It was easier while learning and speaking Spanish."

"But why did you use it with the Angelists?" Kestrel pressed. "What's wrong with Miguel?"

"Because 'Michael' is whiter," I said, simply.

Luke started banging around in the fridge, but I saw the glance. And I knew he understood.

"Ah." Tui nodded. "Gotcha."

Finally, Kestrel's eyes dropped. "Oh. Sorry, Condor. I thought it might have something to do with your dad." Awkwardly, she poked at her phone.

"Well, that too," I said, finally taking a seat, crossing my wings behind me. After such a long sleep without moving, I had a crick in my right wing-shoulder. As I tried to ease the ache, I was distracted by two bowls of cereal and a pile of toast being pushed in front of me. "Oh, thanks, Luke. You didn't have to do that."

Luke blushed, and Tui grinned. "We tried telling him that already."

"Don't have much else to do," Luke mumbled, edging around feathery elbows and returning to his seat.

"You've already done so much for us." Kestrel was swiping through the image library on her phone. Then she paused. "Actually, I don't think we said thank you."

"It's nothing," Luke mumbled, but Kestrel took his hand, making him meet her gaze.

"It's everything," she said, firmly. "You couldn't possibly have known, but you've given us our friend back. We can remember him happy, and free, instead of..." Clearing her throat and dashing her other hand across her eyes, she forced a smile. "It just caught us off guard, last night."

"My timing has always sucked," Luke joked, weakly.

Tui smiled, idly spinning her own phone on the table. "Actually, I think it was just what Raven needed. She didn't have a chance to put up her guard, or shut down. Maybe she'll finally be able to grieve properly."

Kess nodded. "And start talking again."

Already halfway through my first bowl of cereal, I swallowed and nodded. "It was really brave of you to stand up to the Angelists by keeping our phones safe. Especially when they weren't being nice to you."

Luke shrugged. "I tried to fit in. I tried to do what they wanted. Then, when I thought they'd finally invited me along to some kind of youth leader thing, it turned out to be their version of conversion therapy. Although it felt more like an attempt at exorcism." Kestrel gasped, and Tui muttered in Māori. Luke smiled thinly. "When Mom and Dad found out ... well, here I am."

"Sorry, bro. We know what it's like to be abused just because of who you are." Tui flexed her dark brown wings. Luke scrubbed at his eyes.

Awkwardly, I changed the subject. "Where are your mom and dad?"

"Food shopping," Luke, Tui, and Kestrel said together. We laughed, the tension easing.

"I had thought I'd misremembered how much you guys eat." Luke ventured a gentle tease, seeming relieved when we chuckled. "Why do you have to eat so much?"

As I finished my breakfast, Tui explained how and why we need a huge amount of energy to fly. Luke's shyness disappeared as Tui easily answered all his questions in detail. But, as that detail became more and more technical, digging into biology and physics, the cereal and toast sat heavier and colder in my stomach.

"I'd been wondering why the Whi – Céline couldn't fly properly," Luke said, as he accepted Tui's invitation to peer closer at her feathers. "And what those things were on your legs when you arrived. I asked Dad, but…" Luke hesitated, and glanced at me.

"Has God told your dad anything since, uh, we left?" I asked, failing to keep my pulse at a resting rate.

"I don't think so." Luke began clearing the table. "You'll have to ask him when he gets back."

"Which should be soon," Kestrel said, rising to help.

Tui's head turned to the door. "*Kia ora*, sis," she said, brightly. "Have a good sleep?"

Raven stood in the hallway, blinking. Her re-growing black hair was all spiky, and the spare T-shirt the Carters had provided fell to her knees like a nightdress, but twisted around the hole that had been ripped at the back for her wings. At Tui's gesture, the tiny Chinese girl entered the kitchen, allowed our Māori friend to give her a hug, and then hold her at arm's length.

"How are you feeling?" Tui examined Raven's pale face.

Raven rubbed her upper arm, and, after a long pause, whispered, "I am okay."

Kestrel and I sighed in relief, and Tui nodded. "*Ka pai*, sis. You're going to be fine."

Hearing an engine pull up outside, Kestrel and I followed Luke to the front door. We hung back, out of sight, as Luke greeted his parents and helped them bring in the huge load.

The noise brought Dove running, asking for news of her parents, and finally woke even Falcon and Hawk. After a few moments of chaos, Marlene took charge, directing me and the girls where to store the food, sending half-dressed, half-coherent Falcon to transfer our wet, clean clothes into the dryer, and Hawk and Luke to stock the bathroom.

Marlene also handed Tui a large container of painkillers, which she'd requested. The Flight's medic promptly dosed Kestrel, then took her off to their shared bedroom to change her abdominal wound dressing.

"Is Kestrel okay, love?" Marlene asked me.

"She's better now than a few weeks ago," I said, my voice low. "We heal fast, but she had, uh, surgery. The rest of us just have scars now, but Tui says Kestrel still has a couple of weeks to go."

Ex-Bishop Carter put his hand on my shoulder, regret in his eyes. "I'm sorry we couldn't keep you safe, son," he said, sadly. "I honestly believed the Angelists would be enough."

"It's not your fault," I said, uncomfortably. "And you're helping us now, more than the Angelists ever did. Thank you for coming so far to meet us. You didn't have to do that."

Carter smiled. "It was the right thing to do. I might not belong to my own church, anymore, but the Lord's teachings are still clear."

"Did … has God…"

As I floundered, Carter gently steered me out of the room, not even blinking when my wing bumped his arm in the narrow doorway.

"Have a seat, son," he said, waving at the sofa and closing the living room doors. "I'm afraid I won't have the answers you want, but please, ask me anything you need to."

Perched on the edge of the cushion, my hand twisted. "Sir, I … I wasn't always Christian. My father, he … he's an atheist. My mom wasn't very religious until she took me to Mexico City to live with my Abuelita. She was Catholic. She made us go to church, but I never … I didn't…"

Shame strangled my throat, and I couldn't look the preacher in the eye. He sat back in his own seat, relaxed, and waited.

When I still failed to speak after several minutes, he prompted, kindly. "Did you come to consider yourself Catholic?"

I forced out the words. "Mama died suddenly, and I … didn't cope well. I made some mistakes. I sinned. Badly. But Abuelita saved me, and I've been trying to earn redemption ever since." Finally, I looked up. "When my wings were growing, I thought I was being punished. It was so painful. But Abuelita believed they had been given to me by God. Just before she passed, she told me I had a purpose. I've been trying, but I can't figure out what it is. So … I hoped you would be able to tell me."

Carter went to stroke his beard, his hand closing on empty air. Shaking his head, he chuckled at himself. "I thought I knew, once.

Then I realized my wife and my son were suffering because of my arrogance."

"You don't believe you were being tested?"

"We are always being tested, son. But not by God."

I frowned. "Huh?"

"The Lord doesn't expect us to live as though we are on trial, son. The Lord wants us to love Him and to love each other the way He loves us. It is other people who place us in trying situations. God gives us the guidance to overcome those challenges, if we listen. He watches to see what we will do, and to help us if we ask. But the idea that He actively sends people and things to test us..." Carter chuckled, ruefully. "It took me a long time to realize this, but that idea is completely incompatible with God's gift of free will."

Blinking, I tried to understand. "So ... does He have a plan for me? For us? For our wings?"

"I believe that the Lord has a preferred outcome, to which he will guide you, if you ask."

"But I *have* been asking!" Frustrated, I threw up my hands. "At first, I thought his answer was the Angelists, and Dove. Céline. But that led to us all getting tortured for weeks. My friend was murdered. Now Hawk's brain-injured and Kestrel has been mutilated, and Céline is leaving and the Flight is homeless and I don't know what to do!"

Jolting out of my seat, I began pacing, feathers dragging along the carpet. My wings bumped the rental's 'minibar' liquor cabinet as I spun on my heel and paced back.

Carter sighed. "I can't say what you should do, but Marlene and I will make sure you have a roof over your heads long enough to decide for yourself. And, yes, Céline has made her choice. Perhaps you could follow her example?"

I paused with a foot off the floor. "Sir?"

The man gestured. "You mentioned your father. Céline is going home. Maybe you can do the same."

My mouth opened to protest that I could never go back to my dad. Not after what he had done.

But after my own sins, how could I judge him? Adultery was nothing compared to the harm I'd caused others.

Then I shook my head. I'd never been good enough for my dad while normal, so I doubted I could live up to his expectations now.

"Actually, sir," I said, respectfully, "I have to make another choice."

"If I can give advice, I will, but I can't make the decision for you," Carter warned.

"I know, sir." I took a deep breath. "I still consider myself a Catholic. I might not be a very good one, but I'm trying."

"That's all the Lord asks, son."

I tried to smile, and continued. "So I have been wondering, for a while, if I should seek sanctuary with the Catholic Church."

"Why haven't you?"

"Because Abuelita told me to find Hawk. To help him. And then the Flight came together, and we were happy. Even when we were in Hell on Earth, and everything seemed hopeless, we held on for each other. Now, it's falling apart. Owl's gone. Céline's leaving. And she's asked me to go with her."

Saying it out loud finally tipped it from a vague idea into a terrifying reality.

Pursing his lips, Carter nodded thoughtfully as I collapsed into the nearest sofa. "And your friends?"

"I haven't told them," I confessed.

"Because you're afraid they'll want you to stay, or will tell you to go?"

"Uh. Both?"

Carter chuckled. "When did Céline – Dove, did you call her? – when did she ask you?"

"About a week ago." I kicked at the carpet. "A day or two before we contacted you."

"And have you discussed it with her since?"

"Haven't really had the chance."

"Well, then." Carter stood up. "I suggest that would be a good next step."

Slightly bewildered, I let him shuffle me towards the door. But, before he could open it, I had to ask one more thing.

"Sir, is it true that Jesus really loves us, no matter what? No matter what we've done?"

"Yes, son."

"And God really will forgive us, if we are truly, truly sorry?"

Carter placed his hands on my shoulders. "Yes. If a person truly seeks forgiveness, then they will be given it."

"Even … murderers?"

Carter didn't flinch, but he did pause. "Yes, son. God loves us all."

The door opened beside us, bumping my wing.

"Oh, sorry!" Hawk said, sticking his head through. "Marlene wanted me to tell you … um…"

"It's breakfast time!" Falcon called.

"Lunch," Tui corrected him.

"I would have said dinner..." Luke added, and there was a jumble of laughter from the kitchen.

"Point is, food," Hawk said, smiling.

Moving to allow the door to open properly, I insisted Carter exit first.

"Does Dove know?" I asked Hawk as I joined him in the hallway.

"I think she's in her room," Hawk said. "I was going to get her next."

"I'll tell her," I said, quickly, and Hawk nodded, following Carter towards the incredible smells now coming from the kitchen.

"*Oui*," Dove answered when I knocked. "Come in."

She was sitting on one of the twin beds with her legs and wings crossed, reading. The other bed still had some of Raven's black feathers tangled in the blankets.

"Food is ready," I said, shifting from foot to foot.

Dove smiled, and closed the book. It was a Bible. I guessed it had come from the nightstand drawer, like in motels, but the sight still made me feel strangely uncomfortable.

"So? Are we going?"

Blinking, I looked down at Dove, standing next to me.

"Yeah, uh, I just wanted to ask you something."

Dove waited, still smiling. "*Oui?*"

"Do you still want me to come with you? To France?"

The smile faded a little. "Yes, of course."

"Can you just tell me why?"

Dove frowned, and my heart flipped. "Because you are my friend, and you want to be with God, too. You will not be happy with the Flight forever. The American churches, they are too greedy. In Europe, we will find answers."

My chest and legs felt heavy. "You're inviting me because I'm the only other Christian Icarus?"

"And you are my friend," Dove insisted.

Part of me wanted to run away, but I had to ask. "You don't think we could ever be anything more?"

Her wrinkled brow furrowed a little more, and then cleared. "Oh, Condor! I have not been able to think of anything but going home since the Evolutionaries stole us. You are so sweet. And *oui*, I think you are cute." Her hand cupped my face, and I stopped breathing. "Maybe one day. But now, I am not ready for any love but God's."

My throat was too tight, so I nodded, and stepped back, gesturing for her to go first. I followed her giggle down the hallway, towards the kitchen, and the remains of the Flight.

And I realized I was still no closer to a decision.

# 9

# KESTREL

"It looks better on you, sis."

"No, definitely suits you better. It goes so nice with your beautiful brown skin."

"Yeah, nah. We need a third opinion. Raven?"

Our little Flight sister blinked back at me and Tui. She was sitting on the bed with her wings leaning on the wall, surrounded by the huge pile of second-hand clothes. Marlene had cleared the local thrift store racks of everything in our size, and the haul was nearly bigger than Raven.

"Does it look better on me, or Kess?" Tui held out the red hoodie we'd cut into our usual Icarus super-cropped style.

Raven stared, and then shrugged.

Tui sighed. "It's a lost cause asking Hawk or Falcon. And Dove and Condor are busy with Mr Carter. You just have to take it, Kess."

"I know, I'll get Luke," I said.

I found him in the living room, messing around on his phone. "What're you reading?" I asked, leaning over the back of the sofa.

Luke jumped. "Oh, um, an ebook."

"I need a new read. What's it about?"

"Uh, it's a dystopian sci-fi thing set in a future where there's no internet or planes, only mobile off-road libraries driven by ninja librarians, and digital ghosts, and airships."

"Sounds awesome."

"The main character reminds me of Tui," Luke said, then blushed.

I chuckled. "Really?"

"Yeah, super-smart badass teenage girl of colour…"

"Sounds like Tui, all right. I'll have to check it out. But now, we need your help."

I chivvied Luke along to the bedroom and explained our problem.

"You do realise that being gay doesn't automatically bless me with a sense of style," Luke said, guardedly.

"Real fashion feedback isn't required, bro. Just sit there and say we look pretty," Tui said. Obediently, Luke sat.

When Tui pulled on the red cropped hoodie, to my delight our new human friend agreed it was a great colour against her brown skin.

"I like green better than red, anyway," I declared. "Luke, what do you think of this?" I held up a teal T-shirt.

"It's cute?" Luke hazarded.

I grabbed the scissors. "Good enough for me."

As Tui and I turned our selections into Icarus-appropriate clothing, Luke seemed to relax.

"You know," he commented after a while, "when you messaged me the other day, Kestrel, I wondered if it was an Angelist trick."

"Nope, it's actually me," I said, as I searched inside an XXL nightie for the information tag. Certain synthetic blends got really itchy at 5,000 feet up.

"Yeah. And the way that I knew that…" His voice broke.

"You okay, bro?" Tui asked.

"Yeah." Luke's hands were strangling each other. "I knew it wasn't the Angelists because you talked to me like I was a normal human being. I guess I just want to say thanks."

My heart flinched. "Luke, I'm so sorry they were so awful to you."

Tui moved, but Raven got there first, throwing her arms around him and squeezing.

Luke's expression flickered through shock, joy, fear, and confusion. Awkwardly, he placed a hand on her arm.

"And I know you keep telling me that you're not really angels," he said, choking up, "but…"

"You're our friend," Tui said, firmly, her dark wings resettling.

"Proving that, in fact, humans of all types, including mutated ones like us, can get along," I said, trying to lift the mood.

The door opened. "I sense drama!" Falcon said, poking his head in. "Everything okay?"

"Yeah," I said. "We're good."

"Aw. Boring."

Tui's feathers cuffed him around the head. Falcon chortled and briefly withdrew, giving Raven just enough time to release Luke before Fal returned with Hawk.

Hawk was video calling his sister, Cherie. "See, here she is," he said, and aimed the phone camera at me. "Wave, Kess!"

I heard the squeal as I did so, but I couldn't follow the torrent of words.

"Slow down!" Hawk laughed. "Cherie's trying to tell you about karate class, Kess."

I came around to Hawk's shoulder. "I bet you beat all the boys."

Cherie bounced up and down, jolting the phone. "Yeah and then when the mean boy at school tried to take my pencil again I was able to go HI-YA and get it back and he ran away and cried like a baby and I got in trouble but it's okay because he's never going to be mean to me again!"

"This kid is almost as badass as Tui," Falcon said, impressed.

Hawk grinned. "Well, obviously. She is my sister."

Cherie paused and listened to someone. "Okay, Mom. Tyler, I gotta do my homework now. Daddy wants to talk to you. Bye!"

I followed Hawk as he left the room with his phone. The first time he'd called his parents, I'd given them privacy, but ever since Hawk had asked me to listen in so I could later remind him of anything from the conversation that he'd forgotten.

Even so, I only kept half an ear on what they were saying, as I wanted to check in on the latest news from my favourite singers and movie franchises. It was part of Tui's We Are Still Normal plan.

My full attention returned when Hawk began talking about the Icarus twins we'd met online. His dad listened without comment until Hawk mentioned Hawaii.

"Describe them to me again?"

"The girl is a redhead, and the boy has black hair. His skin is more like mine, and she's a bit paler, but really they're both shades of native Hawaiian."

The Air Force colonel nodded. "I think I know their parents."

"You do?" I blurted.

"Put it this way: I remember a couple – who very closely match that description – at the Beijing clinic. She was Scottish, a doctor, I think, and I knew the husband through work. Commander Drew Richardson, from the Navy. He was actually the one who recommended the clinic to us. Your mom and I tried to contact him after your accident, but he was on leave and we couldn't track him down."

Hawk and I glanced at each other. "Rory said their mom is a doctor," Hawk said.

"What did the dad look like?" I asked.

"He's Japanese-Hawaiian, I believe."

"That must be them," Hawk said. "That's crazy."

"This might be the breakthrough we need," Colonel Owen said. "With our combined contacts, we should be able to find this Schmidt/Goldberg woman and finally get answers."

"We can ask them to call you, Dad. I'm sure Rory and Ben will pass on a message to, uh…"

"Commander Richardson," Hawk's dad said, patiently. "If he took leave because his kids grew wings, and I'm still on medical leave with my shoulder, then I'm sure we could find time in our busy schedules to liaise." He grinned.

"I'll send your details now," I said, sliding my phone out of my jeans pocket.

My wings twitched restlessly as I typed. It was the same instinct as jiggling your leg. I wasn't sure why I was suddenly anxious; but then, this was the first time we'd had a lead. At least, one that didn't involve Evolutionaries.

*Hey, is your dad Commander Drew Richardson of the Navy?*

The reply came back in under a minute.

*How the HELL did you know that????*

Shaking, I answered as quickly as possible. *Hawk's dad knows your dad. Colonel Robert Owen of the Air Force. They went to the IVF clinic at the same time or something. Can you give your dad Colonel Owen's info please? He wants to talk.*

I copied in the contact details and sent it.

*Sure,* came the reply. *I mean, you could have opened with that and not given me a heart attack lol. I'll let him know.* This was followed by emojis that included a cross-eyed face, a crying-laughing face, a silly tongue face, and a skull-and-crossbones.

"Oops," I muttered, and sent: *Thanks :-)*

As I went to update the Flight, I wondered why Richardson and his doctor wife hadn't contacted the Owens sooner. Surely they, along with the rest of the world, would have seen Hawk (and by extension, his parents) go viral months ago. What were they hiding?

Then I snorted. They were hiding their kids. The Richardsons wouldn't have contacted the Owens for the same reason we hadn't let Dove immediately and openly call her parents and/or the Angelists.

I sent another quick message.

*PS that's Colonel Owen's secret burner phone and alias email he recently set up to talk to us safely. It SHOULD be free of surveillance. We've sent him the link to the encryption app too.*

Aurora or Benji, whoever currently had the phone, replied in seconds. *Thanks, that helps! Talk soon.* Going by the number of cheerful and slightly crazy emojis that also followed this message, I had a feeling it was Rory.

Tuning back into Hawk's conversation with his dad, I heard Colonel Owen say, "...he's the one who assaulted you?"

"Yeah." Hawk's voice was low, quiet. "Hope Sensei Kasumi never finds out."

His dad harrumphed. "She's been asking after you when we drop off Cherie at training. But I won't mention it."

"Thanks."

"Too bad we don't have any proof of the bastard's crimes."

"Even if the cops believed us and got a warrant, Dad, the Evos will have erased all security footage and evidence," Hawk said. "Every trace of our presence, even the slightest hint of Owl's body, will be gone. There's nothing we can do about it. Which is why we've been trying to ignore it. Him. Them."

"Mm." Clearly unconvinced, Colonel Owen was tapping at his computer on the other end. "I'll keep an eye on these updates for you, anyway."

"What updates?" I asked.

Owen's eyes flicked to his phone, apparently propped up next to his computer. "Sorry, Kestrel, I didn't realise you were back."

"It's okay, Dad," Hawk said, at the same time as I said, "What have I missed?"

The Colonel hesitated.

"I'll tell her, Dad. Probably time to sign off, anyway."

A big sigh. "All right, son. We miss you."

"Miss you too, Dad. As soon as we get Dove sorted out, I'll try visit."

"Or we could come to you."

Hawk grinned, his jaw tight. "We'll figure something out."

"Love you, son."

"Love you, Dad."

Colonel Owen's image froze, then disappeared.

"What's been going on?" I asked, immediately, crossing my arms.

Hawk shoved his phone into his pocket. "Don't get mad at me, okay?"

"How can I possibly promise that?"

Hawk sighed and ran his hand through his mess of brown hair. "Short version: the Evolutionaries have been making regular press releases about their charity and public-good projects, presented by Junior Flockface himself. I didn't want you or Raven to see him again."

The wounds in my lower abdomen spiked with pain, and freezing adrenaline flushed through me. While I had, by some mercy, been fully unconscious at the time, I was certain the main mutilator had been Frederik Larrsson, Junior. The thought of that psychopathic maniac slicing my body open, digging around in my insides, stealing parts of me that could never be replaced...

Hawk had been right. I didn't want to see. Didn't want to know.

After a long pause, during which I stared at the wall just past Hawk's head, my boyfriend put a wary hand on my arm. "You're not mad at me?"

With a shiver, I unlocked my arms and wings from their tense folds. "I'm not mad. I ... Thank you. I don't want to know any more."

Hawk pulled me close with his arms and wings. I tilted my head, instinctively, needing comfort. His lips met mine and poured warmth into me, washing away the icy fear until only a few traces remained in the deepest recesses of my heart.

"Do the others know?" I asked.

"Falcon and Tui have seen the videos," Hawk said, without loosening his arms or feathers around me. "Condor and Dove refused, and we've been hiding it from Raven too. We didn't think she'd want to see either Owl's brother or her own sister."

"Yeah." I rested my head on Hawk's shoulder. "Good call."

"But, if you need to, you know you can talk to me, right?" Hawk said, awkwardly, after a while. "About anything."

"I don't know if there's anything left to say."

Hawk's chest moved as he shrugged. "I don't know. Isn't it supposed to help? Talking about it?"

"If I ever feel the urge, I'll let you know," I said, aiming for wry, though I'm sure it came out bitter. Hawk just pressed his mouth to mine again.

We automatically parted when the front door slammed. Luke's mum was back.

Everyone appeared in the hallway, rushing to help Marlene and succeeding only in clogging up the narrow passageway.

Laughing, Mrs Carter easily took charge. Knowing by now Hawk's tendency to 'forget' that he wasn't supposed to sample the food on the way, he and most of the others were sent off to other chores, whilst Condor, Luke, and I remained in the kitchen as her extra hands.

"I hope this will be enough," Marlene said, brightly, but with a touch of anxiety, wiping her hands off on her fluorescent floral skirt.

Biting my lip, I surveyed the stuffed pantry. It would be a week's worth, if that, at the Flight's current rate. Not for the first time, I felt terribly guilty for how much we were costing the Carters. "How long will you be gone?"

Marlene looked to her husband, and Carter smiled at her before answering me. "It may take us a few days to speak with Céline's parents. It may take a few days more to convince them. And then, another few days to arrange their safe exit and transport ... possibly a week, maybe two."

Two weeks! We'd have to go back to rationing. Even after only a few days of regular large meals, it seemed impossible to survive. But we would. We'd survived far worse than a warm, safe, anonymous house with a stocked larder before.

"What about online grocery deliveries?" Luke suggested.

Carter rubbed his chin. "A good idea, son, but they can hardly answer the door."

"I could stay," Luke offered, quietly. I wasn't even sure I'd heard him correctly. Condor glanced at him and then me, as his parents frowned.

"Pardon, love?" Luke's mum asked.

"I could stay," Luke said, louder. "I can drive, I can leave the house, and I can safely answer the door. I help the Flight while you rescue Dove's mom and dad."

Mr and Mrs Carter hesitated. "Are you sure, sweetheart?" Marlene said.

Luke shifted from foot to foot. If he'd had wings, they'd have been fidgeting and resettling. "The Flight have already been better friends to me than anyone at school, or at the Angelists. I want to help them."

His parents exchanged a meaningful look. But eventually, they nodded.

"I think it's a good idea, son," Mr Carter said, warmly. "If anything, you'll be safer here than in LA."

And so, it was decided.

The Flight and Luke saw off his parents later that evening. It would take a couple of days for them to drive the 1000 miles from Colorado to California, so they were getting a couple of hours' head start before stopping for the night nearer the Colorado-Utah border.

Afterwards, the Flight decided to watch a movie. I snuggled up with Hawk on a sofa and, shielded by his sturdy brown wing, his hand wandered in such a way that I was completely unaware of the screen and desperately wanted to follow him into his bed when it was time to say goodnight.

However, I had to settle for a lingering kiss in the living room before following Tui to our girls-only bedroom; Dove and Raven went into theirs, while Hawk and Falcon half-tackled each other as they good-naturedly fought to be the first through their own door. Condor retired in a much more dignified fashion into the twin-bed room he insisted on sharing with Luke, rather than banishing the poor guy to the sofa. Without parents around, it felt more like a dorm than the 'staying with distant relatives' feeling the house had had previously.

I wondered how long the current arrangements would last – and if, maybe not tomorrow but perhaps the next day, I'd be brave enough to suggest an adjustment to the rooming list.

# GROUP CHAT

RORY created the group.

RORY:

Hello, the Flight!! How's things??

KESTREL:

We're fine. Still no ETA, sorry. Waiting to get Dove sorted. And laying low.

RORY:

Totally understand. Benji's the impatient one.

BEN:

Don't project your flaws onto me. We're fraternal, not identical.

RORY:

hehehe

What are you guys doing while you wait? I'm super bored. Mom and Dad won't let us out!

KESTREL:

> We're stuck inside too. I can get some of the others on the app too, then you'll have at least one person to talk to anytime.

RORY:

Yes please!!

KESTREL added HAWK, FALCON, TUI, and CONDOR to the group

RORY:

Aloha everyone! How are you?

HAWK:

Like Kestrel said, we're bored too, being stuck inside and only going out at night. And Falcon keeps making bad vampire jokes.

FALCON:

Do not!

I keep making EXCELLENT vampire jokes

RORY:

Such as??

TUI:

Please don't encourage him.

FALCON:

Too late

What do you get when you cross Dracula with a bird kid?

BEN:

I'm afraid to ask

RORY:

I'm not!! What?

FALCON:

A VAMPIRACUS

RORY:

HAHAHAHAHA WTF!

TUI:

I tried to warn you.

HAWK:

It's not too late to cancel our rendezvous…

RORY:

Are you kidding?? I've just found my Icarus name and everything!!

KESTREL:

Oh yeah?

RORY:

Lory! Small but loud and brightly colored bird, related to lorikeets. Easy to remember because it rhymes with Rory

But if you guys don't like it, or if it doesn't fit with the rest of the Flight, I can find something else.

KESTREL:

Sounds perfect! :-)

HAWK:

I like it. Hi, Lory :D

RORY changed their nickname to LORY.

LORY:

Hi, Hawk! :-D Hi everyone!!

TUI:

Kia ora sis :)

FALCON:

Hiya Lory! B-)

What about you, Ben?

LORY:

Ben is part fish as well as part bird, so I reckon either Petrel or Tern for him

BEN:

Yeah. I'm not convinced.

FALCON:

Someone got out of the wrong side of the nest. What's up, Benny Boy?

HAWK:

> Shut up Falcon

TUI:

> Don't mind Fal. He thinks he's the clown of the group.

LORY:

> I think he's hilarious. Feel free to send me puns ANY time, Falcon ;p

FALCON:

> Will do!

CONDOR:

> Wow, I'm in the kitchen for five minutes and my phone blows up

BEN:

> Know what you mean. My phone was almost unusable for hours after I posted that video online.

KESTREL:

> Same here. But hey, it worked, right?

TUI:

> Have you guys had any other messages from potential or proven Icari?

BEN:

> No DMs. And nothing obviously posted online. Only the same rumors you've probably seen.

HAWK:

Honestly, no, we've been avoiding it. All the weirdos and their creepy messages put us off

BEN:

Check these out:

Medical Report Leaked: Australian Teen In Hospital With Suspected Wings

Chinese Officials Deny Bird-Kid Cover-Up

Russian Hunters Stumble Across Winged Body

FALCON:

Flocking hell!

HAWK:

Holy crap

CONDOR:

:-(

LORY:

Way to kill the mood, Ben.

BEN:

I felt like you guys should know.

KESTREL:

Yeah, I don't think I need to read the articles, but thanks for the heads-up. Makes you realise it's better to be bored and safe

TUI:

I've had more than enough stress to last me a long time

LORY:

Makes you wonder how many more of us are out there in hiding, though…

BEN:

I don't think we'll be wondering long. The Internet is on the case.

KESTREL:

The "Icarus Truthers" or the Flight Fam? Or are there others now?

BEN:

There are definitely more. And it's not just random people playing detective. Here's a bit of one report:

The find has stirred up even more controversy online, as it appears that more and more of these so-called "Icari" children will continue emerging. Hospitals and radiography centers around the world are reporting a significant surge in parents seeking x-rays, ultrasounds, and MRI scans of their children, paranoid that the bizarre mutation might be contagious or perhaps due to some widespread contamination. Government officials and the World Health Organisation are pleading for calm, insisting it is impossible this is a random coincidence, or due to some naturally occurring pathogen.

The CIA, Interpol, and WHO are working closely together to compile information, supported by the efforts of amateur sleuths. In the wake of recent events, including the formation of the Church of the Angelists in the US, multiple public websites and social media groups have dedicated themselves to solving the winged teen mystery. There are already four fairly complete profiles available, starting with the first to go viral, Tyler Robert Owen of Los Angeles, California.

HAWK:

I'm not sure whether I'm terrified or flattered that I'm first on the list

FALCON:

Here come the men in blaaaaaack!!

TUI:

So, what's the number for the CIA? I have a crime against comedic timing that I'd like to report

FALCON:

If I go missing, come look for me in Area 51 where I'll be learning to speak to the aliens mwahahaha

BEN:

...are you guys always like this?

CONDOR:

This is Falcon on a good day

HAWK:

Again, not too late to postpone indefinitely. Just saying.

LORY:

If you guys cancel on us, I will actually cry

BEN:

She actually will.

TUI:

Don't worry, we will make the rendezvous eventually, sis. We just have to help Dove first.

LORY:

Of course! :)

Doesn't she want to join the group chat, too?

CONDOR:

As everyone in the room at this end is looking at me, I guess that's my cue to answer

Dove is here, reading over my shoulder. English is her second language, so she finds it hard to keep up with text chats.

She says hi.

LORY:

HI DOVE!!!

BEN:

Aren't there 7 of you?

TUI:

Raven's shy. And she's dealing with some stuff at the moment.

KESTREL:

Maybe once she meets you in person :-)

LORY:

Which takes me back to my first point: HURRY UUUUUUUP

HAWK:

haha

TUI:

Even if we left tomorrow, it would take us a while to fly that far. And we have to keep stopping to eat and sleep. But we've made it this far. We'll get there.

LORY:

You've been flying across the whole country??

BEN:

How far can you fly in a day? The furthest we've gone is about 20 miles.

HAWK:

Yeah, it's more like 200 miles for us. 250-300 if we get a good tail wind and no rain.

LORY:

W. T. F.

And I thought WE were fit

TUI:

That's a best-case scenario. We are getting healthier and fitter again, though.

LORY:

Why? What happened?

CONDOR:

A conversation best had in person, I think.

FALCON:

You guys can't see it, obviously, but Condor is giving us the WORST stink-eye right now haha

LORY:

**@Ben** if Mom and Dad ever let us out of this house, we have some SERIOUS laps to do so we can keep up with these guys

BEN:

No kidding

FALCON:

WE SHOULD HAVE RACES

HAWK:

YES

TUI:

NO

I've read that bloody fanfiction too you know

I know how that ends

KESTREL:

#fawkforever

LORY:

BAHAHAHAHAHA

I love you guys

Hurry up so I can hug all of you

CONDOR:

Didn't your parents warn you about meeting random people off the internet?

FALCON:

Did CONDOR just make a JOKE??

Hold me Hawkie-bae, I think I'm going to faint

LORY:

HAHAHAHA

BEN:

wtf

KESTREL:

The bromance is real.

TUI:

**@Kestrel**, let's go help Luke before our boyfriends start re-enacting scenes from that bloody fanfiction.

BEN:

Who's Luke?

LORY:

Ok I HAVE to know more about this fanfiction!

CONDOR:

No, you really don't.

FALCON:

You're just jealous

HAWK:

I think Con's jealous

FALCON:

Snap!

HAWK:

We're just meant to be

KESTREL:

I'm out of here before I puke all over these two lovebirds

Bye Lory, bye Ben. Promise we're not actually insane

TUI:

What she said

And I'm confiscating Fal's phone.

ttyl guys

FALCON:

BYEEEEEEEE

LORY:

OMG you guys hahaha

Bye!!!

BEN:

But who's Luke??

# 10

# HAWK

Yawning, I shut the bedroom door on Falcon's snoring. An odd glow filtered into the hallway from the kitchen. Maybe someone had left the fridge open. I walked softly toward it, hoping nothing would creak and wake the others.

Surprisingly, it was Luke's laptop. The cold screen light fell across the shoulders and wings of one of my friends, head on folded arms, apparently asleep, breathing heavily.

Forgetting about midnight snacks, I approached the kitchen table. Tui's brown skin looked sickly gray in the digital light, her hair all messed. White earbuds, still in place, were just visible through the dark waves. As a tinny, distant beat pulsed, the cable snaked beneath her forearms and into her phone, lying on Tui's notebook. Its scribbles, question marks, calculations, and doodles in English and Māori were almost illegible.

My gaze travelled to the laptop. The screen was full of dense scientific text that, even after advanced biology classes, I struggled to make sense of. Something about physiology and gerontology, whatever that was.

Tui sighed, her breath shuddering. Instinctively, I put a reassuring hand on her shoulder.

She jerked upright. I flinched, and glimpsed the glinting tracks on her face before her hand swiped her cheeks. She hadn't been asleep. She'd been crying.

"You scared the shit out of me, bro!" She yanked the headphones out of her ears.

"I scared *you*?" My heart still vibrating with adrenaline, I tried to smile. "What the flock are you doing up, Tui?"

"Could ask you the same thing, Hawk." She flipped her notebook shut and closed the web browser.

"Midnight snacks make much more sense than studying," I said, trying to tug the notebook from under her hand. "What is so important that you couldn't wait for daylight?" *And then made YOU, of all people, cry?* I thought.

Unexpectedly, Tui slumped, her wings hooked awkwardly over the chair back, her face drawn.

Without further resistance, I sat next to her to inspect the notebook.

Scanning across the pages, I found unfamiliar acronyms – BMR, RDEE, RQ – and complicated formulas I'd never seen before, as well as a few more familiar notations. Heart rate. Kilocalories, kilojoules, and kilograms. Energy expenditure. *Elevated metabolic rate* was underlined, and linked to the words *stress, temperature, food,* and *illness/injury.*

One final note, previously hidden beneath Tui's phone, had been overwritten and circled several times.

I gazed at it, horror slowly inflating my chest.

*MPLS = 45-50 years*

Slowly, and quietly, I asked, "Tui, what does MPLS mean?"

Tui's voice was dull and thick. "Maximum potential life span."

"For who?"

"Us."

Hands trembling, I put down the notebook like it was explosive. "Why would you think that?"

"We're living faster than we should be." Every word seemed to be an effort. "Pulse, digestion, healing ... hair." She pulled at the dark strands around her face. They'd once reached to her waist, before the Evolutionaries had shaved us all like runaway dogs, only weeks ago. "We are wearing out our bodies. We're extremely fit, but flying is so physically intense ... we're not designed for this."

"Are you saying we're basically middle-aged already?" I frowned, reflexively rubbing my face. Still smooth, apart from the odd childhood scar and spot of acne.

I nearly laughed at myself. What did I expect? A sudden ageing, like someone had dropped a filter over my head? "And I thought I was still a teenager. Must have missed a few birthday parties."

Tui shifted, her wings rustling, and she answered my half-assed joke with a half-smile. "I'm prob'ly wrong, bro. Never actually went to medical school." She paused. "Don't tell Falcon, eh? He's convinced our so-called super-healing means we're immortal, or something. He's so bloody sure this is some kind of superhero origin story. I don't want to ruin it for him. Not yet. Not now everything is finally..." Impatiently, she dashed her hands across her eyes.

Gently, I said, "Tui, you're exhausted. Don't stress about it right now. Anyway, you probably just forgot a decimal point somewhere and we'll actually live till four hundred and fifty, or five hundred, or something. If you can put up with Falcon for that long."

Tui chuckled, briefly. "Yeah, nah, we'll see. Especially if he keeps making those bloody awful vampire jokes."

Grinning, I stood up. "See? We'll be fine. You'll be fine. At least, you will be once you've had a decent sleep."

On cue, Tui yawned. "Yeah. Okay."

Finally closing the laptop, Tui stretched, her wings briefly filling the kitchen as huge shadows against the striated streetlight coming through the blinds.

"Night, Hawk."

I squeezed her shoulder as she passed me. She flashed a weak smile and was gone.

She'd taken the notebook with her, I realized. Chuckling, I shook my head. Tui was too smart for me. She was much too good for Falcon, too, but because he knew it, he'd never take her for granted.

I wondered how the rest of the Flight would take the news, and then quickly decided not to think about it, resuming my aborted trip to the fridge. We had to survive the next few months before a reduced life expectancy would become a concern.

And with twisty badly formed thoughts like that, it was definitely time for bed.

*

"Mom and Dad are on their way, with Mr and Mrs Deslandes," Luke said, upside-down on the sofa. The Flight sprawled around him in various states of stupor, staring at their phones or the

TV. "They'll be here tomorrow afternoon." He received a few half-mumbled acknowledgements.

The last week had developed a weird, surreal quality. Stuck inside, hiding from both the surrounding population and the weather, we'd sunk into a muted state. The emotional and physical exhaustion of the last few weeks, let alone our time in the Evo cells before that, was finally replacing the adrenaline in our poor abused bodies. Now we were just sitting around, waiting for Dove to leave.

Tui hadn't brought up her life expectancy research again, and I'd avoided mentioning it too. Either that or it had succumbed to my brain glitch.

Falcon returned from the kitchen. "These are the last corn chips," he announced, the bowls clonking onto the coffee table next to the rest of dinner. "And we're all out of guac."

"What about sour cream?" Tui asked, tossing her phone aside.

Falcon already was crunching on a mouthful. "Huh?" As his girlfriend glared at him, he swallowed. "Sorry. Again."

Rolling her eyes, Tui waited for everyone to sit up and pay attention before she launched into the quick *karakia mō te kai*, which roughly translated into 'prayer for food', and was a traditional acknowledgement of those who'd worked to put the food on our table. She'd done it ever since Mr and Mrs Carter had left, and Luke had felt too awkward to step in for his dad and say grace in front of the Flight.

"*Mauri ora,*" Tui said, ending the now-familiar recitation.

Falcon attempted to echo her, like an amen. "Morry aura!"

"Mow-ri or-ah," she corrected gently, and smiled when Falcon tried again and got it right.

After a minute or so of wordless munching, Kestrel asked, "How can we be running out of food already? It's only been a few days."

"I did accidentally waste some the other night," I reminded her, wincing. I'd attempted to take a turn at making dinner, and then forgotten halfway through. However, as the blackened and inedible (even by Falcon) meal had resulted in the Flight permanently banning me from cooking, it wasn't entirely a bad outcome from my perspective.

"Maybe it's time we tried ordering online," Condor suggested.

This received the most enthusiasm anyone had shown in the last few days, so after dinner and dishes were done, everyone crowded around Luke and his laptop to make sure their particular favorite was on the list.

As the digital cart become fuller and fuller, however, I saw the tension growing in Luke's jaw.

The moment the total hit $400, I said, loudly, "That's enough."

Everyone looked at me, including Luke.

"Guys, we can't abuse the Carters' hospitality like this. They're already forking out a fortune to rent this house, and Mr Carter is currently unemployed. I know we've gotten used to taking whatever we want, or can find, but that doesn't apply to a digital supermarket and someone else's credit card. Okay?"

The Flight's guilty faces, and Luke's relief, were enough of an answer.

Condor shooed Luke away and took his seat, his black wings flicking. "Everyone gets one treat," he said, "and then it's essentials only."

"Fruit and vegetables," Tui said, immediately.

"Exactly. We have to get this total below three hundred dollars." He looked to Raven, hovering by his elbow. "Raven, what's your must-have?"

"Chocolate," she said, shyly.

"Of course." Condor gave Raven a one-armed hug. "Dove? Want something for the road tomorrow?" There was a slight catch in his voice, but the French girl easily smiled back.

One-by-one, the Flight reduced their demands, and Tui helped Condor cull the rest of the digital cart.

Leaving them to it, I returned to the living room with Kestrel. "I wish we had money to give the Carters. It's not fair."

"I know." Kestrel sighed. "I couldn't get any of my savings before I bailed. Mum had control of my account. Bet it's all been spent by Gavin on Stephanie, now." She chuckled. "Although, I definitely cost him a lot more on his credit card, so I guess we're kind of even."

"I couldn't withdraw all of my cash either," I said, dropping moodily onto the sofa, automatically throwing my brown wings to the side. "At least my mom and dad will have protected it."

Then I jerked up. "Hang on! I can talk to them now!"

Kestrel wrinkled her nose. "And…?"

"They could send us my savings."

"How? Without the Evolutionaries tracking it?"

"Uh…" I hesitated. "Digital gift card? Or something?"

"But when we use it, they'd be able to track the code." Kestrel leaned on her elbows, crossing her wings, frowning in thought.

"If anyone can figure it out, you can, babe," I said, cheerfully. After all, she was our cybersecurity expert, and was doing a great job so far.

Later, in the middle of a rowdy late-evening card game, she yelped.

"Got it!"

"Got what?" Falcon said, irritably. "It's my turn!"

"I think she means something else?" Luke said, warily.

Dove's wings twitched anxiously. "Kestrel, what is it?"

Kess turned to me. "Your parents buy stuff online, right? From second-hand listings?"

"Uh, yeah, of course," I said.

"I can set up some random auctions and listings across different websites, using burner emails. We'll send the links to your parents, and they can 'buy' the non-existent items with their regular accounts. Then we can send them the Carters' accounts as payment details. No one will look twice at it. Obviously, we'll have to be careful with the details, because listing a paperclip and your parents paying five hundred bucks or whatever would be a bit weird, but–"

"You're a genius." I kissed her hard, in front of everyone. In my peripheral vision, I saw Luke, Condor and Dove blushing, Raven staring at us with interest, and Falcon and Tui chuckling and rolling their eyes.

When I finally let Kestrel breathe again, she was flushed and giggling. She tried to compose herself.

"Can you get your parents' account details for us, Luke?"

"Sure," our friend said, fidgeting with his cards. "They have several with different banks, and I've got the details in the apps on my phone."

"Perfect. Thanks, Luke. Message me the info?"

"Will do."

I tried to interpret Luke's expression as the game resumed. Relief, certainly. Amusement or bemusement – wasn't sure which. Possibly both.

Although he was a year older than us (in human terms, anyway, and not counting Raven), his smaller frame and relative naivety made him seem younger. An Icarus tended to occupy more space than a non-winged person, but with us all at the table, and Condor's and Falcon's wings flexing and overlapping behind Luke, he didn't look out of place. Even his normal-sized eyes seemed unremarkable.

"Earth to Hawk! Your turn!"

I slapped the cards down. Then I heard myself say, "Contact lenses."

"What?"

The Flight stared at me.

"What?" I echoed, staring back.

"You said 'contact lenses'," Tui said.

"Um … yeah?"

"Any reason why, or will you leave us hanging?"

"Because … I was … thinking about eyes?" I hazarded.

Somehow, Kestrel put together my fragmented body language, direction of gaze, and word dribbles, and made sense of my brain-mouth malfunction. "Do you mean we could use contact lenses to disguise our eyes as human?"

"Yeah," I said, although I had a brief flash of a glitched thought about Luke wearing contact lenses to pass for an Icarus. Why I'd thought he'd ever need to do that, I couldn't say. Kestrel's version made much more sense.

"I think our eyes are the least of our disguise problems," Condor said, dryly, flexing his wings, the feathers rustling against the carpet. "Wings don't exactly look normal, anywhere."

Falcon snorted. "Except Comic Con. We'd fit right in there."

While poor Dove tried to ask what Comic Con was, Falcon jumped to his feet, wings flaring. "That's it!"

As the rest of the Flight were yelping and grabbing at the wind-scattered cards, the response was not what he expected.

"Won't you ask me what brilliant idea I just had?" Fal demanded, hands on hips.

Tui sighed. "Will it get you to sit down, bro?"

"Go on, Fal, tell us," Kess said, patiently.

"Drumroll please ... going to Comic Con can be our cover story!"

Condor leaned back on his wing elbows and folded his arms. "How, exactly, is that helpful?"

"We get some obviously-fake contact lenses, some crappy-looking devil horns and halo headbands, old trench coats, put big straps around our shoulders and wings, pin on some loose feathers in a really sloppy way, and *voila!*" Falcon flourished wide. People slapped their hands onto their cards to catch them again. "A bunch of harmless nerds with fake wings!"

A long pause.

"That's actually not a terrible idea," Tui said, slowly.

"Aw, babe, you say the sweetest things." Fal grinned.

I put up my hand. "How do we explain wearing our pretend costumes every hour of the day? If, say, we wanted to check into and out of a motel, why would we be wearing the big, heavy, awkward wing set? Let alone wandering around Walmart, or whatever."

Falcon hesitated, then brightened. "Precisely *because* they're so heavy and awkward. We're getting used to it before the convention."

The others began prodding and poking the idea from all angles, searching for weaknesses. Raven whispered in my ear. "Cars or flying?"

"Good point." I squeezed her hand before relaying her thought. "Raven and I want to know how you imagine us traveling with these so-called costumes? It won't make sense if we're wearing fake wings when we get out of a car, and arriving by air would make the whole charade a waste of time."

"Driving long distance in cars would be even more uncomfortable now our wings are so big," Kestrel said.

Falcon threw out his wings and his hands. Everyone gave up on rescuing the cards. "I don't know, we'll get a bigger vehicle. Like a bus, or something."

"You could get an RV," said Luke, and then blushed as every mutant eye turned to him.

"Oh my god," Kestrel said. "We'd have a whole house with us. We wouldn't even need a motel."

"We could park almost anywhere," I said, trying to think it through. "We could find campgrounds, or pull over on a back road. Be gone again by dawn."

"We'd take literally everything *and* the kitchen sink with us!" Fal chortled. "Permanent road trip in luxury! Luke, I think I love you! Sorry, Hawkie-bae, we're over!"

"Oh, no," I said, dryly, as Luke's blush deepened. "How will I ever get over you?"

Tui was tapping at her phone. "We can't afford it. Look. We'd need a campervan that could sleep seven–"

"I am going home to France, tomorrow," Dove interrupted, then glanced sideways at Condor.

"Of course, sis, sorry. But a six-sleeper vehicle is still bloody expensive, and I refuse to steal one. It's not like nicking a few muesli bars and biscuits. Even renting an RV is way out of our league."

"Um," Condor said.

His hands twisted at his flight coat. Although we'd ditched the harnesses on arrival, and hadn't worn our tails in days, he wasn't the only one still wearing his cropped leather jacket. They were comfortable, felt warm, and looked cool. What other excuse did we need?

My mental muttering faded as the pause stretched out.

"Yeah?" Tui prompted Condor.

Dove's hand was on his leg. Not his thigh, where a potential girlfriend might touch, but the 'safe' zone of his knee.

"Dove has asked me to go with her to France."

Dove gave his knee one tiny pat, and then removed her hand. Interesting.

I realized the Flight were asking questions and giving opinions over the top of one another. Their agitation finally made Condor's words sink in.

Condor might leave the Flight?

Tomorrow?

I felt like I'd been hit by the big rig again. First Owl had been killed. Then Dove had decided to leave. And now Condor. The first other Icarus I'd ever met. My first friend in this new life. Dove, I could understand, but Condor? It wasn't just popping over to Dove's house for a visit. The arrangements for sneaking across the Atlantic were so complicated, it would be almost impossible for the Flight to follow, or for Condor to return.

We'd probably never, ever see him again. Not in person.

I couldn't believe he was even considering it. Dove hadn't ever shown much interest in him. Not in that way. Or had she?

Had they been hiding a relationship?

The Flight was airing the same thoughts, but I was struggling to keep up.

Then Kestrel's question cut through. "Condor, are you sure it's safe?"

Defiantly, Condor crossed his arms. "If it's safe for Dove, then it's safe for me."

"What will you do? Seek sanctuary with the Catholic Church?"

"I – I don't know."

As the interrogation continued, Raven tugged on my sleeve. I bent down.

"What is the Catholic?" she asked, in her innocent little voice.

"I'm sorry, Raven, it's too complicated to explain right now. Can you Google it or something?"

Soon, she tapped me again. "I do not know the letters."

After spelling the word for her, I tried again to tune into the discussion.

The third time, I struggled not to snap at her. "What, Raven?"

Wordlessly, she held her phone screen to my face.

"Oh, shit," I said, weakly.

The headline read:

*POPE CONDEMNS FALSE ANGELS*

# 11

# CONDOR

"Condor! Breathe!"

Someone shook my shoulders.

"Just breathe. Let me give back Raven's phone."

My friends tried to peel off my fingers, but they were gripping so hard I couldn't feel them anymore. Since the moment I'd grabbed the phone from Hawk, I'd had no control over my body.

"Please, Condor."

Finally, it was removed, and I was gently but firmly pushed onto a sofa.

Muttering, the Flight skimmed the article. Raven's little arms tried to wrap around my shoulders. Dove sat on my other side, patting my knee. She was wearing that same faint smile she'd worn when I'd asked her why she wanted me to come to France.

"What does it say?" I asked, hoarsely.

The others hesitated.

"Just tell me." Waiting for a few extra minutes wouldn't make it hurt any less.

Hawk cleared his throat. "The Catholic Church basically says that anyone who believes we're real angels speaking for the Lord is being deceived by the Devil. And that it doesn't matter if the Angels were created by a human messing with Creation, or if it's the work of the Devil. It's still sacrilege."

The Pope had decreed I was the creation of evil.

I was damned.

Staring at the floor, I waited for it to crack open and the flames to drag me in. I tensed against the agony, my heart exploding with every stuttered beat.

But the dark carpet remained still. A few dust motes drifted in the yellow light from the overhead bulb. The Flight's murmurs were soft, anxious. A car passed on the dark, icy road outside with a swish.

Life continued.

The surge of terror subsided like a wave, leaving me naked and shivering, my body numb from the cold acceptance.

I was completely, utterly, eternally, fucked.

*

After a time – maybe two minutes, maybe two hundred – I became aware of the Flight surrounding me.

"Come on, Condor," Hawk said, forcefully cheerful. "The wind's died, and the moon's not up yet. We're going for some exercise. We've been stuck inside way too long. You'll feel better with clean air in your lungs and feathers."

I didn't answer. Hawk tried again. "Dove, you'll come for a last flight with us, won't you?"

"It would be nice," Dove said, standing, her pale blonde wings nudging my leg. How could she be so calm? Wasn't France mostly Catholic too?

"Come on, Con," Kestrel said, bumping my foot with her own. "It'll help."

"You guys go," I said, distantly. "Don't mind me."

There was no way I could summon the strength to lift myself. To force my blasphemous wings to separate me from God's Earth. Those few pitiful feet of air would be the closest I would ever get to Heaven. To Mama and Abuelita.

"Come on, dude," Falcon said, grabbing my arm.

"No!" I threw him off, suddenly angry. "Just leave me alone!"

He backed off. "Jeez, all right. Just trying to help."

"Argh. I'm sorry." Just as quickly, the anger drained away. Exhaustedly, I rubbed my face. "I'm not feeling well. I'll just go to bed."

"Are you sure, bro?" Tui peered at me. "Exercise will give you an endorphin boost."

"No, I – look. I appreciate your concern, but I'll be okay. After all, I survived this, didn't I?" I touched my chest.

"That was totally different–"

Cutting Hawk off, I sighed heavily. "No, not really. Junior said I was going to hell around about the same time he set me on fire."

Behind the Flight, I saw Luke's round eyes and hand-covered mouth. I dropped the rest of what I was going to say and forced a weak smile instead.

"You guys go catch some air. I'm going to bed."

"We're not going without you," Kestrel said, sternly. "We're not abandoning you just after, uh, you get bad news. That's not what friends do."

Heavily, I stood up. "I'm going to bed," I repeated. "What you do with your evening is your business."

Judging by their twitching wings, they were desperate to get in the air. Only a few minutes ago, I would have felt the same.

But now I just wanted to be alone. I couldn't even look at Dove.

The Flight finally gave in, agreeing they'd go flying, and that they wouldn't force me to join them. As they filed out to fetch their flight gear, Tui nailed me with her stare.

"Don't do anything stupid," she said, sharply.

"I'm not–"

"Just don't."

Luke's quiet voice came from my side. "I'll be here, Tui. I'll look after him."

"Thanks, bro." Tui smiled at Luke, then glared at me and held out her hand. "Phone."

"What?"

"Hand it over."

"Are you serious?"

"Deadly."

"But I–"

"Give. Or I'll make the Karate Cadet take it from you."

Spluttering, red-faced, I found myself doing as I was told.

"Good. Now, I suggest you have a nice long shower, then straight to bed. Okay?"

From the corner of my eye, I saw Luke bite his lip. In amusement? Concern? Anxiety?

"Yeah, yeah," I said, sullenly.

Tui squeezed my shoulder as she passed, my phone in her other hand. If she'd been a few inches taller, she'd probably have ruffled my hair instead. "We won't be long. If you change your mind, you can still join us. We'll just be overhead."

Grunting noncommittally, I went and locked myself in the bathroom.

Staring at my reflection, I listened to the Flight gearing up and slipping out the back door.

The house fell silent. All I could hear was my own rapid and inhuman heartbeat.

I didn't feel like a demon. I didn't feel like an angel, either.

Right now, I didn't feel much at all.

Vaguely, I wondered what emotions a normal person would be suffering. Fear? Anger? Horror?

I'd felt all of the above before, at world-shattering levels. The freezing, quaking fear that spiked my feet and hands. The deep, white-hot, blinding anger that trembled through my whole body. The stomach-twisting, chest-punching horror that made every breath an impossible effort.

All of these marked the worst times in my life. When I had been sinned against, and when I had sinned beyond all redemption.

A knock on the door. I flinched.

"Condor?"

Luke's voice.

"Are you showering, or coming out?"

I glanced at the shower. The thought of exposing myself to the water made my gut shrivel. My dark wings flicked.

Instead, I opened the door. Luke was waiting, eyes still wide, mouth tight. He seemed to relax a little when he saw I was still in one piece.

He needn't have worried. Self-harm wasn't my style. No. I inflicted harm on others.

And now I was paying for it.

I couldn't meet Luke's gaze. He was too good for someone like me to even look at. He'd followed his father and mother, obedient, loving, selfless. He'd already given the Flight so much. And here he was, spending more of his life and energy fussing over me. When I was a lost cause.

Drifting into the living room, I found my usual place on the sofa, and resumed staring at not very much.

A clock ticked, somewhere. Probably that one sitting on the liquor cabinet that functioned as the rental's minibar.

"It's not fair."

Luke's voice snapped me from the daze. "Huh?"

"It's not fair." He sat in front of me with a flump. "This isn't your fault."

Idly, I watched more dust motes fluttering from his movement. "It is my fault," I said, distantly, watching them twist in the air with my evil sharp sight.

"You didn't ask for the wings. You didn't make a deal with the Devil, and you've never insulted the Lord. You've only ever tried to spread His love. They don't even know you. How can they decide you're evil?"

"Because I sinned," I said, blankly. "These wings are punishment. Not a blessing. I should have known."

"Don't say that!" Luke grabbed my hands. "What about the rest of the Flight? You can't have all sinned so badly that you're eternally damned. God is supposed to love, and to forgive, isn't He?"

"I guess?"

Luke was right. If I was being punished, why were Dove, and Hawk, and all the others being 'punished' in the same way? Dove didn't seem affected by the Vatican's announcement. And the rest of the Flight had never been interested in the 'angel' possibility and didn't seem to believe in the idea of Heaven and Hell.

If God had really intended for a bunch of teenagers to become angels, wouldn't He have picked those who were actually interested in the job, and sent us an opportunity to step up by now?

If we were the work of the Devil, wouldn't the Adversary have tried harder to seduce us into sin?

Abruptly, I realized the whole thing just didn't make sense. And I felt some tension leave my shoulders and wings.

"Anyway," Luke went on, carefully, watching my face. "I kind of understand how you're feeling right now, because the Church hates me too."

"What? Why?"

"Because I'm gay, remember?"

"Huh."

Luke was right. Everything that had been drilled into me over the last few years, as I tried to transform myself the way the Church and Abuelita demanded, had told me homosexuality was evil. But I knew Luke wasn't evil. He couldn't be. He was too kind, and caring, and *good*. But the Church said he was a sinner. And the Church was never wrong.

Was it?

"I think the Pope is okay with gay people," I said, vaguely. "Isn't it something like, you might be gay but as long as you don't act on it, you'll be all right?"

Luke blushed. He did that quite easily, I'd noticed. "I, uh … I have had a boyfriend before. A while ago now."

"Oh, well then, you're screwed too, I guess." The comment just slipped out. I slammed my hands over my mouth. "Oh my God – I mean, not God, I just – well, shit."

Suddenly, uncontrollably, we started to laugh.

"You're right," Luke gasped. "We are so screwed."

"I'm hungry," I said, between snorts. "Is that weird?"

"Little bit." Luke pushed off the floor. "I'm suddenly craving pizza. Want some?"

"Sounds great." Then I frowned. "Where were you hiding pizza? Falcon practically vacuumed the pantry."

Luke waved his phone. "I'll pick it up. Mom's car needs a run after sitting in the driveway for so long. It's just around the corner."

In moments Luke had ordered and was reversing out of the driveway.

For the first time in months, I was truly alone.

The gaping chasm still seemed to be right behind me. Hell was waiting.

Maybe.

Either way, it seemed that keeping to the rules, stressing about the rightness of everything, controlling the urge to swear and fight and be angry hadn't done much.

I was doomed to an eternity of torture simply because of who I was, or … maybe I wasn't doomed at all.

Ugh. I was so tired of triple-guessing myself. Of beating myself up for slipping a toe over an imaginary line that my friends didn't even care about.

Maybe God just didn't care about me. He had much bigger things to focus on. Climate change, child abusers, genocide.

Why would He care about me, all alone, here in this room, where I couldn't hurt or help anybody?

I gazed about, looking for some hint of something. Anything. But there was no demon lurking in the corner, no angel with a clipboard.

Instead, my eyes fell on the liquor cabinet.

Fuck it.

Why not?

*

"Sorry, Condor, I forgot to ask if you're for or against pineapple on…"

Luke's voice faded halfway through the doorway.

I was already into the second bottle of hard liquor. To be fair, the first one was nearly empty when I found it. As I hadn't touched alcohol in a few years, I'd been expecting an easy buzz. But as the third glass went down and my eyes streamed, I'd remembered my metabolism was quite different now. And had another drink.

Now I struggled to my feet, intending to help Luke with the pizza boxes, and nearly fell over the sofa, wings flailing.

"Aw, jeez." Luke avoided catastrophe by half tossing, half dropping the boxes onto the coffee table and grabbing my arm. "I shouldn't have left you alone."

Weakly, I tried to snort. "Not your repons – reponsib – responsibility. I'm a big boy now. And I've done way worse things than booze." My face fell as Luke nudged me back to the sofa. "That's why she doesn't want me, I think. Even when I need someone ... she doesn't ... I don't know."

As I reached for the rum, Luke guided my hand to the pizza instead.

"What do you mean?"

Cramming a slice into my mouth while sighing heavily was not a good idea, as it turned out. "I thought maybe Dove ... I've been trying to figure out if she might ever like me back. You know. Like, *like* like." Luke tried to cover his laugh and I rolled my eyes. "You know what I mean. I mean, she asked me to go all the way to France, but then doesn't even try to comfort me when my whole existence is condemned by the Pope himself."

I was sobering up already, and I was nowhere near done with my self-pitying binge. My attempts to get another drink were almost thwarted when Luke seized the glass before I did, but then I shrugged my wings and swigged straight from the bottle, pirate-style. It was going down easier now, more like I remembered. From that time. "I mean, it was like she didn't even understand what it meant. And she's supposed to be Christian too, you know?" I blinked at Luke. "You're the only other person in the whole damn Flight that would know."

Luke took his time finishing his mouthful of pizza before answering. "I do know what you're feeling, but I also understand Dove's position. The Angelists were playing with her head long before they noticed my own 'deficiencies', and started messing with me, instead." He made the air-quotes with a disgusted face. "You know what it's like when you're scared, and alone, and someone tells you it will be okay – as long as you do what they say."

A sob nearly caught me by surprise. "Yeah. I know."

Luke poked at his pizza. "I'm so lucky I had Mom and Dad. What the other Angelists were trying to do to me is illegal. In California, anyway."

"In my case, my so-called saviors were making *me* do the illegal things," I said, moodily. "Assholes."

Unexpectedly, Luke chuckled. My confusion obviously didn't help, as he took one look at my face and it became laughter.

"I'm sorry, Condor. It's just so weird hearing you swear."

Rolling my eyes, I snatched another slice. "You should've heard me a few years ago. Would've made a ... a ... sailor! That's it. A sailor blush. That's what Bianca said, anyway."

"Who's Bianca?"

The question was innocent, but still bruising. "She was my girlfriend."

"I guess that was before the, uh…" Luke gestured, and my wings twitched.

"Before my wings, but after Mama died." My hand wrapped around the bottle neck. "She was older than me. Gorgeous. Played me like a guitar. I knew it, and I didn't care. I did anything she or her father wanted. In return, she gave me everything I wanted. Sex. Drugs. Alcohol." I drank. "Revenge."

Another swig, but this time, the burning was horrible. I forced myself to swallow, then leaned over and put down the bottle as far away as I could.

Luke quietly moved it out of my sight before answering. "Revenge?"

"For Mama."

There was a blob of spilled liquid on the coffee table. Somehow, at some point, I'd slipped off the sofa and onto the floor, so it was nearly at my eye level. My finger started spreading the small puddle into twisted, spiraling shapes.

"Anyway," I said, without looking up, "even though they convinced me to do bad things, they were still good to me. They wouldn't have just … left."

"The Flight haven't left you, Condor," Luke said quietly. "You said you needed space. They'll be back any minute."

"But Dove is leaving," I said, mournfully. "Is she testing me?"

"Testing?"

"To see if I'm serious. If I agree to go with her, she'll know I'm truly in love with her. Then maybe she'll love me back."

My friend's voice was still soft. "But do you love her?"

The answer died on my tongue, stillborn, malformed.

And it all became clear.

Luke yelped as I jerked, my arms and wings struggling to lift my rum-soaked body to my feet.

"I have de-de-decided," I announced to my audience of one, "I'm going to not France." I frowned, tried again. "I'm not going to France."

"You're sure?"

Luke's face faded in and out of focus. "Yes," I said, and tipped sideways.

I have only a vague memory of Luke hooking himself under my arm and wing. I heard heavy flaps, or maybe it was just my thudding heartbeat, as I bumped off the doorframe and somehow landed on my bed in the room Luke and I were sharing.

Luke said something, and I think I answered. I wanted to thank him for looking after me, but I'm not sure if the words actually came out.

Then I was gone.

# 12

# CONDOR

"Condor, hurry up! We gotta go or we'll miss the bus. Metaphorically speaking."

Falcon hammered on the door. Wincing, and wiping my mouth, I flushed the toilet for the seventh, and I hoped final, time.

"Have some sympathy, bro," I heard Tui say through my pounding headache and the whoosh of water. "Have you never been hungover?"

"Nope," Falcon said, proudly. "Unless you count a sugar crash."

"Uhuh. Okay, so multiply that by ten and throw in a migraine and that's about what Condor's probably feeling. He's trying to throw off some serious alcohol poisoning right now. Have some compassion."

"I'm impressed he's even functioning," Hawk's voice joined in. "Well, relatively."

"I can hear you," I grumbled, my own voice clashing with the throbbing pulse in my raw ears. But, as I forced myself to swallow another glass of water, I thought it *might* be easing.

After pausing to confirm the water would stay down this time, I washed my hands and face, and then took a deep breath.

I opened the door.

Most of the Flight wore sympathetic or amused expressions. In Raven's case, it was more like bemusement. But Dove's lips were tight as she frowned.

It was only further confirmation that I'd made the right decision.

Mrs Carter's car was not technically big enough for eight passengers. Especially when seven of them had fourteen- to seventeen-foot-wide wings. However, once we'd packed our feathers into the bulky winter jackets, moaning and complaining as tight tendons resisted the 'full fold' of our wingtips bending like an index finger, we needed only slightly more space than a human of the same body build. Raven was packed into the center between Kestrel and Tui, Dove took the front passenger next to Luke, so Hawk, Falcon, and I climbed into the trunk of the station wagon. All of Dove's possessions fit into a rucksack at her feet.

It wasn't light yet, and half-melted snowdrifts glowed orange in the streetlights. Luckily, the roads were still clear. With hunched shoulders, Luke turned the key. The old car complained, but started within moments.

"Here we go," Luke muttered, and reversed us onto the road.

To get Dove and her parents safely out of the country, we had to get Dove to the meeting point with the Carters and her parents by six o'clock. More than an hour before sunrise. Wherever we were going, it was along the most direct route they could organise from LA to their exit point on the Atlantic coast. Or something.

I was too busy convincing myself that I didn't need to throw up for an eighth time. Falcon and Hawk kept their conversation to occasional whispers, thankfully, and the rest of the car was almost silent. Even if we had been talking, no one outside the car could have heard us – not that there was anyone there to hear. All the sensible people were still in bed.

But we had an appointment. And, as Falcon had pointed out with glee when I'd threatened to vomit on him after he pulled me out of bed, I was now pretty far from the usual definition of 'sensible'.

The only slightly brighter side was that the vicious hangover kept me distracted from the shame, and the sorrow of losing Dove.

I may have nodded off for a bit (or, as Falcon teased later, passed out again), as we seemed to reach the meeting point very quickly.

Like a scene from a movie, as we pulled into a snow-covered, tree-dotted reserve, one of the cars on the other side of the clearing turned its lights on, and then off again.

"It's Mom and Dad," Luke said, relief oozing from his voice.

As he pulled on the brake, Dove threw open her car door and sprinted across the icy grass. Two bundled-up adults emerged from the other car and did the same.

"Maman! Papa!"

My stomach lurched in a way that had nothing to do with alcohol. I looked away before the loving little family was reunited.

The car swayed as the others got out. Falcon and Hawk waited by the open tailgate for me. I took gulps of the fresh, freezing air. The hangover had eased. I nearly thanked God for the blessing of the fast Icarus metabolism, then remembered.

"Come on, Condor," Hawk said. "We have to say hello and goodbye."

Falcon peered at what he could see of my face between jacket and hat. "You gonna be okay?"

One deep breath in; one breath out in a cloud. My hand half-lifted to my chest, then fell back. "Yeah."

Ice crystals crunched as we approached the Carters, the Deslandes, and Raven, Tui, and Kestrel. Dove was barely visible between her parents, all three laughing, crying, and talking in rapid French. Kestrel and Tui had an arm around each other, and Tui had her other arm protectively around Raven.

As Falcon, Hawk and I approached, Mr Carter patted his son's back and moved to greet us.

"Boys, how are you?" he asked, smiling, but with anxious lines around his eyes, visible even in the dull streetlights.

I didn't miss the quick glance that Falcon and Hawk exchanged, and then threw my way. "We're fine, sir," Hawk said.

Carter nodded. "We don't have much time, so if you still need to say goodbye to Céline, better do it quickly." As my friends turned, Carter took my padded shoulder. "Condor, may I have a quick word, son?"

My heart would have sunk, except it was already a cold lump and could fall no further. "Sir?"

Carter drew me to the side, his eyes piercing mine. "How are you?"

Half-shrugging, I felt constricted in the jacket. My wings ached. "I'm okay."

"Is that so?"

I couldn't hold his honest, concerned gaze. "I'm staying with the Flight. Obviously."

"Indeed. And the announcement from the Vatican?"

"I … didn't take it well. At first."

"And now?"

Dove's laugh tumbled across the snow. Hat gone, her short blonde hair was being tousled by her father, while her mother clutched her face, presumably in horror at the loss of her daughter's golden curls.

Sighing, I made myself meet Carter's eyes. "Luke helped me survive the shock. He's the true angel."

The ex-Bishop's gaze softened. "That he is."

"Sir, what should I do now?"

"What do you mean, son?"

I waved at the Flight. Hugs, laughter, and tears were being shed all round, while Luke stood back awkwardly, and Falcon mischievously tried to convince Mr Deslandes to give him a fist bump.

"The church threw me out. Dove – Céline's leaving. What do we do now?"

The man sighed. "I really did believe, and in some ways still do, that you are angels. Everyone is on this Earth for a reason. But very few of us know for sure what that is."

"But why?" Trying not to cry, I curled my fist, hard. My hands were going numb. I'd forgotten my gloves.

Carter smiled. "Because it is up to us to choose."

Blinking, I stared at him, then remembered I needed to breathe.

"But–"

"They're here!" someone called. A van had pulled up with one sharp honk on its horn. I flinched, but the morning traffic was already building.

Sorrow clenched my heart. Tui was handing Dove her bag, which her father took and added to the suitcase he was carrying. And I hadn't even said goodbye, yet.

"Excuse me," said an unexpected voice. "So sorry to interrupt."

Adrenaline spiked in my heart. Carter and I turned.

A man in heavy winter clothes approached, one hand raised in a wave.

"Good morning. Can I help you?" Gently, Carter nudged me towards the Flight, and the final farewells.

But my feathers were bristling. I hesitated.

"I hope so," said the man, now only a few yards away. "I'm looking for…"

His last few words were indistinct as he rummaged in his pocket.

"Pardon?" Carter said. He tried to push me again, but I stood my ground, eyeing the newcomer over his shoulder.

The man's voice was garbled again. "I'm looking for–"

Now within reach, he raised his phone, looked at the screen, then at me.

"What?" I demanded, impatiently. "You're looking for what?"

"You, actually."

He punched me in the arm.

Something plunged through my jacket and stabbed into my flesh.

My bellow cut through the chatter. Silence.

Then, loud pops.

The Flight yelled and cried out.

"Nobody move!" shouted the man, springing back. The phone had disappeared. A pistol was now aimed directly at my face.

Slowly, I raised a hand to yank the empty syringe from my arm.

"Don't touch it, freak!" growled the gunman. "I said, *nobody move!*"

My heart raced. I waited for the familiar numbness to spread, for the blurring tranquilizer to reach my eyes, my brain.

Three armed, balaclava-wearing men emerged from the trees, almost surrounding us.

Over my pounding pulse, I heard one mutter, "Why isn't it working yet?"

"Dunno."

"It's supposed to be knocking them out by now—"

The leader jabbed the pistol at me. "Get back, freak."

My muscles tightened, my mind racing. They'd obviously been sent by someone. Someone who had given them tranq darts and our IDs, and orders to bring us in. And that someone could only be one person. But these guys weren't acting like the usual Evo mercenaries, and apart from the sting in in my arm, I felt no effect from the dart. Something didn't add up.

Hawk was trying to distract or stall them. "What the hell is going on? We didn't sign up for paintball!"

"Shut up, freak!"

"Why do you keep calling us that?"

"I said shut up, you winged freak! On your knees!"

Slowly, as the gunman advanced on me, I backed toward the rest of the Flight.

"You've got the wrong guys," Hawk insisted.

The leader sneered over his two-handed grip. "I don't think so, weirdo. We've been watching those two for weeks." He jerked his chin past me at the Deslandes. "Followed them here from LA, so we know exactly who you are, Tyler Owen. Yeah, that's right, they gave us the full dossier, freak."

"Who's 'they'?" Hawk asked, although the shaking in his voice suggested we'd all figured it out.

"Someone with a lot of money," said a balaclava guy, his voice also trembling, from nerves or excitement.

"No more talking!" screamed the leader. "Get down on your knees or I'll blow your heads off!"

Out of the corner of my eye, I saw the Flight shifting very slowly, hands creeping to jacket zips. But we'd never remove our coats in time to launch and escape into the air.

Dove's blonde head was visible behind her parents, as they backed to the rear of the huddle. Toward the van.

Carter, his hands raised to his shoulders, spoke with no trace of anger or stress. "Let's talk. There's no need for violence, son. These children have done you no harm."

"Shut up, Grandpa!" The man's hand wavered, swinging the gun between me and the preacher. I could see it shaking. This guy was no professional. My muscles clenched, old instincts surging.

Then Dove's parents ran for it. Dragging Dove, they barged past a man, knocking him over. His gun fired into the dark air.

The leader flinched. His finger twitched. Pulled the trigger.

I tensed, but no impact came.

The gunman's eyes were wide, his mouth working silently, staring in horror. At Carter.

Luke's dad fell to his knees. His hands touched his chest. Red dripped from his fingers, onto the snow.

Time stretched.

Distantly, I heard Tui's yell. Saw her shoving through the Flight toward Carter. My gaze dragged from Carter's bloodied hands to the terrified face of the man who had shot him.

I took one step. The gun swung to me as he backed away, but the barrel wavered.

"Stay back, freak," he squeaked. "Or you're next!"

My jacket fell into the snow. Black feathers filled the dying night. The man's eyes couldn't widen further, but his words were strangled as he retreated. He tripped on a snowdrift. He staggered. I leapt.

One beat of my wings and he was flat on the ground. The gun fell. I snatched it up as he scrabbled for it, sobbing.

Instinctively, automatically, my bare hands assessed the weapon in a heartbeat. I felt the balance, the gauge, flicked out the magazine, counted the rounds, primed the weapon. Never took my eyes off the terrified, pathetic little shit in the snow.

I raised the pistol. Aimed at his head.

A screech of tires.

The van was leaving, carrying Dove and her parents to safety.

I glanced up. Just for a second. A white face in the van window. Blonde hair. Wide eyes staring straight at me.

Then she was gone.

My jaw creaked as my tendons tightened past human limits. My hand shook for only a second as I returned my gaze to the man on the ground.

The hot stench of urine stained the frigid air. He was crying. "Please, please, I lost my job, my girlfriend's pregnant, I just needed the money, man, I didn't mean to actually shoot anyone, they said the darts would make sure no one got hurt—"

"HEY!"

Without moving the pistol, I turned my head. The last of the bounty hunters was aiming his own gun at Tui, bent over Carter, frantically trying to save the man's life. Luke and Marlene were at his side. The rest of the Flight were frozen in place.

"S-s-step away from Harley, or I'll sh-sh-shoot the black b-b-b-bitch," said the man, trying to snarl.

A flash of fury burned through my veins and tightened my hand on the gun.

Then, an icy moment of clarity.

I met the man's gaze over his pistol. He was only yards away. The two others wild-eyed in their masks. All seemed younger than thirty. All were white. All looked terrified.

And all still aimed weapons at my friends. My family.

The man opened his mouth, but I beat him to it.

"This is your one chance," I said. Even to me, the words were freakishly calm, empty. "Put down the gun."

He took a deep breath. I saw the decision click in his eyes.

"Fuck you, fre–"

My hand swung. Pulled the trigger. *Crack.*

The man hadn't even started screaming before I shifted the gun again. *Crack.*

*Crack.*

The three men dropped their weapons and fell into the snow, shrieking, moaning.

The urine-soaked wretch at my feet was crying. "Don't kill me, please, don't kill me–"

*Crack.*

I stared down at him. Watched the shock pass through his bare, screwed-up face. Then, realizing he was still alive, the pain of the bullet in his leg reaching his brain, he screamed. The stench of urine intensified.

The smell of blood, gunpowder, and piss finally snapped me back into myself. Nausea boiled in my gut.

Sirens split the air, racing closer. I dropped the gun into the blood beneath the man I had shot. The man who had shot Carter.

Oh, shit.

Suddenly, I felt how hard my heart was pounding. I half-ran, half flew back to the Flight, huddled around the Carters.

Hawk, Falcon, and Kestrel looked up. I saw the fear flicker across their faces.

Stumbling to a halt, my heart skipped out of time. They knew. They'd seen me.

Dove had seen me. The last thing she'd seen of me was–

I was on my knees, struggling to breathe.

"…keep pressure on it. Right here. Don't let him fall asleep. Keep him talking, eyes open. All right, Mr Carter? I need you to look at me, right now. *Ka pai*, that's it, *Matua*. You'll be okay. The ambulance is coming."

"So are the cops," Hawk said. "We have to go."

Through blurred eyes, I watched Falcon bend over Tui. "Time to go, babe."

Hawk grabbed someone. "Luke, your dad's going to be okay. If Tui says so, it's true, all right? Go with your mom and dad to the hospital."

"I … I…"

"Can I have the car keys? Thanks. Text us, okay? We don't want to bail on you, but if we're here when the cops and EMTs arrive, it'll only make things worse."

"But what do I say?" Luke sobbed. He gestured at the men who had attacked us, moaning and groaning, dragging themselves through the snow.

"They tried to mug you, got into an argument, one accidentally shot your dad…" Hawk hesitated.

"Then they all just happened to shoot each other in exactly the same place at the same time? All four of them?" Falcon demanded.

"Just go," Luke said, through his tears. "I'll think of something."

Hawk slapped his shoulder. "We'll find a way to help. We'll be at the house. I promise we're not running away from you. Okay?"

"Okay."

Falcon and Kestrel hauled Tui away as she yelled to Marlene. "Keep the pressure on! Keep him awake!" Her gloves were drenched in blood.

Hawk grabbed Raven's arm, began to run for the car. Then he looked back.

"Move your ass, Condor!" he bellowed. Red and blue lights flashed across the snow. His gaze flickered from me to Raven, and back. With a groan that echoed, even under the sirens, he picked up both Raven and his pace. "Come ON, Con!"

Adrenaline forced me to my feet, and I followed.

# 13

# TUI

"Sit."

I pointed at the armchair.

Condor sat.

The Flight, or what was left of it, slowly settled around the lounge of the rental house. It was still barely dawn, but there was more than enough light for us to see by. To see how pale and tense Condor was. We all were.

However, anxiety and stress were reasonable reactions to the last hour.

I rubbed my chin. Despite throwing away my ruined gloves and scrubbing my hands for five full minutes with household bleach, I imagined I could still smell blood.

There was silence for some time, and the day grew brighter.

Falcon leaned back next to me, one ankle resting on the other knee, arms and wings across the back of the couch, in his best manspreading position. He kept eyeing Condor, then shaking his head with a silent chuckle. After the fourth time, I took an elbow off a knee long enough to jab him.

Hawk stood nearby with crossed arms and a deep frown. Occasionally his brown wing twitched. At least his memory glitch didn't seem to have erased the most recent events. One less thing to worry about.

Kestrel hugged Raven on the other couch, legs tucked beneath them and wings behind. Raven's little face was barely visible under her beanie.

And that was it.

That was all that was left of the Flight.

And now we stared at Condor, wondering if we'd ever really known him.

His wings awkwardly splayed, his hands clasped tightly, he awaited interrogation.

I could feel Falcon starting to get restless. But I put my hand on his, and he settled back. Condor had to come to us.

He had to convince us we could still trust him.

Finally, he took a deep breath. The Flight tensed.

"Hawk," Condor said, and his voice cracked. "I need to ask you something."

Hawk didn't move. "I'm listening."

"Do you remember when we escaped from the Evolutionary building? And you got some guns off the Security assholes?"

There was a collective flinch when Condor cursed, and a long pause before Hawk answered. "I've been standing here trying to remember the details, but I don't know why. I just … somehow … knew it was important."

"What do you remember?"

Falcon grunted. "Is this relevant?"

Condor's dark gaze shifted to Falcon. Even though he wasn't staring at me, I still shivered. "Yes."

Fal lifted his hands. "Okay."

"What do you remember, Hawk?" Condor repeated.

"I know we landed on the plane, and we shot through the cables so it would swing and smash the glass wall. I know the facts of what we did, but I can't recall it personally," Hawk said. "All I can remember clearly is seeing Owl ... you know."

"Okay. When you gave me the pistol, I already knew how to use it. And you made me promise to confess how I knew it. I crossed my heart, but I was too chickenshit to go through with it."

"Hearing you swear is creeping me out. Just saying," Falcon said, grinning nervously.

Condor smiled. It was thin, joyless. "I used to do much worse than swear."

"Please get to the point, bro." I sighed. "Or Falcon will explode."

Condor took one last deep breath.

"When I was nearly thirteen, Mama found out my dad was having an affair. They had a screaming argument that lasted for hours. Then she sneaked us out of the apartment about three o'clock the next morning, and took me to Mexico City to visit her mother. Mama hid from Dad using Abuelita's maiden name. It was tough, because Mama refused to use her American bank account so Dad couldn't track us down. I wasn't used to being poor. I hated it there, and she knew it, but she kept working awful jobs to look after us. She refused to go home. And I was forbidden to contact Dad. I didn't want to anyway, because I was just as angry. I blamed him for everything.

"Then, after about a year, when I was fourteen, Mama was in the wrong place at the wrong time. A man, so high and drunk that he thought he was in the middle of a rival drug cartel's territory, randomly opened fire. He murdered eleven innocent people, including Mama. He was never arrested."

Condor's voice cracked.

"After Mama's funeral, I ran away from Abuelita. I disappeared into the streets. At first, I was just looking for escape. From pain, from fear, from everything. But then I found Bianca."

Falcon couldn't contain himself. "Who the hell is Bianca?"

I smacked his hand and Hawk cuffed his head with the tip of his wing.

"Okay, okay." Falcon surrendered.

Condor continued, quietly. "Bianca's father was a cartel lord, and she was the princess of the castle. They gave me everything I thought I needed. Belonging, escape. And then they offered me revenge."

A long pause, but we all suspected what was coming.

"They'd found the man who'd killed my mother. They kidnapped him, dragged him in, handed me the gun. And I shot him in the head as he begged for his life."

I felt cold. Dizzy. Condor was a murderer?

In the silence, he stared at the floor.

At last, he explained. "I thought I'd done the right thing. I thought I'd found the only version of paradise that could possibly exist. I couldn't believe there was a God who would take Mama from me like that. No merciful God could allow such evil on the Earth. Bianca said she loved me. I said I loved her. Her father gave us his blessing, and I did whatever they wanted. In return, Bianca gave me fun, sex, and alcohol; the cartel gave me money. Drugs. A purpose. I thought life was as perfect as it ever could get in that violent shithole.

"Then, after months, I found out Bianca was cheating on me. I was so angry. But I didn't know what to do. So, I left the house and wandered the streets, looking for trouble. A rival cartel raided the complex while I was gone. It was a bloodbath. Bianca, her father, everyone. I found them all dead.

"I was sitting outside in shock when the media arrived. The photos hit the news. Abuelita saw me. She rescued me, told me that I'd been spared for a reason. That God had chosen me for something. So, I confessed everything to the Padre of her church. He told me I still had a chance at salvation. If I repented. If I atoned for everything I had done.

"If I never spoke Bianca's name again.

"I did everything the Padre and Abuelita demanded of me. I prayed for hours. I said thousands of Hail Marys. I ate nothing but bread for weeks. Coming clean was torture. Afterwards, I thought I saw the world so clearly. The memories of the cartel, from when I was high or drunk almost all the time, were blurry.

"Instead, I filled my head with gospel. I convinced myself I'd learned humility. I was following the path God set for me. I worked, I cleaned, I prayed. The Church promised me salvation. I promised Abuelita I would be better. My whole existence revolved around her and the Church.

"And then I grew wings."

Condor seemed to grow calmer as the truth came out. He paused for a long time, waiting for us to react. But the Flight said nothing.

Picking at his jeans, eventually, Condor said, "That's why I was so uptight and stressed out about every moral choice we've had to make. I couldn't risk a single slip. But now it's been completely taken out of my hands." He laughed without smiling. His eyes moved anxiously between us.

Hawk spoke first. "Does anyone else know what you did?"

Con shook his head. "After Abuelita died, the only person left was the Padre."

"The priest guy you confessed to?" Falcon shifted higher on the couch. "Who told you how to earn redemption?"

"I wish he *had* told me exactly how!" Condor's wings and hands swiped the air. "He just told me I *could*. If I truly repented."

"But you have, haven't you?" I asked.

Condor now stared at the ceiling. "My mother's murderer was a very bad man. I've tried. But, deep down … That man had hurt and killed many people, not just my mom. If I hadn't…"

Falcon leaned in and muttered to me, knowing the Flight could hear him. "Definitely sounds like an evil mofo."

Hawk's hand shifted to his hips. "Look, Condor, if what you did wasn't so black-and-white, good-or-evil, isn't that when you're supposed to end up in, like, Purgatory or something? Get tortured for a while, then once you've suffered for your sins, you go to Heaven?"

"I'm not sure," Condor said, slowly.

"Assuming that I'm right, and I normally am–" Hawk grinned as both Condor and I snorted, Falcon guffawed, and Kestrel rolled her eyes. "Then Purgatory sounds a lot like the Evolutionary lab to me."

Con blinked. "Huh?"

"I think you've suffered more than enough bad karma for your mistakes," Hawk said. "And after being tortured by Dickhead

Demonface Junior, you saved the Flight by busting us out of the Evo cells."

Kestrel spoke for the first time since we'd got home. "And you just saved all of us again this morning, Condor. If you hadn't shot all those lunatic bounty-hunter-wannabes, we'd all be dead right now. Or worse."

"And you didn't kill them," Hawk added. "You could have, but instead you deliberately incapacitated them with the best chance of survival."

Falcon sounded very satisfied. "I reckon you earned a whole bunch of points right there."

"You guys really don't know how this system works, do you?" Condor chuckled in bewilderment.

"Do you?" Kestrel asked, quietly.

Condor's mouth shut with a click.

There was just one more thing I wanted to know. "Why didn't you tell us earlier, bro?"

Condor's fingers clenched, turning red and white. "Because I didn't want to be just another stereotype."

I nodded.

"You were doing a pretty fine job as the good little Christian boy, though," Falcon said, and I glared. He winced and mouthed *sorry*.

Kestrel slid off the couch, hooking her arms around Condor's neck and shoulders. "You know we love you, Condor," she said. "We're family. None of us have been perfect. We've all made mistakes."

"Speak for yourself," Falcon said, brightly.

Condor was going pink, I assumed with emotion, not because Kestrel was strangling him.

"Remind me to tell you guys about the time I was arrested," she went on.

Falcon gasped, and Condor gaped. I raised an eyebrow.

Hawk laughed. "Can we have breakfast first?"

My phone buzzed, and I snatched it from my pocket.

"Luke?" I said as I answered. The Flight fell still.

"Surgery is going well," Luke said, his voice strained. "The doctors say he's past the worst. It will be a long recovery, though."

"The important thing is that he *will* recover," I said, calmly. "How's your mum?"

"She's calling a few people." Luke sighed. "Trying to make sure our health insurance will cover the bills."

From his tone, I could tell their confidence wasn't high. I gritted my teeth and wished yet again that we were safely in New Zealand. It was insane that, after the horrors of the morning, the Carters also now faced financial ruin. After Mr Carter had quit his job. And had been supporting seven ravenous Icarus teenagers for a few weeks.

"Thank you, Tui," Luke said.

"Huh?"

"The EMTs said that, without your help, Dad would have died."

I tried to reply but Luke kept talking. "I mean, I didn't tell them it was *you*, of course, I just said there was a lady passing by who knew first aid, and her friend called 911. Please thank Kess for me too."

I glanced at Kestrel. She nodded.

"Sure, bro. What about the guns?"

"The cops are coming to take statements in about an hour. Mom doesn't want to press charges. She says they've received their punishment. They'll be in rehab for quite a while."

"But what will they say about us?" I asked, anxiously, more to voice my concerns than to get an answer from my friend. Kestrel let go of Condor, and Hawk tucked her under his wing and arm. Falcon had done the same with Raven.

"I don't know," Luke said. "I'm sorry."

"What will you and your mum say?" I held my breath.

"We were saying goodbye to our friends before they left for France, and then those guys tried to mug us. Some passing strangers jumped in to help, one of them used the guy's gun to knock out the muggers, and then they left as the emergency services arrived."

"Okay." I breathed out. "Try not to lie. We can't ask you to do that. You've already sacrificed so much for us."

"Mom said she'll send me home by taxi once I've seen Dad," Luke said. "I'll tell you all about it then."

"Okay. Thanks, Luke."

Tucking away the phone, I followed the Flight into the kitchen. Both the pantry and the fridge were pretty bare again.

Hawk dropped into a chair, which creaked in protest. As Falcon hassled Condor about letting the 'innocent Icari' get first dibs at the cereal, Hawk took something from his flight jacket pocket and placed it on the table, where he glared at it.

Slowly, I sat opposite him. It was one of the now-empty syringe darts. In all the mayhem, I'd forgotten about the bounty hunters' opening round, especially as it didn't seem to have had any effect.

Now, staring at the needle, I wondered.

"Who got injected?" I asked.

Hawk raised his hand.

"Me too," said Condor.

Kestrel and Falcon shook their heads, and Raven rubbed her arm. "I think me," she said, quietly.

"And me," I said. "Four of us."

"And Luke," said Kestrel. "He was hit too."

My frown deepened. Suddenly, I wasn't hungry. I'd been assuming that, like the hunters had muttered, they'd stuffed up the dose. But if they'd successfully stabbed Luke as well, Luke should have suffered some kind of effect.

Maybe it was just a dud batch? The fricking idiots had clearly been amateurs. So, it wasn't impossible.

Maybe we'd just gotten lucky.

"What about Dove?" Falcon asked. "Did they get away?"

Condor instinctively went for his pocket, and then paled. "I don't have my phone."

"Where was it last?" I asked.

Con's jaw tightened. "I don't remember. But I lost my big coat at the park."

"Don't panic, Condor." Kestrel was already tapping and swiping on her own phone. "I can track it. If it's been lost, I can erase it from a distance. It will wipe itself after ten incorrect tries anyway, for just this occasion. Although, I'll be honest, I was expecting Falcon's would be the first victim."

As Falcon made a show of being outraged, the rest of the Flight resumed their hunt for breakfast. Still, the tension didn't ease until Kestrel chuckled. "It's in your bedroom, Condor. You didn't even take it this morning."

"Oh. Thanks, Kess."

"Don't worry. I've messaged Dove, too. I can't see her on the tracker app, so I guess she's out of range on the plane, or however they were escaping." With an almost-silent sigh, Kestrel put away her phone. "I'm sure we'll hear from her eventually."

The Flight ate, yawned, stretched, and made small talk about how we hoped Mr Carter was doing okay. As much as anyone can be okay after taking a bullet to the lung, anyway. I interrogated Condor, Hawk, and Raven about how they were feeling, and compared it to myself, but there appeared to be no effects from the syringe darts at all. Still, I would keep a close eye on us. Even closer than usual, that is.

To our relief, the daily news updates didn't have many details about the early-morning mugging attempt. With no fatalities and no witness footage, there was no way the incident would be noticed beneath the circus noise from London and Washington DC. The world was changing, and not just for us. I shivered.

By the time Luke returned in the late afternoon, the Flight were preparing to make a break for it. Dove had finally replied, confirming she and her parents had made it, and that she had not been darted. I knew I didn't need to check Luke after he'd been triaged at the hospital, but I couldn't help myself.

"I'm okay, Tui, promise," Luke said.

I stepped back with a sigh. "Please tell me the second you feel a bit off, okay?"

"Promise." Luke stared at the piles of bags. "Do you guys really have to go tonight?"

"Yeah, sorry, bro."

Condor, who seemed almost back to his old self – if anything, he seemed more relaxed, although the swearing had stopped again – entered the kitchen with the last of his gear. He placed his tail on top of his duffel bag. "If we're still around when the Evolutionaries turn up, it would only cause you and your family more pain."

"They shot my dad, too," Hawk said, from inside the pantry. "In the shoulder."

"Are you sure they'd find you here, though?" Luke asked, sadly.

Kestrel reached across the table and squeezed Luke's hand. "We're certain the Evolutionaries sent the bounty hunters. They'll know we're in the city, even if they haven't managed to trace your parents' online booking to this address. The Evos will come to clean up the hunters' mess." She glanced at the heap of supplies. "And we've cost your family enough."

Luke started to protest, but Kestrel cut him off. "I'm serious, Luke. We can't abuse your kindness any longer. Once we're safely away, I will set up a crowdfunding page for your dad's medical expenses. Maybe we can use our virality for some good. Worth a try, anyway. We just have to get out of here before they find us."

Luke's smile trembled.

Then there was a knock at the front door.

# 14

# RAVEN

This time, the Flight were whispering.

"Is it the cops?"

"Is it the media?"

"Maybe you left something in the taxi, Luke."

"What if it's the Evolutionaries?"

"If it was, they wouldn't have knocked first!"

*Knock knock knock.*

Luke stood up. "I'll go–"

"Shhhh!" said the others.

Luke made a "sorry!" face. "I'll go look through the peephole, guys," he whispered.

The Flight watched Luke walk quietly to the front door. He put his eye to the little hole. We waited. He looked at the Flight, then back to the hole. Then to the Flight. And again. To the hole, to the Flight.

No, not to the Flight.

To me.

And I knew.

"Uh," he said.

"What?" Kestrel and Falcon said.

Luke's face was worried. "It's just some lady. On her own."

"What does she look like?" Tui asked. Her hand was on my shoulder. And it went tight.

Luke swallowed. "Like Raven."

It was Her.

*Knock knock knock.*

"You know her?" Luke asked.

The Flight didn't answer him. They were whispering fast. My head hurt.

"How did she find us?"

"Is she distracting us? We have to go!"

"They could have surrounded the whole house *before* she knocked."

"Luke, can you see her hands? Is she holding a gun?"

"Again, why the hell would she knock if she's planning to bust in and pop a cap in all our asses?"

"Shut up, Falcon, not helping!"

"You're sure she's alone, Luke?"

"Yes," said Luke. "Should I open the door, or should I tell her to go away?"

*Knock knock knock.*

"Raven should decide."

I blinked and looked up at Condor. The Flight all looked down at me. My hand squeezed my arm.

"Yeah." Tui nodded. "Raven, it's up to you. Should we let her in? Hear what she has to say?"

"We'll protect you," Hawk said, quickly. "Especially now we know we have Mexican Rambo on our side."

Condor's face was red. "Shut up."

"What do you think, Raven?" Kestrel asked, quietly.

I breathed. In, out.

"Yes."

Luke nodded, and opened the door.

She was wearing a long dark jacket and the blue pants the Flight liked and had boots like the Flight too, up to her knees. She had a big black bag over her shoulder. She did not smile. "Hello. I am Lin JingYing. May I come in?"

Luke looked from Her to the Flight. "Uh, yeah, I guess."

"Thank you."

Falcon said, loudly, "There better not be a gun or a gas bomb in that bag."

"No, Falcon." The Flight twitched their shoulders and feathers when she used Falcon's name. "I did not bring weapons. My phone is protected from being tracked, and no one knows I am here." She said 'no' a little louder. "You have my word."

"For what that's worth," Hawk said.

Luke shut the door behind her, locking it again. "Uh, would you like to sit down?"

"Thank you. And what is your name?"

"I'm Luke?" It sounded like Luke was asking a question.

She nodded. "Thank you, Luke."

She went into the living room, and the Flight followed too. She stood in front of the sleeping TV and looked at all of the Flight, before she looked at me.

She explained without waiting for someone to ask.

"I knew where you were, because I have been tracking Raven since you left the facility in Houston."

"Ohhhh, plot twist!" Falcon yelled, his hands slapping his own face.

"Shut up, Falcon!" Tui said.

JingYing looked calm. Not worried. Not happy. "No one else knows. Not even Frederik."

The Flight's wings shivered and rustled. My feathers felt spiky.

"But how?" Hawk said. "And how come it was only Raven?"

JingYing looked at me. At my hand squeezing my arm. She pointed. "I inserted a tracking device into her arm some weeks before you left."

I felt all of the Flight looking at me. My head felt hot. My arm and my hand were sore. My chest hurt.

I felt Bad. I had been Bad. I had been telling Her where the Flight were. And I hadn't even known it.

But my arm had been hurting. I had been able to feel the sore thing in there.

I should have told Tui.

"How do we know you're telling the truth about the tracker?" Hawk asked, loudly. "Shouldn't it have died days, or weeks ago?"

JingYing nodded. "I have a scanning wand in the bag to show you. I will not take anything else from the bag."

She slowly put her hand into a pocket of the bag on her shoulder and took out a long shiny gray stick. She put the bag on the small table. She showed the button on the stick, and then moved it along all of her limbs. Nothing else happened.

Then she put it on the table, next to the bag, and stepped back.

Hawk carefully picked it up and tried it on his own body. Still nothing. He waved it past my right arm. Nothing. He gently took my hand off my left arm and put the wand there.

A beep, and a green flash. A small screen showed some numbers.

Tui pushed Hawk away. He scanned the rest of the Flight while Tui asked me to take off my jacket, and she felt my arm. She found the lump. She sighed. "Oh, Raven."

My heart hurt more. "S-s-sorry," I whispered.

Tui hugged me. "Not your fault, sis."

"Rest of the Flight is clean," Hawk said. "Or, the scanning thing is programmed to go off only when it tags Raven's bug, or JingYing is messing with us and is pushing a button in her pocket to make it go beep at the right time."

"There is no point in a such an elaborate deception," JingYing said. "I could have told Frederik where you are, and arrived with both him and a full Security complement. But I have not. You know I am telling the truth."

Hawk threw the scanning stick onto the table. "So why here?" he asked. "Why now?"

Falcon sat on a sofa. "Does this mean you're on our side, then?" He bent his fingers in the air when he said the words 'our side'.

"I only learned of Frederik's use of bounty hunters this morning." JingYing's face still did not change. "It seems I am not the only one with my own projects."

"We're not projects," Hawk said, his voice low, loud, and angry. "We're people."

"Yes." JingYing stood still and calm. "You are. And I deeply regret your treatment at the hands of the Evolutionary Corporation's employees. That is not part of our company's philosophy."

Condor was touching his chest. "You didn't exactly do much to stop it."

"I did what I could, where I could, when I could. I am not in charge. Yet."

"But why are you here?" Falcon asked, angry-tired.

JingYing looked at me. "To bring YanWei home."

"No!" the Flight said, very loud.

"You can't have Raven," Kestrel said, grabbing my hand. "Not after what you did to her."

"I did not do anything," JingYing said. So calm. My ears were hurting from my pulse. "I was just as shocked to see my dead sister as she was to see me. I understood what van Scholtz told me, and why he believed his own hypothesis about the data in front of him. But I began my own research. And now I believe I can restore YanWei to her true self."

"What, with a magic memory implanting machine?" Falcon said. I didn't know if he was angry or excited.

JingYing made a small smile, and her hands let go. "No. It will take time, and work, to remind YanWei of her childhood. But I believe that, with the rehabilitation of her memories, YanWei's personality will resurface." She put her hands wide. "You love Raven. And I love YanWei. They are the same person. I will not hurt her."

Falcon made a loud nose noise. "You might not, but what about Flockface Freddy?"

JingYing had a very small face twitch. Angry? Happy? I didn't know. "Frederik will not know YanWei has come home until she is ready."

"How do you know your memory rehab plan will work?" Tui asked.

JingYing small-smiled again. "Because I already started when you were all in Houston." Her hand lifted.

I remembered her lifting her hand the same way, when I had been in the Ob, when she had seen me, and I had seen her. She had asked me for a sign. Said she would get me out of there. And she had made a sign with her hand. Like a Flight sign. But it wasn't a Flight sign.

I had wanted to make the same sign. Had felt the movement in my hand. But I had not moved.

And JingYing had looked sad.

Now, she was looking at me again. And I knew she was going to do it again.

And my hand wanted to move.

So I moved it.

I made the same sign at the same time as JingYing. And the Flight saw.

And they knew.

"What the hell was that?" said Hawk, his voice very high.

"American Sign Language," JingYing said, now smiling properly. "We taught it to ourselves when we were five so we could talk even when Frederik and Aron were dominating the conversation. That was our name sign. For the two of us."

My feathers spiked again.

"Awww," Falcon said. "That's so creepy, but kinda cute?"

Kestrel's and Tui's wings shivered.

"I still don't believe Raven or YanWei will be safe with you," Condor said. "Not after what your boyfriend did to me, and to Owl."

"And as soon as you get Raven out the door, your pet soldiers will move in and grab the rest of us," Hawk said, looking to the window. It was still day. "Junior's little bounty hunter game has put a good man in hospital, and there's no way his family can afford it. You've destroyed us, you've destroyed them."

Falcon's wings were twitching. "And you assholes killed Dr Hux when she helped us escape from your special torture lab! So why the hell should we give a shit about anything you say?"

Tui held Falcon's arm. "Maybe don't antagonise the woman who can call doom on us at any second?"

"Falcon," JingYing said, smile gone. "Dr Huxley's death was genuinely an accident. I could explain it in detail, starting with the moment she crashed the entire building's infrastructure, including that of the experimental weapons factory, but I know you would not believe me. However, I was exceedingly distraught at the loss of such a brilliant mind, and caring person. The world, and the Corporation, is poorer for her loss."

Then she looked to Luke. "Do you have a banking app on your phone?"

"M-m-me?" Luke's eyes were very big, and he backed into the corner. "Why?"

"Please open it."

"We don't have any money!" Luke looked like he would cry. "I can't give you anything!"

"Please open the app."

Shaking, Luke looked to the Flight. Kestrel nodded. Her hands were tight and white.

"Hold out your phone, showing the app's home page, Luke," JingYing said.

As Luke did, JingYing took out her own phone, touched the screen a few times, and held it so the camera could see Luke's screen.

"Account number detected," said a voice in JingYing's phone. "How much would you like to transfer?"

"Two hundred and fifty thousand," JingYing said.

The Flight all breathed in hard, and Luke made a squeak.

"Affirmative. Two hundred and fifty thousand," said the phone. "When would you like to transfer?"

"Immediately," said JingYing. "With instant funds clearance. No hold."

"Affirmative. Immediate clearance authorized. Transferring."

No one said anything for a few seconds.

Then the phone said, "Two hundred and fifty thousand transferred. Would you like to make another transaction?"

"No." JingYing put the phone in her pocket.

Luke's breathing was loud and strange. He looked at his screen. Tapped it a few times. Looked some more.

"There's quarter of a million dollars in my mom's account," he said, and sat down on the floor.

Kestrel sat next to him. "Remember to breathe, Luke." She rubbed his back. "Just breathe."

"But ... but ... but why?" Luke looked up at JingYing.

"Corporation activities have caused you and your family harm. I have gifted you this money as reparation, which will not undo the damage, but it will go some way towards your healing."

Luke's mouth opened and closed, but no more words came out.

"Damn," Hawk said, happy-worried. "That's insane."

"It is the sane response, I assure you," JingYing said.

"Can I have two hundred and fifty thousand dollars too?" Falcon said. "I'd even take fifty thousand on its own. I'm not picky."

JingYing leaned over the bag on the table and pulled the zipper all the way open. "I thought you would prefer your two hundred and fifty thousand in cash."

"WHAT?!"

The bag was full of money paper, in bunches.

"Eh, are you serious?" Tui's mouth was wide. "Is that even real?"

"Genuine, clean, and used bills," JingYing said.

Hawk stopped Falcon moving closer. "Why?"

JingYing sat on a sofa. "Because I want to help you. Once YanWei is home, you should be free to do what you want."

"Oh." Falcon's wings went down. "It's a flocking bribe."

The Flight looked at me, and then at the bag.

"We cannot accept your money, Lin JingYing," Condor said, angry. "Raven is not for sale."

"You misunderstand me, Condor," JingYing said, still calm. "I am trying to help you. You do not have to accept my help. It is your choice whether to keep any of the money. But I will leave with my sister."

"Flight meeting, kitchen, now," said Tui. "You too, Luke."

JingYing looked at her watch. "Do not take too long. If I do not resume communication with Frederik soon, then he will want to know where I am and why my GPS is blocked."

"Feathery arses moving *quickly*," Tui said through closed teeth.

Tui's hand was tight on my right hand and Hawk's was tight on my left.

"We can't let her take Raven," Condor said, as the kitchen door shut.

Hawk's hand was hurting mine. "JingYing will just track her wherever we take her."

"We'll get the tracker out of Raven, just like we got the bugs out of Falcon and Condor's arses back in LA," Tui said.

"How insane is this?" Falcon said, sitting down hard on a chair. Everyone's, except Luke's, wings were big and bumping into kitchen things. His hands were on his face. "Of all the people to turn up and start throwing around hundreds of thousands of dollars! I think I'd only be more surprised if Flockerdick himself had turned up!"

"Shut up, Falcon!" Kestrel said. "Unless you have something relevant and useful to say!"

"Oh, come on, you can't tell me this isn't the weirdest *deus ex machina* you've ever heard of!"

"I don't think you're using that correctly, Falcon, and now is really not the time!"

"Should I give the money back?" Luke asked.

"No!" The Flight all shouted. Luke hid his face.

"JingYing is correct that the Evos owe you, Luke," Kestrel said, touching his shoulder. "Your family needs that money."

"But you guys need money, too," Luke said under his fingers.

"Not from them," Condor said, angry.

"Then why is it okay for my family to take their money?"

The Flight was quiet. They looked at me.

I didn't know why they were even angry-talking about it. The Flight needed the money. JingYing had lots of money. And she was giving it to them. They should take it.

Even after so much time, I still didn't understand my friends. But...

JingYing. My sister. She wanted me back. No, she wanted YanWei back.

And Raven was a danger to the Flight.

I knew what I had to do.

# 15

# HAWK

Stubble rasped my hand as I swiped at my face. Raven gazed up at me with that serious, slightly bemused expression.

"You will be okay, Hawk."

"Me?" My voice broke. "I'm not worried about me! I'm worried about you!"

"I will be okay."

"Call us every day," I said. "Or we'll assume something bad has happened, and, and…"

Falcon snorted. "What, you'll call a SWAT team? Bust in like you're a whole squad of SEALs?" But his eyes were wet too.

Raven's tiny nose wrinkled. "Seals go swimming, not flying?"

I laughed. It was either that or sob. "He means we'll come rescue you if you need us. If you don't like it there anymore."

Raven blinked. "I have been there before."

She had a point. She had been there before. And escaped. Twice.

But she'd never been there on her own.

JingYing took Raven's shoulder. "She will be safe with me, Hawk."

I hated when the too-perfect *Homo sapiens superior* said our Flight names. But I consciously smoothed my feathers and managed not to scream at her. "I'm serious. If we don't hear from her for more than twenty-four hours, I'll hand myself into the police and demand they raid every Evolutionary Corporation facility from here to ... uh..."

"Tokyo," Falcon said, helpfully.

"I have given you my word. Raven can contact you any time she chooses. The only information she may not share is her exact location, in case Frederik has hacked your phones."

"He has not," Kestrel said, quietly, her gold feathers vibrating. She crossed her arms and glared.

"No," JingYing agreed. "I have not, either. Once you leave this property, I will not know where you are. Unless, of course, you want me to."

"Why the flock would we want to tell you?" Falcon exploded.

JingYing checked the time. "Because you might need my help again."

"We've survived fine without you so far," I growled.

"Indeed." JingYing's eyes travelled to Luke then back to me. My fists clenched. "You may also need information."

I couldn't help myself. "Like what?"

"You are not the only ones looking for answers. I have a potential lead on the whereabouts of Dr Goldberg. I am also following every potential lead on emergent *Homo sapiens icarus*. I suspect that information may be of ... use to you."

The phone in my pocket, with Lory and Ben's contact details, seemed to get uncomfortably hot.

"YanWei, the car is here." JingYing moved toward the front door like she hadn't just dropped another truth bomb on us. "It will take Frederik approximately forty-eight hours to retrace my steps to this house. I will inform him of my reparation payment, and that should be enough. But it is likely he will send someone to check. When he does, I suggest the Flight should not be here."

"No shit, Sherlock," Falcon mumbled.

JingYing smiled briefly. "Good luck."

She stepped onto the porch.

The Flight surrounded Raven in a feather huddle for the last time. No, not the last time, I thought – just for a while. Crocodile.

Then the Flight's little sister walked out the door, the tips of her black feathers just peeking from under her oversized winter coat, her bag grasped in her mittened hand.

The door closed.

And then there were five.

No, six. Luke hovered nearby, his face twisted and his hands tangled.

"Well ... shit," Tui said, finally.

Condor's fingers ran through his black hair like he was trying to pull it out. "Uhuh."

Fal stomped into the kitchen. "Do you think she's using us as bait to lure in Lor–"

"Shut up, Falcon," Kestrel said, sharply.

"What did I say this time?!"

Kestrel was already in the living room, gold wings flexing, her hands running along the furniture. She yanked the sports bag of cash wide open, and began throwing handfuls of money bundles into a pile on the sofa like it was confetti, searching every seam and zip and pocket. "She's probably dropped a bug somewhere," she called, distractedly, as she dug. "Don't say anything you don't want her to hear."

"Oh."

Tui was shifting everyone's packs from the kitchen into a heap by the front door. "We need to leave before she changes her mind and sends in her boyfriend and his toy soldiers."

"Same plan as before?" I asked, frowning. I couldn't remember discussing it, although it had probably been our usual. Nocturnal cross-country flights, hunkering down during the day, stealing the bare minimum to survive. Keeping one freezing step ahead.

"Um…" Luke peered through the living room door at the fake-looking mountain of bills on the sofa.

Kestrel glanced at him as she reached under the coffee table. "Haven't found a bug yet. Don't assume anything."

After a moment's thought, Luke pulled out his phone and typed. Then he showed me the screen.

*You could buy a vehicle now. Maybe not an RV, but something easier that makes it safer and easier to carry all your stuff. And the cash.*

"Ha! Good point," I said.

"What?" asked Tui and Falcon from the kitchen as Condor appeared with his duffel bag.

"Hang on."

Quickly, I created a new Flight group chat that included Luke, and he copied in his message. There was a jumble of beeps and buzzes through the house, and a pause as everyone checked the text.

"Yes! Genius!" Falcon shouted. He slapped a high five with Luke as he dashed past. "Gets my vote!"

Kestrel tapped out a message with one hand as she excavated the back of the sofa with the other. *Legal paperwork? Registration and insurance?*

Luke hesitated. *If you guys promise not to get any parking or speeding tickets, you can register it in my legal name. The Evolutionary people won't know to look that up.*

"Told you he's a genius!" Falcon called. Sounded like he was under his bed. Probably looking for his other flight boot or something. And I used to think I was messy.

*It's a bit late to go vehicle shopping now,* Tui texted. *We could research tonight and head out first thing tomorrow.*

*Just two or three of us,* Kestrel added. *And a good cover story for why a bunch of teenagers have $250,000 in cash?*

*And we're not spending all of it on a car,* Condor typed quickly.

I heard Tui's snort. *Agreed. There's heaps I want to get.*

*Me too.*

*Me three!*

*I have some ideas…*

I grinned. *I'll start a shopping list.*

*

"It's like a truck and a campervan had a baby," Tui said, staring out the kitchen window. It was one of the few rooms that couldn't have been bugged by our unexpected visitor the day before, not that we'd been able to find anything.

Kestrel giggled. "Is there some kind of law requiring all RVs to be brown and white and squiggly?"

"It's a forty-foot super class C bunkhouse with cab-over, and the design is called a swoop," Falcon said, with an attempt at dignity.

"And we'll blend in," I said. "We nearly got lost in the RV yard and there were only about twenty there. Imagine a campground or trailer park with a hundred or more."

"No trouble from the sales reps?" Condor asked, his arms crossed tightly and black wings twitching.

"Nope, Luke was awesome!" I said, playfully punching the guy's shoulder. "He kept the dealer distracted with so many questions, I don't think the man looked at me and Falcon twice."

"Especially as Luke came up with this brilliant story about how his grandma just passed away after hoarding cash for decades, and she left it all to him because he'd been caring for her for so long, and now he wants to get out of town before all the relatives come looking for him," Falcon added, enthusiastically. "We were his friends helping him choose."

"That story sounds familiar," Kestrel said, glancing at Luke and then Condor.

Luke's face warmed. "Condor's story gave me the idea," he admitted. "I'm sorry."

"Don't be," Condor said, smiling. "It was clever."

"Luke is a genius," Falcon declared, for about the tenth time in the last twenty-four hours. "We'd have been screwed without him. He even convinced the guy to give us a discount for paying cash! Turns out, it's super handy having a pet human around! Almost wish we could take him with us!"

"First of all, stop talking about Luke like he's not here, bro," Tui said.

I glared at Fal. "Secondly, *pet* human? Seriously?"

"Oh, come on, I was joking!" Falcon grinned, unrepentant.

"Thirdly," Kestrel said, "that's actually not a bad idea."

"Huh?"

Everyone stared at her.

Kess shrugged her golden wings. "Falcon's right. Without you, Luke, we'd have been sunk. Or, at least, we'd have had a lot more drama." She smiled. "Seems to me like the Flight needs a human representative. I realize now isn't the best time, but maybe when–"

"Why not now?" Falcon interrupted, bouncing in excitement. "I didn't even get to the part where the truck is a six-sleeper! We've got room!"

"Maybe we should talk about this first?" I said, dazed, wondering if I'd glitched part of the conversation.

"What is there to talk about? It's a great idea!"

Luke frowned. "I'm confused."

"You're not the only one," I muttered.

"Flight meeting. Now." Tui dragged Falcon into the back bedroom by his wing, with me and Kestrel following. Condor reassured Luke we'd only be a few minutes, and shut the door behind him.

"We have to take Luke with us," Falcon said, immediately. "He's practically part of the Flight anyway. We can't pass for human. We need him."

Tui crossed her arms and wings. "So do his parents."

"He's not an Icarus, though," I said, warily.

"So?" Falcon demanded. "I'm not species-ist. Are you?"

"Don't be a dick, Falcon." I hiked a thumb over my shoulder. "How will he feel when we keep flying and he's stuck on the ground? Or we hear and see things he can't?"

"He's no different to the rest of our families," Kestrel said, quietly.

Tui sighed. "And Luke *has* a family already. His dad is in hospital. His mum will need him. We can't take him away."

Condor harrumphed, loudly. "You guys are acting like this is an all-or-nothing, one-time deal," he said, exasperated. "Why don't we just invite Luke along for a few days? Unlike us, he can catch any type of public transport back to his family, so it doesn't matter how far we go. We can even buy him first-class tickets. And later, he can meet up with us any time he likes."

There was a brief silence.

"I like this plan," Falcon announced. "This is a good plan."

"Assuming Luke even wants to come," Tui said. "And his mum lets him."

"Either way, we leave tonight," I said.

"Road trip!" Falcon crowed, and hurtled back to the kitchen, wings banging on the doorframe as he went.

Unsurprisingly, Luke was keen to tag along. The surprising part was that he convinced his mom to let him.

"I'm eighteen," he pointed out, several times, as he paced through the house with his phone. "It's just a road trip for a few days. It will be good practice for when I go college."

Eventually, she relented. *"I suppose a little vacation with friends wouldn't do any harm while your dad's stuck here, love,"* we heard her say. *"I don't want you sitting around, fretting away your youth. But y'all better be on your best behavior, y'hear?"*

"Yes, Mom."

In the background, the Flight added their solemn promise to be good, and Falcon even uncrossed his fingers when Tui cuffed his head with her wing.

So, while the early dusk fell and Luke went to the hospital to say goodbye to his parents properly, the Flight loaded our few possessions and tons of food into our new moving home.

On the outside, it looked like any other grannymobile, with the gross brown squiggles, as Kestrel had noted. Most of the RVs we'd seen had also been brown, brown, and brown with a few highlights of brown. But the inside of this one had been redecorated by the previous owner with white paint, gray glass and tile, and stainless-steel handles, faucets, fridge, and stuff. The paint was peeling in places, revealing the 'cherry' (or whatever) paneling underneath, and some  handles had been screwed on wonky. The amateur renovation was probably why the RV had failed to sell to its usual target market; sitting on the lot for over a year before we'd shown up, tired from visiting three other dealers along the way.

However bad their handyman skills, though, the previous owner's tech upgrades were awesome. And so, as soon as me, Falcon, and Luke had stepped inside, we knew it was The One.

Color-changing LED strip lighting had been installed on every straight edge, and along a few curves as well. There were solar panels, an internet satellite dish, two massive flat screen TVs (one of which could be stored against the ceiling), enough charging ports for four devices each, a *sweet* Bluetooth sound system, and even a heads-up projector display for the driver. Falcon and I were disappointed that the gaming system hadn't been included with the RV, but we consoled (pardon the pun) ourselves with the knowledge we could now afford to buy a brand new one and put it in the air-conditioned closet retrofitted for that purpose. If we could convince the girls and Condor to add it to the Essentials shopping list, anyway.

There were two 'bedrooms' with double beds: one in the loft space over the cab, and one at the rear of the truck, past the kitchen and bathroom (more like a bath closet). Two of the super comfy sofas converted into beds for the fifth and sixth sleepers. Obviously, considering the current social structure of the Flight, Tui and Falcon would get one double bed, and me and Kestrel the other. Condor and Luke would have the single foldouts, but also, as I pointed out, the easiest access to the toilet and to the fridge.

Every now and then, I'd look around for Raven, or even for Dove. But their absence would drop a cold stone into my stomach.

Occasionally, the others would do the same. Then the same sadness and anxiety would cross their face, and their shoulders would droop.

I knew everyone would have traded the vehicle for Raven back in an Icarus heartbeat.

All we could do was keep moving.

After living with next to nothing for so many months, the amount of storage was much more than we needed. Falcon insisted we'd have to do some serious shopping in the next few days to purchase more essentials, like pillows, bed sheets, and 'entertainment'.

However, before that, there were two things we needed to do.

First, get out of town.

Second, make sure we could pass for human.

Then, and only then, we would have a Flight Freedom party.

# GROUP CHAT

KESTREL:

Hi Lory, sorry we've been quiet. It's been a crazy few days. But the good news is... we're on our way! :-D

LORY:

Hallelujah!!!!! Is everyone okay?

HAWK:

Sort of. Dove got away, but our friend's dad got shot

LORY:

WHAT!?!

CONDOR:

He'll recover, but it's going to take a long time. So Luke's coming with us for a while.

BEN:

Will you tell us who Luke is, now?

KESTREL:

Me and Condor met him and his parents at the Angelist church. We got to know them better after they left, and offered to help us.

He's only travelling with us for a few days, so your parents don't have to worry

LORY:

A friend of yours is a friend of ours!

BEN:

But it'll still help calm Mom and Dad's paranoia.

LORY:

Luke's dad got SHOT. It's not paranoia if there really is someone after you!

TUI:

Yeah. And unfortunately, there is.

LORY:

Who?

HAWK:

We'll explain in person. Too hard by text. However, circumstances have changed. Raven's gone home with her sister. It's just five of us extra Icari coming to visit now.

LORY:

Argh, I'm desperate for details. But okay. How long till you get here? Still a few weeks?! How far are you flying each day?

KESTREL:

That's the other thing. We have wheels now. According to the GPS it's a twenty-hour direct drive, but we won't take the most obvious route. We're also planning to stop along the way. We want to enjoy the road trip. Maybe about four, five days?

LORY:

YAY!

TUI:

And we'll bring our own food and other supplies. We have enough money to support ourselves for a while now.

LORY:

Oooooh tell me more??

HAWK:

Again, easier in person

LORY:

PHOTOS OR IT DIDN'T HAPPEN.

CONDOR:

Haha

KESTREL:

The dealer hasn't taken down the listing yet. I'll DM you the link. :-)

LORY:

HOLY CRAP YOU HAVE A HOUSE TRUCK

BEN:

Thanks, guys. Now Lory won't stop jumping on my bed and screaming.

That RV must have cost a fortune. Did you guys win the lottery or something?

TUI:

Sort of. We didn't spend it all on the truck though. We've got a list of other stuff we want

LORY:

OMG YES! What's on your wish lists??

HAWK:

Wrist altimeters

KESTREL:

Comms earpieces

TUI:

First responder kit

CONDOR:

A new winter jacket. I lost mine

HAWK:

Airspeed indicator! And a GPS unit that tells you ground speed

KESTREL:

What about you guys?

LORY:

Um, all of the above? Even the jacket. Mine got ripped >_<

BEN:

If I could get absolutely anything, I'd want some AR smartglasses that has all of those things in one.

Except the jacket and first aid kit, obviously... haha

CONDOR:

AR?

BEN:

Augmented reality. You know, like a heads-up display? Projects information into your field of vision.

KESTREL:

@Condor like Falcon's current app obsession. The one where he 'hunts' mythical creatures and 'finds' and 'catches' them

CONDOR:

Ah. I still don't believe there was a digital dragon egg on my bed the other morning

HAWK:

Hopefully he'll be distracted by the constantly-changing scenery now. Honestly, it was like being locked in a house with a toddler

LORY:

> Speaking of... Falcon doesn't want to chat too?

TUI:

> He and Luke are busy fixing up an ancient Monopoly board he found at a thrift store. Judging by the giggling, it's going to be unrecognisable by the time they're done with it. Sigh...

LORY:

> Can't wait to play it with you guys! I love board games!

BEN:

> Just to make sure I'm following, Luke isn't an Icarus, right?

KESTREL:

> He's our human agent. I'm starting to wonder how the hell we ever survived without his help, honestly. The RV was his idea, and he's been so patient and helpful, collecting all our random supply requests. This morning he picked up a big box of contact lenses to disguise our eyes.

HAWK:

> He's part of the family now. We should give him an honorary Flight name.

CONDOR:

> Or encourage him to choose one, *IF* he wants one.

KESTREL:

Condor's right. We've already asked so much of Luke. I don't want to put any more pressure on him.

LORY:

Well, I'm not afraid of putting pressure on BEN, right **@Ben**? He totally needs to choose a bird name because BEN will really stand out when the whole Flight gets here, **@Ben**.

TUI:

Lory! Chill out, sis!

LORY:

Oh I'm just teasing, Tui. Ben's used to it.

BEN:

...

CONDOR:

I didn't take a Flight name for a couple of months. There's no rule.

But it doesn't take long to get used to, once you find the right one.

BEN:

Well... maybe if this Luke guy takes a Flight name too, then I will.

LORY:

DEAL.

Ok I'm hungry now.

BEN:

You're always hungry.

HAWK:

Us too haha

LORY:

Can you imagine how much food would be needed if there was a huge group of us at a party or something?

KESTREL:

I can't even imagine a whole room of Icari. I'm still wrapping my head around there being ten of us, let alone more

BEN:

Ten?

KESTREL:

Me, Hawk, Tui, Falcon, Condor, Raven, Owl (we lost him a few weeks ago), Dove, now you two.

TUI:

Anyone else tried to contact you?

LORY:

Nothing believable yet. Tons of rumors, and scam messages. Ugh. Fakers piss me off.

BEN:

We'll let you know if anything likely turns up.

HAWK:

I think, if we're ever going to find out for sure, we'll have to find the source

LORY:

The IVF clinic doctor person?

KESTREL:

Once we're all in the same place, we'll pool intel.

LORY:

Sounds like a plan

We have to go to dinner now. Talk soon, guys!

# 16

# KESTREL

There was a knock on the tiny bathroom door.

"Yeah?" I said, around the hair tie I was gripping in my teeth.

"Can I come in, sis?" Tui said.

I gave up on taming my hair. "Yep."

Tui slipped in. "Eh, looking good, Kess!"

I snorted. "Whatever!" I'd turned a thrift shop black T-shirt into a halter top for our Freedom Party. There were a few more holes in it than I'd intended. "I was going for elegant and ended up with failed punk."

"Who cares?" Tui smirked. "Hawk won't."

My cheeks reddened.

"Sis, Hawk's seen you at your worst and he still loves you. You really think he's going to give a crap what you're wearing?"

"Easy for you to say when you'd look good in a sack," I moaned.

"Yeah, nah, you think I just randomly pulled this out of the bag?" Tui shimmied her hips, and her second-hand red skirt flared out around her thighs. She'd turned a white scarf and a black belt into a crop top around her wings and generous boobs, framing her *pounamu* necklace, and looked stunning even before she'd done anything with her hair or the makeup that Luke had so graciously picked up for us.

"I don't think I've ever seen you in a skirt or a dress before," I said. "You look so pretty. And your tattoo looks awesome."

"Thanks, sis. I was never a girly girl before, but I wanted to try something different after … you know. Gotta let our hair down, eh. Speaking of…"

The black waves fell around Tui's face, brushing her ears. All she did was run her fingers through it, resettle the parting down the middle, and she was done.

"Your turn." Tui grinned.

I poked at the kink from my hair tie. "Help me?"

"Okay, try this."

In a few breaths, she had my hair half up, half down, hiding the kink but letting some strands hang around my face. In only a few more weeks, it would reach my shoulders again.

"There," Tui said, satisfied. "Easy as."

Hair done, we moved on to the makeup. However, halfway through applying mascara, I was completely distracted when Tui put on the darkest lipstick I'd ever seen and used the black eyeliner to draw on the traditional Māori pattern I now knew was called *moko kauae* (moh-koh ko-eye) on her chin. She'd explained to me once, ages ago in the desert, that it told a story about her ancestors and where she came from. She'd been gifted the design by her grandmother, and it was deeply personal and sacred. One day she wanted to get it tattooed into her skin, so no one could take it away from her.

I always felt privileged when Tui shared these things with me. I didn't have a sense of connection to my ancestors. I didn't even feel connected to my own mum and dad, let alone England. And now with the wings…

"Eh, Kess, don't look so lost!" Tui grinned, the *moko* enhancing the expression. "Remember our Flight makeup?"

"Oh, right!" Excitement fluttered in my chest. "Should I do that?"

"Hell, yeah!"

After the thick eyeliner, I drew stripes and curls around my forehead and eyes in the design I'd invented for myself so long ago. A tear slipped out and smudged it as I remembered Owl's and Raven's reactions at the time, but I wiped it away and carefully fixed it all. When I asked, Tui assured me that it didn't look too much like her own, or like it was appropriating any native culture other than my own distant Celtic roots, of which I had minimal knowledge.

"Hope Hawk likes it," I said, finally, tightening the black halter-neck wrap. It was weird having bare arms and shoulders again after a long winter, but it didn't take much to warm up the RV, especially with five Icari running hot. It was balmy in the little bathroom.

With a sudden surge of daring, I ripped the neckline of halter top so that it showed a flash of cleavage.

"That's my girl," Tui said, laughing.

"You're sure? It's not too slutty?"

"Sis, you love Hawk, don't you? You like kissing him? Having a bit of a feel?"

"Well, yeah." I blushed. "Not that we've done it much."

"Oh, believe me, sis, I know. There's been no privacy for any of us since we met. But now..."

I blushed harder when I saw Tui's smirk. "Are you going to sleep with Falcon?" My voice instinctively dropped to a whisper.

Tui grinned. "He doesn't know it yet."

"Have you had sex before?"

"Not technically, but I know what I'm doing." She held out her hand. "Ever used one of these?"

It was a handful of condoms. I giggled in shock. "Where the hell did you get those?"

"I added it to the last online grocery order." Tui smirked. "Got to love the internet. And the last thing we need is a couple of pregnant Icari."

My giggles faded. "I don't need birth control anymore, Tui. Remember?"

"Kestrel, you might not have a uterus anymore, but you still need protection," Tui said, seriously. "You don't know if Hawk's had sex before, do you?"

"No," I admitted.

"So, you have no idea what he might be carrying without even knowing it. Also," Tui said, steamrolling over my embarrassed splutters, "it'll help him last longer." She winked, and put one into my jeans pocket. "Promise me you'll use it? Oh, and afterwards, make sure you go to the toilet. All right?"

"What? Why?"

"Prevents bladder infections," Tui said, matter-of-factly.

"Ugh! Gross."

"Yes, so you don't want one. Have safe fun, then pee, *then* you can snuggle up and fall asleep. Okay?"

Meekly, I nodded. "Yes, Mum."

She snorted. "Good. Now, let's go party!"

Falcon wolf-whistled as we appeared in the main section of the massive RV, and Hawk also made appreciative noises. I noticed his eyes straying to my chest, and I tingled wherever his gaze touched.

"I'd completely forgotten about doing that," Falcon said, admiring Tui's face. "You girls look awesome."

"You should put yours on, too, eh," Tui said, holding up the eyeliner.

Falcon, Hawk, and Condor cheerfully reapplied their own Flight-tribe party paint, as Fal called it. His and Hawk's designs were heavily influenced by their distant African roots in the spots and stripes, and Condor's featured Aztec-inspired angles and chevrons. Soon, even Luke had a few party stripes.

By this time the music was loud, and the party had started. Falcon grabbed Tui, they shoved the table out of the way, and they began to dance, dragging Condor and Luke along with them.

Hawk slung an arm around my shoulders. "Looking good, babe. Wanna dance?"

"Not really," I said, wryly. "Not that there's much room left for us right now." Falcon was doing some kind of bizarre wing flaring and wiggling thing, which was apparently based on real-life birds of paradise and animated dragons. Tui, Luke, and Condor were nearly collapsing from laughter.

Hawk chuckled. "That's a relief. As I think we've already discussed a long time ago, I can't dance."

"But you're a master of the meaningful sway, or so I recall."

Hawk kissed my head. "Later, I'll prove it. Right now, I'm hungry. And thirsty. This party stuff is hard work." He towed me between Falcon's and Tui's flailing arms, and into the relatively large kitchen.

"Hey, who already took a bite out of the cake?" he hollered over the music.

"You did!" Falcon and Condor yelled back.

"Did not!"

Fal jumped past the others and brandished his phone with a photo of Hawk caught in the flash whilst shoving the missing piece of cake into his mouth. "Yeah, you did!"

"Busted!" I laughed.

Hawk winced. "My bad."

"You said, and I quote, 'because I was first to come out, I get the first piece of cake'," Falcon said.

"It's my party and I'll fly if I want to!"

"It's the Flight's party," Falcon corrected Hawk. "Things are finally looking up and we get to celebrate."

Tui leaned over the kitchen countertop. "What've we got to drink?"

"What would m'lady like?" Falcon said, smirking, as he began setting out the soda and juice choices on the countertop next to the piles of food.

Soon we all had drinks in hand, tinkling with ice. The music was still blaring, and the LED lights were changing colours with the beat.

"A toast!" Falcon yelled, raising his glass high. "To the Flight and our future!"

We all cheered and drank.

Of course, the food didn't last long, and the table was quickly cleared for the 'entertainment' Falcon had promised, which turned out to be a pack of playing cards and the ancient Monopoly game. Even though half the original cards were missing, Falcon had made plenty of replacements along with amendments to the board, including: Desert Camp, Canyon Road, Aerie Way, Flight Boulevard, and a Chance card that told the recipient to *Go directly to jail, do not pass Go, do not collect $200, and give all your money to Falcon.* Condor nearly snorted his drink out of his nose at that one.

We played cards first, with the stakes being dishes duty. But after a few rounds, Tui's current favourite pop song came on. Falcon immediately rejoined her in the 'living room' formed by the extended slideout, which wasn't sloping *too* much on the flat-ish ground we'd parked on for the night, nearly an hour from the main road in the middle of nowhere. Much mad dancing happened, to my eternal amusement, followed by a couple of calmer, quieter songs to which Hawk and I swayed meaningfully, as promised. My heart double-tapped as Hawk's hands stroked my bare back.

Quite some time later, as Tui, Falcon, Luke, and Condor argued over the rules for playing Flight Monopoly, I snuggled deeper next to Hawk on the sofa. His arm, draped over my shoulders, gently shifted, and he began stroking the feathers on my wings. I hoped the makeup wasn't melting in the overheated RV, and I wished I'd gone for a skirt, like Tui, as my legs prickled inside my jeans. But I hoped I looked as nice as I thought I did. The nicest I'd looked since the Change. Since I'd met Hawk, and the others.

"You okay?" Hawk murmured.

Idly, I traced the edge of my glass with my thumb. "Just thinking."

"What about?"

I resettled my right wing on top of the left, stretched out along the sofa behind and beside me. "The last time I was at a party."

"I sense a story." Hawk took a sip of his OJ.

The confession, which had been bubbling on the back of my tongue since my conversation with Tui, edged forward. "It involves an ex-boyfriend," I admitted, under the music.

Hawk's arm and chest tensed, and his mottled brown wings rustled. He took a longer drink. "The dipshit who kicked you out and wouldn't help you after the Change?"

"We'd been dating for a few months. I was sixteen, Daniel was eighteen. I've no idea why he was interested in me in the first place–"

"Because you're hot," Hawk said. I poked him, and he pulled me closer. "And smart, and funny."

"No one thought so at school, believe me. Either here or in London. The point is," I said, barrelling over Hawk's attempt to interrupt again, "we were dating for a few months, and at this party I think he was trying to get me drunk enough to sleep with him, but instead I just threw up all over him." I giggled, awkwardly. "I was so sure the whole school would find out and that it would be the end of my life."

"But?"

"He never told anyone, and I know that for a fact because Stephanie would have found out and *murdered* me with the gossip. Instead, we kept dating, and..." I took a deep breath. "About a month later, I did actually. You know. Sleep with him."

Hawk was silent for a few horribly long seconds. I couldn't look at him. Just stared at the refractions of light in my glass.

"By choice?" Hawk asked at last, very quietly.

"Yeah. I was sober, and it was awful. I didn't know what the hell I was doing, and I don't think he did either, even though he said he'd done it before. And it hurt a bit. At first. But it didn't last long." I giggled, nervously. "Tried a few more times after that but it didn't get much better. He must have started cheating around then, but I was getting pretty distracted by the Gremlin stuff. Wasn't until I escaped from Gavin's house arrest that I busted him and the girl he was cheating with. Walked straight out again, and hit the road alone."

"And then you met me," Hawk said, forcefully cheerful.

Finally, I looked up at him. "I met you."

Hawk kissed my forehead. "If I ever bump into this guy, he's going to regret ever hurting you."

"If he hadn't, I might never have joined the Flight, though."

Hawk put down his glass, and his fingers lifted my face so he could kiss me properly. The fizz spread from my lips through my chest and stomach. "But I'm still allowed to get mad at anyone who's hurt you."

"You're the first person ever on my side who can actually beat up mean people," I said, grinning. "You and your green belt."

"Purple," Hawk said, with a mock-pained expression under his Flight stripes. "But I'll wear any colour and beat up anyone you want me to." He kissed me, quick and hard.

There was the slapping of cards and a loud whoop from Falcon. As Hawk had another drink, I glanced over and caught Condor's eye. He smiled at me, and I thought I caught a hint of sadness in his eyes before he turned back to the game.

I was genuinely sorry for Condor, and his fifth-wheel status in the Flight. Still, I couldn't help being glad that he hadn't left with

Dove. Maybe she'd miss him and realise she wanted to come back, or maybe Condor and Lory would hit it off. Or maybe there were even more Icari out there, and Condor would find someone. This felt like a real possibility, now. We actually had a sense of having a future.

So, I decided to take Tui's advice, and seize the moment.

A thin line of orange juice glistened on Hawk's upper lip as he examined his glass, apparently deciding whether to refill it. Boldly, I took the cup from his hand and put it down, then climbed onto his lap.

Hawk's eyes widened, but as my mouth touched his, the lids closed. His mouth curved into a smile. Gently, I kissed the juice from his lips and then explored a little further with my tongue.

His hands wrapped around my waist under my wings and my arms slid around his neck. The kiss turned hungrier.

Falcon wolf-whistled. "Get a room!" he hollered.

Hawk and I both lifted our middle fingers at Fal at the same time, and there was an eruption of laughter. As the rest of the Flight turned back to their game, I broke the kiss and met Hawk's gaze.

"What about you?" I whispered.

His forehead creased. "What about me what?"

My heart sighed. "Do you remember what I just told you?"

"About Dickhead getting you drunk and being a crappy lover and cheating on you, yeah. Did I miss something else?"

"No, that's about it." Relieved, I kissed him again. "What about you, then?"

"Have I ever cheated or been cheated on? Hell no, and not as far as I know." He smiled his lopsided smile, and my nerves fluttered.

"But have you ever slept with someone?"

His cheeks flushed. "A couple of times. Two ex-girlfriends. Didn't go very well either, if I'm honest."

With my heart backflipping, I tried to smile seductively while being absolutely certain I looked like a lunatic. "Sounds like we both need to practise, then."

Warily, Hawk raised his eyebrows. "Are you sure?"

"Yes." I nodded, then hesitated. "I mean, only if you want to."

His mouth opened and closed a few times. Eventually, he placed my hand on his chest.

"Can you feel that?" he whispered.

Beneath my palm, his heart was pounding like he'd just sprinted a thousand feet straight up.

Same as mine.

Shyly, I met his gaze. "I'll take that as a yes, then?"

He smirked. "You can take that as a *hell yes*." Then he blinked. "What, right now?"

I attempted to shrug nonchalantly. "We do have our own bedroom, and the rest of the Flight are completely distracted."

Hawk had to swallow hard. "Cool," he said, eventually. "Let's go before Falcon decides we have to play Twister or something."

Trying not to hyperventilate or kill the mood by whacking Hawk in the face with my wings, I untangled myself and slid my hand into his.

Together, we slipped away from the Flight party and into our tiny bedroom. I deliberately didn't look back to see if anyone saw us go.

As we shut the door, blocking out much of the light and music, I began to panic. Had it been too warm? Was I now disgustingly sweaty and smelly? What if my scars turned him off? What if he was grossed out by my unshaven legs? What if his brain glitched halfway through? What if it all went wrong and it ruined our relationship forever?

Then his hands slipped around my shoulders, pulling me to him.

His lips touched mine for only a second. "I haven't … I haven't got … protection."

"Don't worry," I whispered. "I talked to the Flight doctor earlier, and she gave me some supplies."

Hawk suddenly swept his arms around me and lifted me right off the floor. I yelped in surprise and threw my arms around his neck.

"Always wanted to try this," Hawk said.

"Fine by me!"

Awkwardly, both of us laughing, he managed to kneel on the bed before laying me down across the mattress. After a little while, I sat up again so we could unwind each other from our clothing, and then there was nothing between us. Just skin on skin.

In the darkness we explored each other, opening up completely.

And I found I didn't care when his fingers traced the long scars. I didn't care when we clonked skulls going in for another kiss. We just laughed and then kissed harder. I didn't care when I nearly fell off the bed reaching for the packet in my abandoned jeans and Hawk saved me by grabbing me in the most awkward way possible. I didn't care when he accidentally kneeled on my feathers and he didn't care when I accidentally pulled too hard on his. I didn't care when either of us couldn't figure something out, and attempts to ask and explain collapsed into confusion and giggles. It was funny and messy and clumsy and slightly disastrous and totally perfect.

It was Hawk. And he loved me. And I loved him.

And for a little while, nothing else mattered.

# 17

# RAVEN

JingYing put a photo in my hands. It was a screenshot – another new word – from the latest video she had made me watch. It showed Frederik and Aron Larrsson, and Lin JingYing and YanWei. They were all smiling, laughing. They'd just finished filming a pretend documentary about the room they were in. The room I was in now.

JingYing had made it the same as it was before the accident. Before YanWei and Aron had died. Or, their brains had stopped working, and all the scientists called it Death, and called the bodies Vegetables, and started their Tests. When Owl and me had been in the dark place. When it had all been Bad.

But this had been a Good place.

When JingYing had opened the door into this room, into this small house at the top of a very tall city building, she had not said anything. Just looked at me.

It had taken me a long time to walk through the door. I didn't want to, but I did want to.

The soft floor was dark green, like the forests the Flight liked, and Tui's necklace stone. The outside walls were glass. There were big sofas, and a yellow-wood table with five chairs, and a thick TV on the wall. The lights on the ceiling were hung on metal poles.

I walked across the room. It smelled … nice. There were thin sticks in a cup of sand, and they were burning.

"Ba … jiao," I said.

"Yes, YanWei. It is your favorite."

I walked to the glass wall. My feathers were very quiet on the soft floor.

There was a big city. I didn't know which one. But I liked the window walls, because I could think I was flying with the Flight.

I didn't know if JingYing would let me fly again. YanWei could not fly.

There were other doors. I knew they were bedrooms. I didn't want to go there. Not yet.

In the corner was a small stone man with a long beard. I opened a drawer in the table he was standing on. In the drawer was a purple stuffed bear toy.

I nearly picked it up. I stopped.

"That's where you hide Grape when Mother comes to visit," JingYing said. "You convinced Madame to let you keep him when Mother told her to get rid of our baby toys. That's where Grape was the morning that you left."

I pushed the drawer shut, hard. "I am not a baby."

"No." JingYing did not show if she was sad or happy. "You were ten when you left. There were four years of nothing. You have made approximately seven more years of memories since. I will give you back the childhood that you lost. Then, you will have seventeen years of memory. Of life."

Seventeen. The Flight were seventeen.

To have seventeen years, like the Flight, would be Good. Even if it was YanWei who had them, in the end.

I nodded.

So JingYing showed me the memories. The 'diaries'.

"These aren't memories," I said, angry. "These are videos."

JingYing sat down so she was not taller than me. "YanWei, when you think about what happened yesterday, when you access your memories from just yesterday, what are you doing?"

"I was saying goodbye to the Flight," I said.

"No, that is the moment the memory is about. How are you remembering that moment? What is happening in your brain?"

I knew what she wanted. But I pretended not to understand. I just stared at her. Waiting.

Everyone else Owl and I had ever known – the Team, the people Owl and I had met between escaping and meeting the Flight, and then the Flight themselves – always filled the silence after a few seconds. Saying their question again, maybe in a different way, or suggesting an answer. Eventually, I would nod or shake my head, or they would decide an answer.

Not JingYing.

She waited back.

After many hundreds of Icarus heartbeats, JingYing leaned her head to the side. And I could read her face. It said, "I will wait as long as I have to."

So, I answered.

"I remember what I saw, and what I heard, and what I felt. I see it, and I hear it, and I feel it again."

"Then this should be an easy question. What color shirts were your friends wearing?"

My face went hard. I tried to remember again. The Flight hugging me. The smell of their jackets and feathers. I knew what their jackets looked like. Hawk's was black. Kestrel's was dark brown. Falcon's was dark gray. Their shirts ... I couldn't see their shirts.

It was a trick question.

"I don't know. They were wearing their jackets."

"Are you sure their jackets weren't open? You couldn't see their shirts at all?"

"The Flight don't wear shirts. They wear shirt-wraps."

"I apologize. What color were their shirt-wraps?"

"I don't know."

"Why not?"

"Because I don't remember."

"But it was only yesterday."

"It wasn't important."

JingYing sat back. "So, it was only yesterday, and you have already forgotten part of what your friends look like."

My face was hot. My eyes were spiky.

"Why don't you try remembering again?" JingYing said, watching me.

Angry, I shut my eyes. Thought about the Flight. Tried to *see* them from yesterday.

Their faces were sad. Their mouths tight. Dark jackets, dark boots. Maybe Hawk's jacket had been open. The zip had been hard on my cheek when he hugged me. That meant it was open, didn't it? So what color was his shirt wrap?

Why couldn't I remember?

"I think it was white," I said.

"What was?"

"Hawk's shirt-wrap."

"It was white?"

"Maybe gray. He likes gray shirt-wraps." I remembered Hawk laughing about how gray was better than white because it didn't show so much dirt and sweat.

I opened my eyes. JingYing's head was still on the side.

"Are you sure?"

"Yes," I said, annoyed.

"Try remembering again. It was actually blue."

My mouth tasted bad. I closed my eyes again. I pictured Hawk. Sad. The rest of the Flight around me.

A little bit of blue at the end of my nose as Hawk hugged me.

"Can you see it?" JingYing asked.

"Yes," I said, feeling Bad. Why had I remembered it wrong? "His shirt-wrap was blue."

"Oh, did I say blue? I meant green. It was definitely green. But a blue-ish green. I can understand why you would say blue."

Inside my eyes, I tried to see Hawk from yesterday again. And yes, JingYing was right. Hawk's shirt was green.

So why had I seen blue?

I stared at JingYing. I was angry now.

"Did you see his green shirt?" she asked.

"Yes," I said, even though I didn't want to.

"Do you think that is the truth?"

"I saw it!" I said. "I saw it yesterday! And I remembered! I saw it!"

"It was blue, and then it was green."

My throat was sore. "Yes."

"YanWei," JingYing said, reaching out and touching my hand. "You just changed your own memory. And it was only from yesterday. How do you know which is the true memory?"

I pulled away.

JingYing spoke quietly. "You changed the details of your memory to fit with what you believed to be true. This is quite normal. It is impossible for a human, even a *Homo sapiens superior* or *Homo sapiens icarus* brain, to record and recall every point of data it receives every millisecond of every hour of every day. It keeps the important points, and fills in the rest with logical guesswork whenever needed, such as when it is being retrieved, or remembered. Eventually, even the important points become distorted and adjusted to fit."

I did not look at her. I did not want to see her face. I did not want to *remember* her face.

But she kept talking. So calm. So quiet. And I could not stop it.

"Every person in the world, even those who have not had a traumatic experience, has false memories. It is how the brain works. Everyone has a memory they are certain they remember, in detail, exactly as it happened. But it is a memory built on a story they have been told about their childhood, or an event they saw in a home video. Sometimes it's entirely fabricated from nothing.

"People's experiences, their *memories* of their experiences, shape who they are. These experiences inform their understanding of the world, their thoughts and reactions. Few have a detailed, factual record of their lives to which they can compare these memories.

"But we do.

"We made thousands of hours of videos and wrote hundreds of thousands of words together, YanWei, even in our first ten years. You will see, and hear, and read, and you will come to remember. You will rebuild your knowledge of yourself. You will rebuild your memories, YanWei, and you will understand who you were, and who you are. And you will be home."

She stood and turned on the TV. I wiped the warm water off my face. Stupid eyes. Stupid Raven.

"You should message your friends," JingYing said, not looking at me. "Tell them you are okay."

*I am not okay.*

But this strange Not-Me would know that. She knew what I was thinking, and she knew how to change the memories in my head.

I was holding my phone and trying to think of the words, and then I heard his voice.

Owl.

The same as when he was Two. Before the injections that made him so tall and his voice so deep.

I looked at the screen, and it was him.

He was with his brother, and little JingYing and little YanWei. And he was happy.

I forgot the message. I forgot my phone. I watched, and I listened, and I cried.

At the end, JingYing put the photo in my hands. "Memorize this," she said. "Concentrate on what you saw and heard. Imagine what it was like to feel it, to have been there. The more you imagine it, the more real it becomes, and soon, it will *be* real."

Now I knew. I had to. Even if it hurt and it confused me and it changed me and YanWei came back and Raven disappeared forever, it would be okay.

As long as I could have Owl in my head, and in my heart.

*

I sighed. "I don't know!"

"Yes, you do." JingYing pushed the tablet back across the table. "You had a diploma in physics by age eight. I'm sure it was very helpful while learning to fly."

My wings ached.

"Maybe, but then I was dead in the brain for three years," I said, angry. "I remembered one hand sign, four Chinese characters, and three Chinese words. Now you want me to do physics equations after locking me in here for five days?"

JingYing leaned back. "Do you remember the day Aron knocked over the vase?" she said.

I looked to the corner where the bearded stone man was standing, but I shook my head. "You played the video two days ago."

JingYing smiled. "It wasn't clear in the video where it happened. But you've already redeveloped your memory enough to figure it out from context. You didn't even think about it. You remembered it."

"Ugh." I pushed my chair back, and crossed my arms. I would have slid down further in my seat, but my wings were hooked over the backrest.

JingYing laughed. "Have you noticed how much your behavior has developed in the last few days? You're acting like a prepubescent child, YanWei."

"I am not!"

"I rest my case."

"What?"

"A figure of speech. The point is, you are learning and developing very fast. Your language alone has come far in a few days. It proves your brain is just as strong as it was before the accident."

I kicked at the table, wishing my little legs could kick *her* instead. "I didn't learn this fast when I was with the Flight. What are you doing to me?"

"Depends," JingYing said.

"On what?"

"What you focus on. Did you practice talking much with the Flight?"

Kick. "No."

"Why not?"

"Because..." I waved at my throat. "When me and Owl–"

"Aron and I," JingYing corrected.

"It wasn't you, it was me," I said, knowing what she meant and still angry. "When *me and Owl* escaped from your..." What word made Hawk mad? Oh, yes. "...*pet* scientists on the Team, and we had to talk to people Outside for the first time, they always were surprised by my voice. They asked too many questions. And they were mean. So, I stopped talking."

"How did you and Aron escape van Scholtz's laboratory?"

Her voice was quiet, but it made me cold. I didn't want to tell her. But I knew she would wait. And wait. And never give up waiting.

"After Hawk was on the computer screens, and made the Team excited and worried," I said, not angry anymore, "they were not thinking about me and Owl. They were thinking about catching Hawk. They were getting ready and..." Kestrel always had pretty words. "They were running around like headless chickens." Yes, that was it. "They didn't see us take a key card and a Corporation money card, and hide in the vans. We stow-awayed."

"Stowed away," JingYing said.

"Whatever." Falcon sometimes said that. It felt fun to say.

JingYing just smiled, though. That was annoying.

"What happened after you stowed away in the vans?"

"When the van stopped for gas, we sneaked away."

"Just like that?"

No. It had been scary, and hard to breathe, and cold, hiding under the equipment in the van. It had been hugely scary – terrifying – waiting for the time to open the door. Hoping the Team would not see.

The Outside was so big. So smelly. So many people. It was even more than the movies and videos on the Team's computers. Me and Owl had sneaked out to play on the computers at nighttime. Taught ourselves to use the internet by watching the Team. Learned everything we could about the World.

But we never learned or saw anything about people like us.

Not until Hawk was on the news.

"Just like that," I said.

"How did you meet the Flight?"

"We went to the place where everybody was looking for Hawk."

"How did you get there?"

"In a car."

"How did you get a car? Who was driving?"

Wasn't she listening? "We used the Corporation money card. We had seen driving in the movies. Owl practiced and learned how to drive. I'm too short to reach the pedals."

"How long did Aron take to teach himself to drive?"

"A whole night," I said.

"And the rules of driving?"

"We saw what other people did."

"It normally takes people a long time to learn how to drive, YanWei. Aron must have regained his original higher functioning too." JingYing put her chin on her hands and her elbows on the table. "That's fascinating."

"It's not fascinating," I said, angry. That word had always meant more Bad things were coming. "It was hard."

"However, I wonder how much of it was new learning, and how much of it was rebuilt memory," JingYing said. "The boys always loved their driving games. Frederik wanted to be a racing driver for a while, but then gave up because Aron always beat him by at least 50 milliseconds on the simulator."

Although it upset me that JingYing would not call Owl by his chosen name, it made me happy to hear he had been better than Frederik. Maybe that was why Frederik had...

I *remembered* seeing Frederik standing over Owl in the fountain, his wings twisted and broken, and red in the water. I *remembered* hearing the gun. I *remembered* my friends pulling me away as I screamed and screamed and screamed and Owl died.

And I was angry again.

It was my turn for a question.

"Why do you want YanWei back?"

JingYing looked surprised for the very first time. "Pardon?"

"Why. Do. You. Want. Yan. Wei. Back?" I said, again, making all the words short and loud, like Kestrel did sometimes. "You have Frederik. And you like Frederik. He is Bad. Owl was Good. Why do you like Frederik? Why do you want YanWei as well as him?"

I knew my words were not completely right. The ideas in my head were confusing so my words were confused. But I didn't care. I just needed to know.

JingYing looked sad. "I told you, when I came to bring you home. I love you, YanWei."

"I'm not YanWei," I said.

"You are not all of YanWei. Not yet. But you will be."

I felt cold. "What if I don't want to?"

JingYing stood up, and her voice changed. Her face changed. She looked more like Junior.

"My sister wants to come back to me," she said, very quietly, but very hard. It hurt my ears. "I will get my sister back. And you will not stop her. Because you are her."

"NO, I'm NOT!" I jumped up. My wings were wide. "You have Junior! And he killed Owl! Now you have everything, and you have Junior, and now you want to get YanWei too? I just want Owl! And I can't have Owl! So you can't have YanWei!"

"That is enough, YanWei–"

"I am not YanWei!" I shouted. "I'm Raven! And..." I remembered, *really* remembered, hearing Falcon and Hawk. Using the good Bad words. "And you're a bitch!"

I ran out of the living room and slammed the bedroom door behind me.

# 18

# FALCON

I was woken by Condor grumbling about milk. Not my favorite way to wake up.

Not bothering to open my eyes, I tried to move, and found I wasn't feeling overwarm because of my own natural hotness, but because I had a gorgeous half-naked girlfriend curled up against me.

Immediately forgetting to care about the conversation beyond the thin sliding panel, I untangled a hand from the sheet and gently ran it down Tui's bare back, tracing the curves of her skin and tattoo. She sighed and snuggled closer, her dark feathers sliding across the surprisingly-comfy mattress.

My own wings were jammed against the wall, which was also kind of the ceiling. Tui and I had claimed the 'cab-over' bed, and there was only three feet of air between pillow and roof at its highest point. As it turned out, it was just the right size to encourage some very intimate cuddling, without being claustrophobic.

As I pressed my lips into Tui's hair, I heard the others moving about the main cabin of the RV, and I reflected it was a good thing the vehicle had electric leveling jacks, otherwise we'd quickly drive each other crazy with the bouncing and rocking.

I nearly woke Tui up just to turn that thought into a cheeky joke – something about how I'd driven her crazy and rocked her world last night – but because I very much wanted to do said activities again, sometime in the very near future, it was probably better not to.

However, now I was thinking about it, I couldn't stop thinking about it, and part of me was very keen to get started.

My kisses moved down her cheek. Her breathing changed, then her lips turned to mine and her arm slid around my neck.

"*Morena* to you too," she murmured, after a while.

I was too busy sliding my mouth down her neck, and my hands down her back, to reply.

Someone walked closer and rapped on the panel that closed off our little retreat.

"Flock off," I growled, and tightened my grip on Tui's ass.

"Charming," Hawk said, dryly, through the partition. "Put your pants on and hurry up. You've got fifteen minutes left for breakfast, then we're on the road."

Tui put her hand over my mouth and answered for me.

"Thanks, Hawk. Out in a minute."

Then she shivered as I kissed her palm.

"Stop it," she hissed.

"Why?" I asked between kisses. "Don't you like it?"

"I like it too much and you bloody well know it. Now get off me so I can find my clothes."

"Oh, you mean these clothes?" I seized the pile from last night and waved them at her. When she reached out, I shoved them behind me and prepared to wrestle.

To my disappointment, Tui merely leaned over me. As I grabbed the opportunity – two of them, in fact – while it was in front of me, she retrieved her duffel bag from the foot of the mattress, pulled it across me and extracted some fresh clothes, swatting my hand away when I tried to interfere.

I pouted. "You're no fun."

Tui concentrated on fastening her bra under her wing shoulders and wrapping on her shirt. "I save my fun for appropriate moments, bro. I'm going out in two minutes, so if you don't have your pants on by then, you've only yourself to blame."

Sighing, I did as I was told. Although I did pause and offer to help her slide on her jeans in the cramped space. Tui declined. It was hard having a super-independent girlfriend, sometimes.

But I wouldn't change a single thing about her.

As ordered, I had my own pants on by the time Tui slid back the panel and descended the ladder. Hawk saw me sitting there, naked from the waist up, and he blew a mocking wolf-whistle.

Grinning, I blew him a kiss in return. "Morning, Hawkie-bae!" I said, and pulled the first part of my shirt-wrap over my head. I had no shame in being half-naked in front of the Flight. Partly because we'd all been living together for so long, but also because flying had given me a chest and abs I was *hella* proud of.

As I emerged from the shirt, I saw Luke checking me out from the corner of his eye. I grinned and winked. He blushed and looked away, and I chuckled.

Finally, I was all wrapped up and as decent as I ever got. I made it into the kitchen – no, galley – just in time to grab some food before Hawk retracted the slideouts and the RV got a lot more cozy.

"Here we go," he announced, sliding into the cockpit (heh) and taking the driver's seat, his wings slung to the inside. "Next stop, rendezvous with Lory and Ben."

"Aren't we dropping Luke off at the airport?" I asked, tucking myself into the sofa next to Tui.

Luke, sitting next to Condor only a few feet away, thanks to the pulled-in slide-out, twisted his phone in his hands. "I rang Mom this morning. Dad's doing okay, but he's one of the ICU patients who've been put into quarantine to protect him from that new flu virus. Even if I went back now, I wouldn't get to see him in person for ages, and I don't know anyone else in that entire state. And with everyone worrying about a new epidemic or something, Mom thinks I'll be safer in hiding with you anyway."

"We said he could stay," Condor said. "We figured you and Tui would agree."

I briefly considered acting offended, but saw Luke's face.

"Are you guys sure about this?" he said, obviously not for the first time.

"Of course, bro," Tui said, nudging his foot with her wingtip. "We've already explained to Lory and Ben's parents that you're part of the Flight now."

Luke's face darkened as he blushed (again), and Kestrel leaned around from the front passenger seat.

"Everyone ready?"

"Yes, Mom," I said, brightly, and Kestrel stuck out her tongue.

With a jerk and a lurch and some good-natured catcalling as Hawk crunched the gears, we were off.

I'd never been in this part of the US before, so, after getting bored of *I Spy*, I found myself idly scanning the map from northern California up into the Pacific Northwest, where we now were, for random points of interest. Some of my favorite discoveries included: Forks of Salmon, Weed, Friend Place, Surprise Station, Shreck, Mad River, Coffee Creek, and Bonanza King; Falcon Heights, for obvious reasons; Yoder, and, further north, Vader; places where ye olde cartographers had clearly given up, Pysht, Wellpinit and Index; and finally, because I have never pretended to be mature, Black Butte and Red Butte, Humptulips, and Slickpoo. Apparently, yes, they are real places. Would Google Maps lie?

Unfortunately, it didn't have a handy label announcing: 'Sasquatch lives here!' I checked.

Whenever I came across a bird name on the map, which was surprisingly often, I'd suggest it to Luke.

"Wren? Eagle?"

Luke shook his head.

"Pigeon or Goose?"

"Really, Falcon?" Condor said.

Hawk called, "Clearly you've never seen *Top Gun*."

"There's also a Wild Goose. Or what about Loon?" I got a kick for that one. Probably deserved it.

Luke fidgeted. "It doesn't feel right picking a bird name when I can't fly."

"Plenty of awesome birds can't fly, bro," Tui said. "I should know. Aotearoa's famous for them."

"Yeah!" I cried. "Genius, babe! Luke, we need to find you a flightless Flight name."

"Because that's not oxymoronic in the least," Kestrel called.

I pretended to be outraged. "Who're you calling moronic?"

"You!" said Tui, Hawk, and Condor at the same time. I chuckled.

"We'll do more research on flightless birds later," Kestrel said. "We're nearly there."

I suppose it wasn't surprising that it looked similar to the area in which the Flight had originally met. There's only so many ways you can stick trees onto rocks and hills before it gets repetitive. It was nice enough, I suppose. I just hoped there'd be enough room for Hawk to turn the truck around, or an exit that went past and down the other side of the hills. Otherwise, it was going to be a loooooong way to reverse.

Most importantly, as far as we and our about-to-be friends were concerned, there was no one else in the area. We hadn't seen a single other vehicle in quite a while.

The road was in a tree tunnel now. Branches bumped and scraped along the RV roof every now and then, making us flinch. Hawk muttered dark curses about how there'd better be no damage to the solar panels and satellite dish (folded and strapped down, of course).

"Stop!" Kestrel said. Hawk slammed the brake. I fell into Tui and Luke slid into Condor.

"This is the place," Kestrel said, anxiously, peering through the windshield.

"Are you sure?" I asked, taking longer than necessary to detangle myself from my girlfriend. "My phone lost signal ages ago."

"That's what the GPS on my sat phone says."

I kept forgetting we had our old phones back now, and that included Kestrel's heavy-duty, cutting-edge, totally-stolen-from-her-dickhead-stepdad satellite phone.

"There's an old gate," Luke said, peering out the tinted window.

Set way back from the road, almost unnoticeable in the gloom under the trees, an old metal gate guarded a road that was technically paved, but was so damaged and half-buried in rotting leaf litter, it would have made a great location for a post-apocalyptic movie scene. Probably one with zombies.

So, of course, I volunteered to recon. I didn't have an axe, and Hawk refused to let me borrow the brand-new hunting blade he'd purchased the other day, so I improvised in true hero fashion by taking the biggest kitchen knife from its cradle in the galley drawer.

I stepped down from the RV as Hawk turned off the engine. It was silent, except for the wind in the millions of trees, where dozens of birds sang, and thousands of bugs buzzed and – yeah, okay, it was pretty noisy.

But none of the noises seemed artificial, even when I concentrated and stretched my Icarus hearing as far as it could go after hours of being numbed by constant diesel engine droning and Hawk's terrible singing along to the sound system.

Satisfied that no lurching flesh-eaters were about to jump out at me, I paid closer attention to the road. Or driveway. Deep in a bush, I thought I could see the remains of an old mailbox being strangled in slow motion.

Although the pavement was cracked like the streambed in the desert, and the drifts of dead leaves were inches thick, it felt solid enough under my boots as I took a few steps.

Then, my keen hunter's eyes spotted some of the taller weeds were bent and freshly bruised – like a vehicle had recently driven over them. But not too recently. They'd recovered.

And there were scrapes in the brown sludge leading to a discarded, dead branch, now lying in the undergrowth.

Yes, I decided. Someone had recently driven through here.

Step by careful step, I avoided disturbing the evidence (and getting mud on my flight boots) and approached the gate.

"Hurry up, Falcon," Hawk bellowed from the driver's window. "If this isn't the place, we're going to be late."

Hands on my hips (carefully not stabbing myself with the kitchen knife), my wings flicking, I surveyed the gate. It looked like it hadn't been opened in decades. But, as I peered closer at the top rail, I could just make out letters under the lichen and mold.

RICHARDSON'S FARM.

"Hey, guys?" I called over my shoulder. "What's Lory and Ben's last name?"

"Richardson," Tui answered. "Why?"

"This is it."

"I texted Lory," Kestrel said. "She says to come on in."

"What, you couldn't have done that before I risked my life in zombie territory?" I joked.

"I did. It took her a few minutes to reply. You were the one who wanted to play Sherlock."

After I'd reluctantly re-stowed the unused knife, Condor helped me drag open the gate. It moved surprisingly easily, considering how arthritic with rust it appeared to be. We had to hang on to it to make sure it didn't swing back on our no-longer-shiny, forty-foot-long brown monster as Hawk gingerly eased it off the road at a right angle, and through the narrow gap in the trees and fence posts. Lory apparently had promised we wouldn't get stuck.

We shut the gate, and began scouting ahead of the truck, walking along the forgotten road towards our fates.

"You are such a drama queen," Condor said.

"Aw, thanks, Con."

After some anxiety-inducing twists and turns, ear-shriveling scrapes and crunches of branches on metal, and gut-wrenching lurches of suspension through potholes, there was finally sunlight at the end of the tree tunnel.

As we emerged into open air, my wings were suddenly aching.

It was a little mountain valley, cradled by tree-lined ridges, with a clear, grassy valley floor. Derelict farm buildings dotted the fields roughly outlined by broken fences. An old farmhouse with boarded-up windows crouched on one side of the loop at the end of the driveway, with a once-red barn on the other.

And, in the air above, were two flying Icari. As Condor and I stepped out of the treeline, the nose of the RV following like a farm dog, the flyers turned, and headed straight for us.

Without really thinking about it, I opened and stretched my wings. Condor did the same. I broke into a light jog, but didn't try and take off. Instead, we kept up an easy pace, heading for the point where Lory and Ben were clearly aiming – the center of the driveway loop.

The RV pulled up as we slowed to a halt, the engine brake seemingly huffing in relief as Hawk applied the don't-go-anywhere lever.

I shielded my eyes against the almost-noonday sun as Lory and Ben circled overhead a couple times, and then came into land. By the time their red and black wings were back-beating to control the final drop, everyone had piled out of the RV, and the Flight faced our new friends in person for the first time.

Lory's crazy red curly hair was pulled back into a high ponytail, which made her look even taller than she already was. I was not expecting her to be taller than both me and Hawk. Only Condor – and Owl, RIP, buddy – would have had an inch or two more. Benji's black head, on the other wing, was barely up to his twin's shoulder. Ouch. That had to suck.

That was as far as my appraisal got, because by then, Lory had folded away her tail pieces and was sprinting straight at us, shrieking, "Oh my god you're finally here I can't believe it!"

Condor happened to be closest so she slammed into him first, at approximately Mach 2, from what I could tell. Condor nearly assed it backwards as the redhead threw her arms around him and squeezed.

"Uh–" he said, but by then Lory had let go and was launching herself at me.

I kept upright with a few quick half-flaps, and any attempt at verbalizing a greeting myself was completely squished. I had enough presence of mind to register the generous size and shape of the chest underneath her flight jacket – so sue me, I'm a very hot and hot-blooded teenage male, and you can't help but notice these things when they're literally crushed into your own ribs –

and then she was giving the same treatment to each member of the rest of the Flight.

She got to Luke last, as he was standing awkwardly behind everyone else.

"So *you're* Luke!" Lory said. "Awesome!"

And she hugged him just as hard.

"Hi, Ben," Condor said, amused. "Is she always like this?"

A big sigh. "Yep."

I exaggeratedly sidled back to stand next to Ben and Condor, watching in bemused solidarity as Lory whirled between the others, demanding to see tails, flight harnesses, and flight goggles, ask questions about the Change, exclaim about how cute Kestrel was or how smart Tui was. To my surprise, they were laughing with her as they answered, although I wasn't sure if Lory was even hearing them.

Luke appeared at my elbow. "Um," he said.

"Yeah?"

He pointed behind us. "There are people over there."

Condor and I turned, as Lory yelled. "You have to come meet our mom and dad! And I've got a special surprise for you!"

Kestrel gaped and laughed as Lory grabbed Hawk's hand. "Is this the part where I tell you to get your hands off my boyfriend?"

"Aw, Kess, are you taken? Oh, well. We'll see how long that lasts," Lory said, with a wicked giggle, and then took off running along the derelict driveway, Hawk's wing's flicking as he tried to keep up with his kidnapped hand.

"Was she flirting with Hawk, or with Kestrel, just then?" I asked, after jumping out of the way.

Ben snorted. "Knowing Lory, probably both. But she'd never actually try break someone up. She's just…"

"Excitable?" Condor suggested.

"Friendly?" Luke said, shyly.

Ben glanced at Luke, then away, a bit quickly, I thought. Interesting. "Yeah," he said.

Another, even higher-pitched shriek sliced our ears.

"TYLER! TYLER!"

"What the flock?" I said. A little body hurtled out of the dilapidated farmhouse and streaked towards Hawk.

Hawk accelerated, overtaking Lory, flapping his wings to gain precious ground. He met the small person at such a pace that when he scooped her up, they rose into the air. Hawk flapped hard as he spun above the grass, cuddling the little girl close.

It was, of course, his sister, Cherie. I recognized the explosion of dark curls from Hawk's recent video calls with his family.

"Whoa," I said, starting to laugh.

Ben chuckled. "She was supposed to stay inside with her mom and dad while my mom and dad came out and did all the formal stuff. So … surprise, I guess?"

"Definitely," Condor said, grinning.

Ben's parents were shaking their heads and smiling as they waited for Hawk's parents to join them from the porch. Drew Richardson slapped Robert Owen on his good shoulder, and Leah Richardson hugged Julia Owen, a few moments before Hawk (and his sister) landed, and the rest of the Flight and Ben caught up with Lory.

Hawk jogged over to his parents with Cherie in his arms, and the four of them disappeared into a big Owen bundle.

"Hello, sir," Condor said, politely, extending his hand to Drew.

The Japanese-Hawaiian man shook it slowly while eyeing Condor up and down. "Hello, Condor. Please call me Drew."

"Uh, okay, sir."

I elbowed my way forward. "Hi, Mrs Leah. Lory told us you're a doctor of WHO?"

"Falcon!" Tui hissed as the Scottish woman laughed and pumped my hand.

"Indeed, lad."

She looked a lot like her daughter, except for the silver streaks in her red hair, her human green instead of Icarus beige-brown eyes, freckly and pale instead of tanned skin, and no wings, of course. And her height. But otherwise, very similar.

My wing was yanked backwards. Tui took my place and introduced herself to the short but strong-looking woman. Ben and Lory were introducing Kestrel and Luke to Drew.

There was a bubbly, warm feeling in my stomach as I looked around at the conversations, smiles, handshaking and back-slapping. (Or, in Hawk's case, feather-slapping, as his dad clapped him on his folded wings.)

Then there was a brief lull in the conversation, and so it was that everyone, Icarus and human, young and old, heard Drew say something very unexpected to Condor.

"You're Senator Wayne Arrington's son, aren't you?"

# 19

# CONDOR

I couldn't breathe.

However, the intimidating Navy officer seemed amused, not aggressive.

The Flight's sharp gazes were prickling my skin as I cleared my throat and forced myself to answer. "Yes, sir. But we're not exactly close."

"Not now, Drew," Leah said, tugging on her husband's arm. "Let's get the RV tucked away. Plenty of time for interrogation later, right, lad?" She winked at me. I gulped.

The barn was in better repair than it looked, although the big doors were heavy. Drew asked the Flight to drag them open enough for Hawk to drive the RV inside and out of sight. When Falcon asked who could possibly see the vehicle this far away from civilization, or even the road, Drew pointed skyward.

"You're not the only ones with a bird's eye view of the world, Falcon," he said.

The dim barn was illuminated only by the narrow windows and the open hayloft door. The roof, although apparently held together by lichen and rust from outside, let in no light and looked utterly rain proof when viewed from inside.

"When the Richardsons build something, they build it to last," Drew said, with pride. "Even when the farm went bankrupt after World War Two, my uncle kept up repairs as long as he could, and then left it to me in his will. I was already settled in Hawaii with Leah by then, so we left it mothballed. I'm afraid the house hasn't been updated since the sixties. But I think you'll be quite comfortable in your own accommodation." He gave the RV another appreciative glance, and then urged us into the farmhouse.

He wasn't kidding about the décor, but it was clean, well-aired, and clearly loved. As the parents transferred food from the pantry, oven, and containers to the huge kitchen table, I was cornered by Hawk, Falcon, Tui, and Kestrel.

"Your dad's a senator?" As always, Falcon immediately cut to the chase. "Which state?"

I kicked at the wooden floorboards. "DC," I mumbled.

"He's a *federal* senator?!"

"Why didn't you mention this earlier?" Hawk demanded.

"It didn't seem important compared to everything else."

"Then why leave it out?"

"Because he's a dick."

The others blinked, and a couple chuckled. "Okay, then," Kestrel said, putting a warning hand on Hawk's arm. "Was he a senator when you and your mum left?"

"No, it's a recent development. I discovered it a little while before my wings came out. Then I was little distracted."

"Dude, can't we ask him to, I don't know, lobby for us?" Falcon asked, enthusiastically.

"Falcon, he's not the type of guy to risk his position of power for anyone," I said, wearily. "Not even his own son. When Mama found out he was cheating, and threatened to go to the media with it, he threatened to report her undocumented friends to ICE and have them all arrested and sent back to Mexico. I mean, Mama had her green card and was totally legal herself, but we chose to leave anyway after that."

"Oh." Falcon's wings drooped. "Bummer."

Hawk sighed. "Ouch. Okay, Con, we get it. We'll drop it … for now."

"Anyway, bro," Tui said, forcefully cheery, "sounds like these guys have a plan. So let's go find out what it is, eh?"

A wave of gratitude nearly knocked me to my knees. Even now, the Flight still had my back.

Later, I'd have to find out how Drew knew my dad. Did they meet at the clinic? After all, they knew Hawk's parents. Did all our parents know each other?

Had they known Dove's parents?

My heart lurched. If we'd just waited a little longer, or insisted on meeting the Richardsons first, would Dove and her parents have been here now, too?

What if they were still in the country?

What if she could still come back?

No. It was false hope. They were long gone. And the cool, formal tone of Dove's messages proved that the bounty hunters' attack on the Flight – and my response – had forever broken our slim connection.

With a deep sigh, I went to join everyone at the table.

Apparently, I didn't move fast enough. Lory grabbed my hand and dragged me to the long bench seat. There, I was sandwiched between her and Luke. It felt even cozier than in the RV.

With only the briefest hesitation, Tui said the Māori prayer, and then she added (in English), "Thank you so much for welcoming us. Promise we don't expect you to keep feeding us like this. But we're really grateful."

"Hear, hear!" Hawk reached for the potato salad.

"Tyler," his mom said, meaningfully. Hawk swung the bowl towards Leah instead.

It didn't take long to fill everyone's plates. However, the conversation didn't pause as the feast was devoured.

"May as well get right to the point," said Leah, handing a basket of bread rolls down the line. "Here's the deal. We can't go home to Hawaii for a while, so we're preparing the farm for an extended stay. You're welcome to park your fancy bus here for as long as you like."

Enthusiastic nods and muffled "Yes, please!" and "Thank you!" came from the Flight.

Drew nodded. "You can hook up to the power and water in the barn, and we can rig a wastewater pipe to the septic system. As for internet–"

"We have our own satellite dish," Hawk said, quickly. "We won't leech off your bandwidth."

Leah and Drew laughed.

"The barn roof might get in the way, but I'm sure we can sort out a relay," Drew said. "Lory's pretty good with electronic hardware and shopwork."

"Learned from the best, right, Dad?" Lory said, airily, spearing another bread roll with her fork. "Ben's better at the software and coding, though."

"Did you just compliment me?" Ben grinned. Chuckles echoed around the table.

Hawk's dad leaned his elbows on the table, hands clasped above his plate, as he looked at his son. "However, it won't be a free ride," he warned. "No child of mine would take advantage of a friend's hospitality."

Mouth full, Hawk emphatically shook his head.

"Bob's right," said Drew. I nearly choked at hearing Colonel Owen referred to as *Bob*. "In return for room and board, as it were, we're counting on your manpower–"

"People power," his daughter blithely corrected.

"–manual labour," Drew said, "to help us kick this place into shape. If we're to settle here long term, and give you guys the best possible chance at a normal life, maybe even become self-sufficient, we have a lot of work to do."

Lory giggled. "You should see the Bunker."

"Bunker?" Kestrel asked.

"Aye," Leah said. "Storm's coming, lassie. Best to be prepared."

"All the bases are covered for the next month or two," Drew said. "So, in the meantime, we've been working on another project. Bob and Julia? Over to you."

In unison, the Flight turned to Hawk's parents. Even Lory and Ben looked curious and expectant. Hawk tried to eyeball his mom and dad over Cherie's head. From her perch on his knee, she continued pilfering chicken off his plate, ignoring the grown-up conversation.

"While you've been finding your own way in the world," Mrs Owen said, with only a hint of the sadness and worry she must have felt all this time, "we've been hunting for answers. Tyler, when you and Victoria and Miguel dropped by at home, you gave us the doctor's real name. Once we joined forces with Leah and Drew, everything started falling into place."

"We hired a private investigator, explaining we needed to track down the fertility doctor, due to discovering that our child has a genetic 'condition'," Colonel Owen said, with a humourless smile. He picked up a computer tablet from the kitchen counter behind him, tapped and swiped a few times. "To cut a long story short, she thinks she's found our Dr Goldberg." He turned the screen, displaying a photograph.

I nearly spat out my mouthful.

An old, tough-looking woman was caught mid-turn by an extreme zoom lens. Dark hair, a large nose, square jaw set hard over a Chinese collar. Her frown was intimidating. Or maybe that was my imagination.

This woman was the cause of our ... everything?

"Where was that?" Kestrel asked.

"Believe it or not," Colonel Owen said, handing over the tablet, "she's in LA. Or was."

"What?" Hawk yelped.

His mom patted his hand. "We think she came looking for you. All of you, after your Downtown display. The neighbours said she even came to our house, but that was after those *people* came and shot your father and we were living with Nana."

Hawk gaped. "If you'd been home–"

"I don't know what I'd have done if a strange woman had knocked on our door and said, hello, I'm the one who..." Mrs Owen swallowed hard.

"It's okay, Mom. It hasn't been all that bad." Hawk smiled at Kestrel.

"Anyway," Mrs Owen said, after a deep breath, "she's dropped out of sight, but the PI is confident she'll find her again soon. We've given instructions to make contact with Goldberg when she does."

"Are you sure this private investigator doesn't know about the Icarus connection?" Hawk asked, anxiously. "I mean, you guys went viral at the same time I did."

Colonel Owen sighed. "It's entirely possible, but she came highly recommended and the price tag is supposed to ensure her utmost discretion. She's never met us in person, and there hasn't been the slightest mention or question so far in any of her communications. She's been extremely professional."

"I suppose it doesn't really make any difference," Hawk said, poking at the remains on his plate.

There was a short silence, and then Kestrel changed the subject.

"Thank you for lunch," she said. "That was a lot of food, and it was all really good."

"You're welcome, lass," said Leah. "But from tomorrow, we expect some help in the kitchen."

Tui stood up, dragging Falcon with her. "We can do the dishes."

"Aww, I wanted to check out the farm," Fal said, half-joking.

"Off you go, kiddos," Drew said, waving a hand. "Like Leah said, you're on duty from tomorrow."

"I'll show you around!" Lory's wings and elbows bumped me as she sprang from her seat. "Come on!"

I found myself being dragged outside by a wing as Lory listed the farm's features at top speed. I missed most of them, but heard there was a large pond and some 'cool climbing trees' and an orchard gone wild.

"Come on, I'll show you!" She launched into the air with a loud thump.

Dozens of flaps echoed as the Flight followed, Falcon and Tui, then Ben, Hawk, and Kestrel. I was about to jump after them, but I turned.

Luke was leaning on a veranda pole, watching with a wistful expression.

"Who are you?" demanded a little voice. My heart leapt. But it wasn't Raven. It was Cherie, standing behind Luke and glaring with her arms folded.

Startled, Luke looked around. "Me?"

Cherie snorted, sounding so much like her older brother that I had to hold in a laugh with my hand. "Yeah, you. Who are you?"

Luke smiled. "I'm Luke. Who are you?"

"I'm Cherie. Do you have wings?"

"No, I'm afraid I don't."

"I don't either. Why are you here?"

"Because the Flight are my friends," Luke said, showing no discomfort talking to a kid half his size. "They're looking after me, and I'm looking after them, while my mom is taking care of my dad. He's in hospital."

"What happened to your dad?"

"He got hurt."

"My dad got hurt," Cherie said. "The bad guys shot him."

"Oh, yeah, Hawk told me. My dad got shot by the bad guys too."

"But my dad is okay now. Will your dad be okay?"

Luke hesitated. "I think so."

For a moment more, Cherie examined him with all the wisdom of her seven years and then nodded. "That's good. But you still look sad. Don't worry. You can be my friend."

"That's really nice of you, Cherie. I'd like to be your friend."

Cherie was halfway back into the house when she glanced over her shoulder. "Aren't you coming?"

Luke and I shared a helpless smile and a shrug, and then he followed Hawk's little sister inside.

"Everything okay, Condor?" Kestrel called, circling overhead. "You coming?"

In answer, I turned away from the old farmhouse, and broke into a run.

My wings opened wide, and I flapped. Once, twice, three times.

My wings scooped the air. My chest wrenched. My ankles bumped together, twisted. My tail hooked, clicked, and the wind caught my feet.

Flapping hard, I shot skyward, and joined the Flight.

The valley was about a mile long, and half a mile wide from ridge to ridge. I had no experience with real farms, so I couldn't identify the scattered old buildings and rusty frameworks. I could see a few cows, sheep, and some pigs, though. Rutted vehicle tracks peeped through the long grass here and there. A river ran through part of the valley into the pond, lined by dangly trees.

Here in the lower reaches of the Cascade mountains, there wasn't any snow. If we flew higher, we'd see the range stretching away in each direction. The valley was large, but not so big as to feel exposed, or to remind us too much of the glacial mountain lake from which the Flight had been kidnapped by Evolutionary helicopters. The Flight swooped and twisted and enjoyed the first real sense of freedom in a long, long time.

The sun had already left the valley floor by the time the Flight returned to the barn, and it would be properly dark soon. We invited Lory and Ben to join us for dinner in the RV. The parents, although approving of the vehicle, said it was much too small for everyone all at once, and they went back into the farmhouse (towing a very reluctant Cherie with them), and left the teenagers to get to know each other a bit better.

Despite having been left behind during the aerial tour, Luke seemed cheerful, although he mostly just listened to the banter. Between Hawk, Falcon, and Lory, and to a lesser extent, Kestrel and Tui, it was hard for Ben, Luke, and me to get a word in. However, at some point, Ben and Luke fell into a conversation, and I ended up hanging out by myself on the edge of the Flight.

Not that I minded. After our first flight in a couple of weeks, I was tired, and my muscles were even a little achy. I was quite content to kick back on the sofa and let the conversations about the best technique to pull off an aileron roll, which was the best photo to send Raven today, or which streaming service was the best, to flow past.

It seemed I wasn't the only one suffering from the recent lack of exercise. Hawk was yawning, and as soon as Tui mentioned being a little stiff, Falcon had eagerly volunteered to massage her shoulders. She happily accepted, zoning out as Falcon continued chattering over her head to the others.

After the conversation about grooming had petered out, Tui suggested we call it a night. Lory and Ben left, promising we'd have even more fun tomorrow. Personally, I couldn't believe there was someone in the world who could out-talk Falcon. However, Lory's cheerful chatter balanced with her brother's quieter, reserved nature. All in all, I thought, the day had gone well.

I was sure the Flight would be happy here. Raven was sending regular updates as promised and seemed to be okay, wherever she was. Dove was gone, but the pain reduced a little more every day. Surely things could only improve as I got my fitness and energy back.

Right?

# 20

# TUI

"Hey, babe." Falcon grabbed me from behind and squeezed. I yelped and squirmed, but not too hard. He kissed my neck. "I feel like I haven't seen you for, like, three whole hours!"

"That's because you haven't," I said. Because no one else was around, I added, "Babe."

"Ooh, I love it when you call me that." Falcon kissed me again, and I sighed, leaning into him.

Our new friends had worked us hard over the last week. We'd dug vegetable beds and chopped firewood, buried pipes and (with Colonel Owen's and Lory's guidance) built extra furniture from wooden pallets, extending our living space from the RV into the shelter of the barn. Races were run, won, and lost, and camaraderie was high.

But my muscles continued to ache. And no matter how much I slept, I always felt tired.

"We have earned a night off." Falcon slid his hand down my arm until it wrapped around my hand. "Come on."

I let him tug me across the grass and into the barn. Long strings of glowing bare bulbs hung in big zigzags across the new 'indoor-outdoor living room' next to the RV, where the Flight was already gathering. As Falcon messed around with the Bluetooth speaker sitting on one of the crates, Ben and

Kestrel wandered in from their own afternoon chores. Condor, on dinner duty, was already bringing out loaded plates.

Hawk was sprawled on one of the benches, earbuds in and phone in hand, an arm over his eyes. He'd been on wood-chopping duty, so no wonder he was knackered. I'd been assigned to inventory, so I didn't know why I was so physically shattered too. Maybe it was just the concentrating. And, despite all the camping for months, it was harder to get used to sharing a bed with someone than I'd expected. I hadn't been sleeping well, and I couldn't blame all of it on Falcon's snoring.

As Falcon's first choice poured from the speaker, a deep beat quickly developed into a popular R&B hit from last year. I couldn't help myself. I was grooving along straight away.

"Nice choice!" Condor called.

At the same time, Hawk groaned loudly from under his arm. "Some of us were happy with our own soundtracks."

"Some of us have a taste in music too good not to share," Falcon retorted, and turned it up. Then he grabbed my hands and danced with me, making it a party of two.

"I want in on that action!" Lory cried. "What do you say, Condor?"

"Oh, I don't know." Condor fled into the RV, mumbling something about dinner.

Ben dodged Falcon's whipping wings, and retreated to a seat near Hawk.

By then I was ignoring the rest of the Flight, because my boyfriend had some moves! I already knew his singing wasn't the best, but he could rap flawlessly. I did the backing vocals, and the chorus, and before I knew it, we were into the third song.

By the fifth, though, I was out of breath and my voice was tired. I bailed before Falcon could launch into the sixth, waving my hands in defeat.

"You win this round," I said, giggling between the panting.

Falcon struck a Michael Jackson pose, then bowed to his imaginary audience. "Thank you, thank you." He grabbed my waist, and I kissed him hard.

"Ew," Hawk called over the music. "Get a room, you two."

"Flock off," Falcon said, cheerfully, and pulled me to the picnic table. "You and Kestrel suck face just as bad."

"Keeping it classy, as always." Hawk's laugh quickly turned into a coughing fit. He wrapped an elbow around his mouth, but I could see how hard his chest was spasming.

Falcon sat down. "That doesn't sound good."

"Yeah, nah," I said, slowly. "It really doesn't."

Hawk left his eyes shut as the coughing subsided. "I'll be all right," he said. Even under the music, I could hear his larynx was covered in phlegm.

"Just rest," I said. "Falcon, turn it down, now."

"Yes, ma'am."

Hawk smiled weakly. "That's better. I was getting a headache. Thanks, Mom."

"Does that make me the dad?" Falcon asked, cheerfully.

"Yuck, no. My real dad's much better looking than you."

"Bet I got better moves, though."

"No one has moves quite like you, Fal," I said, dryly, as I retrieved my kit from the RV cargo compartment.

Falcon grinned, then frowned. "I'm assuming that's a compliment."

Kestrel perched next to Hawk and put her hand on his forehead. "Tui, I think—"

I was already holding out the new digital thermometer in a plastic sleeve. "Here, sis. Stick that under his tongue, press the button, and wait till it beeps."

Hawk cracked an eye and saw the whole Flight watching him. "Starting to feel like a freak show," he muttered around the thermometer.

"That ship sailed already," Fal said, smirking.

Hawk opened his mouth again, and I cut him off. "Shut up, bro. Let it work, or next time it'll be a rectal measurement."

Hawk's jaw instantly closed. Falcon giggled. I glared, and he waved his hands. "You just threatened to shove a thermometer up Hawk's ass. Of *course* I'm gonna laugh!"

The thing beeped. Kestrel handed it to me, her eyes wide.

Over a hundred degrees. Silently swearing about flocking Americans and their flocking imperial Fahrenheit that made no flocking sense, I pulled out my phone and opened the conversion app.

I breathed out. Hawk was a fraction over 40 degrees Celsius, allowing for the usual variation in sublingual measurements and the cheap digital instrument. Normally, that was ambulance-summoning territory, but our usual resting temperature would be considered a low fever in a regular human anyway. This meant Hawk was only a few degrees out of whack.

"A little higher than usual, for us, but nothing to worry about, bro," I said, and didn't add out loud, *Yet*.

"You know what this means, right, Falcon?" Hawk said, grinning weakly.

Fal covered his eyes. "Go on. Just say it."

"According to your own girlfriend, I'm officially hotter than you."

Falcon groaned. "Enjoy it while it lasts."

Ignoring the banter, I used an antiseptic wipe to sanitise the thermometer and returned it to my kit. Then I pressed my fingers into Hawk's wrist and watched the clock on my phone screen.

I bit my lip. Hawk's heart was beating nearly three times every second. Even for us, that was terrifyingly fast.

Kestrel touched my shoulder. "What should we do, Tui?"

The Flight watched me with various expressions of concern. "Not sure we need to do anything yet, sis," I said. "A temperature like that should cook any normal bug or virus within a few hours, eh. Maybe Hawk can just let his immune system run its course." *I hope.*

"So I get bed rest?" Hawk asked, then sneezed.

"Ew!" Falcon held out his hands in an anti-demon cross. "Should we quarantine him, Doctor Sexy?"

Hawk snorted, and I gave Fal a half-hearted flick with my wing. "Yeah, nah, bit late for that. Either we've already got it, or our bodies already dealt with it, without symptoms."

"So Hawk's immune system is the *weakest*, then?" Falcon's smirk vanished when Kestrel wing-smacked him, heaps harder than I had.

"Enough, Falcon."

Falcon knew when Kestrel's voice got that tough, it was time to bail – and fast.

"Okay, okay." He held up his hands. "Dinner time, anyway."

"You stay put," I ordered Hawk.

He made a face. "But I'm thirsty."

"I'll get you water." Kestrel picked up his drink bottle, and the two of us went into the RV.

"Is it just me," Kess said under the still-playing music and the dinner banter outside, "or is this the first time any of us have been sick since the Change?"

"I think so, eh. I've thought about it a few times, but assumed it was 'cos we were so isolated. No one else to catch germs from."

"Yeah." Kess stared out the narrow kitchen window at the nearby barn wall. "At least his injuries are healed now, I guess."

"Āe, sis. Hawk's a tough bugger. If he survived the worst that Junior threw at him, he'll kick the arse of some puny virus."

"Hope so."

As she returned to Hawk, I swallowed hard. My throat was scratchy, and I couldn't ignore it anymore. I was getting sick too. I had to talk to Leah.

First, though, it was dinner time.

As much as I wanted to pretend things were normal, half of the dinner conversation was me having to explain to Falcon it didn't matter how many antibiotics we could acquire, they wouldn't *work* for a viral infection, and in fact would make Hawk sicker by destroying his microbiome. To my frustration, he didn't believe me till I used the satellite-powered WiFi to search up all the scientific papers that proved it.

"I bow to your superior wisdom, o goddess of germs," Falcon finally said, sighing.

That was one of the many things I loved about him. He never had any trouble admitting he'd been wrong.

Wasn't so sure about the 'goddess of germs' bit, though.

I was feeling a bit better after eating and drinking. Maybe my throat had just been scratchy because I was dehydrated. Hawk had also perked up, and I was starting to think that maybe it was just exhaustion and overexertion, after all.

Then Condor asked to speak to me in private.

And told me he'd been feeling the same.

*Ah, shit*, I thought, and chewed my lip.

Condor noticed. "What, Tui?" he asked, alarmed.

I rubbed my neck and flexed my wings. "I'm achy and tired, too," I admitted. "Have been since the day we arrived."

Condor tightly crossed his arms. "Anyone else?"

I scanned the Flight, spread out around the newly lit firepit, just inside the door of the barn. Falcon was bouncing a ball and taking shots at a makeshift hoop he'd nailed to a support beam, and Lory was chatting to Kestrel. Kess smiled, nodded, and contributed occasionally, as her hand gently stroked Hawk's hair. His head lay in her lap, the rest of him stretching along the bench seat, hidden under a blanket, probably asleep. On the other side of the fire, Ben and Luke were talking quietly, as they often did.

The scene reminded me of previous Flight camps over the past six months, or however long it had been. But those times, Hawk would've been as fidgety as Falcon, in the middle of the action.

It wasn't just the coughing. Hawk had been increasingly subdued over the last week. I hadn't registered it before, because I'd been feeling crap myself. Some bloody nurse I was.

"Come on, Condor," I said. Grabbing my kit again, I moved beyond the radiant heat of the fire, and disinfected the thermometer again before sleeving it and sticking it in my own mouth.

The quiet beep caught everyone's attention. I ignored them.

"Hmm," I said. The measurement was the same as Hawk's, within a few points of a degree.

"What is it, babe?" Falcon asked, chucking the ball into a distant corner of the barn and jogging over.

I didn't answer, instead telling Condor it was his turn as I wiped the thermometer and slipped on another sterile sleeve.

"Do I have to say 'ah'?" he asked, facetiously, and I grabbed his chin. "Ouch."

"Hold still."

It only took a few seconds to beep, but it felt much longer.

"Tui?" he asked, anxiously, as I looked.

"Just a sec." I was tapping the measurements and times into an app on my phone.

Lory hovered nearby, red wings twitching. "Should I get Mom?"

"Not yet," I said. "Flight, line up."

I was both concerned and relieved when it was just me, Condor, and Hawk showing the sore throat and low fever symptoms. Kestrel, Falcon, Lory, and Ben were all normal. For us, anyway.

Luke, however, was also showing a low fever. It took me a second to register, as his low fever was the same as an Icarus baseline. He said his throat was fine, though. He just had a mild headache and felt tired.

"Okay," I said, finishing up my notes. "Everyone get a good sleep tonight, and we'll see how we are in the morning."

As I stood, a puff of cold air blew through the part-open doors. The fire flared. A billow of smoke went up my nose.

My elbow muffled the sneeze in time, but another one was already building in my chest. It was suddenly hard to breathe.

"I need some fresh air." I trudged towards the door, my wings feeling heavy.

Outside, the sky was dark and perfectly clear. Stars arced over the valley. I was having trouble focusing, though, and found myself sitting on the ground, leaning back on one hand and wing.

*I'll just sit for a sec,* I thought. *Get my breath back.*

Distantly, I heard Kestrel shouting at Hawk, and someone else calling my name. Someone was running. Yelling.

"Tui! Tui, I can't wake Hawk up!"

"Oh shit. Where's Tui?"

"Condor, are you okay?"

"TUI! Where are you?"

I tried to get up, but the sudden movement made my head swim. I couldn't breathe.

Last thing I saw was the stars, fading into nothing.

# 21

# TUI

The whisper was harsh in my pounding ears. "Will Tui be okay, Leah?"

It was a bloody effort, but I rolled over. "I can hear you. Could just ask me." But even those few words made me cough.

"Sorry, Tui," Kestrel said. "Thought you were sleeping."

Falcon was sitting on the floor by my head. I was lying on one of the RV sofas. Leah bent over me, stethoscope hanging around her neck. On the other couch, Hawk's eyes were closed, his breathing rapid and ragged. Condor lay on a bed of blankets on the floor, staring at the ceiling.

"What's going on, Leah?" I said, after the spasm had subsided.

"You fainted, lass. Feeling any better?"

My tough side wanted to say yes. But dishonesty wouldn't help anyone. So, I shook my head.

There were voices outside, and Leah said she'd be right back.

As soon as the doctor was out of sight, I shoved back the blanket and put my feet on the floor.

"Whoa, where do you think you're going?" Falcon demanded.

He grabbed me as I tried and failed to stand. My wings flexed weakly as the RV seemed to spin. My pounamu bumped on my chest. The carpeted floor felt prickly through my socks. "I need to pee," I said.

Falcon wrapped the blanket around my shivering shoulders and wings. I knew I was only feeling cold because my temperature was so high compared to the air, but I was past caring about that. The blanket helped, so I took it.

"Who's driving the truck, bro?" I muttered, staggering.

Fal's hands tightened. "No one, babe. We're still parked."

"Doesn't bloody feel like it." I coughed again. Falcon held me up. Leaning my head on his shoulder, I shivered, my feathers rustling under the woollen blanket.

"Need any help?" he asked, as I finally banged into the bathroom.

"I'm not that far gone," I grumbled, and shut him out.

When I emerged, there was an emergency meeting happening outside the RV. Everyone who wasn't sick, human and Icarus, had gathered in the barn. The only absence was Cherie, who I assumed had been in bed for hours.

Someone asked if we were contagious. Leah sighed. "We don't know if the virus can jump from their system to ours, or whether they caught it from us in the first place. That's unlikely. Aurora and Benji have never had these symptoms, and we've effectively been in isolation for weeks anyway."

"I hope we didn't bring it," said a deep voice. Colonel Owen.

"No," Leah said, forcefully. "Rory and Ben would have got it first."

"Is it too late to start that social distancing thing?"

"Depends how the disease spreads. If they're only just now infectious with the coughing and sneezing, then yes. But they could have been breathing it out for days. We just don't know."

"Babe, are you okay?" Falcon said, behind me.

I turned too fast, and Falcon barely caught me before I hit the floor. He half-carried me to the sofa as he shouted for help.

Kestrel knelt next to her unconscious boyfriend, her hand on his forehead. "He's burning! But he's not sweating." She grabbed an ear thermometer I hadn't seen before. Must have been Leah's.

I struggled to sit up. "I have to check—"

"Lie down, Tui!" Falcon ordered, pushing on my shoulders. "We have a doctor. You're relieved of duty."

The thermometer beeped, and Kestrel half-gasped, half-sobbed as she looked at it.

"What's the reading?" Leah strode up the RV steps, Hawk's mum on her heels.

Kestrel showed them the digital display. Mrs Owen gasped. Leah cursed. "We must cool them down. Fast."

"How?" Kestrel asked.

"What's wrong?" Falcon said.

My aching brain suddenly put it together. "Heat stroke," I said, faintly. The RV seemed to spin again.

Falcon held me tight. "It's what?"

"Virus … fever … hyperthermia…"

"Close, lass. Hyperpyrexia," Leah said. "Difference doesn't matter, it's still a medical emergency. We need to cool you down, NOW. Julia, we need ice packs, the hose, and plenty of towels. Send Drew and Bob to the Bunker." As Mrs Owen ran from the RV, Leah turned to us. "And get rid of those feckin' blankets!"

Shivering so hard my jaw clattered, I let go of the blanket. Falcon tugged off my jacket and cropped jumper. Every lost layer seemed to suck away a few more degrees, and the air felt freezing. Ben had to drag another blanket away from Condor.

Kestrel struggled to unwrap Hawk. "He won't wake up," she said, with a sob.

Leah firmly moved her aside, and pinched Hawk's arm. Hard.

Hawk grunted. His eyes flickered, and his arm twitched, yanking away from Leah's assault.

"Good," Leah said. "That's an eight."

"An eight for what?" Falcon exclaimed.

"Glasgow Coma Scale, lad," Leah said, calmly. "He's not awake, but he's not completely unresponsive. Let's cool him off before he sinks any lower."

"A cold shower?" Kestrel said.

"Aye, lass."

"Tui first," Falcon said.

I protested. "But Hawk's worse—"

"Which means he needs more than a cold shower." Leah leaned out of the way as Falcon half-carried, half-dragged me through the kitchen. "But leave that to us."

Then Falcon and I were in the bathroom.

"Clothes off, doc," he said, already unwinding my shirt wrap.

I couldn't argue, or I'd vomit.

Soon I was in my underwear and bra, sitting on the toilet lid. My wings crammed awkwardly against the plastic walls and floor, and Falcon twisted the tap on as cold as it would go.

I shrieked as the water hit my face and shoulder, running down my chest and back, my stomach, my legs. Every instinct screamed for me to escape.

"It-t-t-t-tsss t-t-t-t-too f-f-f-f-k-kin c-c-c-c-cold!"

"I'm sorry, babe," Falcon said, miserably, holding me in place. "But we have to."

He'd ditched his clothes too and was suffering the freezing spray in his boxers.

"I'm s-s-s-s-sorry," I said, trying not to sob.

He kissed my forehead. "It is NOT your fault."

He couldn't hold me close, or it would slow the cooling effect. Instead, my face rested on his shoulder as he knelt awkwardly in the cubicle-sized bathroom, the cold water falling on us both. My hair and feathers were saturated, my skin bumpy. My pounamu was a cold lump.

But as my core temperature reduced, the water seemed to warm slightly in comparison. Slightly.

Still Falcon stayed with me. He stayed through his own goosebumps, and his own violent shivering.

He stayed until the water ran out.

Someone had left towels by the bathroom door. Falcon tried to make sure I was completely dry before he took any notice of himself – and I still had to tell the stupid bugger not to get hypothermia and make everything even harder.

Wrapped in towels, damp feathers sliding along the floor, we went to see what all the shouting outside was about.

"That's a good sign, right, babe?" Falcon asked.

Hawk was sitting on the ground in his underwear, yelping as Lory and Kestrel hosed him down.

"Consciousness is always a good sign, eh," I said, faintly. "Vomiting, not so much."

Lory had to jump out of the way as Hawk rolled onto his knees and puked. Swallowing hard against my own nausea, I knew my temperature was rising again, fraction by fraction of a degree.

"Where's Leah?" I said.

"Here, lass," the doctor said, approaching the RV door. "Feeling better?"

"For now, but I can feel the fever coming back," I said.

She nodded as Kestrel and Lory approached, supporting a dripping Hawk between them, a towel draped over his shoulders and wings. He was extremely pale, but fairly alert.

"Worst … shower … ever," he said.

"At least you're awake," Leah said, briskly.

I realised the blankets on the floor were empty. "Where's Condor?"

"It's his turn under the hose," Leah said, as a yelp echoed inside the barn.

"Ah." So that was me, Hawk, and Condor accounted for. "And Luke?"

Leah frowned. "He's helping Condor. Why?"

"He was feeling yuck too."

Something was nagging at me. There was a link here. I just knew it. I tried to close my eyes to concentrate, but the floor seemed to lurch. Falcon held me tighter. My skin prickled like a thousand needles–

My eyes flew open.

I knew why we were sick.

And that we were totally screwed.

# 22
# RAVEN

*Dear Kestrel, Tui, Hawk, Falcon, and Condor,*

*I'm writing you this email because texting doesn't seem right, somehow. I think you've been busy, because you haven't been texting as much. Thank you for the photos, though. I wish I could see more of where you are, but I understand why you can't.*

*Like I keep telling you every day, I am okay. Physically, at least. Emotionally, and mentally, I'm very tired.*

*It was really strange at first. Which isn't a surprise. I had a weird feeling that I had been here before, but I couldn't remember anything about it. However, Jing Ying wasn't being dishonest when she said she could restore my memories, although there's some abstract theory you have to accept about what actually constitutes a memory before you can accept her definition of "restore".*

*As you can tell, my language skills have developed quite far in a short time. Jing Ying gets grumpy when I forget and I talk about things being Bad, or Good. But most of the time she's friendly enough. She's still not as nice as the Flight, though. She's been asking me about you. I've told her some stuff. Not anything that she wouldn't have already seen or heard from the Lab, I promise. But sometimes she asks me what you would do, or say, in certain situations.*

*I might be wrong, but, I'm starting to think she might be jealous. Of you, and of me.*

*Let me explain.*

*I'm building an understanding of who YanWei was. Who I was. JingYing has thousands of videos, photos, and written diaries from our childhood, and she's making me watch and read every single one, multiple times. It's very strange seeing myself, and Owl, doing all these normal things, and having no memory of it. At least, it mostly seemed normal. It took me a week or so, but I realized what was missing.*

*Friends.*

*I have already watched and read hundreds of these files, recorded from ages 3 to 10. Not once have I, or Owl, or JingYing, or Frederik (yes, he's in these too – he was nicer back then), ever mentioned another child. We never went to school. We were barely allowed out of the apartment, it seems. We rarely saw our parents. We had each other, and our tutor/nanny, and a very, very long list of things we had to learn, and tests we had to take, and exercises to strengthen our minds and bodies. All day, every day. No vacations, no school, no friends.*

*In a way, I've always been in a Lab. This one just had TV and sofas, and big windows, and better food. But Owl and I managed to leave. After The Accident, and again when we escaped the Facility.*

*JingYing and Junior never did.*

*Don't worry, I still hate Junior. He killed Owl, and I will never, EVER forgive him for that. He still has no idea that I'm here. However, I'm beginning to understand JingYing. It was bad enough when we were in here with just the boys, but we had each other. Every time the pressure got too much, we could hide under the blankets and talk about it.*

*But then I was gone, and all she had was Frederik, and expectations that she worried she would never meet. We were engineered to be Perfect, after all. But me and Aron (Owl) turned out to be "flawed", which left just JingYing and Frederik to carry the load. Well, you've seen how*

*Frederik Junior turned out. Now imagine being locked up with him for ten years.*

*That was JingYing's life.*

*Quite simply, she's been lonely.*

*Even when they were allowed out to go to medical school at university, they couldn't relate to the other students, even if they had been allowed to socialize. They were only eleven. They stood out almost as much as an Icarus.*

*I don't know if you remember, Falcon, but when you all found out about me and Owl, you said, "That totally explains your lack of social skills." I now understand what you meant.*

*JingYing is not as kind to me as the Flight was. But, in her own way, she's trying to be. And I'm not the only one she's trying to help.*

*JingYing tells me about conversations she's had with Junior. She's even let me listen to a few phone calls with him to ask for my opinion. I have no idea what she's hearing, or not hearing. To me, he sounds the same as before. But she thinks he's hiding something. Something big.*

*And she's worried.*

*I don't know if you've heard, but there's a new flu virus overseas. There are rumors it could turn into a global pandemic. (I had to look up that word when JingYing wasn't around, because she forgot I didn't know.) This is really important because one of the Evolutionary Corporation's biggest departments is pharmaceutical research and development. JingYing and Junior had to go to medical school so they could work on new lifesaving medicines.*

*Some of those medicines were tested on Owl and me.*

*Junior has been working on a private project for two years, refusing to share it with JingYing. But it must be something to do with viruses, because he is obsessed with the topic. He talks a lot about antivaxxers.*

*Whatever they are, it makes him extremely angry. That's one reason why JingYing is worried.*

*Before the accident, before Aron and I were 'killed', Junior was nice. He never got angry. After all, he was 'perfect'. We all were. That's what we were told. We were supposed to be Saviors. I've looked that up too, but it doesn't make sense to me. JingYing said it will, in time.*

*After Aron and YanWei were gone, JingYing and Frederik had to compensate for us. They could not make mistakes. If they did, they were punished.*

*I know what that is like.*

*They survived, and they achieved everything they were told to. They were the Heirs to the Corporation, and were about to finally start those important things they'd been preparing for their whole lives. That we were all supposed to be working on, together.*

*Then they found out about us. The Icari.*

*And everything changed.*

*JingYing says Junior hasn't stopped working since he was twelve. I don't think she has either. The other night, she was still working at her desk at 3am. I'm worried about her, and she's worried about Junior.*

*I think it might have something to do with the virus. And I think it might have something to do with the Flight.*

*Please be careful. If I learn anything else, I will tell you straight away. Please do the same with me.*

*Be careful. I miss you.*

*Love,*

*Raven*


I sent the email. It was very late, and JingYing was still not back. However, I wasn't surprised. She had finally agreed to go on a 'date' with Frederik. I didn't know if she did love him, or if she felt it was her 'duty' – a concept I still didn't fully understand.

I could not sleep until JingYing returned, so I found my book and sat in my favorite corner of the biggest sofa.

I had read only a few pages when my phone beeped. A text, from Kestrel. That was weird. I hadn't heard from the Flight so late before.

I heard the elevator rising as I opened the message.

My pulse increased as I read the words.

*Hawk, Tui, and Condor are really, really sick. Luke is a bit sick too. We think it might have something to do with the bounty hunters and those syringe darts. Can you ask JY? Please. I don't think they have much time.*

JingYing came in and the door slammed behind her. She was moving roughly, noisily. Normally, she was so quiet and in control.

"YanWei, I have to tell you something," she said. Her cheeks were a little red, almost sweaty. She brushed back her hair impatiently. "Wait, I need water."

She moved into the kitchen and kicked off her high shoes. They crashed into a door.

"I hate champagne," she muttered as she held a cup under the faucet. She drank two full glasses before putting the cup down hard and coming back to the sofa. I watched her, my wings folded tightly.

"First, YanWei, you have to understand something," she said, sitting on the other end of the sofa and reaching for my feet. I pulled them away. She sighed. "You can't hate him, okay? You've forgotten what it's like. I've been trying to remind you, but I just haven't had time!"

She leaned forward on her knees, holding her head. I waited.

"Frederik is not a bad person," she said, to the floor. "He's not. He's brilliant. He just doesn't know when to stop. His father does not tolerate failure. Frederik is terrified of disappointing him, of disappointing me, of disappointing the human race." She breathed deeply. "I thought I'd convinced him to stop taking the stimulants, to stop working through the night."

I knew what stimulants were. They had been tested on me, and Owl. They didn't let you sleep. They made your brain work faster. They made your legs and arms prickle and your eyes ache.

And Junior had been using them by choice?

"Frederik wanted to celebrate over dinner tonight, because his project is nearing its final stages, and he was ready to tell me about it." She took another deep breath. "It's an antiviral superweapon he's calling SunStrike. He thinks it will destroy *any* virus that affects human systems. He's so confident that he's begun the final test before human trials."

JingYing finally turned to look at me. I stared back.

"And he's infected the Flight as his test subjects."

My hands were shaking. I swallowed. "How?"

"He set up the bounty hunters with the tranquilizer darts, but he replaced the anesthetic with the pathogen. He never expected the hunters to successfully capture the Flight. They'd outwitted our best Security squads and escaped from the heart of our Facility. So, Frederik decided to convince the Flight to come to him, instead."

"Why now?" I asked, tears pricking my eyes. "Why tell you now?"

"The incubation period was two weeks. The Flight will now start to get really sick. He estimates they have seventy-two hours until their systems are overwhelmed. Either the Flight will go to a public hospital, where the Corporation can pick them up, or they'll figure out what happened, and call the Corporation directly to turn themselves in for the cure. Or, they'll die."

"But there is a cure?"

"His antiviral serum. The SunStrike."

I frowned. "How do we know it works?"

"Frederik is a genius. It will work." JingYing reached out again. This time I did not pull away. "YanWei, I do not want the Flight to suffer. You must warn them."

Tears fell on the phone in my hand. "They already know."

"How many of them?" JingYing asked, quickly. "Who is sick?"

I showed her the text. JingYing frowned. "But Luke is human – he should not have been harmed."

"The bounty hunters were idiots."

JingYing stood and started to pace. My wings twitched. It was very strange to see her moving so much.

"Four doses," she said. "Maybe I can acquire four doses of the serum. We can reach them in time."

"You will help the Flight?" My chest filled with air, and hope. "But what about Frederik?"

JingYing stopped and faced me. "I want Frederik to succeed. He will succeed. But not like this. I will not let him compromise–"

There was a strange echo to her words as she spoke. A delay.

My eyes widened, and my heart stopped. JingYing turned around.

It was Junior.

He had followed JingYing. His phone was in his hand, and the echo was coming from its speaker. He had put a spy bug on JingYing, and had heard everything she'd said.

And now he was here.

And he was staring straight at me.

# DIRECT MESSAGES

KESTREL:

Raven? Are you there? Does JY know anything??

RAVEN:

Yes.

KESTREL:

Yes, you're there, or yes, JY knows something?

RAVEN:

Frederik just told JingYing about his plan. The bounty hunters were set up to fail. He gave them an experimental pathogen instead of tranquilizer. He's been waiting for you to get sick. He said you have 72 hours.

KESTREL:

72 hours till what?

RAVEN:

Death.

KESTREL:

What can we do??

RAVEN:

JingYing will get some of the antiviral serum. We will bring it to you, if you tell me where you are.

KESTREL:

Are you sure you can trust JingYing?

RAVEN:

Yes.

KESTREL:

Is this the only way of saving them?

RAVEN:

Yes.

KESTREL:

Okay. I'll talk to our friends. I'll send you a location soon.

RAVEN:

Okay.

# 23

# KESTREL

"TRAP!" Falcon yelled, and kicked over a chair.

"No shit," I said, fighting back tears.

Falcon kicked the chair again, hard. It skidded into the corner. He made to attack another piece of barn furniture.

"FALCON! You can't have a meltdown right now!" My voice broke. "Please."

With a half-roar, half-groan, Falcon stomped back. "Look. Either it is Raven texting you, and she's telling the truth, or it's *not* Raven, which means she's in trouble." His wings flared. "What do we do?"

"We go in prepared, I guess." Terror inflated my chest. Choosing to tell JingYing, an Evolutionary, exactly where we were, or where we were going to be? Everything about it screamed WRONG!

But Hawk, Tui, and Condor were dying. And Luke might get worse, too.

*We were supposed to keep him safe*, I thought, the tears finally spilling over. *We were supposed to be safe here.*

*It's not fair.*

Soft footsteps approached. "Oh, Kess," Lory said, gently. "Don't cry. We'll save them. I promise."

She hugged me. I leaned into her, trying hard to control the sobs. "How?"

Benji joined us. "Mom and Dad have an idea, but they'll tell us in the morning. You need sleep. You're no good to the Flight if you're too tired to think straight."

Exhaustedly, I nodded.

We had seventy-two hours.

A lot could happen in seventy-two hours.

*

"The PI found Goldberg."

"What?" Falcon, Lory, Ben, and I gaped at Hawk's dad. But Drew and Leah didn't look surprised.

"You knew?" Lory said to her parents, accusingly. "Since when? Why didn't you tell us?"

"Three days ago," Hawk's dad said, calmly. "The four of us decided it was best to take our time to think everything through."

"And you were all so happy," Leah said. "We didn't want to spoil that straight away."

Hawk's mum patted my hand. "Remember, sweetheart, this woman affected our lives too, not just yours."

I bit back a retort. I liked Hawk's parents. But they clearly felt they were still in charge of their son's life, despite him being Missing for more than half a year.

I guess it made sense they'd wanted to protect him for just a little longer.

Falcon tipped back on his chair, trying to balance with his wings partly out. "So why tell us now? Do you think she can help us?"

"Possibly," Leah said. "Or she might have some information about the Evolutionary Corporation we can use to our advantage."

Falcon and I exchanged glances. It wasn't completely impossible. But was it worth the risk?

"Why won't anyone on base help us, Dad? Did you even ask them?" Lory said.

"Aurora," her dad said, sternly, "we've been through this. The Evolutionary Corporation is a major armament and medical supplier. They have extensive contacts and supporters at the very highest levels of the whole Navy, not just in Honolulu."

"Same with the Air Force," Colonel Owen added. "And they're a megacorp. There have been hundreds of conspiracy theories levelled at them over the years. Nothing has ever come of it. Even if you physically arrived on base in the next hour, Command would take so long to be convinced, it would be too late. They won't risk moving outside of the proper channels. Not even for me or Drew."

"Once we have saved your friends, *and* secured evidence of the Evolutionary Corporation's guilt, *then* we will pull all the strings we can," Drew finished. "Clear?"

The penny dropped. We needed proof. To get that, we had to visit Goldberg, and we had to meet JingYing. Or Junior. Whoever actually turned up. If they brought the cure, great. If not, at least we'd get evidence they were the ones who'd poisoned the Flight in the first place, and *then* we could let all Hell loose.

"Yes, sir," I said, meekly. Falcon tried to salute, but ruined it when he lost his balance and fell off the chair.

"Okay, Dad," Lory said, and Ben nodded. "So what are we going to do, then?"

"Here's the plan."

*

The RV had been converted into a claustrophobic mobile hospital. Three patients were strapped onto makeshift gurneys made from surplus military cots, and wedged into the walkway space. With a lack of hospital gowns, they were in their underwear and a thin sheet for modesty. The air stank of disinfectant.

With the air conditioning blasting at its lowest temperature, its water tanks filled to overflowing, and the freezer stuffed with ice packs, it also felt like a mobile refrigerator.

We were on our way to Los Angeles. It would take us almost fifteen hours, even travelling on the I-5 most of the way. While the Flight were driving, Hawk's family and Drew were, ironically, flying ahead. Leah was travelling with us as our personal Flight doctor, and the Flight would take turns driving. Adding the three invalids meant the RV was technically over capacity, but if we got pulled over, a few extra passengers would be the least of our problems.

There were several reasons why we were making the massive trip to LA. Firstly, that's where Goldberg was. The Flight turning up on her metaphorical doorstep would mean she'd have no idea where in the country we were busy setting up. Ditto for the Evolutionaries.

Secondly, we were seeking safety in numbers. It was easier to hide a huge RV among all the big vehicles in a city, rather than some backwater town or empty wilderness.

Thirdly, LA had already had several outbreaks of winged kids and angels, and there were some big sci-fi/fantasy and anime conventions coming up. Wings and weird outfits would be less remarkable.

Fourthly, LA had one of the largest concentrations of military bases in the US. As soon as we had the whistleblowing info, both Captain Drew Richardson and Colonel Robert Owen could call for help.

At least, that was the idea.

Fifteen hours on the road meant there was plenty of time for triple, quadruple, and quintuple-guessing. However, in true Gen Z fashion, we spent most of it binging on Netflix, streaming through the satellite dish once we were out of hill country. Even Tui, Hawk, and Condor were awake most of the time, thanks to the reminder on Tui's phone that prompted us to replace their ice packs every twenty minutes.

After driving through the afternoon and into the night, we arrived in LA around two in the morning, when Falcon was driving and everyone else was sleeping.

"It's so weird how we keep ending up back here," Falcon muttered as he pulled over on an empty street in a quiet industrial area, nearly hitting two parked cars, a hydrant, a limp advertising flag, and a bus stop before finally hauling on the parking brake.

"It is the City of Angels," I murmured, peering suspiciously into the shadows outside.

"What?"

"Nothing." I patted his shoulder as he yawned. "Thanks for getting us here safe, Fal. Get some sleep. I'll take first watch."

"Cheers," Falcon said, levering himself out of the driver's chair. I heard him check on Tui, then clamber up the ladder into the cabover. Judging by the snores, he was asleep before even taking his boots off.

I 'stood' my watch from the front passenger seat, leaving my post only to change the ice packs every twenty minutes, and shiver occasionally. My friends barely twitched in their sleep, and by now it wasn't even weird switching out the ice packs tucked into their groins, where Leah had explained the main leg arteries were close to the surface. Tui knew the jargon. I was too tired to care, but too wired to sleep.

Nothing moved outside, except the growing fog. It crept in close, unchanging while I stared at it, but doubling in thickness if I glanced away even for a second. It was eerie.

Leah seemed to sleep like a cat, cracking an eyelid every time I climbed past her sofa, but always seeming to drop off again as soon as she'd confirmed I was operating as ordered. I wondered if it was a doctor thing, or a mother thing. Possibly both.

At three thirty, I poked Lory awake for her turn, and swapped places with her on the queen-sized bed I usually shared with Hawk. Ben and Luke, who currently occupied the other half of the mattress, were stretched out fully clothed on top of the blankets. In their sleep, one had draped an arm over the other. As I lay down, I briefly wondered how the hell I'd relax while sharing the bed with two other guys, even if I was still dressed and had my wings between us. But I didn't even register which of them was which before I was gone.

*

Hawk, Tui, and Condor were hard to wake in the morning. But we had to. We had to get food and water into them. Their faces were already thinning, their muscles shrinking, as their bodies burned their own cells as fuel for the fire.

I nearly cried, seeing in Hawk's face the same gaunt exhaustion he'd worn in the Evolutionary torture lab. Of the three of them, his symptoms were by far the worst, and his memory glitch had returned with a vengeance. He kept asking where we were. Once, he even asked who the hell Leah was.

By the time the RV reached the address Colonel Owen had given us, I wanted to scream with anxiety, frustration, and fear. I couldn't lose Hawk. Not now. Not after we'd survived so much.

I wouldn't let him die.

The location was an empty warehouse. By now, the morning fog was so thick, and the vacant parking lot so large, you couldn't see one edge from the other. A huge freeway bridge stood nearby; we could hear its traffic through my open window, but couldn't see it. The honk and roar of the vehicles was strangely muffled.

On the bright-ish side, I mused, no random passers-by could spy on us. Or openly gawk. Or film us...

"There's Dad," Benji said, leaning over my shoulder and wings.

"Aye," Leah said, at the wheel. She parked the RV next to Drew's rental car. Colonel and Mrs Owen also appeared in the mist. Briefly, I wondered where Cherie was, before remembering she'd been dropped at her nana's place for the day, hopefully totally oblivious.

We were fifteen minutes early for the rendezvous with Dr Goldberg. Or the person claiming to be her. As the RV's engine died, the vibrations seemed to continue in my heart and stomach.

"Pants," I heard Hawk say.

I squeezed past Lory and Ben into the main cabin. Luke was helping Tui tie on a loose halter top thing over her bra, as she sat, leaning at a drunken angle, on the sofa. Condor, pale but determined, leaned on the bathroom door. Although he was shirtless, a pair of cargo trousers hung low on his hips, more like an oversized sack than clothes. It was obscene how much weight he'd lost in a matter of days. His wings seemed to have swollen in comparison.

Hawk was still sitting on his cot, in his boxers, repeating the word 'pants' and waving in the general direction of the floor.

"Maybe you should stay in bed," I said, anxiously.

"Flock that," Hawk said. "Gotta tell Goldberg…"

"Tell her what?"

"I'll think of something." Hawk's hand landed on his bare thigh. "Damn it, where the hell is my gear?" He coughed.

"Suffering from a case of being too hot, remember?" I said.

Hawk sighed. "The curse of being me." But his voice wasn't right.

"Here." I reached past him for the pile of folded clothing I'd left nearby. Hawk followed my movement, and nearly fell. As he tipped, I grabbed his shoulder.

"Whoa!" Hawk yelped. "Can someone slow the planet down to its normal thousand miles per hour, please?"

"Come on, Hawkie-boy," Lory said, appearing at my shoulder. "Let's get your pants back on."

Belatedly, Hawk tried to cover his underwear with the sheet.

Lory snorted. "Don't get your knickers in a twist, as Mom would say. It's nothing I haven't seen before. Upsy-daisy!"

Hooking her arms under his wing shoulders, she helped me haul Hawk to his feet, then steadied him as I helped him get his feet into his pants, and pulled them up his legs.

"Normally she's doing this the other way round," Hawk said to Lory, who snort-giggled.

My face burning, I gave his zipper a slightly harder-than-necessary yank, and Hawk yelped at the brief wedgie.

"You are such a dork," I said. "You're literally dying—"

"From being too hot."

"—and we're about to meet our maker and you're cracking inappropriate jokes?"

Hawk shrugged his wings. "What better time?" I groaned, and Hawk grinned his lopsided grin. "But let's face it, it could be worse ... I could be Falcon."

"I heard that," Falcon said from the door. "Are you coming, or not?"

Lory and I helped Hawk down the steps, and into the arms of his parents. We hovered nearby as Fal supported Tui, and Luke and Ben stuck close to Condor. Leah and Drew took up station near the front and to the side. Drew's hand rested casually near a slight lump under his clothing. Just like Colonel Owen's rested on the holster at his belt.

And then we waited.

Only a few minutes later, a passing engine broke away from the invisible traffic, and two bright spots appeared in the foggy parking lot.

"Here we go," Hawk muttered.

I gulped. Even though I was wearing full flight gear, I still shivered, though not as much as my shirtless boyfriend. I snuggled closer inside his brown wing, though whether I was seeking or giving comfort, I couldn't say.

The car rolled closer until we could see its outline in the fog, and the driver could see us. It stopped. The engine cut out, but the lights stayed on.

A figure emerged.

# 24

# KESTREL

Tension rippled through our breaths and wings. High heels clicked towards us. The shadow in the fog coalesced into a silhouette, then a face.

Dr Goldberg stopped a few metres away and steadily met our gazes.

The older, dark-haired woman looked Jewish, not Asian, yet her red silk jacket was decorated with traditional Chinese birds, dragons, and flowers. There was a thick, pale-green bangle on her left wrist, and no wedding ring.

"Dr Goldberg?" Leah said, after a pause. "Or is it Dr Schmidt, these days?"

A brief smile. "Whichever you prefer."

My skin tightened, and my hair and feathers prickled. She sounded so normal. I didn't know what I was expecting. A witch's cackle?

Her eyes lingered on me, then moved onto Hawk. Wrinkles on her forehead deepened. "Is something wrong?"

"You mean apart from the extra genes you spliced into our babies without asking?" Hawk's mum spat, with shocking venom.

Goldberg's hands raised. "I never meant to hurt anyone," she said. "I didn't even know. Not till a few months ago."

Everyone hesitated, angry accusations briefly frozen in the fog.

"Explain," Leah said, sharply.

Slowly, Goldberg took a few careful steps forward. I could see the silver hairs twisting into her dark bun.

"I've been wondering *how* to explain," she said, with a weak smile. "I'll try to keep it brief, and then I'll answer any questions … if I can."

She took a deep breath. We were frozen. Waiting.

"In the 1990s," Goldberg said, "the Evolutionary Corporation lured me from my safe university position with an extraordinary salary and cutting-edge laboratory facilities. The owners, Mr and Mrs Larsson and Mr and Ms Lin, were good people. They were wealthy, intelligent, kind."

"Ha!" Falcon burst out. Tui elbowed him.

Goldberg stammered a bit, then recovered. "I believe they were. They regularly undercut their competitors in the drug market, and their profits were poured into massive free vaccination programmes and into small ethical businesses around the world. But their ultimate goal was to eradicate human suffering at the source. That's why they wanted me to help them."

"With designer babies?" Hawk scoffed, as our friends murmured and shuffled.

"No! At least, not at first." Goldberg's hands waved defensively. "My small team made huge advances in genetic technologies that make CRISPR look like a steam train next to the Space Shuttle. We corrected fatally-corrupted genes in bacteria, then fruit flies, then mice, and so on, until we were curing monkeys."

"Of what?" Leah demanded, hands on hips.

Goldberg straightened her shoulders. "We were editing defects from generations of living in polluted urban jungles with a sixty-seven percent success rate."

"And you didn't publish your findings?" Leah's voice dripped disbelief.

Goldberg sighed. "We were so close. We had to make sure our data was bulletproof. We believed we really could eradicate all human illness and disease by the end of the twenty-first century. But you can't make that kind of claim without first testing every possible angle for weaknesses. To make sure it wasn't a series of incredible flukes. The damage to our reputations, and the Corporation ... not to mention the hopes of–"

"So what happened?" Leah interrupted.

"My team and I were working on the final tweaks," Goldberg said. "Mrs Larrsson and Mr Lin left on a scheduled business trip, which included a philanthropic visit to a small, isolated village, checking on the progress of the school the Corporation was building. That's when they were kidnapped by radicalised extremists and held for an emperor's ransom. Mr Larrsson and Ms Lin immediately arranged for payment, but ... even though they'd sent millions of dollars, their spouses never came home. They were cruelly tortured and – eventually – killed."

A smattering of gasps and fluttering of feathers. Goldberg's voice trembled, but she pushed on, quickly.

"Investigators later found the ransom money had been stolen by an employee of the American-based agency that was supposed to be handling it safely. Whether the kidnappers would have killed the hostages anyway ... we'll never know. But it had been done. Mrs Larrsson and Mr Lin were gone."

"And your research?" Tui rasped. "What's that got to do with us?"

"My surviving employers reclassified the entire project. I was tasked with creating the children they'd lost the chance to have; reconstructing their lost spouses' DNA and combining my technology with the Corporation's IVF research programme. These children were to be the very first of a new, improved breed of human. *Homo sapiens superior.* Stronger, smarter, kinder. That was the mission. We turned to the animal kingdom for inspiration. And we did it. Four perfect children were born. A new hope for a new–"

"Have you *met* the human race?" Falcon demanded. Lory snorted. Hawk swayed and muttered to himself. I gripped him tighter.

Goldberg's lips thinned. "Indeed. Maybe I *had* spent too long in my lab. I was horrified when I discovered my employers no longer intended to share the technology freely. But perhaps I shouldn't have been surprised. Not after what had been done to her husband and his wife – and that was *before* the announcement of our genetic editing breakthroughs. So, they decided to keep it secret, and reserve it only for those they considered worthy enough."

"Don't you mean 'wealthy'?" Leah said, sharply.

Goldberg simply nodded. "I could not be part of it any longer. I couldn't leave this power in the hands of such hurt, angry people. That's why I destroyed everything, and disappeared."

This fit with everything we knew. So far.

"Then where the hell did Owl's and Raven's wings come from?" Falcon demanded.

Dr Goldberg blinked. "Owl and Raven?"

"Aron and YanWei," I said. "Your so-called superior children. They grew wings. Did you know that was going to happen?"

"Aron and Frederik, JingYing and YanWei were all in perfect health before I left," Goldberg said. "The most intelligent and precocious toddlers that–"

"What did you do to my babies?" Leah cut her off. "What did you do to *my children*?"

Goldberg stared at the ground, then sighed.

"I just wanted to help," she said, quietly. "I set up the clinic to help couples like yourselves, and when there were errors in the genetic code, I corrected them. It was supposed to silently spread the so-called *Homo sapiens superior* DNA among the global population. To remove control from those who would abuse it, and let evolution decide which edits were worth keeping. I didn't know that the gene editor itself had been corrupted."

"You mean ... our wings were an accident?" Lory asked, dazed.

People shifted, breath quickened. Feathers rustled.

"That's not possible," Leah said, her voice low and hard.

Dr Goldberg shrugged. "Yet, here we are."

My legs shook, and suddenly it was Hawk holding me up. Distantly, I was aware of an argument, getting louder, until there was shouting.

There was no grand conspiracy. There was no ultimate, underlying, sinister purpose.

We were an accident. We were not meant to exist.

It was the final, painful, cosmic joke.

"...why would I look too closely? I'm only human. I'm subject to confirmation bias just like anyone else."

"Enough," said a voice, and everyone fell silent. And I realised it had been me.

With a brief glance to make sure Lory had hold of Hawk, I walked forward, fog swirling around my wings. I glared at Goldberg.

"It doesn't matter if you did this on purpose, or not. We're running out of time. While you were swanning about in China, or whatever, experimenting on embryos without their parents' permission–"

"I did have permission," she fired back. "I had full permission to correct the errors that were preventing them from–"

"–we were kidnapped by the Evolutionary Corporation and tortured like lab rats by your friend, van Scholtz."

Goldberg frowned. "He's still there? I thought Neil would have given up a decade ago. There's no possible way *he* could have recreated my research–"

"Research that included experimenting on innocent children, you mean?" I asked, icily, but with fire building in my chest. "Don't worry, he recreated that just fine. In fact, you could say he's an expert. And now, your other creations, your *superior* humans, are continuing the great work. My friends are dying, Doctor Goldberg, because Frederik Larrsson Junior wants them to."

Goldberg said nothing for the longest moment, studying my face. I stared her down, refusing to be intimidated.

But when the pause stretched on too long, I couldn't help the agitated wing flick. The movement caught her eye and broke the impasse.

"Tell me more," she said, quietly.

I explained as quickly, but as bluntly, as I could.

"Therefore, as you have nothing useful to offer us," I said, finally, "then–"

"But I do," she said.

Murmurs behind me. "And what is that?" I asked, crossing my arms.

She smiled. "Me."

# 25

# FALCON

"Is Lory still yelling?" I asked, grinning tightly, as Leah climbed into the RV with a tense face.

"Aye."

"What about Ben and Luke?"

Leah moved her doctor's bag from the sofa so she could sit down. "They're giving Drew the silent treatment."

The curtain in the motel room window didn't twitch. It thrashed. Leah and Drew had ordered their offspring into lockdown in the unit, while Kestrel and I took Tui, Hawk, and Condor to get the cure from Raven, or the person – we were certain it was Junior – pretending to be her. Because Luke's symptoms were mild, and his mom and dad weren't around to decide, the other parents had decreed that the motel was also the safest place for him to be. We'd bring back as many extra doses of this SunStrike miracle thing as we could.

But Lory was not amused. Especially as her mom, the de facto Flight medical officer during Tui's illness, was coming with us.

Dr Goldberg wanted to come too. But everyone refused.

Part of me wanted to truss up Goldberg like a turkey and dramatically throw her at the feet of our greatest enemy. But that, as Kestrel pointed out, was a Bad Guy (or at least an Antihero) type of thing to do, and I was definitely in the Loveable Rogue category.

Instead, Goldberg was also in the motel. Drew would guard her, along with Lory, Ben, and Luke, making sure they stayed safely put. We couldn't have all our eggs in one bucket, or all our birds in one hand, or whatever.

If the Evolutionaries truly did value information above all else, then the woman who (deliberately or accidentally) created us would be the ultimate bargaining chip.

We might, just might, manage to save our friends. Including Raven.

Hawk's parents would follow us and watch our backs, calling in reinforcements the instant things turned into pear jam.

That was the plan, anyway.

Kestrel and I checked on Tui, Hawk, and Condor, replacing their melted icepacks. The RV was practically a freezer, but they were still so hot. I mean, Tui usually was anyway, but this type of hot wasn't the good kind. Obviously.

The trip wasn't a long one. We'd told 'Raven' we were in LA, and 'she' sent us an address. I felt like a pinball, bouncing from rendezvous to rendezvous.

As we were fully expecting an ambush, Kestrel and I would come in from the air. It didn't matter if random people saw us. The Evolutionaries knew where we were. In fact, we'd probably be safer if a huge crowd was watching.

Or so we tried to convince ourselves.

"Didn't really work when we used that strategy at the Angelist church," Kestrel said.

Condor coughed. "To be fair, the Evos didn't grab us till the middle of the night."

"I still want to know how the hell they even knew where we were. Bastards." Kestrel shut a cupboard with excess force, jolting Tui and Hawk closer to full consciousness.

"It's still cold in here," Hawk moaned. "Can't I have just one blanket?"

Kestrel smoothed his damp hair. "The colder we keep you, the longer you last."

"Like leftover Thanksgiving turkey?" I suggested, brightly.

"Thanks, Fal," Hawk growled, but I saw the flicker of a smile. I was sure of it.

Tui heaved herself up on her elbow. The meeting with Goldberg had really drained her, and my fists clenched, though I kept my smile on full. "Where are you off to?" she asked, eyeing me in my full flight gear.

"Kess and I are heading to the drug store."

"Uhuh. To get what, exactly?"

"I ran out of tinted lip balm." I grinned as she weakly swatted at me. "To get the cure, babe, obviously."

"They won't have–" Her eyes widened. "Falcon, you are NOT going to–"

A cough interrupted the shout, but she kept struggling upright, clutching the sheet to her bra. I wrapped my arms around her, trying not to squeeze too tight as my heart cracked. My fingers stroked her tattoo and scar.

"Falcon," she wheezed eventually, gripping my jacket with her remaining strength. "You can't bargain with the Evos on this. Not for me, not ever. I won't let you."

"And how will you stop me, exactly?"

"I'll … I'll … break up with you. Or something."

"Babe, you know I didn't enjoy being a guinea pig the first time. I'm not planning to hand myself in for the cure, or anything sacrificial." Though, if it came to that, I would in an Icarus heartbeat, even though it scared the literal shit out of me. I'd been to the toilet at least four times already. "Raven says her sister got the cure off Junior, and we're going to pick it up. That's it. Promise."

Tui glared. "Then it's a trap."

"We know. Look, can we skip the argument in which we explain our plans and you realize there's no other way, and get straight to the part where you reluctantly agree?" I said, my smile feeling too tight.

As I stood up, Tui clung on.

"Are you sure about this, babe?"

"Nope." I kissed her once more. "But don't worry. We've got a plan."

"And that's s'posed to make me feel better, eh?"

As another coughing fit took her, I pushed her back down on the cot. "The plan *is* to make you feel better, yes."

"You–" *cough* "are–" *cough* "such–" *cough* "a–"

"Heroically handsome hero, I know. Now will you stay the flap in bed, please, so I can actually go and *do* the hero thing now?"

I squeezed her hand, then forced myself to move away.

"You better keep your arse in one piece!" Tui shouted after me, breathlessly.

Turning at the open door, I saluted. "Yes, ma'am!" Then I jumped from the RV before she could see my tears.

As I waited for Kestrel, I heard Hawk saying something dopey and completely messing up his emotional farewell. Kess laughed. "I love you too. Dork."

Leah followed Kestrel to the door. As we shook out our wings and pulled on our flight glasses, the doc spoke into her phone.

"One, two, one, two, can you hear me, lads and lasses?" she asked, only the tension in her jaw betraying the sarcasm in her voice, which came to us both through the air and through the new Bluetooth pieces securely hooked into our ears.

"Roger, roger, ten four, Charlie Mike," I said.

Kestrel rolled her eyes. "Don't hurt yourself."

"All right." Leah shut the RV door, and the suspension lurched slightly as she moved into the driver's seat. "Ready when you are, kiddos."

Turning, Kestrel and I began sprinting through the weakening fog. With a leap and heavy double-thump, we were airborne.

Several figures on the sidewalk ducked as we flashed overhead. Their yelps, and the last tendrils of mist, curled in our wake.

The rumble of the RV's diesel engine followed us. Kestrel glanced across at me, and I gave her a double thumbs up.

"Next stop, Raven. Supposedly," Kess said, and tapped her smartwatch.

"*Traffic is heavy. You will reach your destination in twenty-two minutes,*" the map voice said.

"That's what you think, dude," I said to the robot, and accelerated.

"*Route recalculation…*"

"Cut left, over that office block," Kestrel called.

"*Route recalculation…*"

A hundred and fifty feet up, and the noise and exhaust from the morning traffic still assaulted my senses. It made me want to cough. Or was that the virus kicking in?

I gritted my teeth and pushed on.

Kess and I reached the fog-free park about five minutes ahead of the RV. We immediately spotted the Chinese woman sitting unnaturally still on a bench beneath a twisty art sculpture. She had a large coffee cup in her hands, a pile of empty fast food boxes neatly flattened and stacked next to her, and a satchel at her feet. Plenty of people were passing through the park on their morning commute, but none seemed to hang around nearby.

We circled the park a few times. Commuters began to notice, glancing up as our shadows flickered past. Mouths opened, hands pointed, then phones lifted. Typical.

Still, they might just be our unwitting safety net.

"Parking now," said Leah. Through some trees, I saw the brown beast pulling over. A few hundred yards away, the Owens' car also took up station.

"Here goes everything," I said, and tilted my wings into a descending spiral.

Civilians scattered as Kestrel and I swooped low, heading for the grass in front of Lin JingYing. I'd been practicing my landings, and felt like a total badass when I lowered my feet and shifted into a walk without a hiccup or wasted flap.

I still hadn't quite gotten the hang of nudging my tail shut without breaking stride, though, so I had to lengthen my steps to catch up with Kestrel.

"We have an audience," I muttered.

"Yes. I know. That's the idea."

But I saw the shivering in her blonde feathers that had nothing to do with the way her primaries were sweeping dramatically across the ground.

JingYing stood as we approached, but Kestrel spoke first.

"Where's Raven?"

I crossed my arms and tried to look mean, even though the cold, intelligent gaze of the 'Superior' human made my gut freeze.

"YanWei couldn't come this morning," she said, softly.

"Shocker," I hissed. "Did you at least give her a bed in her cell this time? Or did you just cut her open on the floor?"

JingYing's nostrils flared. "I love my sister. I have not harmed her."

My heart double-tapped. "Then what has Junior done to her?"

"He has not harmed her."

Kestrel's eyes narrowed. "But?"

JingYing picked up the satchel. Her shoulders were weirdly hunched, tense. Guess she didn't like the audience. Good. "How many are infected?"

Blonde feathers flicked. "Where is Raven?"

"I have enough antidote for the whole Flight," JingYing said, "but I will only give you as much as you actually need."

"Answer. The. Question," I said, my voice low, my neck muscles tightening painfully. My wings were twitching worse than Kestrel's now. "Where's Raven?"

"*Don't risk losing the cure,*" Leah said in our ears.

JingYing's eyes glanced at the Bluetooth pieces. She'd heard Leah? But how?

"How many doses do you need?" she repeated, her gaze locking onto mine. Then, strangely slowly, she lifted her hand and scratched her ear.

"But where's–" I began, but Kestrel wing-elbowed my arm.

"Three Icari are sick," she said. "And one human friend."

JingYing frowned. "*Homo sapiens?*"

"Oh, my god!" I rolled my eyes. "Yes! Whatever! A regular, non-genetically-edited dude who was shot by your pet bounty hunters! He's sick! Give us the flocking cure!" I hesitated briefly. "Please!"

"Is it safe?" Kestrel asked, quietly. "Will our friend be okay?"

JingYing lifted the satchel handle over her shoulder. "I must examine the human," she said, calmly.

"Why?"

"The experimental SunStrike treatments are prepared for an Icarus metabolism. I need to see your sick friend before I can adjust the dose," JingYing said, as blandly as if she was commenting on the nice day out.

"What if you could talk to another medical professional?" Kestrel asked. "And discuss the dose with that doctor instead. You wouldn't have to bother examining him yourself."

As JingYing paused, Leah said, "*On my way.*"

The Superior's gaze again rested on my ear, before glancing over my shoulder at the distant sound of yelps and curses. The redheaded WHO doctor was barging her way through the crowd of smartphones.

"Hello," JingYing said, as the fierce little Scottish woman arrived. "Dr...?"

"What mechanism?" Leah said, brusquely, her sunglasses dark under her hat pulled low. "Analogue? Inhibitor?" She rattled off a few complicated chemical terms. JingYing responded in kind, and I swear they were actually speaking another language for a minute.

"Fine," Leah said, abruptly, and held out her hand. "I'll take it from here."

JingYing tilted her head and studied the shorter, older woman. "Where is your child?" she asked, softly.

Leah's outstretched fingers twitched. "That is not your concern."

"My concern is for the safety of your child." JingYing looked at Kestrel and then me. "And the company they are keeping. You never know who is … watching."

An icepack seemed to slide down my spine.

JingYing stared through my eyes and out the back of my head. "I suggest you retrace your steps. Quickly."

Finally, she put the satchel in Leah's hand, turned, and walked away, slipping easily through the crowd.

Leah already had phone in hand, tapping on Drew's name. It rang, and rang and rang.

No answer.

Kestrel and I exchanged a single glance.

"Keep trying," Kestrel said. "We're on our way."

Leah nodded. With the phone at her ear, she shoved back towards the RV.

Few paid her much attention. Kestrel and I had opened our wings and bent our knees to launch.

Gasps, yells, calls, even a smattering of applause sounded as we shot into the sky, wings slicing through the weak sunlight.

I barely heard them over the thudding of my heart.

When the motel came into view, the door of the Richardsons' unit seemed fine. But as Kestrel and I swooped closer, we saw it wasn't sitting right in the frame.

"Shit, shit, shit!"

This time, there was no grace, no badassity. Just two thuds and two desperate Icari shoving past the dumbstruck motel janitor.

"Lory? Ben!"

"Luke?"

"Mr Richardson?!"

"Oh my god, Luke!" Kestrel ran to the crumpled figure lying in the bathroom doorway.

Shoes stuck out past the end of the bed. I jumped over the mattress and nearly landed on Drew. A nasty cut was bleeding over a black eye and into his hair. His mouth, hands, and legs were duct taped.

As I yanked open kitchen drawers, banging and crashing as I searched for scissors, a knife, anything to cut Drew loose, Kestrel was dialing 911.

"Ambulance," she said.

The second I'd torn the duct tape on his wrists, Drew ripped the strip off his bearded mouth and grabbed the phone off Kestrel.

"Home invasion by armed intruders." His voice was terrifyingly cold and calm. "My children have been abducted." He continued snapping out information like he was on the bridge of a Navy ship. But this was no drill.

Lory, Ben, and Goldberg were gone.

# 26

# HAWK

Everything was too bright, too loud. It moved too fast one moment, and then in slow motion the next.

If I tried to run, my legs felt like they were wading through mud. If I tried to yell, only a wheeze came out. If I tried to see, my gaze would fall to the ground, eyelids grinding shut like tombstones.

The nightmares were unstoppable waves.

I was back in the Evolutionary cell. Owl stood in the corner, hollow and cold, pale. Blinking at me with unbearable grief.

Raven, chattering away like Cherie, in a language I couldn't understand. She took off her wings and placed them in a box.

Luke laughing. "Surprise! I was an undercover reporter all along! Thanks for giving me the scoop of the century!" Devil horns sprouted from his forehead.

Kestrel, descending from the sky with a flaming sword.

Falcon and Tui, fighting. Trading vicious blows, blood beginning to gush from their faces, arms, wings.

Condor, bound to a burning crucifix, drowning under a tide of crazed Angelists in white robes.

Kestrel. Lying broken on the ground.

A baby. Screaming.

Then

darkness

Warmth. That was the first sensation I noticed. I felt warm, comfortable.

I couldn't remember the last time I'd felt so cozy.

As soon as I'd had that thought, the second one arrived. My nose was itchy. Damn.

I tried to scratch it, but I couldn't move. For a few heartbeats, I panicked. Was it the nightmare again?

Then the weight on my arm shifted, and my hand tingled with fresh blood. Immediately, I tried to reach my face, and accidentally whacked someone.

"Hey!" Kestrel cried.

Finally, my eyes opened. "Sssss?"

Frowning, I tried to see my own mouth. Eventually, Kestrel's laughter reached my muddled brain.

"I love you, Hawk," she said. "Don't ever scare me like that again."

"I'll try not to," was what I tried to say, but dry gibberish came out.

"Here." Kestrel put a water bottle in my hand, and I drank as though I'd been flying for seven hours in the desert.

At last, I cleared my throat. "Sorry. I love you. I promise I'll try not to accidentally bump you again."

"That's all a girl can ask for, really." The comment was light-hearted, but there were bags under her gray eyes, and her hair was roughly tied back in that low ponytail she used whenever she'd run out of flocks to give.

Dragging in all my limbs, I tried to sit up. "What happened? And, uh, where the hell are we?"

It appeared to be a big white tent. I was on my side on a narrow gurney, surrounded by piles of equipment and machines going *bing* and *shhh*. Voices came through the plastic walls, and beyond, rumbles of engines. Huge engines.

"A field hospital?"

Kestrel, giggling nervously, glanced around at the 'ward' from her perch on the edge of my bed. "The LA base."

"Whoa, what? Which one?"

"There's more than–?"

Falcon came skidding around the partition. "He lives! The Hawk breathes to fly another day!"

"That entrance was not as clever as you think it was," Kestrel said, ducking as Falcon aimed a hearty slap at my shoulder.

"Ow."

"Well done, Hawkie-bae. You survived. And, not that it was a competition or anything, but you're totally the last to wake up."

"Flock off, Falcon."

He sighed dramatically. "Well, I would, if I could. But, as you may have noticed, we're not in Kansas anymore."

I looked at Kess. "What is this idiot on?"

"Pure adrenaline, Hawkie-bae, and my natural abundance of testosterone."

"Shut up, Falcon," Kestrel said. "I haven't had a chance to explain, yet."

Finally, I managed to sit up. "But Tui and Condor are okay?"

"They're doing much better. The antiviral thing from JingYing actually worked. But..." Her golden wings, folded neatly and draping over the side of the gurney, twitched. "While we were away, the Evos … they…"

Her face twisted. My heart tightened.

"Who got…" I didn't know how to finish my question. Hurt? Taken?

Killed?

Kestrel blew out a large breath, and Falcon dropped into the folding chair in the corner.

"They took Lory and Ben." Kestrel picked at the hospital sheet.

Fal muttered something obscene. "And Goldberg."

"Luke and Drew tried to stop them, but they broke Luke's leg in three places and knocked Drew out before duct taping him up."

"Wait, what?" My brain was already hurting. "Goldberg was there?"

Kestrel looked at me sharply. "Do you remember meeting her in the parking lot?"

"It was foggy," said Falcon, as though that helped.

Groaning, I rubbed my eyes. "Nope. Nothing."

Impatiently, Kestrel waved it away. "We'll catch you up later. Point is, Lory and Ben are missing. Drew and your dad have called on every single contact they ever made in the Navy and the Air Force, the LAPD is going gangbusters – there's a huge manhunt on."

"Why?" I asked. "We already know who did it. Just bash down Junior's door and–"

Kestrel's head dropped into her hands. "It's not that simple. The Evos own hundreds of properties under dozens of subsidiaries and shell companies, and that's just in the States. Even if the whole US military was involved, they couldn't search them all, even if they could get the warrant for it."

"Isn't JingYing helping?" I demanded.

Falcon was ripping a piece of paper into tiny shreds. I hoped it hadn't been important, like my doctor's notes, or something. The flakes drifted across his slumped chest and knees, and onto the floor. "We think Junior is holding Raven hostage so JingYing won't betray him," he said, dully. "The cops are trying to get through the Evos' lawyers, and *they* keep going on about their thousands of employees' jobs and charity projects they have to protect."

"But we know it was Junior who took them! Isn't there security footage, or cell phone data, or something?"

"They're trying," Kestrel said, her voice catching. "The cops … it's literally their job. They have the tools and contacts. It's completely out of our hands."

"And this?" I waved at the white plastic around us. There was even plastic sheeting on the floor.

"We're in quarantine," Falcon growled. "Like it will make any flocking difference." He copied my wave around the room, but gave me a hard look as he changed the gesture at the end, flicking his fingers towards a tiny gray security camera taped into the corner of the tent. Without Icarus sight, I doubt I'd have been able to spot it. I wouldn't have noticed it at all without Falcon's heads-up.

So, we were being monitored. No surprise there, really, but it did make my feathers prickle.

"Well," I said, resettling my wings, "it's still more comfortable than the Evolutionary prison cells." I pulled at the hospital gown. "Not sure this is an upgrade from the inmate uniform, though."

Kestrel slid off the bed and retrieved a familiar bundle from the floor. "Your clothes are here. As well as your ankle braces."

As my mouth opened, her look scared the question back down my throat. "Great," I said, taking my clothes and folded tail pieces. "Awesome. Okay. That's a relief?"

Falcon snorted, and Kestrel's eyes widened in that warning way. "Yup. Had to explain how having wings, and flying everywhere, means our legs aren't as strong as humans'. Bit embarrassing."

"They took all our flight gear, though," Falcon grumbled, a bit too loudly. "We're stuck in here."

"Huh." Trying to process all their hints, I absently began pulling off the hospital gown.

Falcon shot to his feet. "That's my cue to leave," he said. "I do not need to see your bare ass a second time in twenty-four hours." Chuckling, he ducked out of my personal ward.

"Wha...?"

Kestrel sighed as she helped me disentangle my arms. "We met Goldberg and got the cure from JingYing yesterday."

"It's been a whole day?" I nearly fell over trying to shove my boxers and pants on at the same time.

"You nearly died yesterday, Hawk," Kestrel said, grabbing me. "Even for us, it takes time for drugs and immune responses to work. Please take it easy, okay?"

"What about Tui and Condor?"

"When you're dressed and got your, uh, braces on, I'll take you through to our new home away from home."

I groaned. "Not another one."

As soon as I was shirt-wrapped and tail-strapped up, Kestrel took my hand. She led me through the white plastic tunnel, its sides flexing and rustling under frequent wind gusts. We passed a couple more single wards like the one I'd woken up in, but they were empty.

The big room at the other end held military camp cots, military folding furniture, a few military crates of food, and the rest of the Flight. Those that weren't missing, anyway.

Luke was in a wheelchair, his cast leg sticking straight out in front. He looked like he hadn't slept in four days. Tui and Condor were there too, already dressed. Leah ordered them to stay put in their chairs as I came in with Kestrel, and continued typing furiously on her rugged-looking laptop. Falcon, predictably, was bouncing a trash ball off the plastic wall, and Drew was sitting next to Luke, talking quietly and earnestly. He nodded to me.

"Hey, bro," Tui said, as Kestrel installed me in the canvas chair next to her. "You look like hell."

"Thanks. Rather look like it than be back there."

"Amen," Condor said, wryly.

Something went *ding*. Instinctively, I patted my empty pockets and the places where my flight harness pouches should be before I saw the machine in the corner. "A microwave?" I asked, shocked.

"Yes," said Kestrel, and placed the bowl in my lap. "We've been given enough MREs for about a week. If we eat like regular human people, anyway."

Anyone watching would already realize that scenario was unlikely. I swallowed with difficulty. "Where's my phone?"

Kestrel nodded to the corner. "Over there, with everyone else's. It's the one place in this quarantine tent with reliable signal."

I frowned. "There should be great service on base."

"The Air Force people said the big storm moving in is affecting reception everywhere," Falcon said, "but I think they don't want to admit they're using jamming technology."

"Storm?"

"The Pineapple Express – the atmospheric river – is bringing a massive weather system, lad," Leah said, shortly, without looking up from her computer. "It's hampering search efforts."

"But it will also hinder the abductors," Drew said, and the food soured in my mouth as I remembered Lory and Ben had been kidnapped.

At first, I couldn't believe how calm their parents were. But, as I paid attention, I noticed the tension in their movements, the lines around their eyes and mouths, their flinches at a particularly loud thump of wind against the tent.

Guilt twisted a knife into my heart as I remembered their children would still be safe if the Flight hadn't turned up.

"So, uh, thanks for not letting us die," I said, awkwardly. Leah gave me a brief, joyless smile.

Kestrel took the empty bowl and replaced it with another full one. Being in a coma or something for a full day explained why I was so hungry that my chest was aching. I also felt sick as I thought about all the terrible things Junior was probably doing to Lory and Ben right then, but I forced the food down. I had to get back to full strength so I could help.

Somehow.

"When are we allowed out of here?"

"When they're sure we're not contagious, I guess," Condor said, fidgeting with his 'ankle brace'.

A nearby engine was briefly louder than the wind-blasted tent, and I remembered where we were. "Has anyone seen my dad?"

"He is liaising for us," Drew said, sharply. "Obviously, this is his turf. I've been in contact with my people. Now we have to wait for the message to get through the right channels."

My head dropped, and I resisted the urge to say yes sir, sorry sir.

After my hunger was finally sated, the Flight moved a table over Luke's leg, and we began a reluctant card game. No one really cared. Falcon was staring off into the corner so long that we just skipped his turn three or four times in a row. Luke looked like he'd burst into tears any second. Tui barely spoke, constantly glancing over to Lory and Ben's parents.

Drew and Leah were whispering in the other corner, and the wind and tent noise meant we couldn't listen in.

I tried to think of something to boost morale. Briefly, I considered congratulating Luke on his guts at trying to stand up to the Evolutionary kidnappers, but seeing as the encounter had ended with him being thrown into a wall and his leg being stamped on so hard that it broke in three places, and our friends being abducted, it was probably the wrong angle to take.

Suddenly, there was a discordant chorus of beeps. Everyone jumped, yelped, swore, gasped. Then Leah, Kestrel, and Falcon practically dived for the phones.

"Huh?" I blinked.

"It's not Lory or Ben," Leah said, her voice heavy, as she swiped through her phone.

"Or Raven," Falcon said. "But..." he frowned.

Hope was rising on Kestrel's face like the morning sun.

"I don't know who, but someone is sharing their location with us," she said, practically vibrating with anxiety and excitement. "Someone is showing us where to go."

# 27

# RAVEN

The girl with the red wings and the boy with the black wings were scared. The bruises on their arms and faces looked like shadows on their skin. Even though it wasn't cold in the dark room, they shivered.

The girl, Lory, held on to her brother, Benji. I recognized them from the video calls with the Flight. They huddled on the floor in the corner. As far away from me as they could get.

When they had been thrown into the room the night before, they had been surprised to see me, then excited, and then quickly became suspicious. I did not know what to say to make them feel better. And I did not see the point in trying.

So I continued to sit on the chair, and they sat on the floor in the corner. There was silence for many hours.

I did not know where we were, only that it was another apartment in a tall building in a different city to the one where I had stayed with JingYing. Where we had grown up with Aron and Frederik. That apartment had been old. This one was new. It was not even finished yet. There was no carpet, no paint, no kitchen. The windows did not open. There was a toilet and a sink, and lights hanging on wires from holes in the ceiling, and light switches hanging on wires from holes in the walls. There was a table made from planks of wood, spotted with splatters of many different paints. There were four metal chairs. They were also old, splattered, and wobbly.

From this chair, I could see the only three doors in the apartment. The front door, which was locked and bolted on the outside. The bathroom door, which stood open. And the bedroom door. It was also locked.

On the other side was a woman. I did not know who she was. But I knew she was important.

In the middle of the night, I had heard soft sobs coming through the door, and murmurs in a language I did not know. But I recognized the patterns from when Condor would whisper to himself. The woman had been praying.

I did not sleep. I sat, and I listened, and I watched. My wings slowly flexed in time with my breathing.

As the morning came, and the city outside became gray instead of black and orange, Lory and Benji became braver. Or bored. They stood up, stretched, and began to explore in the new light.

"Hey, Ben, are we still in LA?" Lory's voice bounced oddly as she pressed to the window.

"How would I know? We've never been to LA before yesterday, and now it's raining. I can't exactly read the street signs from up here."

"Yeah, but I'm sure that I recognize that skyscraper."

"But you've never seen it before."

"You'd know the Eiffel Tower or the Taj Mahal or Stonehenge if you saw them."

"That's an office block. Not a world-famous monument."

"It was in a viral video a while ago."

"And why would you remember that?"

Lory turned and looked at me. I looked back.

"Because," she said, "it showed the Flight playing hide-and-seek with a bunch of helicopters."

Slowly, I stood up. Lory and Ben backed away as I approached the window. I looked out. And I saw Lory was right.

"Okay," Benji said. "We're still in Los Angeles. How does that help? Unless Raven still has her phone?"

I shook my head.

Lory sighed. "It's so cruelly ironic. If we could just open one of these frickin' windows…"

"Tails gone," Benji said, sadly.

"We could still glide from rooftop to rooftop."

Suddenly, Benji ran across the room. He grabbed a chair. Lory and I jumped out of the way. He threw it at the window.

There was a loud *crack*.

But it wasn't the glass. One leg of the chair had broken.

With a yell, Benji picked it up and slammed it into the glass again. And again. And again.

"Benji!" Lory shouted, but her brother continued, yelling and crashing the chair into the earthquake-proof glass. "Benji!"

At last, he threw the chair across the apartment. He fell to the floor, sobbing.

"Benji, Benji, I'm sorry." Lory fell to her knees beside her brother, wrapping her arms and wings around him. "It'll be okay."

"No, it won't," Benji choked. "They hurt Dad. And they hurt Luke. I don't know if he – what he–"

"Shh," Lory said, rocking her brother. "Shh. They're okay. Mom's saved them. I know it."

"We're going to die, aren't we?"

Benji was looking straight at me.

I saw Owl in my memories. Frederik's face as he executed the monster he believed had taken over his brother's body. The blood that swirled into the water as Aron died at his feet.

Frederik hated us so much because without Aron, without YanWei, it was only him and JingYing left to be perfect. To save the entire human race. And the Flight were in the way.

He would not let us remain there for long.

None of this would make sense to Lory and Benji. So I said nothing.

"Come on, bro," Lory said, dragging her brother to his feet. "Let's find another exit."

I watched them explore the half-finished apartment for a long time. They looked for any missed builders' tools, for any loose pieces of drywall or ceiling tile. They pulled at the corners of every small hole in case there was something more behind.

They were on their knees, picking at the base of the far wall, when the lock clicked, and the front door opened.

Frederik walked in, and I briefly experienced atrial fibrillation as I saw, again, Aron's face.

Then I saw the woman behind him. And I stepped back.

Madame was wearing her usual skirt suit, the pearl necklace, and her gray hair in the smooth bob cut. I knew these terms now, after JingYing and I had discussed the hierarchy of the Evolutionary Corporation. JingYing and Frederik were the heirs to the company. Now they were twenty-one and had come of age, they commanded vast fortunes and armies of employees. There were only three people with more power. Two were Mr

Larrsson, Senior, and Ms Lin, my mother, who lived in Shanghai, and still did not know I was alive.

The third was Madame.

Lory and Ben held each other and watched as Frederik locked the door's extra bolts and put the keys in his suit jacket. He wore a business shirt with no tie and the top buttons open, casual trousers, and quiet shoes. He moved almost silently, but Madame's heels clicked on the rough floor.

She looked at the three of us and sighed, shaking her head. "Not again, dear."

But I saw the tightness in her face. I saw how sharp her movements were as she set down her bag on the table. And I knew she was angry, and afraid.

Frederik kept smiling. It was a Bad smile.

"This entire situation is of your making, Madame," he said. "If you had not authorized the experiments on Aron's and Yan Wei's bodies following brain death, I would not be constantly reminded of everything I lost, every time I look at this disgusting child-monster." He grabbed my hair and yanked my head back. I forced myself to meet his gaze, and not fight back. My wings twitched.

"Do you see her, Madame?" he asked, louder. He shook me. My scalp stung. "Do you see the remains of Yan Wei in her face? It's worse than locked-in syndrome. Knowing that part of her consciousness is possibly still in there, trapped behind the new mutant personality that has taken over her body? A fate worse than death." He threw me to the ground, and walked away.

Gasping, I lay on the floor. It felt like Frederik had punched me. Was that why he'd killed Owl?

To set Aron free?

"My sole purpose in life was, is, and ever will be, to provide you with the best possible opportunity to achieve your goals, dear." Madame walked over to one of the chairs, and placed it at the table as though it was a fancy restaurant, before sitting down with a brush of her skirt. "Van Scholtz proved there was zero neural activity. If Aron and YanWei had been taken off life support, the bodies would have ceased functioning in minutes."

"As should have happened," Frederik said, his voice low.

"Dear, we've been over this. Your own existence was still a mystery. To provide you and JingYing with appropriate companions, or children, we needed to learn how you were created in the first place. With their bodies, we suddenly had all the time, and all the research material in the world. It was the best hope we had of recreating Goldberg's editing machine."

"Your team had ten years of experimentation and research," Frederik said, standing opposite Madame, his hands behind his back. "What results did you deliver in that time?"

"You've seen the list of FDA-approved pharma–"

"Not drugs. Genetic advances. DNA breakthroughs. Where is the editing machine?"

Madame coughed lightly. "Well, dear, as you know, no one was able to figure out what Goldberg had done. That part was, admittedly, a failure. When she died, the knowledge died with her."

Frederik smiled, slowly. "Do you know what it was like for me and JingYing, Madame, when we were suddenly faced with people we believed had been dead for over a decade?"

"I can only imagine–"

"It felt something like this."

Frederik turned, and unlocked the bedroom door. Opening it, he said, "Please, do join us, doctor."

Slowly, the woman emerged, moving stiffly. Her red jacket was wrinkled, her hair a little messy. But she stood with a straight back, and nodded to Madame.

Madame stood up so quickly, her chair fell over. No one reacted as it clattered to the floor.

"Doctor Goldberg?" Madame said, her voice high. She cleared her throat, and waved her hand at one of the other chairs. "What a ... pleasant surprise. Do sit down. Tea?"

I stared as Dr Goldberg sat. Madame picked up her chair and sat opposite.

"I'm afraid I only have two cups and the one flask, dear," Madame said to Frederik, taking a fat bottle from her bag. "I wasn't aware we'd have company."

Still standing, Frederik waved his hand. "The two of you mature, esteemed ladies should share it. You have so much to catch up on, after all. Don't mind me."

Madame's hand shook slightly as she poured the tea into the two cups. My stomach ached. I had not eaten since the day before, and I didn't know if it was longer for Lory and Benji.

"So, Doctor," Madame said. "Where have you been for the past twenty years?"

Goldberg, the woman who had created me and Owl, and the rest of the Flight, didn't answer at first, as she drank. I remembered she had not even been able to access water, unlike me, Lory and Benji. If I had known who was in that room, I could have talked to her. Asked her through the door. Finally learned the answer to...

Why?

# 28

# RAVEN

"Answer Madame's question, Doctor Goldberg," Frederik said. His voice was low. Tight. "Where have you been?"

"Here and there," Dr Goldberg said, at last. "Mostly in China." She glanced at me, then quickly looked away. "How about you, Madame?"

"Fulfilling my duties," Madame said, sharply, but she had that terrifying, Bad smile. "Guiding the children you created as though they were my own. Nurturing them to their full potential."

"Weren't you and Arthur talking about starting a family, when these little angels were starting to toddle?" Dr Goldberg nodded towards Frederik. His lip curled when Goldberg said 'angels', but he did not move.

Madame picked up her cup but did not drink. "I was spending so much time with the super twins, I was never home," she said, brightly. "Arthur didn't like the arrangement. And his buddies thought it amusing that his wife was earning five times as much as he ever could. So, he left."

"Oh, I'm so sorry, Geraldine."

"It was for the best, *Christine*. Besides, the rascals kept me so busy, I didn't have time to miss him. How about yourself? Meet anyone special while you were dead?" Goldberg opened her mouth, but Madame kept talking, in the bright, Bad way. "Anyway, dear, why on Earth did you have to be so dramatic? Faking your death is a little extreme, don't you think? An ordinary resignation letter would have been sufficient."

Goldberg looked at Frederik. "You know as well as I do that was not an option."

"An extended vacation, then. The Corporation does take very good care of its employees."

"Yes. I'm quite sure I would have been taken care of." Goldberg sipped her tea.

Madame laughed. "I would ask what kept you busy all those years, but I think the cat is rather out of the bag now, dear. Or is the bird out of the cage?" She tilted her head at Lory and Ben, who tried to shrink further away into the corner. "What on Earth were you trying to achieve?"

"The same as you, Geraldine. Supporting other couples to have the children I would never have."

Frederik grunted with annoyance, and shifted his weight, crossing his arms.

"Did you tell them their children would be perfect? Or did you warn them they would mutate into freaks as they aged?" Madame's voice was still bright, but was getting tighter.

Goldberg sighed, and looked around the room. "I know you all want me to cackle over my tea and reveal some great master plan. But there is none. I didn't know."

"Didn't know what, dear?" Madame put down her cup. "That your creations would suddenly develop a mysterious illness that manifested in a hunger that was never sated, that made their eyes and ears supernaturally sharp, that made their bodies swell and deform beyond human limits until alien limbs burst out in a shower of blood and gore?"

Madame was standing now. Goldberg leaned away from her, her face white.

"Those perfect children became demons," Madame said, quietly. "Their bodies were tortured until they broke. I was driving them to the Corporation hospital, hoping we could save them, and they were screaming in pain, Christine. They were dying. And then their bodies exploded, and they went insane. They attacked me. The car crashed. And they died. I died. I was resuscitated four times. They were not."

Goldberg was breathing hard. "I didn't know."

"Didn't know that two of your superior children had time bombs wired into their DNA? Or didn't know that it wasn't just their lives you ruined?"

The room was still.

"That was not supposed to happen," Goldberg said, eventually, quietly.

Madame slowly sat down. "Then, do tell me what was supposed to happen."

"You know what. I thought I had fulfilled my brief as dictated by my employers. By our employers."

With a long sigh, Madame made herself more comfortable. "And yet no one could replicate your results. Or so we thought. Then these … specimens began appearing." She pointed at Lory and Benji again. "Why don't you talk me through the process?"

"I can't."

"Why not?"

"Once I realized, I destroyed it. Years ago."

"Then," Madame said, through closed teeth, "walk me through what you remember. I'll even record it, so you don't have to repeat yourself."

She placed her phone on the table between them, tapped and swiped, then sat back.

Frederik unfolded his arms and checked his watch. "Carry on, Madame," he said. "I need to make a call. I'll be back in a few minutes, but continue your little chat. We need that information." He gave Goldberg a long look. "And we will retrieve it by any means necessary."

He left and locked the door behind him. There was silence.

"More tea, dear?" Madame asked, in her bright voice. She poured without waiting for Goldberg to answer. "Oh, and I quite forgot to offer you sweetener! How rude. Allow me."

She took a small bottle from her bag and poured a thick liquid into Goldberg's cup, then her own.

"Personally, I prefer sugar cubes, but trying to cut down and all that," she said, with a little laugh. "You know how it is when we get to our age!"

Goldberg picked up her cup. "Quite." She took a sip, wrinkled her nose, but drank again.

An Icari behind me whimpered.

"There's water in the tap, dear," Madame said sharply. "You can get it for yourself." She smiled at Goldberg. "I think that's where I went wrong with Frederik, you know. I did so much for him, so he could focus on his studies. I may have coddled him a little too much."

Goldberg nodded, and yawned. "Excuse me. I didn't get much sleep last night."

"I understand, dear. Ever since the accident, I haven't been able to sleep without a little help, if you know what I mean."

Goldberg nodded again, and rubbed her eyes.

"Drink up, dear, the tea will help."

As Goldberg drank, and Madame watched, I stood. Lory and Benji hesitated, but I held out my hands. After a moment, they took them.

Keeping our distance from the two women talking at the table, we edged around the apartment to the single functioning sink.

As I bent my mouth to the faucet, Lory whispered, "We need to get her phone."

Benji glanced over, and the corner of his mouth smiled. "Yeah. Time to spill the tea." He touched my shoulder. "Okay, Raven?"

I thought about JingYing. If I escaped, or helped the others escape, Frederik would hurt her. If we stayed, he would hurt Lory and Benji. I didn't want that to happen. And I thought, maybe, JingYing wouldn't want that, either.

I made my decision.

My legs were shaking as we walked towards the table. My feathers twitched.

Madame looked sharply at us as we stood next to her. "Go and sit in the corner," she said.

"But we have questions, too," Lory said, with a high, annoying voice.

"Move away before Frederik comes back."

Benji leaned forward. "I'm so hungry," he moaned. "You look like a granny. Grannies always have snacks in their bags, don't they?" He reached for Madame's bag.

She slapped his hand away. He yelled, and his arm bumped the flask of tea.

"Sorry!" Ben grabbed for it at the same time as Lory. They knocked over Madame's cup and the flask. Tea flooded the table. Madame shrieked.

"Oh no!" Lory grabbed Madame's bag and phone and Benji tried to pick up the cup. I put my hands on the table and wiped the puddle. Most of it poured onto Madame's lap. She jumped up. Goldberg sat with her drink in her hand, blinking rapidly.

"Stop!" Madame grabbed my wrist. "Move away. Now. You." She pointed at Lory. "Give me back my bag."

"I'm trying to get the tea off," Lory said, shaking the bag.

Madame swung around. "Where's my phone?"

"I'm trying to get the tea off, too," Benji said, using the corner of his shirt-wrap to wipe the back of the device. His thumb was tapping urgently on the screen.

"Give. It. Here."

Lory held out the bag. Just as Madame reached over, she dropped it. Its contents tumbled across the floor.

"I'm sorry, I thought you had it!" Lory fell to her knees and tried to pick everything up.

"Why did you make half of them idiots?" Madame said to Goldberg, trying to wipe tea off her skirt. She snatched the bag from Lory. Some things were still scattered on the floor beneath the table, including makeup containers and the bottle of sweetener. Ignoring them, Madame grabbed her phone from Benji. "Why couldn't you just make them all the same?"

"I did." Goldberg blinked, giggled. "They are identical twins."

Madame paused. "What?"

"They *are* twins. Frederik and Aron, YanWei and JingYing. Their DNA is the same."

My stomach felt cold, and my pulse rapidly increased. My genes were identical to JingYing's?

And Frederik's were identical to Owl's?

"Oh, shit," Lory muttered. "Pretty boy is not going to like this. Raven, did you know?"

"I was starting to suspect," I whispered. "But JingYing would not answer my questions."

Benji swallowed, and tried to drag his sister and me further away from the dangerous women at the table.

Slowly, Madame sat down, staring at Goldberg. "But van Scholtz told me their DNA was different. He'd found differences. He was trying to unravel them."

"Ugh," Goldberg said. "Van Scholtz is incompetent. He couldn't figure it out, so he probably invented a reason to keep experimenting and cover up his ignorance."

"Then why did only two of them develop the mutation?"

Goldberg slouched in her chair. "Ask van Scholtz. He was researching growth hormones for a while there. He probably gave them something experimental that triggered it. It'd be his style to only administer it to one half of each pair." She lifted her cup and drank the last of the tea. "And never admit it."

"Then why are all the wild specimens so consistent?" Madame demanded. "Why did they all mutate at the same time?"

Goldberg shrugged. "They didn't," she said, slowly.

"What do you mean, they didn't?"

"Not all at the same. Time." She yawned. "This is good tea. Can I have more?"

"It's all gone," Madame said, sharply. "How many of these freaks did you make?"

"Umm ... fift ... fifty."

I gasped, Lory squeaked, and Benji flinched.

"You made fifty of these freaks in your little clinic?"

"Mm-hm."

Goldberg's eyes closed, and her head fell back on her chair. Her breathing was loud.

"But why?" Madame asked, bewildered. "Why?"

"So they ... wouldn't be ... alone."

She seemed to fall asleep.

We waited. Madame sighed, looked at her phone, stopped the recording. Locked the phone. Put it in her bag.

The lock clicked. Lory, Benji and I backed away. Frederik entered, and stared.

"What the fuck happened?"

"Language," Madame said.

Frederik looked at Goldberg, unmoving on her chair. "What the fuck is wrong with her?"

"I guess she's had a little too much truth-telling for one day," Madame said, coldly. "And mind your language, Frederik!"

Frederik stared at her, at the tea stain on her clothes, at the wet table, the puddle on the floor. The dropped items from her bag.

He saw the bottle of the liquid that she'd poured into Goldberg's cup. He tilted his head.

Somehow, he read it from where he was standing. And it seemed he could not speak for a moment.

"You spiked her tea with sodium thiopental?" Finally, he bent down and picked up the little bottle. He shook it. "How much did you put in?" His voice rose. "Do you realize what you've done?"

"I was getting the truth!"

His fingers were on Goldberg's throat. "With a poisonous overdose?"

"You said to get the truth by any means necessary!" Madame cried. "I had the means, and it was necessary!"

"There's no such thing as truth serum, you stupid old woman! And now she's dead!" Frederik smashed the little bottle on the floor. We flinched. "You have overstepped your authority, Madame."

Madame stood up, the chair crashing over again. When she spoke, her voice was low, quiet, and vibrating with anger. "I am sick and tired of taking the blame for your foibles, *dear.* This company would have fallen apart without me. Yet you, JingYing, and your parents all treat me like I am expendable. I have cleaned up your messes, handled the hush money, visited the families left behind. I did what needed to be done. I have sacrificed my entire life for you. And you have treated me with contempt since you were old enough to spell the word. You might be physically and intellectually superior, young man, but you will never have the love you so desperately crave."

Frederik grabbed the table, lifting it easily. Madame's bag, phone, tea bottle, and cups clattered to the ground, skidding across the floor towards us. Frederik threw the table at the wall. Goldberg slowly fell off the chair.

Lory's hands were squeezing me too tightly. Benji was trying to drag us further into the corner, as Frederik turned on Madame. His arms tense. Fists clenching.

Madame backed away, towards the windows. "Frederik…"

Then his phone rang. Frederik didn't take his eyes off Madame as he answered. "What?"

I clearly heard the man on the other end.

"*Sir, I believe your location has been compromised.*"

"Why?"

As the man said it, we heard it coming.

"*There is a helicopter approaching your building.*"

"Yes, you idiot. I summoned it."

"*This is not a Corporation chopper, sir.*"

Frederik frowned. "LAPD?"

"*Unmarked, sir.*"

"What type?"

A pause. "*Military.*"

# 29

# CONDOR

"Like *fuck* I'm staying here while my kids are in danger!"

Leah's yell, aimed at the anonymous hazmat suits just outside the quarantine tent, briefly made the Flight smile.

Drew spoke next. "I'd listen to her, if I were you."

"But ma'am, you're a doctor, not–"

"Corporal, I've been in more war zones than you have, and armed only with a stethoscope. You can check with Colonel Owen. We're authorized and we're going, laddie."

A sigh. "Yes, ma'am. But the … other patients have to stay here."

"What?"

"No!"

"Are you kidding?"

The Flight put on a really convincing outraged act, I thought. We'd expected this.

Falcon flopped dramatically onto a chair. "Ugh. Not like we can fly at the moment, anyway," he said, loudly.

Leah and Drew briefly returned to the quarantine lounge. Drew was carrying a box. "Here's the extra food your dad sent, Hawk," he said, as Leah grabbed the Bluetooth earpieces for their phones.

She pointed at us. "You lot, stay together. We'll keep in touch."

"Okay, okay," Hawk grumbled.

As soon as Leah and Drew had left, and the tent had been re-sealed, we had the box open. On top of the food packets were our flight glasses. Of course, we already had our 'ankle braces'. We'd have to do without the rest of our gear, but it would be enough.

I hoped.

"Ready?" Hawk asked, rummaging deeper and extracting one last piece of kit with a satisfied grunt.

"Aye aye, Cadet Captain Sergeant sir," I said, sliding my phone into my pocket and the thingy into my ear.

"All set, Luke?" Kestrel asked.

"Ready to be our guy in the wheelchair?" Falcon added.

With laptop balanced on the cast-bound leg, phone in one hand with his earbuds and mic set wired in, Luke held up his thumb.

"Location hasn't moved," he reported. "All of you are showing, too."

"Thanks, Luke. Keep us posted." By now, Hawk had strapped on the holster that his dad had smuggled back to him. He slipped out his knife and flipped it over in his hand. He grinned. "Let's go."

In the horrible weather and the chaos of the scrambling rescue forces, no one saw us cutting out of the tent and launching into the rain until it was too late.

An airfield spread out before us, with neat rows of small aircraft and large helicopters. A cluster of low buildings stretched away alongside it. A stubby air traffic control tower stood as sentinel.

People in fatigues ran through the rain with purpose – then some saw us.

Voices yelled, barely audible over engines and wind.

"Hey! Wait! Stop!"

"What the hell are those?"

"But you're sick!"

Hawk took point, flipping a salute to his dad at the controls of the helicopter lifting from the tarmac. It was carrying Drew and Leah, and a whole military squad. Whether they were Army, Air Force, Navy reserves – I had no idea.

I was just glad they were on our side.

"I got rain down my neck already," Falcon grumbled, his voice vibrating into my ear. Wincing, I adjusted the volume with one hand as I swiped water off my flight glasses with the other, all the while flapping hard to gain altitude.

Hawk's snort was less painful. "I'll pass your complaint on to the manager."

"Condor, Tui, how are you doing?" Kestrel glanced back from her position at Hawk's right wing.

My lungs, still raw from coughing, felt like I was breathing in sand. But it was still better than yesterday. And Lory and Benji needed us. I was not stopping for anything. I'd found my purpose.

It was the Flight.

"I'm fine," I said.

"Yep. If I don't talk much," Tui added.

Falcon grunted. "Less chatting, more flying. We've got Flight to save."

The helicopter could have easily outpaced us, but due to the low visibility and the proximity of LAX, Hawk's dad kept it slow.

Still, our destination was so close, we were preparing to land on the skyscraper only minutes later. I hadn't even had time to think about the fact that we were probably dropping in on Junior himself.

I was glad we had a small army on our side, this time.

The chopper was loud. Everyone in the building must have noticed its arrival. However, there was a helipad – so maybe they wouldn't think much of it?

"Luke?" Without the earpiece, there was no way I'd have heard Kestrel over the weather, traffic, and helicopter landing below us. Despite the wind crackling in the mic, her words were clear enough. "Found anything useful about the location?"

"A news article. Grand opening of the apartment tower is set for next month. No one has moved in yet," Luke reported from the base. "Being a weekend, it might even be empty of contractors."

"It would be nice if we had a bit of luck, for once," Hawk called.

Falcon pointed. "At least we've got backup for a change."

Far below, two convoys of screaming police cars and a couple of SWAT vans were converging on the building.

"Holy shit," Hawk said.

"Where were these guys when we needed them the first seventeen times?" Falcon said.

"Probably here in the city, while we were faffing about in deserts, mountains, and swamps," Tui said, breathlessly.

Luke suddenly reported: "The locator's disappeared."

"What?"

"Crap!"

"Where'd it go?"

"Don't know. It just cut out."

By now, the military chopper was on the helipad. The heavily armed adults piled out, ducking under the spinning blades and running for the access door. Drew had his hand on his wife's back as they followed, Leah clutching a medic's kit.

We didn't have a radio to listen in on the commands and conversation, but we knew the gist. The LAPD would form the perimeter, the SWAT team would enter from the ground and work their way up, while the military volunteers swept the building from the top down. Hawk's dad would stay on alert in the chopper – especially in this weather, which could blow it off the rooftop. I wiped my goggles again.

"I need to land." I hated feeling weak, but knew I needed to rest, or I'd be no good to anyone.

By the time our formation had wheeled around and descended toward a part of the roof that didn't have spinning blades on it, the military team had forced open the access door and disappeared into the building.

I messed up my landing, partly due to the crosswind and partly due to fatigue, and staggered into Tui. She grabbed me, and we steadied each other.

"Me and my weak ankles are very grateful to be on the ground, eh," she said, with a strained grin. "Relatively speaking."

"Oi! Get over here!"

Hawk's dad beckoned from the chopper. We had to tuck in our wings as we crossed the helipad so we didn't get blown away.

"You look like half-drowned chickens," Colonel Owen said, grabbing his son's jacket and half-hoisting him into the cabin, before reaching a hand to Kestrel.

"Thanks, Dad." Hawk crossed the cabin, nearly tripped on the strapped-down piles of search-and-rescue equipment, and peered out the opposite window. "Are my ears ringing, or can I hear another chopper?"

As I climbed past him, Colonel Owen leaned out of the side door into the lee of his helicopter. "Looks like it. Hard to tell in this crap. But it should be easing shortly."

"It's probably heading for the tower across the road," Kestrel said. "The one a few storeys taller."

Luke's voice added, "Satellite photos show it has a helipad, too."

"Keep an eye on it," Colonel Owen said, slowly, then clambered into the cockpit. He flicked a few switches, and then a radio conversation was blasting over the cabin's speakers.

"*–penthouse level clear. Moving down one level by northwest staircase to floor forty-nine.*"

"*Affirmative.*"

Over the next few minutes, as we watched the other helicopter land through gusts of rain, we listened to the clipped voices announcing the two ground floors, the top three floors, and the first basement clear of anything weird.

Then:

"*We have a locked door on the forty-seventh floor.*"

"*Copy that. Break it down.*"

"*Affirmative. Forcing entry.*"

Even the wind seemed to hold its breath.

"*We have two unresponsive adult females, repeat, two unresponsive adult females, requesting urgent assistance on level forty-seven, northeast corner.*"

*"Affirmative. Doctor Richardson en route from forty-eight with escort."*

"What the hell?" Falcon said. "One must be Goldberg. But who's the other?"

Kestrel bit her lip. "JingYing? Maybe?"

"They would have mentioned wings, right?"

I twisted my jacket. "They wouldn't refer to Raven as an adult."

"Shh," Tui said, impatiently, as the radio crackled again.

*"Confirm doctor's arrival. Resuscitation attempts underway."*

*"Copy that. Ambulance en route. Do you need further backup?"*

*"Negative, but forensics will want to take a good long look."*

*"Explain?"*

*"For one thing, I've never seen feathers this big before."*

The Flight collectively gasped.

*"Uh, could you repeat that?"*

*"There are two feathers here that are easily four feet long, and they're not from a fucking peacock."*

There was a painful moment of radio silence.

*"Acknowledged. Apparently, this proves we're on the right track. However, it also indicates that suspect and hostages are on the move."*

*"They can't be far. There's a beverage flask here that's still warm."*

*"Acknowledged."*

"Hey, Dad," Hawk said, not moving his eyes from the window. "Can we get your buddies at the NAA to check the registration number on that helicopter?"

"Not in the next ten minutes," Colonel Owen said. "What did you see?"

"Not enough," Hawk said, frustrated. "The rain's eased, but the angle's wrong. It's still idling. It hasn't shut down. I think it's loading up and preparing to take–"

Luke was suddenly shouting in our ears. "The locator's back! It's in that other building, the one you said the helicopter was landing on!"

The Flight rushed to join Hawk at the window. "What the flock?" Hawk said. "How the hell could Junior have got them to that building without–"

*"Two armed adult males in Basement Three. Claiming to be security guards, demanding ID and search warrant. Please advise."*

*"They can come up and see the fucking warrant for themselves. What the hell are they guarding?"*

*"Seems to be a pedestrian tunnel."*

The silence seemed to stretch for minutes. But it was only a few rapid breaths.

I lunged for the door.

"It's taking off!" Hawk yelled. "Flight in the air! Go, go, go!"

As the Flight catapulted from the military chopper, I was sprinting for the edge of the roof. The other helicopter tilted forward as it accelerated, giving me a glimpse inside.

Junior was at the controls.

I dived. My wings snapped wide. Caught the wind. Swooped up. Twisted.

Junior's helicopter buzzed past my head. I reached. Grabbed the helicopter skid.

My arm was nearly yanked from my shoulder. I dragged in my wings and managed to hook my legs and other arm over the skid.

"Hold on, Condor! We'll catch you up!" Hawk hollered. I could just hear him under the helicopter.

Without unhooking my arm, I stretched my hand and turned my head to dial up the volume on the Bluetooth earpiece again. "Don't take too long," I grunted. Straining to peer beyond my folded wingtips, I caught a glimpse of the Flight before the rain closed in and they disappeared like smoke.

But at least I could still hear them.

"Where the hell is he going?" Falcon asked.

Luke reported, "The locator just dropped off again. But Condor was right on it."

"More like I'm right under it," I said, trying to shake raindrops off my glasses as I stared at the belly of the helicopter a few feet from my nose.

"What—" Hawk started, then paused.

"What's going on?" I yelled.

No reply. My regular arms, not used to holding my weight like my wings, were already burning. My head ached from the rumble.

Kestrel finally came online. "Sorry, Condor, Hawk's dad was picking us up. It'll be easier to catch up in the helicopter."

"Makes sense," I grunted.

"You have to hold on. Without your GPS signal, Junior's chopper will be invisible in this weather."

"Got it."

Tui's breathless voice joined Kestrel's. "You're doing awesome, bro. Just a bit longer and we'll take over, okay?"

"Yup."

"Luke?" Hawk called. "Any idea where this psycho is headed?"

Luke began to answer, but multiple voices suddenly shushed him.

A crackle and whine of interference. Then I could hear the military radio again. Someone had somehow patched it into the Flight's comms – or had simply shoved their earpiece into a helicopter headset.

"*–said they were just following orders. Both claim they have no idea where the boss was heading.*"

"*Charges of aiding and abetting kidnapping not jogging their memories?*"

"*I suspect that's not the worst thing on their rap sheets.*"

"*How many on the helo when it launched?*"

"*Just 'the boss', whoever he is, the lady pilot who brought it in, and three, I quote, 'freak monsters'.*"

"*Which direction did the helo go?*"

"*West,*" said the cop on the radio, at the same time as Luke broke in.

"Towards the sea. Condor's GPS signal just crossed over Venice Beach."

Craning my neck, I saw I was now dangling over gray, violent water. Somehow, while clinging on for my life, I managed to shiver.

Drew's voice joined the others in my ear. "Luke, find an AIS tracking website. Quickly!"

"A what?"

"Automatic Identification System. All ships of a certain size and type by law must have a transmitting AIS. There are dozens of free tracking websites. We might see exactly what he's aiming for."

"On it."

Rain battered the helicopter, wind sliced past, and the rotor thunder was blurring my vision. There was water all around me now. Water shredding the air, and water churning below.

"Wow, that's a lot of boats," Luke said. "Um, Mr Drew, sir?"

"Go ahead, Luke."

"There are three boats directly ahead of the Evolutionary helicopter, at least, as it's currently pointing."

"What ship types?"

"When I hover over the dots, one says it's a tanker, one says cargo, and one says pleasure craft."

"Click on the pleasure craft details," Drew said, immediately.

A pause. "It's a yacht called *Superiority Complex*."

"That's it," Hawk said. "That's where he's heading. Bet it's a superyacht."

Drew obviously agreed. "Good job, Luke. I'll alert the Coast Guard. Is it anchored or underway?"

"It's moving, uh, southwest. Ish."

"Copy that. Bob, how's … visibility?"

"Zero," Hawk's dad said, as the call began to cut in and out. "Rain clutter … killed radar and FLIR … -ying on faith here."

"Faith in what?" Falcon said.

Colonel Owen's reply was broken by a chuckle and the dying signal. "That no one … mad enough to … this weather."

"I'm losing Con…" Luke said. "…over the ocean … not … cell towers in the … signal's cutting…"

"–him!" Falcon shouted. "Dead ahead!"

Under the rain and the wind and the thundering rotors, I could barely hear myself think, let alone another approaching.

"Hurry up," I begged at full volume through gritted teeth.

"A hundred-seventy-five knots not fast … you?" Hawk called.

An enormous, flat-topped ship slipped by. The tanker, I guessed. "Not if I'm being dragged along at two hundred!"

"Don't worry, son," Colonel Owen said, calmly, as the signal briefly strengthened. "We're faster."

"Heads up!" Falcon cried.

Suddenly, the Evolutionary helicopter banked. Hard. Rain stung my cheeks. Through the splatter, a huge gray shape materialized, only yards away.

It seemed to slide sideways through the air as the Evolutionary dodged. A feint left and then a jerked acceleration right. I groaned.

Whatever Junior tried, Colonel Owen matched it. The military helicopter cut off every manoeuvre, even when the Evo punched it straight up. The Flight's helicopter was so close I could see their faces at the window.

The gigantic waves shrank until they had disappeared in the thrashing rain. The wind whipped my head and shoulders. My arms had gone numb.

Then, the Evolutionary helicopter stopped. It hovered in the storm, bucking in the wind, but holding position.

Slowly, it turned, until it was broadside to the Flight.

Something appeared, dangling beside me. The ends of dark wings. A pair of legs, no tail. Bound tight. Struggling as they hung over the drop.

Raven!

Frederik Larrsson Junior's voice crackled over the radio. "Back off, or I drop the mutant!"

The Flight threw open their helicopter door, staring in horror across the rain-streaked abyss. Hawk, Kestrel, Falcon, and Tui flexed their wings, tensing, ready to jump.

Junior sighed loudly, audible in my full-volume earpiece even over the storm and the helicopters. "I know you won't use those guns, and you won't ram me, so you have ten seconds to BACK OFF."

Should I let go? Drop a few feet, swoop up and into the open door? Could I slam into Junior and knock Raven back into the cabin?

I couldn't see. I couldn't know. I couldn't risk it.

There was a painful knocking and scraping, and then Lory's distant voice.

"Hey, pretty boy! You'll want to hear this."

I flinched. Instantly, I recognized the voice from our imprisonment in the Evo laboratory.

Madame.

*"Give. It. Here."*

Strangely, she was answered by Lory. *"I'm sorry, I'm sorry, I thought you had it!"*

*"Why did you make two of them idiots?"* Madame snapped. *"Why couldn't you just make them all the same?"*

*"I did."* What? Goldberg? *"They are identical twins."*

*"What?"*

*"They are twins. Frederik and Aron, YanWei and JingYing. Their DNA is the same."*

"We're not freaks," Lory yelled. "We're people! Like you."

Junior roared. "You are nothing like me!"

And Raven fell.

I let go. Free fall rushed through my veins. With a flick of a wing, I rolled. Aimed for Raven's tumbling form. No arms or legs flailed. Her wings didn't open.

I had seconds.

I flapped. Hard. Flapped again. Reached forward. My ankles clicked, my tail opened. I nearly grabbed her legs as she rolled. The water rushed upwards.

With a bellow, I flapped harder, and snatched feathers. My other hand seized Raven's shoulder.

I wrapped my arms around her and threw out my wings.

Pain tore my back and chest as I tried to pull up. The air dragged on my feathers. We were curving, away from the water, nearly parallel, but still falling.

"Incoming," Hawk yelled in my ear.

Something red slammed into my head. I grabbed it with one hand. It was a big loop. A rescue sling.

"Hold on!" Tui cried.

She and Hawk flashed past overhead. The sling nearly jerked from my grip. They were trailing a rope each, both tied to the sling. Their wings tilted, swooping upward.

Flapping hard, the extra boost from the towline was enough to keep me and Raven above the waves. Just. Sea spray soaked my legs as we aimed for the sky.

As my momentum faded and gravity dragged at me, I twisted my wings into a treading-air thrash, slowing our fall.

It was just enough. As Tui and Hawk hovered overhead, keeping some slack on the line, I hooked the sling around Raven's body. Her eyes were wide.

The last thing I did was to rip the duct tape off her mouth.

She swung away from me, Tui and Hawk sagging as they took up the strain.

Only then did I notice the shouting in my ear.

"She's okay," I reported, hoarsely. "Tui and Hawk have Raven. She's okay."

No one replied.

My breath, which had been easing, quickened again.

What was going on up there?

# 30

# KESTREL

"Back off, or I drop the mutant!"

We'd been dreading this moment. As soon as Junior had opened the helicopter door, Hawk and Tui had the sling and ropes in hand. The rest of the military rescue supplies lay strewn around the cabin.

Behind Junior, in the luxurious, cream-coloured cabin of the private helicopter, Lory and Ben had been dumped on the floor. Their legs, wings, and wrists were bound. There was some luggage tossed onto some of the seats, spare radio headsets thrown on another, and, in the far corner, was JingYing. She stared at Junior and Raven.

But she didn't move.

Unseen by the Evolutionaries, Condor clung to the skids of their chopper, a dark lump with a pale face. The two helicopters lurched like boats over waves as they hovered in the storm.

We'd hashed out a rough plan. Hawk and Tui weren't happy about it and, honestly, I wasn't either. But in their depleted states, Falcon and I insisted this was the only realistic chance we had of saving our friends.

Hawk's knife felt hot in its holster against my leg.

As the Flight watched, tendons and feathers quivering, ignoring the rain slashing our faces, Lory struggled partly upright, her brother's bound feet pushing at her back. She had something between her tied hands. A phone?

The one that had been sharing their location?

Junior gave a dramatic sigh. "I know you won't use those guns, and you won't ram me, so you have ten seconds to back off!"

Lory lunged awkwardly for the pile of spare headsets. She hooked one. Stabbed at the switch.

Everyone flinched at the sudden knocking and scraping on the radio.

"Hey, pretty boy!" Lory yelled. "You'll want to hear this." She held the phone to the radio mic.

A familiar, terrifying voice.

*"Give. It. Here."*

Raven kicked and struggled, but Junior was frozen. JingYing's eyes never left them as the helicopter lurched.

Goldberg's voice. A confession?

Hawk shifted his weight beside me. His wings flexed. "Get ready," he said to us.

*"They are twins. Frederik and Aron, YanWei and JingYing. Their DNA is the same."*

"We're not freaks," Lory yelled. "We're people! Like you."

Junior bellowed. "You are nothing like me!"

And he dropped Raven.

Hawk and Tui dived. Condor had already fallen from the helicopter, accelerating after her.

Falcon and I threw ourselves out only a second later. The Evolutionary helicopter bucked upwards, hiding the door.

"Come on!" Falcon roared, and we sprinted for the Evo machine. As we strained up, the chopper dipped. Contact.

Grabbing the doorframe, giving another messy, wing-bumping flap, we shot into the cabin of the executive helicopter.

Lory was sprawled across her brother, her bound wrists pressed to her bleeding nose. Benji was trying to commando-crawl and drag his sister out of the way. Falcon and I nearly fell over as the helicopter lurched again. I glanced into the cockpit. It was empty.

After missing a few rapid heartbeats, I spotted the glowing diagram of the helicopter, parts of the image flashing under the words AUTOHOVER.

Okay, so we weren't on a crash course with the sea. But where was–?

Junior was on his knees in front of JingYing. "I had to. I had to do it. To save us both. You'll understand when I show you what Goldberg–"

At last, I saw JingYing was tied into her seat. She stared at Junior, emotionless.

But her pale wrists were red raw where she'd wrenched against the bonds. Her shirt hung askew on her shoulder, the thin fabric rippling in the howling wind.

Falcon and I tried to lunge for Lory and Benji, to get the seats between us and the Superior psycho.

Junior's hand whipped around, aiming a pistol at Falcon's head.

"I am having a *conversation*," he snarled.

Falcon yelled over the noise of rotors and rain. "She'll never listen to you while you've got her all tied up like a fucking rapist."

Junior stood, sneering. "What would you know?"

"A lot, actually! I have the best relationship in the world, and she knows I'd do anything for her!"

Junior swayed. "I have killed for love."

"And I would die for love!" Falcon's wings flexed.

"Which proves how stupid you are."

As Falcon held Junior's attention, with every lurch and sway of the helicopter, I eased a little closer to the cockpit.

Falcon tried to put his hands on his hips but had to grab a seat to steady himself. "I'm not the one who's tied up his girlfriend because he's afraid of her."

"Only an idiot wouldn't be afraid of Lin JingYing." Junior took an uneven step towards Falcon. "And only an idiot wouldn't be afraid of me."

"I am afraid of you," Falcon said. "But I'm here anyway.'

Junior steadied his aim. "Then you're still an idiot. I should remove you from the gene pool. For the good of your *species*."

With the next lurch, I opened my wing. Stabbing my feathers into the cockpit, I rammed a dozen controls and switches.

The autopilot died.

Everyone staggered. The helicopter lolled, caught the wind, banked into a tight turn. Junior stumbled. Falcon hit his head and tumbled onto Benji and Lory. As he fell, his wing flicked high and whacked Junior. Hard.

Junior careened towards the still-open door.

I caught myself on one seat as Junior grabbed another, halting his slide into the void.

The helicopter's spiral picked up speed. Falcon and I could still bail and flap to safety, but Lory and Benji were bound and tailless.

JingYing's dark hair whipped as she wrenched at the rope, her shoulders hunched, face contorted. She was screaming, unheard under the roar of the storm and the dying helicopter.

Then, I heard: "*She's okay. Tui and Hawk have Raven. She's okay.*"

Fighting the whirling gravity, I clawed along the seat and grabbed JingYing's seatbelt. Bracing my legs and wings, I snatched Hawk's knife from the holster.

"She's alive," I shrieked in JingYing's ear. "The Flight saved Raven. She's alive!" And I cut the Superior woman free.

She shoved me aside. I went tumbling through the cabin. Bruised and dizzy, I landed between Lory and the luggage. Blearily, I watched JingYing's form climb into the cockpit. The helicopter jerked. Seemed to flinch.

The whole world flipped. My eyes closed.

And then it was calm.

"Are we dead?" Falcon yelled.

Warily, I cracked an eye. The wind and rain still battered the craft, and its rotors still roared.

"Don't think so." I tasted blood. Trying to move quickly, I rolled to my knees, and nearly sliced myself with the knife I was still clutching in a death grip. It nearly had been a death grip, too, I realised. I'd almost stabbed myself while crashing through the cabin. Instead, blood oozed through my jacket sleeve and from my forehead.

"Holy flock, Kess. Gimme that." Falcon snatched the knife and sawed at the ropes around Lory and Benji.

Lory was sobbing. As she didn't have a Bluetooth or radio headset, I had to lipread. "I'm sorry, I'm sorry…" She clutched the phone to her chest. "I didn't think he'd really … I'm so sorry!"

My eyes widened, and I grabbed her shoulders. "It's okay!" I shouted. "The others saved Raven. She's alive."

Lory gaped. Then she flung her arms around me. "Oh, thank god…"

Falcon had his hand out to Benji. But as the pale, bruised Icarus went to take it, he looked past us. He cried out. Pointed.

Junior was dragging himself back inside, although he struggled to gain purchase on the wet exterior of the helicopter. His headset was gone, his blond hair plastered to his face. There was no fear in his wild blue eyes; only apoplectic fury.

Beyond him, the military helicopter descended into view through the lashing rain.

If we didn't go now, he'd slam the door closed, and we'd be trapped.

Wiping blood from my eyes, I braced my legs, tensed my wings. Aimed for Junior's rising figure.

If I could knock him out of the helicopter…

JingYing blocked my path. Shoulders hunched, she reached for Junior. I'd lost my chance.

With JingYing's help, Junior climbed into the doorway. But, before he was safely inside, her arm became a rigid bar, holding him just on the cusp of safety.

"We are them," JingYing said, her voice rough over the radio, loud enough for Junior to hear. "They are us." Under her rain-soaked shirt, I saw her hunched back ripple and flex.

And two small, blood-drenched wings ripped from her shoulders.

I yelped. The others swore, and gasped. Over the radio came the Flight's shocked yells.

Junior's mouth opened. He flinched, wrenching himself from her grip. Backwards.

There was no slow motion, no horrific moment in which he hung in the air. He was just there one second and had vanished the next.

Frederik Larrsson, Junior, fell.

And was gone.

For a long moment, we stared at the empty space where he'd been, now filled with nothing but knives of rain.

Then Falcon said, quietly, "Bet he wishes he had wings now."

Benji slapped a hand to his mouth, and Lory gasped. "Falcon!"

I stared at him, felt the pressure rising in my throat. Then I burst out laughing and crying, all at the same time.

And I didn't stop the whole way back to land.

# 31

# HAWK

I spiraled lower, scanning the waves. The storm had briefly eased, the rain now less voluminous than the sea spray accumulating on my feathers. The wind was steady, but it would soon pick up again, more ferocious than before.

There.

Junior's body, half-submerged, slid up a wave and down the other side.

This was not a job the Coast Guard should risk their lives for. Not when we were right here with the correct equipment. So, the USCG boat watched from a distance, and I focused on the practicalities of the task.

Grief and horror could come later.

Angling into the strong wind, I barely needed to flap as I hovered above the body, waiting for Dad to bring over the HH-60. Soon, the powerful downdraft and rescue basket were descending beside me.

It didn't take me long to guide the basket into the waves and underneath the body. I made the circular hand motion and the line went tight, winching its sorry cargo out of the water.

The whole time, I avoided looking at its face.

The rain and wind were picking up as I climbed back into the HH-60. With the rescue basket winched close to the fuselage, Dad turned the helo for home.

Jing Ying, piloting the Evolutionary craft, was as good as her radioed word. With Lory, Benji, Falcon, and Kestrel on board, she kept precisely 500 yards ahead of the HH-60 the whole way to the Joint Forces Training Base. It was, as Dad said, the least political place to land, as well the site of the tent prison. Sorry, I meant field hospital.

Personnel were already on hand to deal with the fallout (excuse the terrible pun) of the rescue mission. The basket was unhooked, covered, and carted off at top speed, so the HH-60 could land within minutes of arrival. By then, the Evolutionary helicopter had been grounded, the door had been cleared to open, and our friends were sprinting through the pouring rain toward us.

Leah and Drew bolted from the cover of the nearest hangar and ran for their children. Coming from the HH-60, I wasn't far behind them as I crashed into Kestrel. Falcon and Tui reunited a step later.

"What happened? Are you okay? Does Junior have to die a second time?" I asked, trying to hold Kess tight but also inspect the congealed runnels of blood on her face.

Crying, laughing, she shook her head. "Self-inflicted, I'm afraid. With your knife, actually."

Cold shivered through my arms, spine, and wings. "I'm never lending it to you again."

"Fine by me. I'll never steal it again, either." She buried her face in my soaking jacket.

"Deal."

Condor approached, his arm around Raven. From the other direction, JingYing walked towards us. The LAPD officers, who'd been waiting to arrest anyone who looked suspicious, followed her at a distance.

"Uh, Kess?" I murmured.

"Mm?"

"Did I hit my head again? JingYing looks like she has wings!"

Without loosening her grip, Kestrel wriggled so she could see the young Chinese woman approach. "Uh, yeah. It happened while you were rescuing Raven. It scared Junior to … well, death."

"Huh."

"I'll give you the replay later," she whispered, as the Flight faced the newest, and most unexpected, Icarus on the planet.

"Thank you for saving my sister." JingYing's voice was hoarse, like she'd been screaming.

"Thanks for saving us," Falcon said. "Didn't really want to be on a helicopter that wanted to be a submarine instead."

"I have questions," Tui said. "Heaps of questions."

"Yes. I know." JingYing sighed, and shivered. Her new, small wings twitched. I felt a sympathy twinge in my own. "I have many questions too. So do the police. And now that Frederik…" She wiped at her eyes. "I will need some time."

"We'll take care of Raven until you're ready to talk," Condor said, quietly.

JingYing looked at Raven. Raven looked steadily back. They nodded at the same moment; the movement eerily similar.

As the Evolutionary Icarus heir left with the LAPD, Falcon said, "I bet there's a team of lawyers already waiting at the station."

I snorted. "I'm pretty sure she can afford bail."

"Junior kidnapped her too, you know," Lory said, as the Richardsons came closer. "She landed the helicopter as Junior's soldier boys dragged us up the stairs. She ordered them to let us go, so Junior had them tie her up as well."

Benji was glancing around. "Where's Luke?"

After Dad joined us and used his Colonel voice to summon a guide, a bemused but polite airman escorted us into a nearby building. Luke had been stashed by a huge window.

"About time you guys remembered I was–" He and his wheelchair disappeared under the Flight group hug. When he was visible again, he was blushing.

"This guy," Falcon said to Lory and Ben, while pointing at Luke, "is the best damn mission slash air traffic controller a Flight could ask for. If he hadn't been so frickin' onto it, we'd never have locked onto you guys so quickly–"

"Literally, in Condor's case," Tui said, grinning.

"–and we might have lost you."

Lory threw her arms around Luke's neck. "Thank you, Luke!"

Benji limped over to shake Luke's hand. "Thanks."

"Are you hurt?" Luke asked, holding on just a little too long.

Ben shrugged, dark feathers rustling. "Just a bit banged up. Nothing like what they did to you."

"Oh my god, get a room, you two!" Lory laughed.

The two guys immediately dropped their hands and turned almost identical shades of red.

"Let's go, lads and lasses," Leah said. "The sooner I've checked you up, the sooner we can all check out."

Lory insisted on pushing Luke back to the field hospital, where Leah promised we would *not* be sealed in. But Ben's pained, limping gait proved too slow for his hyperactive sister.

"You should ride with Luke!"

"Uh–"

Ben was suddenly in Luke's lap and they were being accelerated across the concrete at high speed, Lory laughing at full volume, oblivious to the audience of astonished military personnel.

"Does that girl ever slow down?" Kestrel blinked. "I thought she'd just been rescued from a highly traumatizing hostage situation?"

"Oh, believe me, she'll crash soon, and crash hard," Drew said, with an affectionate sigh.

"Hopefully not while she's pushing those boys, though," Leah added. "We'd better catch up. See you shortly."

They dashed after their rogue offspring.

Dad's work phone rang. "Owen," he answered. "Yes?"

As Dad talked, Condor beckoned to Falcon, Tui and Raven. "We'll see you guys there," he said to me. "Say thanks to your dad from us." They headed after the Richardsons and Luke's hijacked wheelchair.

"Yes, sir," Dad said. "I'll be there in fifteen minutes." He put the phone away and pulled me into a bear hug.

"You've got to go?" I guessed.

"The general wants a full explanation about why I abandoned the rescue platoon in town and went on a joyride over the harbor." Dad chuckled. "I don't think I'll get in too much trouble, seeing as we successfully rescued Captain Richardson's children, and the Air Force's reputation along with them."

My wings fidgeted. "And there was no fighting, right?"

"No. The Evolutionary security guards were uncooperative, but not idiotic. And when the Coast Guard caught up to that superyacht, its crew were so shocked that they surrendered immediately. The yacht is impounded and awaiting full forensic investigation – along with that fancy helo over there."

"What about the two women they found?" Kestrel asked, timidly. "Are they dead? Do we know who they were?"

Dad's smile faded. "We have to wait for the coroner's report, of course, but Dr Richardson identified Christine Goldberg. Although no handbag or phone was found for the other, she's been unofficially identified as a member of senior Evolutionary management known as Madame."

"Whoa," I said, feeling lightheaded.

Kestrel flicked a thumb at the private helicopter, already fenced with police tape. "I think you'll find her stuff in there," she said. "Lory had a phone. I think that was the locator that we were following, till Junior wised up and turned it off."

Dad nodded. "Makes sense that the bastard would grab it – and that he could unlock an employee's phone. I'm sure it has even more juicy evidence. The LAPD will find out and let us know." He checked his watch. "Got to go. Ty, please call your mother. I've already told her it's over, but she'll want to hear it from you, too."

"Yes, Dad."

"I'll remind him," Kestrel said, with a faint smile.

One more hug for both of us, and Dad was gone.

With noticeable sagging of our shoulders, Kess and I headed for the hospital tent. But it seemed we weren't done quite yet.

"Tyler! Hey, Tyler! Over here, you weirdo!"

"Huh?" Stumbling to a halt, I swung around, brown feathers brushing the wet pavement. Two very familiar people in CAP uniform strode towards us.

"Holy crap! It is him!" the shorter, darker figure said to the taller blonde one.

She eyed me as they came closer. "Yep. It's Tyler Owen, all right. You've got a nerve showing up here after the stunt you pulled, Lieutenant."

I sensed Kestrel easing nearer. Heard the indignant vibrating of her feathers. And I suppressed the grin.

"I don't report to you anymore, Cadet Captain Blondie," I retorted, glaring at the college student.

Her hands lifted threateningly. "You'd better show some respect, or you'll get your ass handed to you."

"Yeah?"

"Yeah."

"Yeah," chimed in the smaller one with the hopeful attempt at a moustache.

Glowering, we squared off for a heartbeat more.

Then we all burst out laughing. Nico and Hayley closed the gap, grabbing my hands and pulling me in for a shoulder bump and back slap.

"Look at you!" Nico chortled. "I always said you were a freak!"

I pulled a mock salute, flexing my wings. "Guilty as charged."

"You could have at least texted to confirm you hadn't busted your head open," Hayley said, reproachfully. "Do you know how long it took me to build up the courage to climb into a plane again, after seeing you fall past me to your apparent death?"

"About twenty-four hours?" I grinned.

Nico snorted. "Close. She was back in the air after a week."

"Would have been sooner, but all skydives were cancelled for investigation." Hayley crossed her arms. "Thanks for messing up my schedule."

"You're welcome." Then I raised an eyebrow. "How come you guys are here?"

"Sightings of flying people were all over social media," Nico said. "We had to come see for ourselves."

"And they nearly didn't let us on base," Hayley complained.

"Like you'd ever take no for an answer." I chuckled. "You're the toughest human female I ever met."

"Human female?"

"Nico, Hayley, meet Kestrel. Smartest, bravest, and modest-est woman I know." I hooked my wing around Kess, nudging her closer. "And my girlfriend."

"Hi," she said, a little shyly.

Nico and Hayley's eyes widened at Kestrel's battered and bloodstained appearance. "Uh, hi, Kestrel, are you okay?" Hayley asked, warily.

"You should see the other guy," Kess said, almost controlling the tremor in her voice.

"Who's the other guy?" Nico asked, through a tight grin. "Not Tyler, is it?"

I squeezed Kess's shoulder. "Nah. He was a super-rich super-genius super-brat, who kidnapped our friends, murdered a few people, and is currently on his way to the morgue."

"Thanks, *babe*, now they think I'm a killer," Kestrel said, with false brightness, as Nico and Hayley took an unconscious half-step back.

Shaking her head, Hayley held out her hand. "No, we're just impressed. I hope Tyler's doing enough to deserve you."

The tension in Kestrel's wings eased as she accepted the handshake. "Yeah, he'll do."

The girls laughed as I shrugged at Nico.

"Oi, Hawk! Kestrel!" Falcon bellowed from a distance. "Hurry up!"

"Sorry, guys. Duty calls." I saluted my old friends, and they automatically returned the gesture.

"At least text us, this time?" Nico called, as Kestrel and I walked away.

I made the 'okay' sign, then took Kess's hand in mine.

And it hit me. I actually *could* text them. I could take back some parts of my old life, like my family, my friends. All the stuff I'd missed so much.

I glanced down at Kestrel's damp, messy blonde head, and wrapped my wing around her. I'd take the good parts of my old life, and blend them with the best parts of my new life.

Finally, the danger was over.

We were safe.

# 32

# HAWK

Falcon, Tui, Raven, and Luke were sitting in the tent's 'living room'. The voices of Lory, Ben, and their parents echoed down the tunnel.

"Took you guys long enough!" Falcon jeered at me and Kess. "You missed out on the big event!"

"Uh…" I glanced at Kestrel, who shrugged. "Bigger than rescuing Lory, Ben, and Raven?"

"Yes! Well, kind of." Leaning on the wheelchair handles, Falcon swung the blushing Luke around to face us. "Meet Weka!"

"Wecker?" I repeated, bewildered.

"Weh-kah," Tui corrected. "Luke has been offered and accepted a Flight name. A weka is a ground-based bird. It's curious, intelligent, and a good swimmer."

"Aw!" Kess said, clapping her hands together. "It's perfect!"

Lory bounced in, trailed by a distant "*Take it easy, lassie!*"

"Yes, Mom!" Lory did a victory lap of the plastic room, hugging everyone as she went.

"You okay, sis?" Tui managed, as the hug nearly choked her.

Lory giggled. "Everything hurts but I don't care! I have neeeeeews!"

I dropped into a folding chair. It creaked ominously. "Not you, too?"

Lory posed by the tunnel entrance, cleared her throat, and made a series of almost-musical 'dah, da-dah!' noises, accompanied by jazz hands.

"May I introduce … TERN!"

Her brother entered, red-faced. "Thanks, Lory," he muttered.

"Eh, nice!" Tui said.

"My turn!" Falcon cried. He imitated Lory's intro. "Lory, Tern, may I introduce you to … Weka!"

As congratulations and exclamations flowed, I leaned over to Kestrel.

"What a bunch of weirdos," I joked, quietly.

She nudged me. "You can talk." She kissed my cheek, then she stroked my jaw. "You need to shave."

A huge yawn forced its way out. "I need a nap," I grumbled. As I came down off the adrenaline rush and the serotonin high from saving our friends, I agreed with Lory.

Everything hurt.

I stayed semi-upright long enough to accompany Kestrel through her own check-up, wound-cleaning, stitching, and bandaging. And then I crashed so hard, I have no memory of anything that happened after that.

\*

Unsurprisingly, as soon as Mrs Carter heard about Luke's 'adventures', she rushed to retrieve him. She insisted she didn't blame us, and totally believed everything was safe now the Big Bad Guy of the Evolutionaries was gone, but she really needed to take Luke to see his father. Mr Carter was being transferred to Sacramento, and Mrs Carter was working on getting their old home back.

Privately, I doubted our friend Weka would be content to stay in that small town, especially when I noticed how long he and Tern hugged each other goodbye.

We were released from medical supervision a few days later, when JingYing provided proof that Junior's virus was only contagious by blood, and only induced mild symptoms in regular humans. Why Icari had been more susceptible would probably be debated for years.

It could join the list.

The Flight were more interested in the job offers coming in. Apparently, someone on the USCG cutter had filmed my retrieval of ocean flotsam, and word had got out about our dramatic air-sea hostage rescue. This had led to the crazy idea that we flying freaks might actually be useful. The offers ranged from search-and-rescue training opportunities, to security patrol positions, to urgent medical courier roles.

Dad had even hinted that his superiors were *very* interested in talking to the Flight about our opinion on surveillance drones. After all, Icari couldn't be hacked, and if our communications were jammed, we still had a brain.

However, Tui and Leah each put their foot down. We needed to rest and recover, they said, and the serious offers would still be open when we were ready.

Unfortunately, Raven didn't stay to recover with us. She was still small, and her voice still sounded young, but something else had changed. Something deeper. And it wasn't just the strangely adult vocabulary and speech patterns, either.

She knew it, too. At first, we all tried to treat her the same as ever, but we could feel the slight stiffness and tension when we hugged her, and saw her withdraw when we asked too many questions about her time with JingYing.

"I'm not Raven anymore," she said, sadly, a few evenings after the big rescue. "And I'm not YanWei. I don't know who I am."

"You're both, I think, sis," Tui said, gently, touching her hand. "It's part of growing up. It's normal."

Slowly, Raven nodded. "I need to see my sister," she said, quietly.

Condor smiled. "Bet she's impatient for flying lessons, too."

"I still think it was a trick," Falcon declared. "There's no way she could have busted out a real pair of wings at the perfect dramatic moment like that."

Kestrel calmly laid down a winning hand of cards, and Falcon the drama queen fell off his chair, clutching his chest. Kess ignored him. "I bet JingYing compared her DNA with Raven's and saw the match. She may have tried to recreate the chemical trigger, and tested it on herself."

"I think stress hormones also have something to do with it, eh," Tui said. "When the time is right, and our bodies are on edge for an extended period, then bam! The Change kicks in."

"I was building up to my solo skydive," I remembered.

Condor's voice was low. "Abuelita had been deteriorating for a while."

"I was under house arrest," Kestrel said, casually.

"What?!" Falcon exclaimed.

Kestrel met his gaze with a raised eyebrow. "What about you, Fal?"

"My dad was having a rough patch with his recovery," he begrudgingly admitted. "Money was tight, Mom had to work too much, I felt like a burden. That was pretty stressful."

Tui nodded. "I was studying for major scholarship exams."

"JingYing knew she was losing Frederik," Raven said, softly. "She did love him. The way he was before. Before ... the Flight. Then he changed, and she was lonely."

"She must be even more lonely now," Tui said.

Raven nodded. "I must go home."

"We'll have to go soon, too," Tern said. He and Lory had been unusually quiet, perhaps sensing this was something the original Flight needed to discuss.

"Yeah," I said. "We'll miss you, Raven, you know that."

She smiled. "But I will call, and we can visit all the time." Her smile turned wicked. "And I have a private jet now."

JingYing picked her up on that private jet the very next day. It was bizarre seeing a bunch of Evolutionary security guards who weren't trying to catch or kill us. I supposed I'd get used to it eventually.

It was also hard to re-adjust to city living. The constant noise, the smog, and the presence of other people and their questions and stares were tiring. And I wasn't the only Icarus who thought so.

So, after some time with my family in LA, the Flight retreated to the Richardsons' farm and settled in for the winter.

Now that we actually had a future, we could take our time deciding what it would look like.

★

"...but *centrifugal* force is fictional, says right here. Should be centripetal."

"Yes, but it depends on your point of view. If you're the thing that it's affecting, then it's called centrifugal to–"

Yawning, I thumped out of the bedroom. "Guys, it's way too early to be arguing about physics."

"It's never too early for education," Lory said, grinning.

Tern grumbled. "Imaginary invisible forces make my cereal taste bad."

"It's not imaginary, it's relativity," Lory said.

"But–"

"She's right, Tern," I said, yawning again. "Because we're describing it from our point of view, and our frame of reference is rotating, then it's centrifugal. Like spinning on the roundabout at a playground. You feel the centrifugal force pulling at your arms and legs, but the school bullies call it centripetal as they spin it faster and faster and don't let you off."

Condor snorted. "Speaking from experience?"

"I wasn't always tough and badass."

"And you're still not," Falcon said, his head emerging from the cabover bunk.

"Flock you, Falcon."

"Good morning to you too, Hawkie-bae."

"All right, how about this." Lory leaned her elbows on the table, reading off her phone. "An insect has six limbs. An Icarus has six limbs. Therefore, Icari are insects. Discuss."

Rolling my eyes, I flicked a wing and buried my head in the fridge as Falcon howled with laughter. Behind him, Tui grumbled about oversimplification of science and internet trolls and, judging by the muffling halfway through, yanked the pillow over her head.

As the Flight continued debating the most bizarre random crap trawled from the depths of the internet Icarus insanity, Kestrel appeared, still warm and fuzzy from bed, and snuggled under my arm.

"Morning," she said, as I kissed her head. "What are we doing today?"

Lory swung around, green eyes sparkling through her reading glasses. "Oh, you will enjoy this."

*

"Ready, Hawkie-bae?" Falcon yelled.

"More than you are!" I hollered back, my breath smoking through my face shield and curling away in the headwind.

Tui's voice crackled in my ear. "We're wearing comms, bros. You don't have to shout anymore."

Falcon chuckled, which I heard both from his position a hundred feet off my right wing and through the thing in my left ear. "Yes, Miss."

"The wind reduction is working well at cruising speed," said Lory, also in my ear. "Are you boys going to test it, or are you still busy making googly eyes at each other?"

There was a jumble of loud snorts and chuckles.

"Would the good ship Fawk set sail already, please?" my girlfriend said, over the comms. "I'm tired of testing, I'm freezing, and now the sun's setting, it's only getting colder."

"Thought you Brits were used to the cold," Falcon teased.

Lory laughed. "You should visit Scotland sometime."

"I think my wings have frozen shut," Tui said. "Please hurry your feathery arses up, bro."

Falcon chortled. "Don't you want us to hurry our feathery asses DOWN?"

"You've got ten seconds to start or I'm going back in the RV and locking the barn door behind me."

"Okay, okay. Time to dive, Hawkie!"

"Uh…" Dragging my eyes from the ice-crusted farm far below, I tried to swipe at my smartwatch to check my reminders, but my gloves didn't work on the touchscreen. Or on the second watch I appeared to be wearing right next to it.

There was a long sigh on the Flight channel. "I propose buying Hawk a whiteboard to hang around his neck. All in favour say, aye."

"Shut up, Falcon," Kestrel said, calmly. "Hawk, we're testing the altimeters and the new deadcat on your headcomm blimp. I got that right, didn't I, Lory?"

"Oh, definitely."

"That's the fluffy thing currently stuck in my ear?" I said, nudging it.

"Yes. The wind noise was dreadful, so we're trying the fluffy things to see if they'll reduce it without attenuating vocal clarity. And the altimeters got reset, so we're testing the accuracy of their descent acceleration with the new GPS security updates."

"I love it when you talk tech-sy to me."

Falcon mock-gasped. "Flirting with someone else in FRONT of me? How could you?!"

"Shut up, Falcon," Tui, Kestrel, and Lory all said. Tern and Condor laughed.

I followed Fal in a wide curve above the north point of the valley. The ridge sprouted a group of new wind turbines, all spinning in the steady breeze and packing electricity into the farm's vast bank of brand-new batteries – one of the many awesome new features that were transforming this place into the perfect Flight retreat.

We were safe, we were well-fed, and we were actually able to have fun. It was pretty much heaven. Apart from the flocking freezing winter temperature. Now I was flying with the wind, it was sliding up my flight jacket. I shivered.

"All I got to do is dive?" I asked, trying to re-focus.

"Yup! Even you can manage that!" Falcon waggled his dark brown wings. "*Toru, rua, tahi!* Go!"

I was taken off-guard by Falcon's use of Tui's Māori language. His dark tail was already a hundred feet ahead and accelerating, the tips of his folded wings stretching back past his boots.

With a yelp, I gave chase. Freefall tingles rushed through me, then the wind was trying to yank off my aviator hat, the chinstrap digging into my throat. The freezing air streamed through my feathers.

Scraps of frozen cloud whipped by, and the valley grew bigger. The rushing air stripped the warmth from my face shield and every breath stung my lungs. But the exhilaration overrode all pain. I whooped.

The wind turbines zipped past, and still Falcon dived. I kept up, nudging a wing-elbow every few breaths to slalom around a particularly tall conifer. The wind dragged on my wing bones, and my chest muscles burned. I yelled in joy again.

"Hi, babe!" Falcon bellowed.

Five figures waved as we shot overhead. Tui, Kestrel, Lory, Condor, and Tern were so bundled up, the only way I could tell them apart was by the color of the wingtips that brushed the snowy barn roof they stood on.

The Flight and the farm buildings were wiped away by the fields as Falcon and I careened down the valley.

"Last one to the waterfall is a rotten egg!" Falcon's wings flapped hard, wispy treetops surging in his wake.

"You're on!"

As Falcon threw his left wing high to swing around a tree, I twist-dived.

Falcon yelped, his wings faltering as I whipped through his personal airspace.

"Cheat!" he howled as I took the lead.

"Nah, I'm just the better flyer!"

Falcon's flaps accelerated, right on my literal tail.

I sprinted for the south end of the valley, cutting Falcon off. There was the little waterfall, snowmelt gushing from the peaks above. Less than half a mile away now.

As I was distracted by the way water twisted in the air, Falcon finally overtook me with a high-pitched giggle. He shot over the waterfall. I flashed past only a second later.

"I win!"

"Because I let you!"

"Did not!"

"Boys," Tui said over the comms, "can you at least pretend you're nearly grown-ups?"

Falcon spun through an aileron roll. "Why do today what you can put off till tomorrow?"

"You'd better not put off cooking dinner. It's your night on duty."

Condor came on the line. "And I'm starving after beating you three races in a row."

"Yeah, yeah…"

The good-natured banter continued as Falcon and I returned to base. Technically, Lory and her brother Tern had bedrooms in the old farmhouse. But seeing as their parents were on the front lines of the current health crisis and wouldn't be home for a while, they preferred to hang out in the RV barn with the rest of the Flight.

The satellite broadband connection and massive TV might also have had something to do with it.

By the time Fal and I sauntered into the barn, where we now had a big barbecue, sofas, and a proper basketball hoop, Condor was deep in discussion with the girls about the day's equipment tests, and Tern was swinging idly in the hammock strung between two barn poles. He was video calling someone, and I didn't need to see the screen to know who.

"So," I murmured, slipping into the seat next to Kestrel. "Have Tern and Weka finally succumbed to the inevitable and made it official?"

"Not yet." Kestrel grinned as she removed the dead-fluffy-cat-thing from my ear, switched it off, and packed it away in a charging case. "Want to adjust your bet? Sweepstakes now include power of veto on Movie Night."

"Nah. Within the next two days. I'm sure of it. They've called each other every morning and night for the last week."

"Long distance relationships are hard, though."

"Not as hard as some other stuff we've lived through."

"True."

Falcon began yodeling along to some pop hit in the RV's kitchen, and I crossed my eyes in exaggerated pain. "Can I have the earplugs back?"

Kess just laughed.

"What's next on the shopping list?" I asked, louder, to the rest of the table.

Condor leaned back on his wings. "The cash won't last forever, you know. We can't keep splurging on gadgets."

"Are we nearly out already?" I pulled a sad face. "And I was so looking forward to those AR smart goggles that Tern was talking about."

"Once you get a job, bro, you can spend your money on whatever you want." Tui stood and stretched.

Lory shivered theatrically. "In the meantime, you're on fire duty. And we're still cold. Hint, hint."

"Aye aye." Chuckling, I went to light the evening's blaze in the barn's 'fire bin', 'rustic brazier', or 'hobo drum', depending who you asked.

Condor wandered over as I fed kindling to the infant flames.

"Hey, Hawk," he said.

"Yo."

Quietly, we watched the flames twist and crackle. Falcon's distant racket continued drifting from the RV; the girls chatted at the table, and Tern swung idly in the hammock.

And I thought, *This is nice.*

Eventually, Condor resettled his black wings. "Can I ask you something?"

"Yeah, obviously." I snorted. "I might not answer though. Depends on the question."

Con laughed. "Fair. It could be a little personal. So, you don't have to."

Curiously, I studied him across the glowing mouth of the fire drum. "Okay?"

"You and Kestrel ... you guys are good together. You seem happy."

"Because we are," I said, a little guardedly.

Condor smiled. "Oh, I know. That wasn't my question."

"Then what is? You're starting to worry me, now."

"Sorry. My question is, how did you know?"

I frowned. "Know what?"

Condor's wings resettled again. "That she was interested in you, and that you were genuinely interested in her. That it's real."

"Real love?"

"Something like that."

I poked the fire with the old iron rod we'd found on the farm. "It just fits. I can just be me. She's my best friend." I glanced up. "We know the best and the worst things about each other, and she still likes me, so you can bet this farm I'm not letting her go."

Condor sighed. "I'm happy for you."

"But sad for yourself?"

"Not sad. Just confused."

I dropped a couple of split logs on the fire. "What's really up, Condor?"

He showed me his phone. It was a message from Dove.

*Mon amie, I miss you. I hope you are okay. Text me back?*

"And this is confusing because?" I said, slowly.

Condor scrolled up, showing the messages he'd sent every other day over the past few weeks. They were all friendly; sharing genuine Flight news and hopes for Dove to respond sometime soon.

"I was getting worried because she wasn't replying," he said. "Then she does, and it's like she never received any of my earlier texts."

"Maybe she didn't," I said. "Maybe they got lost in cyberspace, or she got a new phone, or they were blocked by the French government for being too hot to handle." That got a smile. Phew.

"I guess so."

"So, what's the problem?"

"I don't know. I just don't know what to say."

"Flocking hell, you're asking me? What do you want, a pickup line? A romantic song to sing under her window? A sonnet?"

"Uh, what?"

"How about this: Roses are red, the sky is blue, Junior's dead, and I *like* like you."

Condor couldn't reply. He was laughing too hard.

"You are terrible," he said, eventually.

"Told you I wasn't an angel." Smugly, I dropped more wood into the now-roaring fire. "If, now she can't have you, she's realized she does actually want you, then she'll soon make it obvious. Otherwise – well, there might not be plenty of fish in the sea, but it turns out there's about fifty bird kids on the planet. There are still forty we haven't met yet. Chances are, one of them will be willing to put up with you."

Tern's laugh, at something Weka had said or done, made us both glance over.

"Or," I added, dropping my voice, "it appears there is hope for at least one Icarus-human relationship in the very near future. So, you never know what will happen. Just let it happen! You're still only seventeen, you know."

Condor smiled. "You're right. Thanks, Hawk."

"You were wise to seek my counsel," I quipped.

"Now you sound like Falcon."

"You're right. I must be light-headed from hunger. Let's see if Falcon's stopped trying to sing long enough to finish dinner."

# 33

# TUI

The Flight looked up from their laptops, then Falcon ran over.

"Hey babe, I missed you!"

"I've been gone two hours, bro," I said into his shoulder, but hugged him back just as tight.

"But I still missed you! Didn't you miss me?"

"Yeah nah, of course." Although, Leah's instruction style was so rapid and intense, I hadn't had time to think about anything except the exact steps for emergency blood transfusions since I'd entered the training 'clinic' she'd set up in the farmhouse. "How was school this morning?"

"We were supposed to be doing maintenance on the wind turbines but because of the rain, Drew postponed that to tomorrow. We had to do electrical engineering research in the meantime to get ready for the maintenance lesson," Hawk said, reading off a page in his exercise book.

"Remember any of it?" Falcon teased.

Hawk flipped him his middle finger. "I was the one teaching you, remember?"

"Yeah, *I* remember."

I sat in one of the Icarus-customised seats; chairs with low-cut backrests.

"What've you been doing, babe?" Falcon asked, sitting next to me.

"Blood stuff," I said, suddenly exhausted. As much as I loved learning from Leah, the no-nonsense Scottish doctor was somehow cramming months' worth of training into my brain in a matter of weeks.

Lory dropped onto the stool on my other side and squeezed my free hand. "You've got the afternoon and a couple days off now, Tui," she said, brightly.

"We've got self-defence with Dad tomorrow," Tern said, looking at the timetable on the wall.

Hawk flicked through this notebook. "Am I–"

"Yep, you're helping me tutor the others," Lory said, jumping up again. Her red feathers bumped my arm. "Sorry, Tu!"

I leaned my head on Falcon's shoulder. "Any other news?"

"Raven messaged us," Condor said. "JingYing's flying lessons are going well. No surprise there. Raven sent a video too. You'll never guess where they're training."

"Tell me, then."

"In the hangar-sized wind tunnel at the Evolutionary HQ."

"What? The one they tortured us in?" My hand slipped to the pounamu around my neck, and I shivered.

"Yeah, that was a bit creepy watching that. But I suppose it makes sense. No one can fly a drone over, or video them, if they're in there."

"A desert worked pretty well, I thought," Hawk grumbled. "No walls to bang your head on, either."

"Will Raven visit soon?" Kess asked, changing the subject.

"I hope so," Lory said. "I'd love to get to know her better in person."

"We all need to get to know the new Raven a bit better." Kestrel swiped her screen. "No other major news, though, Tui. No sightings or media posts."

"And the latest update to the Fawk fanfic is totally disappointing," Falcon said, irritably. "Everyone can skip it."

Lory giggled. "You're just annoyed they had Hawk winning the Flight Games and you coming last."

I didn't bother asking. After the number of conspiracy theories, Icarus Hunt websites, and other online stalker activity had passed into the hundreds, I refused to listen to any of it. I relied on the rest of the Flight to keep me updated with the critical points.

The Falcon-Hawk slashfiction saga did not meet the criteria.

As the others finished packing up the laptops, tablets, notebooks, and spare electric parts that were scattered around the homeschool room, my phone buzzed. It was a reminder: *Video call with Mum in 5 minutes.*

"See you guys at lunch," I said, grabbing a laptop.

Kestrel half-smiled. "We'll make sure Falcon and Hawk don't eat your share."

"I would never!" Falcon protested.

Hawk snorted. "Yeah, you would."

Falcon folded his arms and sat next to me. "I'll prove it by waiting till–"

"Go on, bro." I nudged him with my wing elbow. "I'm just catching up with Mum. I won't be long."

After a show of protest, Falcon left with the others, blowing kisses at me on the way out. His PDAs were ridiculous but, secretly, I loved it that he loved me that much. That he didn't feel any shame in being such an affectionate lunatic.

I'd introduced him to Mum weeks ago, but only let him sit in one out of three calls a week since, otherwise I never got a word in to my own mum on the other side of the world.

"There's my Tui!" she said, speaking in te reo Māori. "Baby, I miss you so much. I love you!"

"I love you too, Mum," I said, also speaking our native language. "How are you? How's Ria?"

My little sister was fine, apparently, but was with her dad for the weekend. "Aw, I wanted to see her," I said.

"I know, baby, but I wanted to talk to you privately."

My feathers stood on end. "Oh, yeah?"

"Tui, darling, I'm sorry it's taken me so long to answer you, but I'm ready to talk about your father now."

Shivering, I resettled on the stool, re-angled the laptop screen, and brushed back my hair. "Okay."

At the beginning, my calls with Mum had been super emotional, and I'd struggled to explain everything that had happened without too much traumatic detail. Besides, half of the first call had been her yelling at me for not telling her about the wings and then running away, and the other half was both of us crying (not that I would ever let anyone, even Falcon, know that). I guessed it had taken her this long to accept that I really had wings, and that I was in America.

I wanted to go home. So much. But even if I did make it through the airport with my wings and without the right documents, the whole world was being turned upside down right now. There were no planes to take. It was safer to stay put.

But I missed my mum. I missed my whenua and my whānau. And I knew they missed me.

"Tui, baby, just remember everything I ever did was to protect you, all right? Because I love you. You know that, eh?"

"Yeah, Mum, I know. But I realised something dodgy must have happened." I flexed a wing. "But I guess you had a real good reason."

"Darling, here's the truth. After this, no more surprises, I promise."

I braced myself, and Mum began telling me the true story of my birth.

When my mum was twenty-two, she'd met a handsome Samoan boy who was studying computing and information technology at university. They fell in love, and had been together for over a year by the time of my conception.

So far, so good. I knew this already. Then came the kicker.

After graduating with honours, my dad wanted to set up his own IT business. He was experiencing some challenges in Auckland – at that time, no one believed a Pasifika boy could be as tech-smart and business savvy as he was, not even his own parents – so he hatched a crazy plan. He would go to China and find a business partner there. With the booming Chinese economy, and their active interest in the Pacific, he was certain he'd find success. Then he could bring that back to Auckland, establish his IT empire and marry his sweetheart. My mum.

I listened with my mouth open as Mum explained that, because my dad would be away for ages, she insisted on accompanying him to Beijing. Things were going so well, they ended up staying for much longer than expected – and my Māori mum was lonely, unable to speak the language, and cut off from her whānau. She and my dad had the technology to communicate, but no one at home did.

So, they decided to try for a baby.

However, after multiple miscarriages, they found themselves in a little IVF clinic. The fertility doctor was super friendly to international couples.

Of course, I now knew 'Dr Kris Schmidt' had really been Dr Christine Goldberg, but I said nothing as Mum described how absolutely thrilled they were when, a couple of months later, they learned she was pregnant. With me. The IT business was booming; the Chinese partners loved my dad. Everything was perfect.

Then my dad was killed in a car crash.

The company collapsed; Mum flew home, unmarried and pregnant. My dad's parents took his body back to Samoa and refused to let Mum come to the funeral. They were upset that Mum and my dad had been living together 'in sin' for so long. They thought she'd corrupted him. When she told them she was pregnant, the pregnancy was still so early, they thought it wasn't possible. They believed Mum was lying to get her hands on his money – because they weren't married, and my still-young dad hadn't thought about making a will, his parents got everything, and Mum was left with nothing.

My mum's whānau rallied around, of course, but life is tough for a single mum. Politically, legally, emotionally, it was easier to tell people that I was an accidental pregnancy, that I was her miracle to remember my dad by. It was easier to not even mention Beijing, or the money. The gossip and misunderstandings were too painful.

So the story became simpler, and simpler, until it became the version I'd always known; my dad died in a car crash, and my mum discovered she was pregnant with his child only after he was buried in Samoa.

After Mum finally ran out of words, I stared at the table for a while. "Huh," I said, eventually.

"Forgive me, baby?"

Shaking myself, I looked up. "Nothing to forgive, Mum. It's not like you just told me my dad was in the All Blacks and, surprise, he's still alive!" Mum giggled, and hiccupped. "It wouldn't have made any difference to my life to know all the details. I mean, knowing I was conceived in a tube in Beijing might have cleared up heaps of confusion a lot earlier, but..." I shrugged all four shoulders. "My story now checks out with everything else I know, so it's actually a relief."

"I love you, Tui," Mum said, wiping her eyes. "And your dad did too. So much."

Swallowing hard, I managed to smile for my mum. "I know. I love you too."

"I'm sorry about what happened to you, baby."

"It's not your fault, Mum. You couldn't have known."

"If I ever meet that Schmidt bitch again, she'll get her arse kicked! Messing with my baby!"

I paused, wondering what to tell her. Then I just shook my head. "Don't worry, Mum. I know for a fact that karma's a bitch, too."

My phone buzzed. A message from Falcon: *Hawk's going to eat your food. I'm fighting him off, but I'm not sure how much longer I can last… argh blargh wham pow argh!*

My stomach gurgled. "I have to go. I love you, Mum."

"Love you, Tui."

The call ended, and I sat back.

The pieces of the puzzle were falling into place. I finally had the full outline of my past, and the shape of the future seemed brighter … except for that long, but not-long-enough shadow.

I realised life was too short for secrets. And my friends didn't know just how short.

It was time.

*

"I need to tell you guys something."

Conversation and eating paused. All eyes turned to me. I took a deep breath.

"I've done some calculations and research, and I've checked with Dr Leah. I'll have to run it by Raven and JingYing as well, but … here's the thing."

I hesitated, but Hawk caught my eye, and nodded. With relief, I realised Hawk remembered our midnight conversation from weeks ago.

The Flight waited expectantly, silent except for the fidgeting of feathers against the rough barn floor. The knowledge that Hawk had my back gave me the courage to spit it out.

"Being alive as an Icarus is pretty hard on our mostly-human bodies," I said, calmly as I could, not rushing, not revealing any anxiety. I hoped. "So, we'll wear them out quicker than most other people. And that means we'll hit the Icarus equivalent of old age a bit sooner than our human friends and family."

"How much sooner?" Condor asked, suspiciously.

My wings flicked. "To be honest, bro, I'll be impressed if we live to see fifty-five."

To my surprise, there was a sudden easing of tension.

"Jeez, Tui, don't scare me like that," Lory said, leaning back on her wing elbows with her hands clutched to her chest. "I thought you were going to say we had a life expectancy of twenty-five or something."

Falcon made a show of counting on his fingers. "That means we've still got thirty or forty years left. That's ages!"

"Well, not really–"

"It also means that, in Icarus years, we're already adults," Fal said, enthusiastically.

Kestrel chuckled. "Some of us, anyway."

Hawk put his arm around her. "It gives us plenty of time to enjoy ourselves, and maybe even track down those other kids that Goldberg tweaked. See if we can collect the whole set."

Falcon snorted.

Abruptly, Tern stood up. "I have to call Weka," he said, and made for the barn door.

"Uh, it only applies to Flight members with wings, Tern," Falcon called.

Tern ignored him and disappeared out into the long chilly shadows of the late winter afternoon.

Hawk held out his hand. "I'm cashing in my bet before bedtime. I guarantee it."

"You guys really aren't upset?" I asked, just to be sure.

"Tui," Condor said, gently. "We've been through so much, every day's a blessing. We will be fine."

"Especially as we have you looking after us, babe!" Falcon said, and planted a big sloppy kiss on my face in front of everyone.

"Thanks," I said, and wiped my cheek.

Just to make sure Falcon really was okay with the news that we were the opposite of immortal, I coaxed him into a late afternoon flight, just him and me.

After coasting around the valley, we landed above the little waterfall that was fast becoming one of the Flight's favourite spots. It offered a great view of the farm, and an elevated peek at the mountains beyond.

"…and they said as soon as the industry is back up and running, they want me to come in for training!" Falcon finished his massive exposition about his latest Hollywood job offer from a bigshot cinematographer, who'd seen Tern's edit of Fal's sports camera flying footage on YouTube. Something about stunts and steady cams had been mentioned. I had zoned out early, as Falcon got excited about a different job every week.

"Hollywood is trying to put on a more diverse face, I guess," I said, absently. "You don't get much more 'minority' than us."

Falcon pretended to pout. "And my hardcore flying skills have nothing to do with it, of course."

I snorted. "Of course not."

He chuckled, and my heart felt warm as I finally accepted that Falcon was truly comfortable with our 'life sentence'.

"Hey, check this out, babe," Falcon said, handing over his phone.

A regular teenager had photoshopped themselves to look like an Icarus. However, instead of their wings realistically matching their hair colour, they'd digitally painted fancy blue tips to their feathers. Beneath the images, a bunch of self-named 'Flight Fam' fans were heatedly debating how many bottles of hair dye it would take to colour an Icarus's wings.

"I never thought about colouring our feathers before," I said, swiping through the photos.

"You don't need to, babe, I love you just the way you are. You're hot." Falcon kissed my neck, but I nudged him away. He sat back, caressing my wings. "I mean it. Your feathers and hair are gorgeous."

"Imagine if we could dye our feathers as easily as hair, though," I said. "Not just blonde, but purple or green, or something."

"Rainbow wings!" Falcon laughed. "Flocking hell, yes! I'll have to try that one day!"

"I can imagine what Mum would say if I came home with purple hair and feathers."

"Oh yeah, what did your mom say?"

Leaning forward, elbows on knees, I picked some weeds from the rock and began knotting them around my fingers. "Actually…"

Falcon was uncharacteristically silent as I told him the truth about my conception.

"So … what do you think?" I said, a long time after I'd finished, and he still hadn't spoken.

"I think it's about time I called my mom, too," he said, quietly. "And I'm sorry about your dad."

Shrugging my wings, I flicked the shredded stems away. "I never knew him, so it's hard to miss him."

"Yeah, but his parents, your grandparents. That's rough."

"I have my mum and Ria, and my aunties and cousins and the rest of my whānau. I know my whakapapa. I'm okay."

"But they're so far away. Your kāinga is so far away."

"Eh, you said it right!" I kissed his cheek.

"Of course I did!"

"See, that's why I'm okay. I've got you. So, I can't be all that mad at Goldberg."

"Did you just say something mushy?" Falcon grinned. "This really is a significant day!"

"Oh, shut up. The point is, if Goldberg hadn't picked us for her project, then I'd never have met you."

"I have to take you home to meet my mom and dad. They'll never believe I managed to catch someone as awesome as you."

"Yeah, whatever."

"Although…" Unexpectedly, Falcon frowned and his dark wings flicked. "It suddenly occurs to me that my parents might have met your parents. In Beijing. In the clinic."

"Huh." I stared out at the valley. "I never thought of that either."

"We might have been next to each other as little lumps of cells in test tubes. That's crazy."

"Yeah."

Falcon got up and threw his arms and wings wide. "It means we're meant to be!" He spun around, and landed on one knee, grasping my hand with That Grin.

Quickly, I yanked it back and stood up. "We've talked about this! We're not even eighteen yet!"

"We will be, like, next month or something," Falcon said, refusing to get up, grabbing my hand again. "And you said yourself that our lives will be a bit ... concentrated. Why waste what time we've got?"

"We're not in some crappy teenage romance book, Falcon!"

My cheeks were burning even though there was no one else around. I covered my face with my free hand, still trying to tug the other out of Falcon's grip.

"Aw, come on, babe, you know I'm just teasing." Finally, he stood up, and his arms and wings surrounded me. I rested my face on his shoulder, taking deep breaths. "But I do love you."

"I know," I mumbled. "I love you, too."

"Cool. So, wanna get married then?"

"FALCON!"

My boyfriend laughed and kissed me hard. The sun was setting, the sky was decorated with pink and gold clouds and, way down deep inside of me, a little warm part glowed with happiness at the soppy romance of it all.

The rest of me ignored it, and I kissed Falcon back.

"Tui," Falcon said, between kisses.

"Don't ruin this, Falcon."

"I'm not. I'm not going to propose."

I sighed. "Then you may speak."

"But when I do propose ... promise to say yes?"

"Hmm. I'll think about it."

"Okay. I can live with that a little longer."

Things were getting more interesting when both of our phones beeped.

Sighing, I checked the group message from Hawk.

*Where the flock are you guys? Weka and Raven are online for our Flight video hangout.*

Falcon replied for us. *Coming now.*

I re-tied my hair since Falcon had messed it, and resettled my flight jacket around my wings. Out of habit, I also ran my fingers over the buckles around my lower legs. All as it should be.

"Let's go," I said, and jumped off the cliff.

The wind streamed past my feathers as I plummeted. My ankles hooked together. My tail opened, and my legs lifted. My wings opened with a thump, the sudden scoop of air wrenching on my chest and back muscles. A sickening lurch tugged on my stomach as I swooped skyward. There was a distant *Geronimo!* and a second thud above and behind me.

Laughing with pure joy, Falcon and I zoomed across the valley.

We didn't know exactly what would happen in the future. But that was normal. As long as we had each other, we'd be okay.

Life would never be perfect, but for now, it was close enough.

# Author's Note

This concludes the original trilogy of the Flight.

When the first edition of this book came out in 2020, I had been writing and rewriting this series for nearly a full decade. The first version of *Air Born*, which was called *First Flight*, was written in 2011 and sort-of initially published in 2012, and then again in 2014. See my website or the back of *Air Born* for the full story. So by 2020 (because, you know, *2020*), I felt it was time to let the Flight rest. I had other projects and characters I wanted to work with for a while.

However, since then, I have heard from *Generation Icarus* readers and fans who want to know – what happened to Dove? How did the Flight find their place in the world? Did Condor find his own happy ever after? And what about the forty other unknown *Homo sapiens icari* that Goldberg mentioned?!

I hope you feel that the ending to this book answers most of the burning questions and narrative arc that occur in this trilogy, but, if you also want to know what happens next, I think the Flight is about ready to tell me...

So, if you would like me to write another in the series, then please SHARE the books with friends and family. If enough people want it, then I won't be able to put the Flight off any longer (they've been trying to get my attention again recently).

Otherwise, please keep reading for further info about my other books and worlds!

*PS:*

I am aware of a certain other set of books that, in 2020, started a spin-off series with the main character (and first book) called Hawk. It also had a graphic novel adaptation called *First Flight* come out in 2015.

As mentioned above, my Hawk, and *First Flight*, came first.

# MORE BY J L PAWLEY

Want to read the book Weka (formerly known as Luke) mentioned in Chapter 9? The "dystopian sci-fi thing set in a future where there's no internet or planes, only mobile off-road libraries driven by ninja librarians, and digital ghosts, and airships", with a "super-smart badass teenage girl of colour" as the star character? Presenting:

### ARID EARTH #1:
### *THE KNOWLEDGE KEEPER*

**In a climate-changed world, the Library is the lifeblood of civilisation. And it's about to have a heart attack...**

If it hadn't been for the man in white body paint appearing out of the darkness, my Bus would now be a broken steel carcass in a smoking hole.

Someone set a landmine in ambush for the Library vehicle, a mobile repository of information saved from before the War. A beacon of knowledge in the ashes of civilisation, and my sole responsibility. Someone tried to take it from me. To stop the flow of free information. To steal from the people scratching out a living on the dusty frontier, just one cloudship delivery away from desiccation.

Now, other Keepers are missing. And not just Keepers. People have been disappearing from camps and settlements scattered across the outback. Why didn't we know about it? The Library is supposed to know everything. That's its whole purpose, to save and share knowledge. Isn't it?

I have to warn New Pearth. After all, this is what I was trained for. Though the Library could never have predicted a plot this savage, or this well-organised.

But first, with only a psychotic ex-slave and a digital ghost to help, I have to survive the trip...

*The Knowledge Keeper* is perfect for scifi fans who are looking for a fresh, more optimistic and less dystopian take on a post World War Three and climate change action thriller. Featuring a diverse cast of characters, from cranky airship pilots, snarky AIs, and badass teenage warrior librarians to a snakeskin-tattooed soldier called Gladys, it's been described as "*Mad Max* meets *The Magic School Bus*" – you've never read anything like this before!

## THE CHRONOZOOLOGISTS #1:
### *THE FAIRY HIVE*

It was just like any other day at school – and then Ellie Hapstead found a lost baby unicorn behind her classroom!

Recruited by a time-travelling animal rescue agency, 12-year-old Ellie steps through a glowing portal into the year 2361. Here she learns the truth about mythological animals from all over the world: Bigfoot, unicorns, flying monkeys and more – they're all real! But they aren't supposed to be... and the STARR Agents must sneak into the past to rescue as many as creatures can, before they become more than just legendary.

Now, with a sassy Chameleon Bird as her new best friend and partner, Ellie's on her first mission as a Chronozoologist Cadet. As a nest of venomous fairies is threatening a village in Victorian England, Ellie and the team must race to find a missing child and retrieve the hive – before it's too late...

Warning: These fairies bite!

## FOR ADULTS:

### *THE COMMONWEALTH COLLECTION* ### BY CHARD PAWLEY

**Book 1:** *ORION RISING*

### A.D. 2080

It has been sixty years since the Wars. Most of Earth is an uninhabitable wasteland. The remaining human population is crammed into Australia, New Zealand, and the ruins of the Indonesian archipelago.

In the Commonwealth, most believe the Wars to be long over. Technology has saved them from extinction. Colossal sea-rises clutter the coasts, housing entire cities. All food is supplied from vast fleets of floating farms moored at sea.

But tension is rising in the northern Fringes, where for many the Wars never ended.

On board the *Cassiopeia*, second mate Orion enjoys a life battling the waves and weather to tend the crop barges in New Zealand's eastern waters. But his world is soon shattered by the news of a friend's supposed suicide. With the help of Sam, the new trainee, Orion embarks on his own investigation, uncovering secrets that someone will go to any lengths to keep buried, including in his own past...

All the while, a far greater threat is looming, one which threatens to fracture the fragile peace between the Commonwealth and the Fringes, and reignite the Wars... Orion doesn't know it, but his actions might decide the fate of the entire human race.

**ORION RISING and its sequel SCYLLA BURNING are coming SOON!**

# ACKNOWLEDGMENTS

**TO YOU, THE READER** – Without readers, writers are just people with really vivid daydreams. Thank you for supporting me by reading *Generation Icarus*. Since I finished the first draft of the first book in 2011, it's been a long rollercoaster of a trip to get here today. The story is on my website or in the back of *Air Born*, so I won't repeat it here, but please know that I appreciate every single person who has ever taken the time to read even a page of my work. I hope you enjoyed it! If you did, please share it with a friend!

**Sue Copsey** – I'm so glad we were able to work together again on the edit of the Steam Press edition in 2020. Thanks for all your support over the years. Any errors in this edition are entirely my fault from messing with the manuscript again in 2024!

**The Flight Fam** – Without your undying love, this story never would have been finished. Hope you liked your cameos!

**Mum & Dad** – For having my back. Always.

**My soulmate and our crew** – You're my everything. Thank you. I love you.

www.ingramcontent.com/pod-product-compliance
Lightning Source LLC
Chambersburg PA
CBHW031053260626
47172CB00001B/50